ALEXANDRA BRACKEN

Quercus

For all those history has forgotten.

QUERCUS CHILDREN'S BOOKS

First published in 2017 by Hyperion
First published in Great Britain in 2017 by Hodder and Stoughton

1 3 5 7 9 10 8 6 4 2

Text copyright © Alexandra Bracken, 2017

Jacket art © 2016 by Michael Heath. Lettering by Molly Jacques.
Reprinted by permission of Disney • Hyperion Books.
All rights reserved.

A CIP catalogue record for this book is available from the British Library.

ISBN 978 1 78654 002 7

Printed and bound in Great Britain by Clays Ltd, St Ives plc

The paper and board used in this book are
made from wood from responsible sources.

Quercus Children's Books
An imprint of
Hachette Children's Group
Part of Hodder and Stoughton
Carmelite House
50 Victoria Embankment
London EC4Y 0DZ

An Hachette UK Company
www.hachette.co.uk

www.hachettechildrens.co.uk

Not I, nor anyone else can travel that road for you.
You must travel it by yourself.

It is not far, it is within reach.
Perhaps you have been on it since you were born, and did not know,
Perhaps it is everywhere on water and on land.

WALT WHITMAN

LONDON
1932

PROLOGUE

She'd had a doll once, with a painted-on smile, and pale hair and eyes like her own. For a long while, it had been her constant companion—a friend for tea when Alice was traveling with her papa, a confidant when she overheard her parents whispering secrets, someone who had to listen to her when no one else would. Her name was Zenobia, after the desert warrior queen Grandpapa had told her about. But one day, while Henry Hemlock chased her around the garden, the doll had fallen, and she'd stepped on her neck, shattering the fragile porcelain. The dreadful sound it made had sent her heart up into her throat.

Now, the sound of her mama's neck breaking under the heel of the man's boot made her vomit into her hands.

A pulse of fiery power washed through the room like an errant wave, carrying with it all the crushing chaos of the nearby passage as it collapsed. Rose was thrown back against the compartment's wall. The trembling air made her bones shiver, her teeth ache.

Dead.

Rose held her breath, clenching her eyes shut as her papa howled from where the shadowed man had him pinned to the floor, a sword driven through his shoulder. She knew better than to scream with him,

3

to try to reach for her mama the way he was reaching now. The hidden cupboard built into the wall behind the bookshelf would protect her, just as Grandpapa had promised, but only if she stayed *silent*, stayed *still*. The thin crack between the backing of the shelf and its frame was just enough to see through and not be seen.

Somehow the afternoon had slipped into night. Their dinner sat downstairs at the table, nearly untouched—their only warning of the intrusion had been the growls and whimpering of their neighbor's dog before it was quickly silenced. Her papa had just had enough time to light the office's lamps and fireplace, her mama to stow her away, before footsteps fell on the stairs. Now the lingering warmth and glow made the darkness in the room feel as though it was breathing.

"I told you to cooperate." The man wore a fine black overcoat with silver buttons, engraved with some symbol she could not quite make out. A thin black scarf had been pulled up to cover the lower half of his face, but it did nothing to muffle the silky tones of his voice. "It need not be this way. Relinquish your claim to it, give the astrolabe to me, and our business here will conclude."

Broken glass and scattered papers crunched beneath his boots as he circled around her mama . . . her mama's . . .

No. Grandpapa would be back soon from his meeting. He had said he would tuck her in, and he didn't break promises. He would make everything right again. This was . . . it was all a nightmare. It was her silly little mind, dreaming up all those stories about the shadows that came for traveler children. All of this would be over soon, and she would wake up.

"Bloody—*monsters*—the whole lot of you!" Papa tried to pull the sword out of himself by the blade, leaving a smear of blood. The man hovering above him only leaned onto the ornate golden hilt, driving it down further. Her papa thrashed, his legs kicking at nothing but air.

Mama did not move.

The sharp, hot edge of Rose's scream began to tear up her throat.

4

The river of stinking blood had soaked through the rug and was beginning to creep toward her mama's bright hair.

Her father tried to surge up again, one hand gripping a stone paperweight that had fallen from his nearby desk in the initial scuffle. With a yell that ripped from his lungs, he swung the stone toward the masked man's head. The man caught it easily and, in turn, retrieved another thin-bladed sword from the second masked man standing guard at the door. With a grunt, he stabbed it through her father's arm, keeping that in place, too. When her papa let out his bellow of pain, it was not nearly loud enough to drown out the masked man's laughter.

You must watch, Rose thought, curling her knees up toward her chin. *You must tell Grandpapa what happened.*

Stay silent, stay still.

Be brave.

"You—you tell Ironwood that he can die knowing—he'll never—he'll *never* have it—"

Ironwood. Always the Ironwoods. The name was hissed in her family, always edging into their lives like a shadow. Grandpapa had said they would be safe here, but she should have known. They had never been *safe*, not since her aunts and uncles and cousins and grandmother had been stolen, one by one, across the centuries and continents.

And now Mama . . . and Papa . . .

Rose bit her lip again, this time tasting blood.

The other man kicked off from where he'd been leaning against the door. "Finish this. We'll search the floors and walls unhindered." And then, as the figure prowled forward, Rose saw that it wasn't a man at all, but a tall woman.

Her mama had once said that Ironwood liked to collect the girls in his family and keep them on shelves like glass figurines, never taking them down, not even to be dusted. He must have seen this one as unbreakable.

Mama was unbreakable, too.

Until . . . she wasn't.

The first masked man reached into the inner pocket of his coat and affixed a long silver blade to his index finger. It curved like a gleaming claw, pricked at the air.

Rose's eyes shifted away from the weapon, back to her papa's face, only to find him looking at the bookshelf—at her—his lips moving soundlessly. *Be still, be still, be still.* . . .

She wanted to scream, to tell him to fight, to tell him that *she* would fight, if he wouldn't. She had the bumps and scrapes on her hands and knees from tussling with Henry to prove it. This was not Papa. Papa was brave; he was the strongest person in the whole world, and so very—

The masked man leaned down and slid the blade into her papa's ear. His body jerked once more.

His lips stopped moving.

In the distance, false thunder broke against London's sky as another passage crumbled. It was fainter this time, but it still made every inch of her skin feel rubbed raw.

Papa was still there in his suit that smelled of tobacco and cologne, but Rose saw him disappear all the same.

"You start with the bedroom," the masked man said as he wiped the blade and stowed it back in its place.

"It's not here," the woman replied slowly. "Wouldn't we be able to feel it?"

"There may still be a record of it," came the gruff reply, and the man began yanking the desk drawers out one by one. He tossed out ancient coins, papyrus, tin soldiers, old keys, scoffing, "These ingrates are *collectors*."

The woman crossed in front of the bookshelf, making the floor-board squeal. Rose pressed her filthy hands against her mouth again to hold in her scream. She tried not to breathe in the smell of her own sick again, but her parents' blood was already making her stomach churn.

The dark woman's eyes swept over the shelves, and she came to a stop directly in front of where Rose was hidden.

The moment caught in her mind like a leaf on the surface of water. It trembled.

Be still.

But she didn't *want* to be still.

It would be so easy, she thought, to be as brave as Mama—to break through the compartment and try to throw the woman to the floor and run. To pick up one of the swords and slash and slash and slash until she cut the darkness away, the way Papa would.

But Papa had told her to *be still*.

In the corner, the grandfather clock carved out the lost seconds. *Tick, tick, tick . . . dead, dead, dead . . .*

The hot, tangled, thorny parts of herself began to twist around her heart, tightening again and again until Rose finally closed her eyes. She imagined her veins, her ribs, her whole chest hardening like stone to protect the parts of her that hurt so very badly. She was too little to fight them now; Rose knew this. But she also knew that one day she wouldn't be.

The woman's eyes flicked away, toward something on the next bookcase over. Rose let her fear be ground down to pure hate.

Ironwoods. Always the Ironwoods.

"How many place settings did you see on the table?" the woman asked. She backed away from the bookshelves, holding something—a picture frame—out for the man to see. Rose's throat squeezed as her fingers clawed at her dress. That was her papa's photograph of the three of them.

The old house groaned around them. The masked man placed a finger to his lips, his head cocked in the direction of the bookshelves. He stepped over her papa, crossing the distance between him and the woman.

Be still.

7

"We'll take the child," the man said finally. "He'll want her—"

The bang of the front door as it cracked against the entryway's wall carried up the flight of stairs. There was a furious bellow from below—*"Linden!"*—and the bones of the house trembled with the heavy footsteps that spilled up the stairs. Rose looked toward the door just as three men burst through it. The man in the front, his imposing form sweeping in like a thunderstorm, made her recoil. Her papa had shown her a photo of Cyrus Ironwood as often as he could, so she would know him by sight at any age. Know when to run and hide.

One of the men toed at her mama's face. "Well, now we know why that passage closed behind us."

Rose nearly threw herself out from behind the shelf to shove him away, but she realized something suddenly: the masked man and woman were gone. She hadn't seen or heard the window open, nor had she heard the flutter of cloth or their footsteps. It was as if the masked ones had melted into the shadows.

From the shadows they come, to give you a fright.

From the shadows they come, to steal you this night. . . .

"The scum got nothing more than what they deserved," Cyrus Ironwood snarled as he leaned down and yanked the sword up out of her papa's arm, only to shove it down again through his chest. Rose jumped at the sound as the tip of the blade struck bone and wood, felt the soft growl leave her throat.

"This is one bounty I'll *relish* paying," Ironwood said. "I knew it would be the only motivation needed to put this into motion. It's only a damn shame Benjamin wasn't with them—what are you standing there for? Start searching!"

Ten thousand pieces of gold. Rose wasn't supposed to have seen the notice Grandpapa had brought home in a fit of rage. She wasn't supposed to know that Ironwood had put a price on the value of their lives, but Papa didn't—*hadn't* always locked his desk drawer.

The youngest man picked up the same gilded picture frame the masked woman had, only this time from the corner of the desk. He pointed at the picture of Rose sitting primly between her mama and papa. "And her?"

Ironwood spat on her papa's face before he took the photograph. Rose's vision washed over with black, the temperature beneath her skin boiling until she was clawing at her soiled dress to keep herself still. His eyes swept around the room; she could make them out from where she crouched, the color as bright and burning as a lightning bolt. Then, without a word, he returned to her papa's side, crouching down to study something—his ear?

"Boss?" the other young man queried.

"We should leave this place at once," Ironwood said, sounding distracted by his own thoughts. "Take the bodies. We can't risk a change if they're discovered."

"But what about the astro—"

Ironwood spun, throwing the picture frame at the man behind the desk, forcing him to duck. "If the bloody thing was here, it isn't any longer. Now *take the bodies*. I'll be in the car."

He took his poisonous rage with him as he left. Rose let herself breathe for the first time, watching as one man retrieved the pink sheets from her nearby bedroom and, with the other man, went about the business of covering and wrapping first her mama, and then her papa.

The rug was carried out last, leaving nothing but scars in the wood. Rose waited until the front door shut and then counted to ten, listening for something to stir in the shadows. When nothing—and no one— did, she shoved the bookshelf forward and scrambled down the stairs, out the back door. Her eyes stung as she opened the gate, swung her leg over the bicycle that was propped against the fence, and began to pedal.

Rose felt nothing. She pedaled and pedaled and pedaled.

Her vision blurred, hot tears slipping past her lashes onto her cheeks, but it was only because it was so very cold and damp out.

Ironwood's lorry gleamed like the shell of a beetle under the street-lights as she trailed after it, staying back at a distance. All along the way, she remembered one of the fairy tales Grandpapa had read to her, about the man transformed into a monster by his own ugly heart, and she understood it for the first time. Rose imagined her nails turning to claws, her skin to a knight's armor, her teeth sharpening like a tiger's.

Rose had always known it would be a matter of time before Ironwood came back to stamp out the last of her family, but she wasn't like all of those Jacaranda or Hemlock children who had let Ironwood take them in after their own parents gave in, or were executed.

How sad for them, she thought, that they had grown up without any thorns with which to protect themselves.

One day she would take everything from Cyrus Ironwood. She would demolish his throne of hours and his crown of days. She would find him and finish what her mama and papa had started. But tonight Rose would only follow this monster through the shadows.

Because someone would need to tell Grandpapa where Ironwood had hidden the bodies.

TEXAS
1905

ONE

ETTA WOKE TO THE RUMBLING CALL OF THUNDER, HER BODY wrapped in ribbons of fire.

Her mind launched into sharp awareness. The skin was burning off her bones, peeling back to expose every tender nerve and vein to pure, unflinching agony. She choked as she inhaled, her lungs too tight to bring in more than a small gasp of air. She knew she wasn't in water—the ground was stiff and ragged beneath her—but the instinctive flare of panic, the way her body felt heavy as stone as it jerked, felt like drowning.

Etta turned her head to the side and tried to cough up the dust that filled her mouth. The small movement sent a fresh ripple of pain through her shoulder, down her ribs, and then back up her spine.

Fractured pieces of memories burst through the feverish haze of heat and delirium: *Damascus, astrolabe, Sophia, and—*

Etta forced her eyes open, then squeezed them shut again at the intensity of the sun. That single second was enough for her to absorb the image of the bone-white world around her, the way it flickered and shimmered as heat rose up from the pale dust. It made her think of the way sunlight played on the ocean waves. It made her think of . . .

Passage.

That was the thunder she was hearing, then. There was no storm coming—no break from the heat. She was surrounded by desert—everywhere, for miles—broken up by distant, unfamiliar plateaus instead of ancient structures and temples. Then this wasn't—

Not Palmyra. The air smelled different here, burning her nostrils as she breathed in again. There wasn't that hint of rotting, wet greens carried over from a nearby oasis. No camels, either.

Her chest tightened, fear and confusion knotting around her stomach.

"Nic—" Even that sliver of a name felt like broken glass in her throat; her dry lips cracked, and she tasted blood.

She shifted, pressing her palms against the rough ground to push herself up. *I need to get up. . . .*

Drawing her elbows in close to her side, she got no further than lifting her neck when the dull pain in her shoulder burst like a blister. A scream finally broke loose, ragged in her throat. Etta's arms buckled beneath her.

"Good God, shriek again a little louder this time, will you? It's bad enough the guardian's on his way, but by all means, bring the cavalry galloping up with him."

A shadow fell over her. In the few seconds before the darkness reached up and dragged her back down, Etta thought she caught a glimpse of bright, almost unnaturally blue eyes that seemed to widen in recognition at the sight of her. "*Well.* Well, well, well. It seems like this Ironwood does have some luck left to his name, after all."

NASSAU
1776

TWO

Nicholas leaned back against the chair, lifting the wilting corner of his hat to survey the crowded scene at the Three Crowns Tavern again. The air in the establishment was sweltering, giving its rum-soaked patrons a look of fever. The proprietor, a former ship captain by the name of Paddington, was an eager participant in the merrymaking, leaving his sturdy wife behind the bar to coordinate the drinks and meager food service.

Neither seemed to have a care for the fact that the gaudy emerald paint was curling off the wall in clumps, as if eager to get away from the overpowering stench of men deep in their cups. A defaced portrait of George III loomed over them, the eyes and sensitive bits scratched out—likely by men of the Continental Navy and Marines, who had raided the island for munitions and supplies seven months before.

Nicholas weighed the odds, as he impatiently turned his now-warm pint of ale between his hands, that the "three crowns" in the tavern's name referred to the three vices that seemed to reign over it: avarice, gluttony, and lust.

A lone fiddler huddled over his instrument in the corner, trying in vain to raise a tune over the bawdy singing of the men nearby. The knot in his throat tightened, aided by the knot of his stained cravat.

"Jolly mortals, fill your glasses; noble deeds are done by wine. Scorn the nymph and all her graces; who'd for love or beauty pine! Fa-la-la-la-la . . . !"

Nicholas jerked away from the sight of the bow gliding over the strings, lest his mind start chasing memories down that unhappy trail again. Each second was chipping at his resolve, and what patience he had left seemed as insubstantial as a feather.

Steady, he coaxed himself, *steady.*

How very difficult, though, when the temptation to claw at the table and walls to release the bottled-up storm in him had him so close to surrender. He forced himself to focus on the men hunched over their tables, slapping down cards in perfect ignorance of the onslaught of rain pounding against the windows. The dialects and languages were as varied as the ships out in the bay. There were no uniforms present, which was a welcome surprise to him and a boon to the men at the tables around him, as they shamelessly attempted to unload their contraband.

Little wonder that Rose Linden had chosen this place to meet. He was beginning to question whether the woman courted villainy, or if she merely felt at home in it. If nothing else, her choice ensured that the Ironwood guardians watching the hidden passage on the island would not be likely to step in—their sensibilities were too delicate to risk brushing up against the scruffy charm of the seamen.

Settle yourself.

Nicholas reached up to press his fingers against the cord of leather hidden beneath his linen shirt. Against the outline of the delicate earring he'd strung through it for safekeeping. He didn't dare take it out; he'd seen the look of pity and disgust Sophia had fired his way last evening, when she'd caught him looking at it by the light of their small fire, studying the pale pearl, the gold leaves and blue beads attached to the gold hoop.

It was a safer thing by far to keep his eyes forward, rather than fixed on the evidence of his failures.

Etta would find this place agreeable. He could not catch the thought before it escaped, nor could he stop himself from picturing her here. She would have delighted in watching the room, soliciting whatever stories she could about the island's sordid history as a pirate kingdom. He might have lost her, even, to an ill-fated treasure hunt or a smuggler's crew.

Lost her all the same. Nicholas exhaled slowly, packing the ache away again.

On the worst of days, when the restlessness and fear turned his blood to squirming spiders and his inaction became unbearable, his thoughts turned to nightmares. *Hurt. Gone. Dead.* But the very simple truth, the one that remained when every doubt swirled around him, was that Etta was simply too clever and stubborn to die.

He'd purposefully extinguished the lantern hanging on the wall beside them, and he'd ordered just enough small plates of food and ale to allow them to keep their table without question. But his pockets had lightened as the hours wound down, and Nicholas knew that what little pay he'd scraped together from a morning's work unloading cargo on the docks wouldn't keep for much longer.

"She's not showing," Sophia growled at him from across the table.

Nicholas pinched the bridge of his nose, trying to tamp down the swell of frustration before it carried him off.

"Patience," he growled. The night wasn't over yet. "We aren't finished here."

Sophia huffed, downing whatever was left in her pint before reaching over and snatching his, drawing appreciative looks from the next table over as she gulped the remainder of the ale.

"There," she said, slamming the tankard down. "Now we can go."

In his twenty-odd years of life, Nicholas never could have dreamt he'd see the day when an Ironwood looked so utterly disreputable. Owing to the presence of Ironwoods on the island, and owing even more greatly to the fact that the Grand Master himself had likely put a bounty on his and Sophia's heads large enough to purchase said island, they were in disguise.

Sophia had sullenly—but willingly—sheared her long, dark, curling locks to her shoulders, and braided the remainder into a neat queue. He'd secured clothing from a sailor who shared, approximately, her small stature, and she wore it as comfortably as she did her own skin—unexpected, given her past proclivity for silk and lace.

Most surprising, however, was the leather patch over the now-empty socket of her left eye.

Nicholas's fears of her losing her eye after the brutal beating she'd suffered in Palmyra had been well founded. By the time he and Hasan had brought her back to a hospital in Damascus, the wound had become infected, and her sight in that eye was already gone. Sophia had elected for slow death by rot and fever rather than willingly let any of the physicians remove it, no doubt for vanity's sake.

Yet, when they at last had been forced to remove it, some part of her must have wanted to survive, because she had not retreated from life even in the fiercest clutches of agony. In fact, she had healed quickly, and he had to begrudgingly admit her force of will, once she had made a decision, was something to be feared.

It was a lucky thing, too. While she recovered in Damascus, Nicholas received an unexpected note from Rose, left inside Hasan's home for him to find.

Circumstances prevent me from waiting the month out, as discussed. We will meet on October 13th in Nassau or not at all.

At some point during her ride back to Damascus from Palmyra, where they had agreed to their original meeting, something had clearly changed in Rose's evaluation of these "circumstances." Without details, however, Nicholas hadn't the slightest idea if he should be afraid, or merely irritated she expected them to be able to travel so far, so quickly. As sympathetic as he was to Sophia's wounds, the idea that her injuries might cause them to miss their opportunity to discover the last common year had ignited a sickening panic, and no small amount of resentment, in him.

But her bruises and cuts had faded over the nearly two weeks since her beating, until, three days past, she'd been strong enough to begin to navigate them through a series of passages. And, finally, after one short chartered voyage from Florida, they had arrived to find Rose . . . nowhere.

"She's not bringing Etta with her, if that's what's got you looking like a puppy about to piddle on the floor," Sophia said. "Don't you think we would have seen them by now if that were the case?"

He hadn't expected Rose to arrive with Etta, safe and healing from her own wound, in tow . . . at least, not since that morning. Hope, as it turned out, dwindled like sand through an hourglass.

Nicholas forced himself to take a steadying breath. Her hatred of him minced the air between them, and, over the past weeks, her feelings had scarred into something far uglier than he'd known before. It made sleeping near her at night somewhat . . . uncomfortable . . . to say the least.

But he . . . How bitter the word the word *needed* was, when it was attached to Sophia. He *needed* her assistance to find passages, and, in exchange, had promised to help her disappear from Ironwood's reach once their ill-fated adventure was at an end. It seemed obvious enough to him that the true reason Sophia remained with him was because she had not fully given up her designs on the accursed object.

And he had to live with the knowledge of this, because he, God help him, *needed* her. Damn his pitiful scraps of a traveler's education. Damn his luck. And damn all Ironwoods.

"So eager to go back out in this weather?" he asked, narrowing his eyes. She narrowed her one eye right back, then scowled, turning toward the tavern.

Nicholas ran his fingers along the edge of the table, feeling each groove in the wood. Even two days ago, the idea of abandoning his deal with Rose had been inconceivable. Yet, if she couldn't honor their agreement, what tied *him* to it?

You know what, he thought. Discovering the last common year between the previous version of the timeline and whichever this one might be. Etta would have been shoved through the passages, through decades or centuries, until they'd ultimately tossed her out somewhere in that year, stranding her there hurt and alone. He should have fought to flip their aims, so Rose was searching for the astrolabe, and he Etta, but it had struck him, even exhausted and raw with emotion, that Rose would have the contacts needed to quickly sort out the timeline changes.

Nicholas was already preparing for her cold fury when she found out that he had not spent the two weeks searching for the blasted astrolabe, as she'd asked him to. He could start in earnest, once his mind was no longer haunted by his fears for Etta's life. Until then, he would never be able to fully concentrate on the task at hand.

As much as he had, in the privacy of his own heart, toyed with the idea of playing the selfish bastard and disappearing from this story, his whole soul railed against the dishonor of it. Once the astrolabe was found and destroyed, and Etta's future mended, he would be happy to leave Ironwood to his hell of knowing he'd never have it.

But more than honor, more than responsibility, was *Etta*. Finding her, helping her, sorting this disaster out *with her,* the way they were meant to. His partner.

My heart.

He would finish this, and make his own life, as he'd always intended. The traveler's world had never belonged to him. He'd never been granted access to its secrets, or allowed to explore its depth. He'd never been anything other than a servant.

Even Etta's future had been like a distant star to him; he'd marveled at what she'd told him of its progress and wars and discoveries, but it had remained too far away for him to seize, to hold in his heart as something truly real, not wild fiction. Never mind something he could lay claim to. But whether or not they'd go there, or find a home elsewhere, he wanted to restore that world she had known and loved.

The merrymaking in the tavern was occasionally punctuated by the bang of the door, battered both by the force of the storm's winds and the poor wayward souls who stumbled in for shelter. Nicholas returned his gaze to that spot, waiting for the telltale flash of golden hair, the pale blue eyes.

"Can you at least make yourself useful and dispose of the degenerate in the corner?" Sophia grumbled, crossing her arms on the table and resting her head on them. "If he keeps staring at me, I'm going to start charging him by the minute."

Nicholas blinked, swinging his gaze around to each corner in turn, then back at the girl in front of him. "What the devil are you talking about?"

The scorn rose from her like a tide of fire as Sophia sat up from her slouch, nodding toward the far side of the tavern, at a table in their direct line of sight. A man sat there, dressed in a dark cloak, a cocked hat jammed down over his wet wig, as if prepared to bolt out into the storm again at the first opportunity. Catching Nicholas's gaze, he quickly turned back to stare at his pint, his fingers rapidly drumming on the table. It was only then that Nicholas noticed the sigil of the familiar tree stitched in gold thread on the back of his glove.

Something that had been clenched inside his gut finally relaxed. The derelict man was a Linden. A guardian, if he had to guess.

Or an Ironwood trying to lure us out.

No—the past month had made him suspicious, perhaps beyond reason. An Ironwood would have confronted them directly. While his father's family suffered from a drought of subtlety, they were gifted with a rare love of lethality. Still, he felt for the knife he'd slid into the inside pocket of his jacket all the same.

"Stay here," Nicholas said.

But of course Sophia followed him on stumbling, drunken feet. The man still didn't look up as Nicholas and Sophia sat down in his table's empty chairs.

"Those are taken," the man grunted out. "Waiting fer company."

"I believe it's already arrived, sir," Nicholas said. "We seem to have a mutual friend."

"Do we now?" The man turned his pewter pint around in his hands. Turned it again. And again. And again. Until, finally, Sophia's hand shot out and slammed down over it, beating Nicholas to it by a sliver of a second.

"Test my patience further tonight," she bit out. "I *dare* you."

The man recoiled at her crisp tone, blinking as he looked at her face—her eye patch—closely. "That a costume you've got, luv, or just . . ."

Nicholas cleared his throat, drawing the man off that dangerous path. "We were waiting for . . . someone else."

The man's skin looked as if it had been left beside a fire to dry out for several hours too long. It was a familiar texture to Nicholas, one that marked years of working by or on the sea. The man's green eyes flickered across the room as he reached up to tug his hat off and his wig forward.

The man confirmed it as he said, "Saw some . . . let's say I saw some faces I usually try to keep clear of. Scouring the beaches and town real close and the like. Gives a man some second thoughts about helping a lady out."

"Can't be too careful," Nicholas agreed. "Where is this lady?"

The man ignored him, continuing in his tetchy way: "Said there'd only be one of you. You seem to fit." His gaze shifted toward Sophia. "Don't know about this one here."

Sophia narrowed her eye.

"She's an associate of mine," Nicholas said, trying to move the

24

conversation along. He could understand the necessity of secrecy, but each second that passed without searching for the astrolabe was a second too long. "Are you to take us to this lady, then?"

The man took a deep drink of his pint, coughing as he shook his head. With one more furtive glance around, his hand disappeared into his cloak. Nicholas's own fingers jabbed inside his jacket again, curling around the hilt of his blade.

But instead of a pistol or knife, the man pulled out a folded sheet of parchment and set it on the table. Nicholas glanced down at the red wax seal, the sigil of the Linden family stamped into it, then back up at the man. Sophia snatched it up, turning it over and shaking the folded parchment as if expecting poison to trickle out.

"Our . . . *flower*," the man said, emphasizing the word, "had other business to attend to. And now I've repaid her favor, and I'll be off to see to my own—"

"Favor?" Sophia repeated, the ale making her even more brazen than usual. "Aren't you supposed to be a guardian?"

The man pushed himself back from the table. "Used to be, before another family killed nearly the whole lot of them. Now I do as I please. Which, in this moment, is leaving."

Nicholas stood at the moment the Linden guardian did, dogging him through the thick crowds until he was close enough to grab his arm. "What other business did she have? We've been waiting for her—"

The guardian wrenched his arm out of Nicholas's grip, bumping into the back of another tavern patron. Ale sloshed over the edge of the pint and onto Nicholas's shoes. "Do I look like the sort Rose Linden would tell her bleeding secrets to?"

Actually, given his rumpled state and the rather impressive scarring around his neck, which could only have come from surviving a hanging, he seemed like the *exact* sort.

"Did she give you *any* other information?" Nicholas pressed, annoyed he had to raise his voice to be heard over the squealing fiddle and the boisterous laughter of the men and women around him. "Is she still on the island?"

"Are we not speaking English, lad?" the guardian continued. "Do I need to be giving it to you in French, or—?"

A feminine shriek broke through the loud roll of deeper male voices. Nicholas spun, searching out the table he'd just left, only to find a serving girl frantically trying to pick up the pieces of several broken glasses that had smashed across their table. Another small figure in a navy coat helped mop up the liquid as it rushed over the edge onto the floor.

"You—you *cow*!" Sophia shouted, snatching a rag out of the flustered serving girl's hand to mop down her front.

"An accident—so sorry—stumbled—" The poor girl could barely get a word out.

"Are you *blind*?" Sophia continued. "I'm the one with one eye!"

"Best of luck with that one," he heard the guardian say, but by the time Nicholas turned back, the man was on the other side of the tavern, and a sea of bodies had filled the space between them. The wind caught the door and slammed it open as the guardian disappeared into the night. The Three Crowns proprietor was forced to abandon a tray of drinks to bolt it shut before the rain flooded in.

"What's this about?" Nicholas asked, moving toward the table. Sophia dropped back into her seat, glowering as the serving girl swept up the last of the glass into her apron.

"Someone," Sophia emphasized, as if that someone weren't standing directly beside them, "decided to be a right and proper fool and waste perfectly good rum by making me bathe in it—"

Truthfully, the liquor had improved her smell.

"I'm not a fool!" The serving girl's face reddened. "I was watching where I was going, sir, but something caught my foot!"

She stormed off before he could tell her it was all right. And, of course, Sophia only seemed further infuriated by her absence.

"What? She can't take a hint of criticism?" she snapped, then yelled after her, "Stand up for yourself, you sodding—"

"Enough," Nicholas said. "Let us have a look at the letter."

Sophia crossed her arms over her chest, slumping back against her chair. "Hilarious. You couldn't even let me hold on to it for a moment before you took it."

"I don't have time for your games," he said. "Just give it to me."

She returned his sharp look with a blank one. A cold prickling of unease raced down his spine.

"The *letter*," he insisted, holding out his hand.

"I. Do. Not. Have. It."

They stared at each other a moment more; Nicholas felt as though her gaze was slicing him to pieces as his mind raced. He stooped, searching the floor, the chairs, the area around them. The serving girl—no, he saw her kneeling, and surely she wouldn't have hovered by the table if she'd just stolen something. She hadn't swept it into her apron, either. He would have seen that. Which left—

The other man. The one who had wiped down the table.

"Where did the man go?" he said, spinning on his heel.

"What are you on about?" Sophia grumbled, pushing herself back up to her feet. As she spoke, he caught sight of the deep blue jacket he'd seen before, but the wide-brimmed hat did nothing to disguise the slight man's distinct features. The Chinese man stood, watching them from the landing of the staircase leading to the private rooms above. Nicholas squinted through the tavern's dim lighting and took a single, cautious step in his direction. A flicker of a movement, really, but the man bolted with all the ease and speed of a hare.

"Hell and damnation," he groused. "You wait—"

Sophia slid a pistol he had never seen before out from under her jacket, aimed wide, and with a single, careless glance, fired in the general direction of the staircase. The ringing silence following her shot swung the attention of the room toward them. Pistols, knives, and the odd sword rang out and clattered as they were drawn. And with that small explosion of powder and spark, the fight Sophia had been looking for, the one she'd tried a dozen times to get from him, from the serving girl, from whoever so much as looked at her the wrong way, broke out in earnest.

One man, limbs clumsy with rum, elbowed another man in the back of the neck while trying to pull his own weapon out. With a strangled cry, *that* sailor swung his fist around, knocking the first clear across the nearest table, scattering cards, dice, food, and ale in every direction. The card players rose and charged into the nearest throng of gawking men, who were forced, of course, to push back lest they be trampled.

A sailor emerged from the fray, swinging a chair up from the floor, aiming at Sophia, who stood where she was, smirking.

Blind to it, he thought in horror, in that short instant before he bellowed, "On your left!"

Sophia's hat flew off as she jerked around. Her foot rose instinctively, her aim true: the powerful kick landed directly on his bawbles. As the sailor crashed to the floor with a shriek, she relieved him of the chair and smashed it over his head.

The fiddle shrieked as the bow jumped off the strings. The fiddler himself dove to the floor, just in time to avoid a chair hurtling toward his head from a whiskey-soaked doxy trying to hit her rival across her rouge-smeared face.

One lone drunk seaman stood in the center of the chaos, eyes shut as he swayed around in some odd reel, holding out his rum bottle as if it were his dancing partner.

"Damn your eyes!" Nicholas hollered.

"I think you mean *eye*," Sophia said, reloading the last of their powder into the pistol, pausing only to steal the half-empty rum bottle from the next table over when its occupant turned to the sprawling fight.

Nicholas shoved his way through the thrashing tangle of limbs, dodging to avoid a sword winging its way through the air. The proprietor climbed to the top of his counter, and, instead of stopping the fight with a well-timed shot into the room, leaped onto the back of the nearest man, tackling him to the floor with a loud cry.

Nicholas had seen more civilized tar-and-featherings than this.

He arrived at the stairs in time to see a man, while fleeing the fight, shove a doxy out of his way and send her tumbling in a mass of skirts down the stairs. He managed to catch her, narrowly preventing her from breaking her neck.

"Christ!" he gasped, coughing as he waved away a cloud of her wig powder.

"Thank ye—thank ye—!" The woman kissed whatever patch of skin she could find, moving to block his path up the stairs, even as he tried to gently push her away.

"Ma'am, please—"

"Move, wench!" Sophia stood at the bottom of the stairs, pistol aimed at the doxy's face. "He doesn't have two coins to rub together, let alone any to waste on you!"

At that the girl ceased her assault, turned in a huff, and marched down the stairs to join the fray.

"Did she kiss you senseless?" Sophia snarled. *"Go!* He's getting away!"

Nicholas took the steps two at a time. He burst onto the second floor, his chest burning as he drew each heavy, uneven breath. Down the hall, at the very end of a length of worn rug, a bedroom door had been thrown wide open, and Nicholas strode toward it. Just inside, a dark-haired girl, wrapped in a knit blanket, leaned onto the shoulder of another girl who patted her back now and then as she spoke in rapid, almost nonsensical English.

"On me—the door—a mite—funny little man—waving his knife— out the window—"

"A funny little man?" Nicholas asked, just as Sophia repeated, "Out the window?"

The girl blinked at their sudden appearance. "Why—short, yes, very small, almost like a child. And he's one of them—he's, how do you say—"

"From the Far East? Chinese?" the other offered. The first nodded, then turned to him, clearly thinking she should be rewarded. But Sophia was right—he didn't have two coins in his pocket. After their drinks and supper, he no longer had even one.

Sophia pushed past him into the room, Nicholas following at her heel. The room was choked with the scents of smoke from the blown-out candles and perfume reeking of flowers. Rain had blown in from the open window and soaked the carpet in dark splotches.

Sophia retrieved a torn piece of fabric stuck to the frame, and inspected it as Nicholas stuck his head out, searching the flooded streets for any sign of movement. He swung a leg over the window frame and climbed out through it, jumping from the ledge to the porch's roof and, finally, dropping to the ground. A heavy thud and curse followed as Sophia landed behind him.

Nicholas ran forward, shielding his eyes against the tropical torrent. Water rushed along the dirt and cobblestone paths, carrying away, just for the night, the grime and filth of the island.

But the thief was gone, and Rose's letter along with him.

"Carter!" Sophia stood a short distance away, at the edge of the tavern, rooted in place. A large dark lump leaning against the brightly painted wall suddenly took the shape of a man.

"What's the . . ." The words shriveled in Nicholas's throat as he took a step back.

The Linden man sat slumped, his eyes open and unseeing. His skin had taken on a white, waxy quality, as if the blood had been drained from it. Between the rain and the near complete dark, Nicholas could see no obvious mortal wound—no gunshot, cuts, marks of strangulation.

"What happened?" he asked Sophia as she knelt beside the body. She turned the dead man's head to the side, where a rivulet of blood was working its way down from his ear and along his jawline.

"There they are!"

Nicholas looked up to where one of the doxies was leaning out of the window, pointing directly at them. Several men at her shoulder turned to run back down the stairs, through the tavern, at the sight of them.

"We need to run," he told Sophia.

"No argument from me," she said, and sprang forward, leading them deeper into the night's storm.

SAN FRANCISCO
1906

THREE

Eᴛᴛᴀ ꜰᴇʟᴛ ʜᴇʀ ᴡᴀʏ ᴀʟᴏɴɢ ᴛʜᴇ ᴇᴅɢᴇ ᴏꜰ ʜᴇʀ ᴅʀᴇᴀᴍꜱ, carried by the soft rocking of memory.

The waves thrashing beneath her suddenly steadied to a gentle pulse that mimicked her own. Faces ringed around her in the dim candlelight, whispering, their rough hands tugging at her bruised skin. She pulled back to the cool silk and shadows of her mind, searching for that bit of light she'd seen: the moon on water stained with midnight.

He found her first, as he always did, from across the length of a ship. The parts of her that had dimmed with loss flared again, flooding the aches and fears until nothing but the sight of him remained. The tide kept the same pace, dipping, rising, with each step they took toward one another.

Then, suddenly, he was there, she was in the circle of his arms, and her face was pressed to the folds of his rough linen shirt. She breathed in his sea scent, her hands sliding along the strong planes of his back, seeking the familiar warmth of his skin. *Here, here, here*— not without, not anymore. The simplicity of it took root in her chest, blossomed into all of the possibilities she had dreamt about. A rough cheek brushed her smooth one and his lips moved against her ear, but

Etta couldn't hear a word, no matter how hard she gripped him, drawing him closer.

The world beneath her eyelids shifted again; the shadows pulled back, just enough to see the others around her, the curve of the Underground tunnel. A violin's notes slanted against the air, and she realized they were swaying to its sound, moving in a slow, endless circle of two. She thought of the way she had taken his arm, stroked the strong veins and ligaments, created a masterpiece of his pulse and muscles and bones. The walls shook and banged and roared, and Etta thought as she looked up, as she tried to see his face, *Let them roar; let it all fall apart.*

He ducked his head down and drifted back, receding. She tried to catch him, his sleeve, his fingers, but he disappeared like a warm breeze, and left her overturned and alone.

Don't leave me, she thought, as the heaviness in her body subsided and she resurfaced in her skin, flushed with panic, *not now, not now—*

Nicholas called back, laughing, *And now, good-morrow to our waking souls. . . .*

Etta opened her eyes.

The fire that had singed her veins in the desert was gone, at least. But she felt as insubstantial as the specks of dust dancing around the flickering lamp on the nearby bedside table. She stayed still, keeping her breathing even, and surveyed the room beneath her lashes.

And there, right at the foot of the bed, slumped in a high-backed chair, was a man.

Etta caught her gasp and swallowed it back. All she could see from the bed was the crown of his head, his thick, dark hair. Candlelight caught the few silver strands mixed into it. He wore a simple shirt and dark slacks, both crumpled from the position he had slept in. One hand rested on the open book in his lap, a loose bow tie woven between his fingers; the other arm had fallen over the side of the chair. His chest rose and fell slowly with each deep, sleep-drugged breath.

Her discomfort at the thought of being watched while she slept, unable to do anything about it, was defused by how weak of an effort this guard had put into the task.

A breeze caught the tears and sweat on her face and ruffled his open shirt collar. The window, framed by long crimson velvet curtains, had been left open.

Slowly, so as not to make a sound, Etta shifted up, biting her lip against the pain that lanced from her scalp down to her toes. Her eyes skimmed quickly around the room, searching for anyone else, but saw no one. A handsome little writing desk was nestled up against the floral wallpaper, a short distance from a bureau that looked so large, Etta had a feeling the room must have been built around it. Both had been carved from the same gleaming wood as the bed; leaves and vines arced along their edges, the pattern weaving in and out of itself.

It was a pretty little gilded prison, she had to admit. But it was already past the time when she needed to be searching for a way out of it.

Several candles were burning in the room: on a side table, on the desk, in a sconce near the door. It was the only reason she could make out her own reflection in the dusty mirror hanging over the bureau, though the image was split by an enormous crack across its center, and distorted from hanging at a crooked angle.

Oh God.

Etta rubbed at her eyes and examined herself again with growing disbelief. She knew her time in Damascus had given her pale skin some color, but now her face, ears, and neck were sunburned to the point of peeling. Her greasy hair had been braided away from her bruised face and hollow cheekbones. She looked ill—worse than that. If someone hadn't cleaned the dirt from her face and arms, she would have guessed she'd been dragged beneath a taxi through Times Square. Repeatedly.

Yet, somehow, the worst thing about it all was that someone had taken her clothes from Damascus off her—while she *slept*—and replaced them with a long, ankle-length nightgown, tied high and prim at the throat with a hideous mauve ribbon. She hoped it was the same person who'd taken the care to wrap and bind her shoulder—the same person who had cleaned her up the best they could. Still, she shuddered, both at how vulnerable she'd been and how badly it could have gone for her.

Unable to ignore the stinging pain a second longer, Etta turned her attention to her left shoulder, peeling the fabric back to inspect the itchy bandage that covered it and her upper arm. Biting her lip, she fought the unhelpful rush of tears that came as she pulled the fabric away from the sticky, healing wound.

It was a hideous, grim shade of pink—not the sheen of new skin, but the furious color of a burn. The splotch was still swollen with an uneven blister. The tightness in her throat became unbearable; Etta heaved in a breath, her gaze darting back over to the sleeping guard.

Let's go, Spencer. Run first; think later.

As soon as she could manage without feeling as though she would vomit from the motion, Etta swung her legs around and pressed her toes into the dusty Oriental rug. Just as she began to test whether her legs could bear her weight, a fast clip of steps drummed out beyond the closed door at the opposite end of the room.

In a rush of motion that smeared black across her vision and made her head feel like it was collapsing, Etta dropped to her hands and knees, ducking down until the bed blocked her from the view of anyone who might come barreling through the door.

". . . have to get . . ."

". . . try telling that to him . . ."

The voices trailed past, disappearing as quickly as they'd appeared, but the faint buzzing in her ears had subsided long enough for her to detect the strains of garbled music rising up through the floorboards. The clinking of glasses cut into the rising voices that bubbled like champagne froth.

"—three cheers—!"

"A toast!"

Fear woke inside Etta all at once, blazing through her confusion.

It seems like this Ironwood does have some luck left to his name, after all.

Both Nicholas and Sophia had warned her that Cyrus Ironwood had guardians watching each of the passages. She hadn't recognized the man who'd spoken to her, but it didn't matter, seeing as that single word, that single name, was enough for her to know she was in serious trouble.

But even that thought was devoured by another fear.

Where is Nicholas?

Those last few seconds in the tomb were splintered in her memory. She remembered the pain, the blood, Nicholas's horrified face, and then—

The only way to describe the sensation she had felt next was as if some invisible rope had knotted around her center and yanked her through a veil of imploding darkness. Etta pressed her fists against her eyes, unknotting the idea inch by inch.

I've been orphaned by my time.

The timeline has changed.

My future is gone.

Panic swelled in her chest, hot and suffocating. It fit—all of these pieces fit with what Sophia and Nicholas had explained to her. Time had reached out and snatched her, tossing her through a series of passages before spitting her back out at whatever the last common point was between the old timeline she had known and the new one they had inadvertently created.

Because the Thorns took the astrolabe? Etta knew carelessness could change the timeline, but not severely enough to cause travelers to be orphaned. That required *intent*. Focus and strategy. Taking the astrolabe from her, preventing her from destroying it—that hadn't been enough to orphan her, but something else had. *They must have used it.* That was the only explanation she could think of. The Thorns had used the astrolabe and irrevocably changed—broken—some event or moment in history.

And now she was here, with the Ironwoods, and Nicholas was not.

Colors burned beneath her eyelids, blood beat between her ears, a crescendo that broke over her in a frenzy of pain and grief.

Mom.

She couldn't think about her right now. Ironwood had sworn to kill Rose if Etta didn't return with the astrolabe by his deadline. *But* . . . She took in a deep breath. Knowing what she did about her mother now, Etta had to believe—she had to hope—that Rose was alive, that she'd already escaped from wherever the Ironwoods had been holding her.

Now it was her turn to do the same.

She forced herself to relax the muscles bunching up her shoulders, to breathe the way Alice had taught her to when her stage fright was at its most crippling. The anxiety, the terror, they were useless to her; she breathed in, out, in, out, until they were chased out of her mind, replaced by a floating, graceful measure of notes. The music was soft, serene, filling the shadows in her thoughts with light. Vaughan Williams's *The Lark Ascending.* Of course. Alice's favorite, the one Etta had played at her instructor's birthday, a few months before . . . before the Met concert. Before she'd been shot just outside the mouth of the passage.

Stop thinking. Just go.

Her guard shifted in his chair as she slowly rose, and adjusted his own position with a soft sigh. The book was on the verge of slipping out of his hands, onto his feet. She didn't let herself wonder at how strange that was, that the guard had felt comfortable enough to take off his shoes and curl up with a book.

It doesn't matter. There was a literal window of opportunity, and she needed to take it now.

Its frame creaked in quiet protest as Etta pushed it open further. She leaned out to assess her options, quickly recoiling back into the room.

The moon was high overhead, illuminating the bruised remains of a city. There were no streetlights, save for a few distant lanterns, but Etta had a clear view of the hills that rolled down beneath her window, of slanted, winding streets that disappeared beneath heaping mounds of brick and wood, only to reappear again, scorched.

The air held a hint of smoke and salt. An insistent wind carried thick fog up from a distant body of water, as if the city was breathing in the clean, cool mist. Skyscrapers had whole sections of themselves scooped out, their windows knocked loose like teeth. But here and there, Etta saw buildings and structures that looked freshly built—all framework and unfinished brick faces. While many streets and patches of ground had been cleared, the sheer scale of the destruction reminded her of what she had seen in wartime London with Nicholas.

She had the ghost of an idea where she was, but it fled before she could grab onto it. The *when* seemed more obvious. The furniture, the expensive draperies and bedding, the hideous Victorian-doll-like nightgown someone had stuffed her into, the destruction . . . late nineteenth century? Early twentieth?

Well, she thought, hoping to prop up her spirits a bit, *the only way out is through.*

She was on the second or third story of a house, though it was difficult to tell by the steep angle of the road below. This side of the house was covered in an intricate puzzle of wood scaffolding that extended from the roof above her to where the long beams were anchored on the ground.

She stuck an arm out, testing the distance between her and the nearest support. Her fingers easily folded around the rough wood, and before she could question the decision, before she could consider all the reasons it was a very, very terrible idea, Etta climbed up onto the window frame and swung her legs around first to its ledge, then toward the nearest horizontal plank of scaffolding.

"This is insane," she muttered, waiting to make sure the wood could at least hold some of her weight. How many times growing up had she seen news reports of scaffolding collapsing in New York City?

Eight. Exactly eight.

The blood drained from her head all at once, and she was forced to wait, heart beating an impatient rhythm, until her balance steadied again. Etta held her breath, arms trembling from the strain, as she scooted off the window ledge and onto the wood plank in front of her.

It didn't so much as groan.

There, she thought, *good job. Keep going.*

In some ways it was like heading down a strangely constructed ladder. Every now and then, Etta felt the structure tremble with her added weight, and some gaps between the planks and beams were almost too wide to reach across. But she gained confidence with each step, even as the wind plucked at her back, even as she realized she had no idea where to go once she reached the ground.

The bay windows on the floor below were longer and jutted out from the house. More dangerous yet, the glass was glowing, light spilling out onto the scaffolding. Etta crawled forward to peer through her cover of darkness; if the room was occupied, she'd have to move closer to the edge of the scaffolding to avoid being seen by its occupants. But first she wanted to know who, exactly, was in the building—the enormous house—and why they'd taken her in.

The room was larger than the one she'd just climbed out of, and lined with stately, dark wood shelves that contained row upon row of books. There was a desk stationed in front of the window and a large broad-backed chair turned away from her, but the room was otherwise empty.

"Come on," she whispered. "Move it, Spencer."

Her lip began to bleed as she dug her teeth into it, trying to keep from crying out in pain each time she dropped down and overextended her hurt shoulder. Gripping the beam she'd been sitting on, as if she were on the monkey bars, she stretched her toes out and felt a tremor of panic deep in her gut as they barely scraped the beam below.

Too far. Her arms strained under her weight as she looked to her right, her left, trying to judge how far she'd have to shift and scoot over to reach the nearest vertical support and slide down it. No—she wasn't going to make it, not with her shoulder on fire and her entire body shaking.

Not going to make it. She looked down again, this time to the ground below, the slant of the street, and tried not to picture what she'd look like lying there in a broken heap of gauzy white fabric and blood. If she could drop softly enough, she might be able to balance, catch herself—

A sudden movement at the window in front of her snapped her attention forward again. A bemused face stared at her through the glass. She blinked rapidly, her breath locked inside of her throat. The window creaked open, out toward her.

"Well, that's a bit of trouble you've gotten yourself into, old girl—"

Arms reached for her, and Etta didn't think, didn't speak, just *kicked*. Her heel connected with something hard, and she took some satisfaction in the surprised *"Cripes!"* laced with pain in response.

"That was uncalled for!" came the same voice, now muffled as he clutched his nose.

The pain in her shoulder and left arm stabbed straight through her fear, and her fingers spasmed and relaxed their grip on the beam. A gasp tore out of her as she dangled there by one arm. Her jagged finger-nails dug into the wood as she frantically tried to line up her footing below before she lost what grip she had.

"Take my hands—come on, don't be a fool about this," the young man was saying. Etta leaned back out of his reach, struggling to pull far enough away, as he climbed onto the frame. "Really? You think the better option is breaking your neck? I'm hurt."

The wind picked up, tossing her loose hair into her eyes, lifting the hem of her nightgown.

"I can admire the intent here, but you should know that all it would take is one shout from me and you'll be swarmed by unhappy Thorns having to climb down to fetch you. I doubt you want to die, either, so let's have it, then—I'll help you back inside, as easy as pie."

"Thorns?" Etta's brows knitted together. *Not Ironwoods?*

She didn't recognize the sounds at first, the odd rumbles and creaks, but the vibrations under her hand—those, she understood. The whole structure of scaffolding was being shoved to the left by the wind, leaning, until she heard a snap and felt something clip her bad shoulder as it fell behind her.

Then she was falling, too.

FOUR

IT HAPPENED TOO FAST FOR ETTA TO EVEN SCREAM. ONE moment she was falling; the next, her arm was caught and yanked in its socket as two hands closed around her wrist and dragged her toward the pale exterior of the house. Her cheek slammed against the rough stone, and she squeezed her eyes shut as the scaffolding began to shudder, folding in on itself and collapsing down onto the old-fashioned cars parked on the street below.

"Reach up, will you?" the young man said, the words strained. Etta shook her head. Her wounded shoulder was too stiff, and the whole length of it, from neck to fingertip, felt like it was filled with scorching, sunbaked sand.

Instead, he released her wrist with one hand and reached down to grab her nightgown. There was a loud grunt overhead as he heaved her up. Etta's feet scrabbled against the wall. She didn't breathe again until her elbows were braced on the windowsill. Then she was spilling through it, onto the young man and the carpet below.

She rolled off him and onto her back as soon as she landed. Her whole body sang with pain and adrenaline, and it was several long moments before her heart steadied enough for Etta to hear anything over its frantic rhythm.

"Well, that was exciting. I've always wanted to rescue a damsel in distress, and you've given me twice the fun on that front."

Etta cracked open an eye, turning her head toward the voice. Next to her, propped up on his elbow, the young man was making an appraising, appreciative study of her. She pushed herself upright and scooted back against the desk to put some much-needed distance between them.

He was young—her age, or a few years older, with short, chestnut-colored dark hair brightened by streaks of red. It was mussed to the point of standing on end, and Etta had the horrifying realization that she really *had* gripped it for leverage when she'd tumbled back into the house. His shirt was open at the collar and inside out, as if he'd picked it up and thrown it on without a second look. He scratched at the shadow of scruff along his jaw, studying her with piercing light blue eyes that warmed with some unspoken joke.

His voice . . . those eyes.

Ironwood.

Etta pulled herself to her feet, but her path was blocked by the desk. He'd claimed they were with the Thorns, which could only be true if he'd defected from Cyrus Ironwood's ranks and joined theirs. Or if he was a prisoner, same as her.

Or it would make him a liar. But if this was the truth, then . . . Etta was exactly where she needed to be.

With the people who had stolen the astrolabe from her.

"I suppose you gave me a bit of a fright, I can be man enough to admit that—"

"Where am I?" she asked, interrupting him.

He seemed startled by her ability to speak, but he stood and retrieved a glass of some amber liquid from a corner table for her. "You sound as terrible as you look, kiddo. Have a sip."

She stared at it.

"Oh, you're no fun," he said with a little pout. "I suppose you'll want water instead. Wait here and be quiet—can't raise the alarm just yet, can we?"

Etta wasn't sure what that meant, but she complied all the same, watching as the young man walked to the door and stuck his head out into the hall.

"You, there—yes, you—bring me a glass of water. And don't bloody well spit in it this time—you honestly think I'm not well versed enough in that fine art to notice?"

The response was immediate and irritated. "I'm not your damned servant."

So there are guards after all. The only question was whether they were protecting him, or protecting themselves from him.

"I do believe the official decree from your master and commander was, 'Give the dear boy what he wants.' This dear boy wants water. And make it snappy. Pep in your step and all that. Thanks, old chum."

Etta's lip curled back. Definitely an Ironwood. And, by the sound of it, definitely working *with* the Thorns.

"I'm not your—" The young man shut the door on the response and leaned back against it with a pleased little smirk.

"They're such a serious bunch that it's all too easy to rile them up," he whispered to her with a wink. "You and I will have the best fun together now that you're here."

She glared back. *Unlikely.*

After a moment the door popped open and a hand thrust itself in with a glass of cloudy-looking water. The instant the young man took it, the door slammed shut. This time, Etta heard the lock click from the outside.

"You use your old bathwater?" the young man shouted through the wood.

"You'd be so lucky!" came the reply.

He was still muttering as he crossed the room again and handed it to her. It was tinged a putrid brown, with a few suspicious particles floating in it.

Seeing her face, he said, "Sorry, the water situation is none too good after the earthquake, as you can imagine. No one's gotten sick from it." And then, after she'd already taken a sip, he added, "Yet."

The water did have an odd taste—a little metallic, maybe, a little dirty too—but she downed it in two quick gulps. Her hands and arms were still trembling as they tried to recover from the strain.

"Where am I?" she demanded. "When?"

"San Francisco," he said. "October 12, 1906. You've been out a number of days. . . ."

Etta's heels seemed to sink further into the rug as the weight of his words slammed into her. Thirteen days. She'd lost *thirteen days*. Nicholas could be anywhere. Sophia could be anywhere. And the astrolabe . . .

"We were briefly acquainted in the middle of the Texas desert, just after you were spat out by a passage. You might remember?"

"Are you looking for a thank-you?" Etta asked.

"Don't I deserve one? You are damn lucky we were orphaned through the same passage. I saved you from both the nearby guardian *and* the coyotes circling nearby, waiting for you to croak. In fact, I'd like to think that if it weren't for *me*, the boss man would be lowering your tattered remains into the ground."

That confirmed her suspicion, at least. Some change must have been made to the timeline that orphaned all the travelers born after that time. Etta closed her eyes. Took a steadying breath through her nose.

"What changed?"

"What changed—oh, you mean the timeline? Judging by the party they neglected to invite me to, the timeline's shifted the way they were hoping it would. The dimwits running this joint said something about

Russia losing but winning. Drunken nonsense. Why we're still in scenic post-earthquake San Francisco is anyone's guess, though. Stay with these people long enough and, believe me, they'll show you the armpit of every century."

"You haven't even tried asking them, have you?" Etta asked, unimpressed. "What year?"

His look was lightly scolding. "I told you. 1906."

She swallowed her noise of irritation. "No, I mean, what year was it in Texas?"

"I'm not entirely sure I should say—"

Etta lunged forward, barely catching the words burning the tip of her tongue before they had the chance to singe him. He wasn't going to keep the last common year from her—that was the only way she could figure out how to retrace her steps to Damascus, and to Palmyra.

"Oh ho—!" He stood and backed away from her. "You've got that wild look in your eyes like you did just before you bopped me on the nose. Believe me, they've removed everything that can be used as a weapon."

Etta looked down at the glass in her hand, then back at him, one brow arching. "I've gotten pretty creative over the past few weeks. I think I can handle one minor Ironwood."

"Minor?" he shot back, his voice wavering between incredulity and outrage. "Don't you know who I am?"

"No. You were so busy congratulating yourself, you never got around to making introductions," Etta said. "Though I take it you know who I am?"

"Everyone knows who you are," he muttered, sounding annoyed. "How far I've fallen that I actually have to *introduce* myself."

He placed one arm behind his back and the other across his waist, giving her a mocking little bow. "Julian Ironwood, at your service."

———

49

HER DISBELIEF MUST HAVE BEEN SPLASHED ACROSS HER FACE, because his smile shifted, becoming sardonic. Clearly not the reaction he had been expecting.

Julian Ironwood? Etta let out a small, lifeless laugh. Time travel had already presented a number of brain-bending possibilities—meeting an eighteen-year-old version of the violin instructor she'd known from the moment she was born, to name only one. But, surprise, experiences like that didn't make it any easier to come face-to-face with the dead. Etta tried to keep her expression neutral, knowing that staring at him in horror was going to raise some flags in his mind.

Nicholas had warned her repeatedly about the dangers of telling anyone their fate, that knowing how and when they would die could affect the choices a person made, and potentially, the timeline. Alice had given her an out, had specifically asked her not to say, but now . . .

The guilt felt familiar as it pooled in her heart. Etta bit her lip. It was just . . . what were the chances of meeting Nicholas's brother, and here, of all places? And why hadn't Nicholas mentioned that Julian had been held at some point by the Thorns?

"Either my adorably sadistic grandfather has done something terrible to you, or you're about to inform me that I've died by—rather stupidly, if I say so myself—falling off a mountain," he said. "Those seem to be the only two reactions I get these days."

"You—" Etta sputtered, whirling back around. "I didn't mean to—it's just—"

"Calm down, will you? You're going to give yourself the vapors for no good reason," he said. "As you can see, I am *not* dead."

"Wait . . ." she began, coming closer to better study his face. His eyes were the same icy shade of blue as Cyrus's, and she could detect, under the scruff and grin, the same high cheekbones and long, straight nose that age had tempered on the old man's face. Julian *also* seemed to have the Ironwood affinity for grappling for control of every conversation, no matter how short.

"You're *alive*," Etta finally managed to get out. "You . . . you didn't die after all?"

He grinned, enjoying the conversation, and motioned down to his body. "Still in one piece. The luck of the devil, as old Grandpops used to say. Rather odd, that, considering he *is* the devil—"

"What happened?" she interrupted.

He gave her an infuriating grin. "Tell me what you think happened."

Etta, with patience she had no idea she possessed, managed to tamp down her temper long enough to say, "There was a storm. . . . You slipped on the path leading up to the monastery, Taktsang Palphug—"

"Did Grandpops really give the world that much detail?" Julian asked, flattening his hair with his hand. "He's usually so quick to defend the family's honor, but I guess even he couldn't resist making me sound like a right idiot."

There was a sharp undercurrent to the words that seemed at odds with his jocular tone. Etta studied him again—the slouching posture, the unkempt clothes, the glint in his eyes she'd originally taken as mischief—and wondered which side of him was the truth, and which he'd simply made a home in.

"I thought he would have . . ." He kept pacing, but this time turned his eyes to the floor. "Did he . . . I never heard anything about a memorial or the like . . . ?"

Etta's brows rose. "I don't know. I'm assuming."

"It's not that it matters to me," he said quickly, shaping the words in the air with his hands, "but it's sort of . . . anticlimactic to disappear into a puff of snow and mist. A chap wants to know that—you know, actually, it doesn't matter. None of it really matters."

"Stop—*stop* pacing, you're making me nervous," Etta said. "Can you stand still for one second and actually explain this to me?"

He popped himself up onto the corner of the grand desk, folding his hands in his lap. Within seconds, his bare feet were swinging, drumming against the leg of it, and Etta realized she'd asked for the impossible. Not only did he not shut up, he couldn't seem to burn off enough energy to stop moving.

"In that instance, the Thorns were *also* responsible for orphaning me," Julian said. "Three years ago, they used a passage to New York in 1940 to set a fire at the New York World's Fair, hitting at Grandfather's business interests in that period. At the same time, I happened to be stupidly falling down a mountainside in Bhutan. Since I was born in 1941, I was kicked through the passages to 1939, which was, at that point—"

"The last common year between the old timeline and the new one," Etta finished. Between tracking the timeline, the collection of years at the mercy of the travelers' actions, and each traveler's personal life that they lived straight through, even when they were jumping between centuries, she thought her brain might explode. "But I was born after 1940, too, and I wasn't orphaned when that change occurred."

"Then the change must have been confined to that year, and not rippled past 1941. I'm sure you've heard this a thousand times by now, but you know how the timeline is about inconsistency."

Etta did know. It had self-corrected as if passing over a speed bump, instead of the road completely diverging. Interesting.

"At least that time I got spat out in the Maldives. Made for quite the vacation. But by the time I located the necessary passages and resurfaced, I caught news of my supposed death and decided I might as well make the most of it."

"And it never occurred to you once—*once*—over the past few years that you might, you know, *tell* someone that you were alive?"

Not Nicholas? Not Sophia? Not any other member of his family?

Julian pushed away from the desk. He moved to the bookshelves, dragging his fingers along the beveled spines of the books as he made his way around the room. It was like watching a cat pace in front of a window, restless and watchful.

If she hadn't heard the words leave Nicholas's mouth, she would never have believed they were related at all. It went beyond their looks. Where Nicholas moved in assured, long strides, even when he was uncertain of where he was going, Julian had a kind of agitated under-current to his movements. He didn't have Nicholas's height, either, and his body hadn't been honed and chafed by the hard work of life on a ship. Julian's words fell over each other, as if fighting over which got to escape first, while Nicholas took careful measure of each and every word he said, knowing how they might be used against him. Julian seemed to be bursting at his seams, and Nicholas had been so careful, so steady, in holding his feelings in check.

Because he had to.

Because he'd had none of the privileges Julian had, born into a family that never wanted him and a society that scorned and disrespected him.

Anger bloomed, vivid as the crooked portraits on the wall. If this really was Julian Ironwood, then it was the very same person who had taken advantage of Nicholas's love for him, the one who'd turned around and treated him like little more than a servant, rather than genuinely teach him the ways of travelers.

I'm the fool, Nicholas had told her, *because in spite of everything, he was my brother. I never saw him as anything else. And it clearly wasn't the same for him.*

Julian hadn't even had the common decency to find a way to tell his half brother he was still alive. Instead, he'd let Nicholas drown in his guilt. He had let him spend years questioning his honor and decency. He had let Nicholas take the exile and rage-fueled beating from Ironwood.

All of this time, Nicholas had been suffering—and for what?

Nothing.

"Well, kiddo, to continue this tale, I floated around for a while, living life as one does—without much money to speak of, which got me into more than a few scrapes. It all became rather tedious and boring. Enter: the Thorns. I thought it might be best to sell some knowledge about Grandfather, try to exchange it for steady meals and a safe place to sleep at night."

He glanced at her, as if expecting Etta to coo with sympathy. She kept her gaze on the unlit brass chandelier overhead, fingers curled so tightly around the lip of the desk that her hands prickled with pain. *Don't do it. He's not worth it.*

"Speaking of," Julian said, swinging around toward her, "I'd like to get back to you—*holy God!*"

Etta relished the throbbing pain in her knuckles as her fist made contact with his cheek and he stumbled back over his own feet, landing in an ungraceful heap on his bottom. He stared up at her with huge eyes, one hand still cupping the red mark on his face as she shook out her hand.

"What the bloody hell was that for?" he howled.

"Do you have *any* idea," she said, voice rising with each word, "what your 'death' did to your brother? Do you have *any* idea what he went through—what your jackass of a grandfather put him through?"

"Brother?" Julian repeated, rather stupidly. Her instinct to give him another kick, this time beneath the belt, must have registered on her face, because Julian scrambled back on the rug.

Then, to her surprise, he said, "But . . . how do you know Nick?"

Etta studied him. He looked genuinely shocked, either from her hit, Nicholas's name, or both. Unsure of how much information to trust him with, she answered, "I traveled with him for a little bit."

His brow creased. "On behalf of Grandfather?"

She shook her head, but before she could elaborate, a key scraped in the door's lock. It should have been enough to send Etta diving behind the desk, out of sight. Instead she stood there, towering over Julian, the door letting out a tortured groan as it was thrown open. Two men barreled in with guns in hand, both dressed in trousers and plain white shirts, coming up short at the sight of her. The one out in front, a dark, bushy mustache disguising half of his face, actually took a generous step back, crossing himself.

"Christ," said the other, glancing at the first. He was somewhat shorter, his pale hair cut close to the scalp and almost gone from balding. "The others were right. It's the bleeding ghost of Rose Linden."

The other one merely crossed himself.

"Aren't you supposed to be protecting me?" Julian complained. "This girl is clearly deranged—"

"*Deranged* is one word for it," the dark-haired man said. Now Etta recognized his voice as that of the man who had sparred with Julian over the water. "How in the hell did you get in here, miss?"

"I think the better question is, why did it take you almost a half hour to realize I was gone?" Etta said, reaching back for the water glass she'd left on the desk. Before either man could answer, she slammed it down on the edge of the desk, shattering its top half and leaving a jagged edge on what was left. For one insane instant, Sophia's lesson on where to cut them, how to slit their throats, floated to the front of her mind.

Get a grip, Etta. She needed to stay here and find the astrolabe, and she wouldn't be able to do that if she was locked away. But part of her hated that these people had seen her at her weakest, her most helpless, and she couldn't ignore it. They needed to know she would fight back if they pushed her.

"Easy there!" Julian cried. He craned his neck up to look at the men. "Aren't you going to do something?"

The pale-haired man raised his small black pistol, then swore, tucking it back into the waistband of his trousers. "Come along, girlie, it's time for you to go back up to your room."

Etta swung her makeshift weapon toward him, ignoring the small, warm pool of blood collecting in her palm from where she'd cut herself. "I don't think so."

Dull footsteps grew to a pounding storm out in the hallway, and the music she'd heard before cut off with a loud scratch. She caught snatches of voices shouting, *"She's gone!" "Find her!"* and a variety of swearing that would have made even the men in Nicholas's crew blush.

"She's here!" the dark-haired man called. "The office!"

The rush of panicked activity ceased, but one voice rang out. "Thank you; that'll be all the excitement for this evening, God willing."

The two guards straightened—the smaller of the two even reached up to fix the limp cloth hanging around his neck into something resembling a bow tie. A man strode into the darkened corner of the room, hands tucked into his trouser pockets.

"We were handling the situation, sir," the dark-haired one said quickly. "I was about to return the girl to her quarters."

"I see," came the amused response. "But it seems to me that she's the one who has this situation well in hand."

The man stepped into the shallow firelight, giving Etta her first real glimpse of him. It was the guard from her room. Dark eyes swept around the room, studying each of them in turn, but his gaze lingered on her, so unflinching that it seemed to wipe everyone else away, leaving just the two of them.

The man's presence made her blood slow, and finally still in her veins, but the trickle of uneasiness she'd felt at his appearance was nothing compared to the torrent of uneasiness that came in the moment where her memory met recognition. Etta wasn't aware that the glass had slipped from between her fingers until it fell, striking the top of her bare foot, and rolled away.

The black hair, cut through with silver strands . . . his rough-hewn features . . . she wasn't seeing him in the high-waisted pants or loose white shirt he currently wore. She saw him in a classic black-and-white tuxedo, wearing silver-rimmed glasses, in the Grand Hall of the Metropolitan Museum of Art. In the twenty-first century.

"You recognize me," he said, with a small, approving note in his voice—like he'd expected she wouldn't?

Not only had she bumped into him, he'd come running when she and Sophia had found Alice dying in a pool of her own blood. Almost as if he'd known it might happen.

Or as if he'd been the one to pull the trigger.

The two guards immediately stepped closer to the man's side, as though they'd been drawn into his orbit.

He looked to Julian and said, this time with a slight edge, "How did I know to check this room first?"

"She dropped in on *me*," Julian protested, pointing to the window. "I was minding my own business. For once."

The man flicked his dark gaze to Etta, and this time she forced herself to meet it. The corners of his mouth tipped up again. "I don't need to ask how you got in here, for I suspect the mountain of scaffolding piled up outside is likely my answer. Tell me, did it ever occur to you that you could have broken your neck?"

He was so calm, his voice so measured, that he made the rest of them sound manic. Even his posture, the way he hadn't once tensed up, made her want to ruffle his composure, just to see how far he could be pushed. To see where the boundaries of his anger began. It would be useful later, she thought, in trying to trick him into saying something about the astrolabe, and where the Thorns might be keeping it.

"You know," Etta said, "you're making me wish I had."

She wiped her slick palms against the horrible nightgown, wary of the man's warm laughter, the spark of enjoyment in his voice. He turned to the bald guard, knocking the back of his hand against the other man's chest. "I told you she had some spirit, didn't I?"

"You did," the guard confirmed. "Sir, I take full responsibility for all of this—"

"Sir" waved his hand before placing it on the guard's shoulder. "I was there and slept through her clever escape. Have Winifred dress her and bring her to me once she's comfortable and presentable, will you?"

"Yes, of course, sir," the guard said, nearly sagging with relief.

"I'm not going anywhere with you," Etta said, taking a step forward. "I don't even know who you are! What right do you have to order me around?"

The man had already begun to turn toward the door, but at her words, his shoulders stiffened. He glanced back over his shoulder, but the candlelight flared in his glasses, masking his expression. Julian coughed, either to hide a laugh or his discomfort.

"My name is Henry Hemlock, and you're here at my mercy," the man said. "You will do as I say, because I am your father and we have *much* to discuss."

NASSAU
1776

FIVE

THE STORM HAD BROKEN AT DAWN, BRINGING A BIT OF MERCY to what had been a night that redefined misery. Nicholas and Sophia trudged and waded through still-flooded streets, following the path of the runoff toward the beach. Servants were waking, appearing on the balconies of bright, two-story wooden buildings to beat rugs and toss out the waste, and the smell was rank enough to leave him feeling as if the small town had become one large chamber pot. After a rather unfortunate splash of something he didn't care to inspect, Sophia's mood had gone from sour to curdled.

They'd spent hours hiding from the tavern owner; the whoreson had sent out a veritable gang of men and Redcoats to find someone to hold accountable for the damage the fight had wrought, and had settled on them. This, despite his own gleeful participation. The dodging and hiding had considerably hampered their search for the man who'd stolen Rose's letter. As it turned out, even a rare Chinese man in the Indies didn't attract the necessary attention to leave a trail of witnesses behind. Nicholas had caught himself wondering more than once if he'd had more to drink than he thought, and made a man out of a shadow.

But the doxies and their customers upstairs had seen him, so surely . . .

He stilled, turning back toward the harbor. Would he make for a ship? If he was an Ironwood, not just some enterprising opportunist looking for possible targets for theft, he'd try to catch the first ship out. The more Nicholas turned over the thought of investigating that area, the sounder it seemed. Information traveled like flies between sailors, and surely someone of the man's ethnicity wouldn't have evaded their notice. Someone might know where he was staying, and if he had any plans of sailing out of port within the next few days.

Damn your eyes, Rose, he thought, not for the first time. *You couldn't have come yourself and saved us the trouble?*

Sophia had charged forward as his steps slowed; a good three lengths ahead, she turned back. "Did your mind suddenly go on holiday? Let's *move*. I'm ready for this hellish cat and mouse game to be over."

"You continue on," he told her. "I'm going to follow another lead—"

No sooner were the words out of his mouth than she came stomping back toward him, sending muddy water shooting up around her already-soaking shoes and splattering him in the face. "What lead is this?" she pressed. "Or have we started redefining 'lead' as 'wild guess'?"

He took a deep breath for patience, and parceled out his words carefully, so as not to reveal anything she might be able to use herself. It would be like handing her the knife she'd later jam into his spine. "I'm headed to the bay, to see if anyone might have information on our thief."

"Fine," she grumbled, turning in that direction. "We'll make it quick."

He shook his head. "You go back to the beach, get some rest—"

"I have to say," she interrupted, her small, pale hands curling at her sides as her stare burned into the side of his face, "I have no idea how Linden tolerated traveling with you. A few hours into our special partnership and I wanted to push you out a window."

Nicholas was surprised by how hard, how fast, fury gripped him. Exhaustion, hunger, frustration—he could make any excuse he liked, but the truth was, she'd touched the one sore on his heart that was still raw. "Utter her name again. Test my resolve, ma'am, please."

Sophia glowered. "I *meant*, I don't know how she could stand this game of evasion and stupid, masculine pride you seem so fond of: *stay here, go back, don't move, go on ahead.* You're not my governess, and I'm not one of the men on your stupid bloody ship, so stop ordering me around. Try to leave me out of this—try to leave me behind—one more time, and I *will* actually shoot you. In a delicate area."

"Do I need to remind you," he said, hating how quickly she seemed to be able to get his temper rolling on stormy waves, "that *you* got so deep into your cups last evening that instead of being reasonable and maintaining our disguise, you *fired a pistol*, and fired it badly, inside of a crowded tavern? That just yesterday, you harassed and abused a British regular because you 'disliked the way he looked at you' and nearly got us thrown into a rank gaol?"

"Would have been an improvement over where we've been sleeping," she grumbled.

She will never respect me, he thought, sick with hate. *She will always see me as nothing.*

"One day they will name a plague for you," he said.

"Hopefully a particularly nasty one," she answered. "A girl can dream."

"From the beginning, you treated me no better than a rat," he continued, ignoring her smirk. "Do you want to know how Etta *tolerated* me? Because we were partners, because we trusted each other, and because she was capable of taking care of herself. You seem to have appointed yourself to the task of getting us both killed. And while you might consider yourself to be expendable, I need to confirm she survived *your* treachery."

Nicholas braced himself for her inevitable snide comment, the smirking condescension she seemed to favor.

Instead, Sophia busied herself by removing her hat, unknotting the

63

small scrap of leather she'd used to secure her short braid. Her hands worked through her hair, mussing the weave in silence. They fell in line with the men stumbling bleary- and beady-eyed out of the inns and taverns, the wreckage of the previous night's frivolities. Some at least were making an attempt to tuck their shirts back into their breeches. Still, Nicholas shook his head. Captain Hall would have knocked each of them in turn off his ship if they'd reported back in such a state.

Hall. He'd sent word that he was alive and mostly well, but had yet to receive a response. And he likely would not until they returned to port. Nicholas didn't resist the small echo of longing for the thought of boarding a ship and disappearing into the horizon—for the simplicity of that life, and how quickly it would welcome him back.

Someone began to whistle, a high, bawdy tavern tune that made the men around him chuckle. All at once, seemingly without him knowing, the port city had shaken off the night. Crimson coats dotted the streets, the prim uniforms and gleaming buttons only looking primmer in contrast to their surroundings. Wagons moaned and rattled with the weight of cargo being drawn up and down the path, coming or going, just like the residents of the island. The green palms and underbrush looked as if they had been painted by the sun, glowing with pleasure in the heat, the way they only did after a hearty storm. The old fort stood above it all like a four-pointed star to the west, high walls winking as the light glanced off its wet gray stones.

"Just go," Sophia said, nodding toward the ships in the bay. "You want an out, you've got—two—three—*four* chances out there."

"What are you on about?" he asked, batting away how bloody unnerving it was that she'd traced his line of thought. "Are you still drunk?"

"Only observant," she sang.

"Whatever you think you know, I assure you, you do not."

"I know you've wasted our time here. I know you don't truly care about the astrolabe, just the first girl who turned her big blue doe eyes on you."

"That's not true," he insisted. "And can a deer even have blue eyes?"

"Then what are we still doing here?" Sophia challenged, hands planted on her hips. "Are you hoping that if we wait long enough, the woman might find her daughter and bring her here to you? We don't *need* information about the last common year. It's irrelevant. If the Thorns have the astrolabe, they're traveling with it, and finding them is our best bet for finding it. But you haven't even considered that, have you?"

He was tired; so tired of the Ironwoods, of travelers, of all the meddling in the lives of innocent people and the hardship they suffered over the greed and demands of his kind. He was inclined to say Ironwood could take the blasted astrolabe to hell with him, if it weren't for the damage he knew Ironwood could do to Nicholas's own time.

"I made a promise," was all he said.

"Promises are for saints and losers. Most of the time we can't even keep the ones we make to ourselves."

He gave her a sour look from beneath the brim of his hat. "You and I are *entirely* different people."

"You don't say!" Sophia scoffed. "At least be man enough to admit that what you really, truly want is to find Etta."

More than my next heartbeat. But it was like swimming out to sea in the rain; no matter where he went, he could not avoid the cold drench of truth. Etta would want him to finish what they'd begun by finding the astrolabe.

And leave her to die?

His right hand curled at his side, and he could almost catch the memory of what it had felt like to have her hand tucked there.

And that was it. That calm certainty in knowing her as he knew himself. There was no point to any of this if Etta didn't survive; the future didn't belong to him, it had belonged to *her*, and had always been tied to her dreams. He wanted that success and celebration for her, the chance for her to resolve the unfinished yearnings in her heart. Everything good in this life was her or meant for her.

At the time, it had felt like an inevitability that they would collide, even in the face of such insurmountable odds. Each time something had blocked their path, it had only served to feed that necessity of staying together. Now and then, though, when he stared into the fire at night, or stole a moment to himself, a passing doubt caught him in its snare. They were both so very, very stubborn. So determined to strike back at the rules of life, the way their situation had confined him, that he worried they had only come together purely as an act of rebellion.

But then her face would find him, as fierce as the moment he'd first clapped eyes on her. When his hands were dry and chapped, he recalled the softness of her skin. When the world shivered at the approaching winter, he recalled the warmth of being beside her. When he felt the sneering judgment of the eyes around him, he recalled the invincibility she'd instilled in him with her belief.

And the doubts, they would recede as quietly as they came, leaving a peace as vast as the deep, dark ocean. Nicholas believed they could find that place she had spoken of, the time that was meant for the two of them. He had to believe that.

It was weeks since she'd been orphaned. If she had survived her wound and found help, as he hoped she had, Etta was strong enough to keep surviving and begin finding her way back to Damascus. Perhaps they'd meet each other halfway and continue what they'd begun, rewrite the rules of this life.

Sophia pressed on. "Go find her, sail off into your sunset, and leave me to . . ."

"To . . . ?" he prompted when she did not continue, already knowing the answer. *Leave me to find the astrolabe alone.* Oh; he stifled the bitter laugh before it could emerge. She would cherish the opportunity to remove him from the playing field; to not have any obstruction between her and whatever she was planning.

Instead of answering, Sophia turned her gaze back out to the tents and stalls and argued, "What about Rose Linden's promise to meet you here? Aren't you sick of sitting here and twiddling your thumbs, waiting for Mummy to tell us what to do? If you want us to find Etta, if *that* will perk you up and get you back on the trail of finding the astrolabe, then we'll start by looking for her. It'll be a risk, knowing Grandfather could get to those Thorns first, but I guess we'll have to take it. The price we pay for you being so revoltingly lovesick."

He studied her carefully, frowning. Being compassionate was at odds with her natural disposition, and she was so entirely resistant to niceties that he couldn't stop the trickle of suspicion inside him—that she was arguing this point for more than what she was letting him see.

"He doesn't necessarily know what happened—" Nicholas started.

"Don't be ridiculous. By now, he knows what's happened. We have the small advantage of him being more interested in finding those Thorns than finding us, and we need to use it. So, ticktock. Let's *go*."

As loath as he was to concede it, she did have a point. Over the last few days, it had become clear to him that he was the only one willing to play this game with any decency, and he'd begun to wonder if decency was merely the trade of fools.

"Where do we begin to look for her?" Nicholas heard himself ask. "How do we go about ascertaining the last common year without turning to another traveler?"

Any Ironwood or Ironwood ally would immediately report them to the old man for the reward. Without Rose's information, searching for Etta would feel like a dead reckoning. He did not enjoy navigating a ship blindly, and the same could be said of his life.

"We go find Remus and Fitzhugh Jacaranda, like I've been telling you," Sophia said. "Grandfather gave them the worst posting imaginable when they came crawling back into the fold after they betrayed him and joined the Thorns. I would bet anything there's no love lost between them and Grandfather, and they might be willing to share what they know for a price. Or you can just tell them your tragic tale, let slip a manly, heroic tear."

Pity. Wonderful. His patience finally slipped its leash. "If they have such a terrible, remote posting, who's to say they'll even have heard about the shift in the timeline?"

"If they haven't heard anything, they'll be able to point us to someone who might know. It won't be a wasted trip either way."

Nicholas released a harsh breath through his nose, considering this.

Sophia, possibly for the first time in her life, was being reasonable. They *were* losing time. He *was* bloody well tired of Rose's games. If the Jacarandas could aid in making quick work of finding Etta, then that was the way forward. If they couldn't help him, at least he could console himself with the knowledge that he was actually moving forward, that he'd broken out of the gaol of inaction in which Rose had locked him.

"All right," he said, relenting. "We will try it your way, then. If nothing comes of searching for Etta, then . . . we'll proceed with finding the astrolabe on our own. I promise you."

Sophia rolled her eyes, moving ahead of him again. "Saints and losers, remember?"

And if Sophia truly was after the astrolabe for her own gain, as he was now doubly certain, then their weak truce would conclude and he would do anything in his power to keep it from her. *Anything* necessary.

"Being good on your word is a core tenet of honor," he called.

"Honor." She looked disgusted. "Good thing I don't have much of the stuff left."

NOON ARRIVED, BRINGING WITH IT A MISERABLE HEAT THAT sagged against him, and seemed unjust for October. They passed their walk back to the camp in blessed silence, Sophia stalking forward,

Nicholas staying several steps behind, not just because he didn't want to encourage any words between them, but because he knew that the white men and women they passed would expect it of a servant, a slave—Nicholas shook his head, rolled his shoulders back, as if he could fling it off. The charade sapped what little good mood he'd managed to eke out of the day. And an hour later, when they finally reached the deserted stretch of beach where they'd set up camp, the last lingering traces of goodwill between them evaporated altogether.

"Bloody *hell*!" Sophia snarled, and would have charged forward had Nicholas not gripped her by the collar of her tattered coat.

Their blankets had been carelessly thrown around, and the hammocks they'd stretched between palm trees had been dug up and left in tangled heaps. Their single cooking pot, the one he'd disguised among the lush greenery to collect rainwater, had been overturned, thereby catching nothing that they could boil and drink.

But it hadn't been the storm that had turned the earth over and washed up what was left of their possessions for anyone to steal: it was a small figure sitting cross-legged in front of the rain-filled fire pit, eating the last few pieces of their jerky, playing with a light Sophia had insisted on bringing, despite the fact that it wouldn't be invented until the next century.

"Drop that at once, sir!" Nicholas demanded.

The small man looked up, a piece of jerky dangling from his lips. His dark eyes were strikingly distinct. Two thick, dark brows were angled over them, as if someone had taken ink and thumbed the shapes across. A surprisingly delicate nose and high cheekbones were sunburned—the only flaw in otherwise clear, fair skin.

His mouth stretched into a shameless smile around the jerky clenched between his teeth. A weathered navy coat rustled as he brought a gloved hand up, fingers dancing in a little wave.

Thief.

SIX

It was several outraged moments before Nicholas was able to collect himself enough to speak. "What is your name, sir? And what business do you have with us?"

The man cocked his head to the side, studying him. After a moment he answered, his voice higher than Nicholas might have expected, speaking a language he'd never heard before. The grating laughter, however, did not need translation.

Sophia answered, barking out a string of words in that same language, wiping the gleaming humor from the thief's face. Nicholas released the grip he'd maintained on her coat, and watched as Sophia lunged toward the small man. He rolled back off the fallen palm tree he'd been perched on, dancing away from her reach again and again.

After everything she'd imbibed last night, he suspected Sophia had a headache pounding like the drums of hell, so frankly, he didn't blame her for reaching into her coat for her pistol and taking aim.

The small man froze. Nicholas caught a hint of gold tucked into his belt—a knife, perhaps? The ceasefire, at least, gave him a moment to assess the risk: the man wore the attire of an Englishman, but the loose fabric of his shirtsleeves and breeches had been rolled and tucked at the ends to account for his diminutive stature.

"Put the flintlock down, *nŭ shén*," the man said.

Sophia lunged toward him, snarling. In two fluid moves, the man had Sophia disarmed and on her knees on the ground, looking stunned.

She growled and, undeterred, rose just enough to try to knock the man's feet out from under him. He simply leaped back out of the way.

Something in the man's face shifted, a feminine softening that arrived with a flurry of delighted, girlish laughter. Sophia seemed to realize their mistake the precise moment Nicholas did, and cut off her next attack, stiffening.

Not a man.

A woman.

Nicholas cocked his head to the side, studying the thief again. He could see it now, of course; how blind and presumptuous he'd been, but the Three Crowns had been dark and his glimpse fleeting. The binding of linen wrapped around her chest peeked out from beneath the loose collar of her shirt.

Her focus shifted off Sophia's face to meet his. "Remove your gaze, *gŏu*, or I will remove your eyes."

"I know better than that," he said, holding his own pistol steady. "I want the letter you stole."

"Neither of your weapons are loaded," the young woman said, flicking her fingers in their direction. "They are too light in your hands. Neither of you carry a powder flask. And . . ." She spared a glance around their pitiful campsite. "Could you afford such?"

"More than one way to use a gun," Nicholas noted. "Would you like to discover how many?"

At that, a small smile curled her rosebud lips. "I suspect I know far more than you, *bèn dàn*."

He tried to quell the tightening in his guts at the knifelike edge to her words.

"Who. Are. You," Sophia managed to get out from between her gritted teeth.

The young woman removed her hat, dropping it to the sand with a look of disgust. She lifted her long black braid from where she had tucked it under her cloak, and then a heavy jade pendant, the length of one of Nicholas's fingers. The image of the tree carved into it looked like an evergreen; it stood tall, arrow-like in shape. Its branches were not as full as several of the other family sigils, but still robust and proud.

Damn it all, he thought, feeling a weariness creep into him. And here he'd been hoping, however in vain, that the culprit would be a random thief, one without ties to their hidden world. Nicholas supposed he would never be so lucky.

"Hemlock . . ." he began.

"Did my grandfather send you?" Sophia interrupted.

The girl scowled. "I will never work for him. Not even if he were to offer a fair price for my services."

A mercenary, then. He'd heard stories about them from Hall—members of the Jacaranda and Hemlock families who had refused to bow to Ironwood once he seized control of their travelers and guardians and absorbed them into his own clan. They offered their services to any traveler or guardian who could pay them. He'd always wondered about the kinds of jobs they took, assuming they were mostly occupied with tracking down wayward family members or lost possessions, or maybe even quietly making small changes to history that wouldn't result in the timeline shifting.

"Call me Li Min," she said.

"I'll call you Jackass if it suits me," Sophia snapped. "Tell me what the hell you're doing here before I take this knife and slice you from gullet to gut."

Nicholas wondered briefly if it was his destiny to be surrounded by women possessing varying degrees of murderous intent.

The girl smiled. "This is no way to speak to one with whom you wish to do business."

Sophia sucked in a sharp breath, filling the bellows of her chest to explode, but Nicholas was quicker on the draw. "We have no business with you beyond retrieving our letter. I don't suppose you'll be so kind as to offer any sort of explanation for why you took it? Who hired you to steal it?"

And why you are here, dangling it in front of us, if someone paid you to take it? Unless, of course, she was angling to dip into two different pots of profit, hoping he and Sophia would bribe her for a look.

"I never said I was hired," Li Min said. "It is in my interest to know the business of the travelers I come across. Work is hard to find, you see, and occasionally I must look for it, rather than wait for it to come to me. Many Ironwoods have traveled here in recent months. But imagine my surprise to see a Linden guardian scuttling around the beaches like a little crab. And then you appeared to conduct your business. . . ."

Unsure of whether or not he'd live to regret it, Nicholas lowered his pistol and returned it to its place at his side. Feeling steadier, he began to consider their situation in this new light.

"If you stole it to ransom it back to us, then you already know we have nothing with which to pay you," he said, sweeping his arms out to indicate their sorry state of affairs.

"I wish to know what the letter says," the girl said. "It is written in a peculiar way. I will give it back to you on two conditions."

"I'll take it from your dead body!" Sophia swung an arm out, her fist barreling through the air. Nicholas saw it happening, felt that wrench of dismay, as Sophia misjudged the distance between her and the other girl by nearly a foot. Li Min easily dodged, her face passive, as Sophia lost her balance and slammed into the sand, sending up a spray of it.

Sophia raised a hand to her eye patch, nearly howling in frustration. It wasn't the first time Nicholas had seen her struggle with her altered vision, and it wasn't the first time his heart had given an unwelcome, involuntary clench at the sight, either.

Li Min forced her dark gaze up from the girl, back to him. "I will give you this letter, and you will show me how to read it."

Nicholas shook his head. "Unacceptable."

If the writing was "peculiar," he had a feeling it was written in the way Rose had coded the other letters to Etta—a calculated risk on Rose's part, because what if Etta *hadn't* shown Nicholas how to decode them?—and he was loath to reveal that secret to anyone outside the family.

The envelope emerged from inside of Li Min's shirt, stained brown by the ale, rumpled and worn, but in one piece. That is, until the girl ripped it in half. Nicholas and Sophia both lurched toward her, crying out.

"If I do not read it, you will not read it," Li Min warned, her voice shifting from its airy tone to flint. And to make her point, she turned the halves to the side and began to rip them into quarters.

Sophia turned to look up at Nicholas. "It's not worth it. Let her have the damn letter. We already have our plan."

But it would save us time . . . tracking Etta would be a simpler thing if we could have the last common year now, without delay, Nicholas thought.

"Don't do it, Carter," Sophia warned, voice low.

"I will not show you how to read it—" Nicholas held up his hand, stilling Li Min. "But I will read to you what it says."

"Unacceptable," Li Min said, mimicking his tone. "You might deceive me."

"You accuse me of being dishonorable?" Nicholas said.

"What does an Ironwood know of honor?" Li Min wondered aloud, waving the pieces of the letter at him.

"My name is Nicholas Carter," he said. "I am an Ironwood by only half my blood, and never in character. If nothing else, I am honor-bound to the Linden family not to show a stranger the sole way they have of communicating with each other without Ironwood being able to discover their secrets. You can understand that, I think, given your line of work."

"The Linden family is dead," Li Min said, eyes lighting up with obvious curiosity. "Only a few guardians remain."

"Their methods work, then," Nicholas said, "if you have not discovered that some of their travelers are still very much alive."

Li Min inclined her head toward him, giving him that much, at least. "I will accept this condition, then. But I have one other."

The girl was smiling again, and within the span of less than an hour, he'd already learned to fear the implications of that expression. His mind began to take tally of what little they had, and he braced himself for the loss of any of it. "Go on, then."

"As my payment, I would like a kiss," she said, glancing between the two of them. "A proper one."

Nicholas paused.

Of all of the things he'd suspected she would ask for—flintlock pistols, shoes, a favor, a signed confirmation of debt—a *kiss*? He stared at her a good long while, waiting for her to give the true price, but she simply gazed back, her dark eyes unwavering.

Nicholas had kissed a number of women in his twenty years of life; not as many as Chase, but then, even Lothario could not top that tally. He was far—*far*—from being a saint, but at some point over the past few weeks, his heart had resolved that it only wanted to kiss one girl ever again, and his whole spirit seemed to retreat at the thought of kissing another.

I could kiss her forehead, her cheek, he thought quickly. She hadn't specified where, or how.

Do it, Carter. He pressed his hands to his thighs, trying to steady the rioting dismay. Get the matter over with, read the letter, and go. That was all that mattered now. He would not think of Etta, the way she'd tasted of rain when she'd kissed him in the jungle. How he could have sworn there were stars in her hair that night in Damascus. The way she made him feel solid, and terribly brave.

Well, *his* mind was unhelpful.

"All right," he said, resigned. "Let's have it, then."

Li Min took a step back, dark brows rising over her forehead in both amusement and disdain. "I was speaking to *her*."

It was physically painful to exist inside the long stretch of silence that followed. *Oh.* The wheels of his mind began to turn again. *Her.*

"Oh. Well, that's . . . it's certainly . . ."

Sophia had begun to collect their scattered belongings, grumbling every curse and oath known to mankind none too quietly. At Li Min's words, she slowly began to straighten.

"Ma'am, I apologize," Nicholas said sincerely, inclining his head. "Forgive my presumption."

Li Min flicked her fingers dismissively in his direction. "It can be hard for men to believe they are not all gods walking the earth, as so many women are forced to fall at their feet."

He lifted a shoulder in a faint shrug. Where was the lie in that?

"And you expect me to fall at your feet now?" Sophia asked, her expression surprisingly even.

"No one expects that," Nicholas said. "It's your choice. As you said before, we have other avenues of inquiry to pursue. She can take the letter and be damned."

"Oh? I have your permission to refuse, then?" Sophia rolled her eye.

"I only meant to make it clear—" He closed his mouth, knowing he'd botched this moment beyond repair.

"Fine," Sophia said, cutting him off. She squared her shoulders, glancing back at him as she stepped toward the other girl. "We could go on without the bloody letter, but if it helps us find the men who— I just want this to be over with."

Nicholas didn't miss the catch in her voice when she said "the men."

"Have at it," Sophia said, removing her hat. She stood straight in front of Li Min, who mirrored her stoic expression. Nicholas had the peculiar sense that he was watching a duel, with neither of the aggrieved parties willing to fire into the air.

He kept a hand on the unloaded pistol at his side, and was startled to find that Sophia was not doing the same. Rather, she was holding her ground, waiting for the other young woman to approach.

Sophia's throat worked as she swallowed with some difficulty. Li Min brought a hand to her face and curled a loose strand of dark hair behind the other girl's ear. With a tenderness that made Nicholas want to avert his gaze, Li Min leaned forward.

"I'll wait," she said, her lips a breath from Sophia's. "One day you may be willing to pay, and I will delight in collecting."

Sophia's face, already flushed from the sun, deepened to crimson as Li Min offered the halves of Rose's letter to her. She snatched the parchment away and thrust it in Nicholas's direction, never once taking her eyes off the mercenary. "Read it."

Nicholas felt the knots around his lungs ease, and briny air filled them, tempered with the scent of the rotting green flesh of the jungle. He moved a short distance away from the young women and sat down on the bowed body of a fallen palm tree. With great care, he lined up the raw, torn edges.

Dear Little Heart, the center of my being . . . It went on to discuss the weather, King George III, and so on, like tiny riots of nonsense across the page.

Nicholas felt his brows rise as he reached up and swiped the sweat from his forehead. The endearment would read as a bit much to the casual reader, but Etta had explained to him that, in the absence of a key to read it, the way to decode the letter was embedded within the salutation. She'd used "star" before, and "heart" was easy enough— though, what to make of "little," and the curious inclusion of "the center of my being"?

Unless . . .

He curled his index fingers and thumbs together, forming a heart, and positioned it at the center of the parchment. The message it revealed was still padded with gibberish, and he couldn't make sense of it until he imagined the shape of a small heart laid over the words at the center of the letter.

Cannot meet you. Will lead the shadows away from you as long as I can. For year, seek belladonna.

Another blasted riddle. The paper wrinkled under the force of his grip as he read the message aloud to the young women. *Bloody Rose Linden.*

"Iiiinteresting," Sophia said, something sparking in her eyes. "Dare I say it, but the woman might have actually come through for us. I hadn't considered it as an option, but she's onto something."

"Foolish," Li Min shot back. "And you were right *not* to consider it."

"I would prefer to know what it is the two of you are referring to, rather than watch you argue the point," Nicholas said with a patience he did not know he still possessed.

Sophia ignored Li Min's look of disbelief, saying, "There are two people in all of time that know the workings of our world—who make it a point to know everything everyone is doing. One of them is Grand— is Ironwood himself, and the other is the Belladonna."

"Belladonna is a she, not a thing?" he confirmed, trying to extinguish the eagerness in his voice.

"Julian never spoke of her?" Sophia asked him, at his look of confusion. "She's . . . I'm not quite sure how to put this. She seeks out treasures lost to time and holds auctions for them; only, instead of paying in gold, you pay for them in favors and secrets. Ironwood has allowed it because, generally speaking, these treasures must stay 'lost' to preserve his timeline."

"What is it that you hope to accomplish with this visit?" Li Min asked. The sunlight gleamed off her coal-black hair as she cocked her head to the side. "Perhaps you might purchase the information from me, instead?"

"What business is it of yours?" Nicholas asked. In truth, he was mildly concerned about what she might ask for next, and whether or not he could trust her answer.

"I told you, it's my business to know others' business."

"We are attempting to uncover the last common year with this most recent major shift in the timeline," Nicholas said. "Is that information you possess?"

There was a single beat in which his hopes shot into the air like a firework, only to crash back down a moment later. Li Min glanced off toward the turquoise water. "No. I could . . . I might seek the answer for you, however."

"For a handsome fee," Sophia burst in. "Trying to poach some business from the Belladonna, are you? No, thank you. We'll go to someone who will actually know, not a second-rate mercenary who can't even decode a message." Sophia ignored Li Min's light laugh and turned back to Nicholas. "The Belladonna knows *everything*. Julian told me that on his last visit accompanying the old man, she rattled off the full scale of *all* of Ironwood's comings and goings, and the supposedly secret changes he'd enacted."

"And your quarrel with her is . . . ?" Nicholas asked, turning back to Li Min. He did not entirely like the sound of this, aside from potentially having a more direct, guaranteed route to Etta.

Li Min lifted a shoulder, but her gaze darted over to Sophia, just for a moment, as she pressed her lips into a tight line.

"She's bought into the rumors that the woman is a witch," Sophia said with obvious ridicule. "That she'll ensnare your soul. Ridiculous!"

Nicholas did balk at that. *Witch* was a strong accusation in his native time, and flung around far too quickly when it came to ladies with unusual interests or predispositions.

Li Min's lips parted, but after a moment, she only smiled. Tossing her long braid over her shoulder again, she bent to retrieve her cape and hat. "You seem to have your path charted, then. Be well."

She was several feet away and retreating into the palms before Nicholas's mind took note that she was leaving.

"That's it?" Sophia called after her. "After all that, that's *it*?"

Li Min didn't miss a stride as she called back, "For now. Until we meet again."

When it looked as though she might try to follow the other girl, to haul her back for further interrogation, Nicholas caught Sophia's shoulder with one hand and used the other to tuck Rose's correspondence back in his jacket pocket.

"Can you *believe* the nerve of that girl—"

"Sophia," he interrupted, "a *witch*? Is there anything else I should know?"

"Oh, we'll be fine," Sophia said, turning from the trail of broken underbrush Li Min had left behind.

"Are you personally acquainted with her?" he pressed.

"Well, no; but she is a legend, and between Julian's stories and the old man's absolute loathing of her, I feel as though I've a handle on her," Sophia said quickly. "I can't believe I didn't think of this. The only thing we have to worry about now is finding a passage to Prague. She operates in the fifteenth century—I think there should be a passage to Spain if we can reach Florida, and from there—"

"Not to interrupt your planning, but how do you propose we buy passage off this island?"

Sophia cocked her head to the side, her lips curling up at the edges as she lifted a fist-size leather bag from inside of her jacket and tossed it to him. "Some thief she is. Didn't even notice when I cut this from her belt."

Nicholas actually laughed, unknotting the laces to reveal enough gold coins to momentarily stop his heart. "She'll be back for this."

Sophia glanced back at the path Li Min had taken. "Good."

SAN FRANCISCO
1906

SEVEN

THEY RETURNED TO THE SAME ROOM ETTA HAD CLIMBED out of, accompanied by a different pair of guards, as well as a maid who her father—she shook her head, clearing the impossible word from it—who the *man* had practically flung at her. Also joining them was a tall, silver-haired woman with posture so severe, Etta wondered if it'd be possible to break a wooden chair against her spine. No one had introduced them, but Etta was reasonably sure this was the Winifred the man had spoken of.

"You may proceed," the older woman told the maid. Etta would have been shocked if the girl was even seventeen; she peered out from beneath a heavy mop of dark curls escaping from a loose braid. The girl was curious, but not at all frightened or overawed, which made Etta think she was likely a guardian, someone connected to the Thorns. The lantern in her hands made fragments of light jump around them on the thick carpets and gilded wallpaper, fluttering like newly disturbed ghosts.

"A little privacy would be nice," Etta told the older woman.

The old blade reached behind her to lock the door. Etta raised a brow, taking in the dark violet of her dress. It looked painfully cinched at the waist, with a trail of small pearl buttons that ran up the bodice to the place her tight collar ended, just beneath her chin. The silk skirt was draped with all the elegant ease of a waterfall, collecting in a slight bustle at the small of her back.

After rummaging through the wardrobe, the maid pulled out a plain white blouse with a little dark embroidery around the collar, and a long gray skirt that looked to be made of wool. It was cut narrowly at the waist and along the thighs, but flared as it got closer to the knees and brushed the floor. The poor girl seemed to realize at the exact moment Etta did that there was an icicle's chance in summer that the tiny waist would fit her.

"I'll let it out, it won't be but a moment," the girl swore, her gaze darting to Winifred.

A moment too long, apparently. With an irritated look, Winifred turned back to Etta and ordered, "Strip."

"Can I get a *please*?" Etta grumbled, eyeing the very familiar garment in the woman's hands. "I'm not wearing the corset. Absolutely not—"

Winifred seized the scruff of Etta's nightgown and yanked it hard over her head. Momentarily blinded by the fabric, Etta reached up, trying to loosen the ribbon before it strangled her or tore off an ear. She crossed her arms over her chest, shielding her body as the woman threw her a thin chemise.

It occurred to Etta that the woman was literally and figuratively stripping her, trying to make her feel as vulnerable as possible, and that she shouldn't simply let her do it without a fight. When she tried to twist away from her, Winifred shoved her off-balance, dropped the corset over her head, and began to lace it up before Etta caught her next breath. The woman handed her another thin, sleeveless top to pull over the corset. Etta resented the little cheerful pink ribbons on it almost as much as the woman's smirk.

"You poor creature. You've your mother's sorry figure."

"Touch me again and I'll show you how alike we are," Etta spat out.

Winifred had already turned away, retrieving the blouse and newly let-out skirt from the maid. She threw them at Etta's feet.

"With *haste*, you stupid child," she said, when Etta did not immediately do as she was told. "The Grand Master won't be pleased if he's kept waiting."

Etta's temper flared at the word *child*, singeing whatever restraint she might have had left. That was the only explanation she had for why she said, "Cyrus Ironwood is the Grand Master."

The slap came so suddenly that Etta could not have dodged it if she had enough time to try. She careened back onto the bed, pressing her hand to the burning skin on her face.

"Look what you made me do," the woman growled. "Such insolence! And after I cared for you! Washed you! Tended to your courses! And with nary a complaint. If he hadn't asked it of me, I would have smothered you from the start."

"You are insane," Etta informed her, fists already clenched. "Hit me again and your friends will be picking pieces of you out of the rug!"

The maid blanched, but Etta didn't care, she didn't—she was shaking now with the full force of her fury, embarrassment, and resentment. She tried to quell the hurricane of emotions swirling in her chest as she finished dressing and was forced to sit at the vanity and have her hair braided. She avoided looking in the mirror, unwilling to see the throbbing red mark across her cheek.

"Hardly acceptable," Winifred said, once the ordeal was over, "but follow me."

Etta knew she needed to go with her if she wanted to confirm the Thorns had the astrolabe, but obeying this woman felt like swallowing seawater: it incinerated her throat, choking her.

"I think I'll stay," Etta said, crossing her arms over her chest.

The woman's hand reached out, and Etta instinctively struck her arm out to block the hit—only, the woman wasn't aiming for another slap. Her other hand came up and fisted into Etta's braid, twisting so tightly that Etta yelped in pain. "Let me go!"

Instead, the woman dragged her across the room, never once breaking her stride as Etta kicked and scratched at her to release her grip. The door opened to the other guard's wide-eyed shock, and, as he fumbled for his words, the woman continued on her path, letting Etta's bare feet drag and burn across the carpet, down the stairs.

There really was some sort of party happening on the first floor. As Winifred hauled her across a gallery hallway, Etta could hear the excited chatter and laughter, even as a man poured himself into playing a jaunty tune on a piano. The smell of liquor and perfume permeated the air as they passed the door to the library, with Julian's amused face peering out.

"Attagirl," he called after them. "Keep fighting, kiddo!"

"Stop calling me that!" she snarled back, gritting her teeth as his laugher chased them down the hall.

And, finally, to another door, this one guarded by three men in fine suits. Winifred released her grip on Etta's hair, and Etta righted herself. Two of the men blanched at the sight of her. The other twitched a heavy brow in her direction, struggling to swallow his laugh as he gave Etta a pitying look.

"Come now, Winnie. She's just a girl. Have a care."

"*Her* girl," Winifred said, pounding on the door. "Never forget this."

"Come in," came the immediate reply.

Not an invitation, of course, but a command. Etta had arrived ready to fight, her pulse raging as she huffed. *Calm down, calm down, remember the plan*—she had to find out if they had the astrolabe, and try to figure out how to get it away from them to destroy it once and for all.

The guards fell back as Etta was pushed inside by the older woman, her hand twisted in the loose fabric of Etta's blouse to ensure, she guessed, that she didn't try to make one last run for it. Instead, she passed through the threshold at her full height, trying not to glare.

This office had been decorated in a similar style to the library—all masculine dark wood and jewel tones. It aimed to be impressive, and hit the mark. The window captured much the same view of the crippled landscape, along with the first hint of dawn brightening the sky.

There were already four people in the room, seated around the stately desk at its center. Etta's eyes landed on the woman first, taking in her tailored skirt suit and the dark hair she'd curled and twisted into victory rolls. The older man beside her wore plain linen trousers and a tunic, both almost entirely hidden beneath his leather chest plate and sword belt. His long gray hair was slicked back from his bearded face, with small silver beads braided into several of the strands that grazed the fur pelt draped over his shoulders. To his right was a young Asian man, wearing a kimono in a shade of blue usually found only in the deepest heart of the ocean.

An incredulous laugh bubbled up inside of her at the sight of them.

Etta inhaled a deep breath through her nose, letting the smell of wax and wood polish settle her. Henry Hemlock sat behind the desk, his feet crossed and propped up on it.

The others turned to look at Etta and Winifred, and then back at Henry, shifting uncomfortably in their seats. Henry Hemlock, however, continued on with what he was saying. "I hear you, Elizabeth. I do. The last thing I want is for your children to go to sleep worrying you won't be there in the morning. So many of us lived through that time and suffered for it. I'll take another look at the postings and see if anyone is amenable to a switch."

The woman's shoulders slumped in relief. "Thank you. *Thank you.*"

"We shouldn't delay in meeting them, sir, if the situation is as dire as the message seems to convey," said the man with long silver hair. "We must help them and secure our advantage before making any changes to our personnel. In fact, I think I should go round up John and Abraham before meeting the rest of you there."

Henry grinned. "Perhaps leaving the fur behind."

The man laughed, stroking the tufts of it. "I think I'd make quite a statement stomping down the Seine."

"And cause a disastrous change for a laugh, I suppose," Winifred said, with ice in her voice.

Etta counted more than one set of eyes rolling in that room.

"You'd try to shoot a star down from the sky for shining too brightly," the man groused back.

"All right," Henry said, taking his feet off the desk and standing. Everyone in the room, except Etta, pivoted to follow his path back and forth as he began to pace. "That's enough. You know how I feel about this sort of sniping. Remember there's a true enemy out there to aim at."

"Yes, of course," Winifred breathed, the very essence of sweetness, even as her grip on Etta tightened.

"I don't think we've considered the fact that he, too, could be dead, and that Ironwood might already have the astrolabe," the Japanese man interjected, leaning over to poke at an open letter. "Who else could they mean by 'shadows'? Who else has the resources to hunt the brothers the way he describes?"

What? Etta felt the moment tilt sharply beneath her feet, the realization its own earthquake.

"If it were so easy, we would have done so decades past," Henry said, turning his gaze onto Etta. "You seem surprised. Almost as if, perhaps, you'd expected to find the astrolabe with us?"

Etta said nothing, only turned her face away, to stare at the place where the wood floors met the carpets. There was a kind of lure in his dark gaze; his focus tracked her every shift and breath. The weight of it registered so strongly, it felt as if he'd put his hands on her shoulders and was stubbornly trying to turn her back toward him. She didn't want him to have easy access to her thoughts, not when her mind was racing like this, trying to keep pace with her thundering heart.

It had been two weeks since the two Thorns, along with Sophia, had wrested the astrolabe from her in Damascus. They should have been able to create a passage directly back to the rest of the Thorns here in San Francisco; but from what she'd understood of their conversation, not only had they not brought the astrolabe, they'd disappeared altogether. And there had been no word at all from Sophia, who'd gone with them.

"All we've seen are the Ironwoods he's sent out to try to rewrite our changes in small ways," Henry said. "Were it in his possession, Cyrus wouldn't have hesitated to use it, to reset the timeline back to his own. It's greed and greed alone that compels his family."

"Let's not forget," the silver-haired man said with a chuckle, "we both have Ironwood on our mothers' side."

"No," Henry said with a quick smile, "*let's*. But my point stands. We must trust in Kadir's ability to get to safety, and in our own to ensure we can get to him in time and retrieve the astrolabe from where he's hidden it. I'm sorry to cut the celebrations short, but tell the others to make ready to travel in the morning. And we'll need to leave at least some travelers to support the guardians staying here to watch the children."

"A wise decision," Winifred gushed.

Etta tried not to gag.

The others nodded, and, sensing they'd reached the end of the conversation, rose as one. They brushed past Etta, one at a time, each stealing a last look at her. For a second, she could have sworn the man with silver hair gave a little shudder.

"Please have a seat, Henrietta. Winifred, thank you; that will be all. Ensure we're not disturbed."

The older woman bobbed a slight curtsey, giving Etta's back a parting pinch, hard enough to make her jump forward a step. Etta waited until the woman had vanished through the door in a swirl of dark skirts before turning to Henry and spitting out, "She doesn't travel through passages, does she? She sacrifices a puppy and flies through the centuries on her broom."

He gave a sharp cough into his hand.

"I assure you, your great-aunt is quite loving," Henry said, only to stop and reconsider. "That is, she's quite loving in her own way . . . every other Sunday. In May. Won't you sit?"

Great-aunt. No way in hell.

Etta didn't sit; her hands curled around the back of the chair so tightly, its joints creaked.

"The first thing I want you to know is that you are safe here," he said, not breaking his gaze. "You have nothing to fear from myself or anyone here. I've taken measures to ensure your safety from Ironwood, as well. Unless you choose to go looking for him, he will no longer concern himself with you."

That seemed unlikely. Before she could press the point, Henry turned his attention to shuffling through the unruly stack of opened correspondence and parchment piled into small, unsteady mountains on his desk. He seemed to find what he was looking for; he pulled a black velvet sack out from under the mess and dumped something into his palm—a gold earring. A hoop decorated with a pearl, blue beads, and tiny gold leaves.

Mom's earring. Etta's whole self seemed to tense in belated panic. One hand rose to touch her ears, only to find both of them free of jewelry.

"Winifred found this in the folds of your clothing when you were brought to us," he said, offering it to her. "I thought you might like it back."

Just one? The question hung in her mind, quiet with devastation. In the grand scheme of everything that had happened, losing an earring was hardly the worst failure she'd endured, but it was another betrayal of trust, another way she had let her mother down.

She couldn't add yet another notch to that tally by falling prey to this man's lies. "You keep it. I found it in some junky old thrift shop."

Henry's lips compressed at that, and, when he did speak, there was a new edge to the words. "I realize you are out of your depth, and I am quite sympathetic to all that you've been through. But one thing I cannot tolerate is lying, and another is disrespecting your family. You did not find these earrings in a thrift store. I imagine they were a gift from your mother, as I know they were a cherished gift from her beloved uncle's wife."

He knows about Hasan.

That didn't prove anything. He and the others had talked about having many sources out there; he could have easily learned about Hasan that way.

Even that his wife was the one who gave her the earrings?

Etta began to bite her lip, but forced herself to stop. She would not give in to the temptation to fill the uneasy silence between them with chatter. Not when Henry seemed so comfortable in it, and was watching her so closely.

"Who did you bribe for that information?" she asked, taking the earring from him.

One corner of his mouth kicked up, and he opened the same drawer, retrieving a long velvet case. Resting inside was a strand of glistening pearls, each slightly irregular in shape. Every third pearl was nestled between breathtaking sapphires. "Samarah made them to match this necklace I commissioned upon our engagement. Is that proof enough for you?"

At that, Etta did sit down. Henry placed the jewelry case between them.

Engagement. *Engagement.*

Memory clouded her mind, dulling all of the certainties with which she had walked into the office.

But, darling, who's your father? Alice had asked her in London. *Henrietta . . . is it . . . is it possibly Henry?*

"I'll have another earring made to match," he told her. "Or we might adjust it to be worn as a necklace. Whichever you'd prefer."

Etta felt like she was barreling down a road at night without a brake pedal. This wasn't right—it wasn't him. This man couldn't be her father.

"I don't want anything from you," she said.

"And yet, it's my duty to provide for you," Henry said. "At least grant me that much. I'm nearly eighteen years behind on the matter."

"I can take care of things myself," Etta said.

"Yes," he said with a faint laugh. "That seems likely, given your mother. It's rather remarkable, you know, the resemblance between the two of you. Uncanny, even."

"Yeah, I didn't miss the folks in the hall who crossed themselves when they saw me," Etta said dryly.

Henry didn't seem to hear her. He was carefully studying her face, his hand absently ruffling his dark hair. "But she gave you my name. . . ."

Is it possibly Henry?

There seemed to be a question buried in the words, but his voice trailed off; he looked away, focusing on the empty bookshelves on the other side of the room. It gave Etta the opportunity to study him again—to prove to herself, and that small, chiming part of her heart, that there was no resemblance there to be found.

"I don't know what to tell you," she admitted.

"'He who dares not grasp the thorn should never crave the rose,' as Brontë said." There was a wry expression on Henry's face as he continued. "She has always been fiercely intelligent and determined, but she held herself apart from most others, for her own protection, to give herself distance if she ever needed to run. Capturing her heart was like wrestling a bear. I still have the scars to show for it."

Etta, not for the first time, or even the twentieth, wished she had a better grip on the timeline of her mother's life—when she had left the Thorns, when she had gone to infiltrate the Ironwoods, and when she had ultimately betrayed both by hiding the astrolabe and disappearing into the future. But it fit. All of this fit.

Is it possibly Henry?

More than possible. Etta brought her hand to her face, pressing her fingers hard to her temples, as if that could ease the pounding there. Her shoulder complained each time she shifted, but the pain only chiseled down her thoughts to their bare truths. Each small argument, each scrap of evidence, was beginning to form an undeniable picture.

She wanted Nicholas—she wanted to see his face, and measure his thoughts against her own until they made sense. Etta hadn't understood how she'd used his steady resolve as a shelter until it was gone, and she was raw and exposed and trapped. When she'd been orphaned, she'd left the braver parts of herself with him, and what was left of her now was too cowardly to admit what she already knew to be true.

"It was for her as it was for me," Henry said, eyes back on hers. "Truthfully . . . I don't know that she named you for me, so much as for a moment in time. I suppose you are a tribute, a kind of memory to who we were. It's—well, it's unexpected, given the way she left us."

Etta didn't trust her voice enough to speak.

Her whole life, all eighteen years of it, her father had lingered as a kind of question mark in the background. A ghost that came around haunting now and then in her thoughts to remind her of the loss—to expand that gap in her family portraits. But there had been *many* ghosts, and *many* gaps, on both sides of her family, and Etta had never let herself dwell on any of them in particular, because it seemed ungrateful in the face of everything and everyone she did have.

Father. A word from a vocabulary of love she'd never learned. Etta couldn't make any more sense of it than she could of the way she felt. An involuntary, panicked elation that left her feeling like she needed to run to him or *away* from him.

"What am I doing here?" Etta asked finally.

"At first, we only wanted to protect and heal you—you were almost dead when Julian Ironwood brought you back to us. From here on out . . . well," he said, "I should like to hope you will aid us against Ironwood, considering all he's done to you. And if I'm lucky, you might tell me a little about yourself, beyond what I know."

"Which is what?" she asked, shocked by the eagerness in his voice.

"That you were born and raised in Manhattan. That you enjoy reading, and were homeschooled from a young age. I know that you have performed across the world in many competitions, and that you feel very strongly about Bach over Beethoven."

"You read the *Times* article," she said quietly.

"I read everything I could find from this . . . *Internet* . . . creation," he admitted. He said *Internet* like he was testing the word in his mouth for the first time. "Not nearly enough. There's one question in particular I've had for weeks now, and I desperately wish you'd consider answering it—but only if you are comfortable."

The way he framed it satisfied her pride and appealed to her curiosity, but there was one weight she needed to remove before she could continue.

"I need you to answer a question for me first," Etta said. "But I don't know if I can even trust your answer. . . ."

"Ask and see."

She took a pacifying breath, waiting until the pain in her throat eased enough to speak normally. "The night of the concert . . . were you or any of your Thorns involved in a shooting?"

There. A flicker of something in his face. Henry's lips compressed and she heard the harsh breath leave his nose. "Do you mean Alice?"

Etta had expected a quick dismissal, an annoyed defense. But that softness in his expression rubbed at the fragile shield she'd constructed around her heart, and the heaviness in his words nearly cracked it altogether.

She swallowed again. Nodded.

It was a long while before he spoke again, and the whole time, he never broke his gaze away from her. Etta could see his mind working, as if deciding how best to continue—or was he deciding what she could handle?

"Never," he told her. "I would never harm Alice, though I'm not sure she felt the same about me. I believed her when she said she tried to stop you from traveling. To protect you."

"She told you that?"

A rebellious thought rose in her. *Alice trusted him.*

"After you disappeared, I stayed with her," he said. The words slammed through Etta's heart, making it throb in her chest with a mess of relief and gratitude and envy.

"Her last thoughts were only of you."

She wasn't alone. Alice didn't die alone.

Etta pressed a hand to her face, drawing in breath after breath to stave off the crush of tears. "She wasn't alone."

"She wasn't alone," he said softly. "She shouldn't have suffered that at all, but at least . . . there was that one small bit of mercy."

Etta heard him shift, his feet moving against the carpet, but he didn't reach for her, didn't feed her comforting lies. He remained nearby, silent, ready, until the metronome of her heart slowed enough for her to find her center again.

"Thank you," Etta managed. "For staying with her until the end."

He nodded. "The honor was mine. Are you satisfied with your answer?"

"Yes," she said. "What was your question?"

"Did your mother give you any sort of traveling education and training?" Henry asked. "The fact that you so willingly followed the Ironwood girl made me think not, and yet it's so unlike your mother not to have thought through something five steps past everyone else, and there should have been any number of precautions to protect you against this."

Etta gritted her teeth at the humiliation that itched inside of her. The embarrassment at being so unprepared for a traveler's life was familiar, but feeling it now meant that she cared what this man thought of her. She didn't want him to somehow think less of her.

"I didn't know I could travel until the night of the performance."

His hand rasped over the faint stubble along his chin and jaw, eyes softening in a way that made her hate herself, just a little bit, for how much she appreciated it. "None of us are born speaking a half-dozen languages or feeling at ease in the Roman Empire. You'll pick it up quickly enough, and there are many here, myself included, who would be happy to help you in any way we can."

Etta raised her eyebrows at that—from her unscientific survey, less than half of the Thorns she'd met had been willing to look her in the eye.

"She did what she had to do," Etta said. "Mom, I mean."

"She did what she was *told* to do," Henry said, rising again to his feet. He was tall, but not imposingly so. Yet, when he moved, he took command over every inch of the space around him. "How can you not be angry with her? How can you defend her after everything she's subjected you to?"

There were so many ways she would have answered that, even a few days ago, but now Etta felt all of her explanations crumbling, slipping through her fingers like the hot dust of Palmyra.

"She didn't come for you when you needed her most." His face was strained as he spoke. "She let you fall into Ironwood's trap."

She had . . . Etta had taken care of herself the best she could, tried to wrest some control from the situation, but it didn't change that simple fact.

"He's holding her prisoner," Etta explained. "There was nothing she could do. He might have . . ." *Already killed her.*

Henry made a noise of disgust, waving the thought away. "Your mother was free of Ironwood's men within days. I had numerous reports of her scampering about, staying well clear of you."

"She's *alive*?" Etta breathed out. The fear released like a sigh, blowing hot, then icy as what he didn't say finally set in. *She's alive and she didn't come to help me.*

"I can forgive her for what she did to us. She betrayed the trust of this group by lying and saying her family no longer had the astrolabe. The Thorns loved her, cared for her, and she took the key to everything we hoped to accomplish." He raked his hand back through his hair again, mussing it further. "We've known each other since we were children, Rose and I. For a time, I truly believed I understood her better than I knew myself. I'm not proud to admit it, but I did not see just how ruthless and hopelessly misguided she had become. She is no stranger to using people, Thorns or Ironwoods, but for *you* to bear the brunt of it is cruel, even by her standards."

Etta didn't like that line of thought, the way it worked her stomach into disarray. She wanted to argue in her mother's defense, to call his own bias into question, but when she reached into her memories, she found she'd already run through what little evidence to the contrary she had.

Making his way to the window, Henry looked out, keeping his face from her. "There's so much darkness to this story, there are times I feel suffocated by it. Our lives became a tapestry of family and revenge and devastation, and it wove around us all so tightly, none of us escaped its knots, not even you. I should have seen the signs, but I wanted to believe she was beyond it. You have to know that if I had known she was with child when she left, I never would have stopped looking for you. I would have gone to the very edges of time to save you from this."

"What are you talking about?" Etta pressed. Her fingers twisted around each other in her lap. She could almost hear the way her thoughts were swelling, racing through the beats of lies and secrets to one final, crashing crescendo. She didn't want to hear.

She had to.

His gaze met hers over his shoulder. "All of this—this journey she's sent you on—is rooted in nothing more than delusion and lies."

EIGHT

Rather than stay seated and speak to his back, Etta pushed the chair from the desk and padded over to him. Sunrise edged ever closer with each second, adding to the unrelenting pressing of time's swift march away from her. The sky near the horizon had lightened to a soft violet and, in the gentle light, she saw what wasn't there: the footprints of the decimated buildings and streets hidden by rubble, streetlights that had been twisted and snapped like dry long grass.

"I—" she began. But the story wasn't about her, not yet.

"I don't know what you know of the Thorns, of us," he said, giving her a sidelong glance as he clasped his hands behind his back. "I cannot claim we are without fault and failures. Many of us lost everything in the war against Ironwood. Families, fortunes, homes, a sense of safety and independence. But the people here are good and decent, and want do something meaningful. We want to protect each other. It was your mother, you know, who came up with the name. It was something she used to say, that she could no longer be a rose without thorns. She nearly destroyed every hope we had of succeeding when she disappeared. Rose turned our castle to glass and left us exposed and one strike away from shattering."

"I know about all of that," Etta said. Rose had infiltrated the

Ironwoods for a time to keep them from finding the astrolabe. She knew now she'd come back to the Thorns briefly before leaving for the future, with child. "I want to know what you meant by *delusion*. That's a strong word."

"I've never told anyone this, the more fool I," he murmured. The reluctance in his tone made Etta step forward, as if to seize the secret he was offering. "After her parents were murdered, Rose claimed she was visited by a traveler, one who warned that if Ironwood were to possess the astrolabe, it would result in some sort of endless, vicious war, which could destroy everything and everyone."

Etta made a sharp noise of surprise. Henry glanced over at her again, and seemed to be measuring her response. "You have to understand that she was deeply, deeply unwell after their deaths. She witnessed them herself as a young child, and they were so gruesome I feel I must spare you the details."

Etta's gaze sharpened on him. "So you just dismissed it? Because she was an *unwell* little girl?"

He held up his hands. "I would never use that term lightly. She described this traveler as shining like 'the sun itself,' golden, his skin and form flawless. She told me once that when he spoke, it was as if she heard his words in her mind, and that he could plant images in her thoughts. That even our shadows served him—*shadows*."

Etta was at a compete loss for words, trying to reconcile this image of her mother with the stiff, immaculately put-together woman she'd grown up with.

So . . . all of this was . . . not a fantasy, but . . . Her mind stumbled over the words. Hallucinations and delusions. If she was following Henry's thinking on this, Rose's parents' deaths had been so deeply traumatic, the psychological aftershocks so damaging, it had eventually ruined not only Rose's life, but compelled her to ruin her daughter's as well.

All of this was a lie.

Her blood was pounding wildly inside of her, like the flapping of a bird's wings struggling against a fierce wind. A tiny figure at the edge of her memory tiptoed forward, hesitating, curling the ends of her bright blond hair with her small fingers. Quiet, as always, so as not to disturb. Perfect, as always, so as not to disappoint. Only watching the careful, meticulous strokes of her mother's paintbrush against canvas from the doorway of her bedroom.

Wondering if the reason her mother seemed to rarely speak to her was because her language was color and form, when Etta's was sound and vibration.

Henry reached out a hand for hers, but jerked it back when Etta flinched.

After a moment, he continued, "As a child, her grandfather helped put her off the notion, but years later, after she'd joined me in trying to restore the original timeline, she had a dream about that meeting with the 'golden man,' as she called him. Her fixation was renewed. The fierce, lively person I knew withered away, and in her place grew someone who was paranoid, erratic. Rose would go for days without sleep, then disappear for weeks, only to return more levelheaded, folding away more and more secrets inside of her. I wanted to help her, but she didn't believe she needed help; not even as her delusions worsened, and she claimed she could feel people watching her from the darkness."

Each word pulled at a new thread in Etta, slowly unmaking her.

"I should have fought her on her plans to spy on the Ironwoods by ingratiating herself to them, but it was like trying to bend steel with my hands. And then she vanished, and for years, I was afraid . . . I thought for certain she had . . . ended her own life."

Her mother would never have surrendered. Forfeited her life that way.

"Are you all right?" he asked, his brow creased.

Who would be? she wondered.

"Why did she hide it, then, instead of just destroying it?" Etta asked instead. "That's the only way to truly keep it out of Ironwood's hands, right?"

"It gets at a struggle we've felt for years, the debate we've been locked in." He reached down to the satchel near his feet, removing a dark leather journal. "This came into our possession almost twenty years ago, when your great-grandfather Linden died. It's one of his ancestors' journals, one of the old record-keepers who compiled information from old traveler journals and tracked changes to the timeline. From her understanding of her old ancestor's legends, destroying the astrolabe would have a nullifying effect on any alternations to the original timeline."

"Meaning," Etta said, "it would revert to the exact thing you and this group are after—the original version of the timeline?"

"Yes, but at a steep *cost*," Henry said, placing the journal back on the desk. "Do you know that passages collapse when a traveler nearby dies outside of their natural time?"

Etta nodded.

"Imagine losing the one thing that could reopen them in the event of someone becoming trapped—being forced to wait out years or decades in an unwelcoming time, separated from your family," he said. "There used to be thousands of passages, and now, there are only a few hundred. Many would argue that, as more of us die than are born, our way of life will vanish as the last passages close."

"But not you."

"Not me," he said. "I understand that not everyone uses the passages for their own selfish ends, the way Ironwood does. Many simply need them to visit members of their family and friends who can't travel, or to conduct studies and research. Even your mother felt that way—unwilling to potentially risk losing her family in other centuries. But recent events have proven to me that this has become a necessity if we're to restore what's rightfully meant to be."

The buzzing static in Etta's ears finally exploded, swallowing his words. Some part of her strained against what he was asking of her;

she didn't want this information, didn't want to know this, or put the pieces together.

"This doesn't make sense," she said, hating the desperation in her voice, as she reached for logic to protect her heart, "none of it. She wanted me to destroy it. She told me that herself."

Unless *he* was lying about wanting to destroy the astrolabe, or what destroying it would do—but then, what was the point? He would be trying to convince her of all the reasons it needed to exist, and what they intended to do with it. But none of her usual red flags were being raised. If anything, he just sounded tired and angry—there was nothing calculating in his eyes or tone. He *believed* what he was telling her.

"Then she should have returned to us the moment she was able, but she didn't," Henry said. "Instead, she concocted a scheme to force *you* to do the work for her. She endangered your life every step of the way, and somehow, worst of all, she kept you in perfect ignorance. Because—my God, because she needed events to play out the way this *special destiny* required. She knew that Ironwood would eventually learn of you and try to use you, and she *allowed it.*"

Etta leaned heavily against the desk, and used her very last defense. "She did it to save my future."

"Ironwood's future," he corrected gently. "I see you struggling with the lack of logic. There's simply none to be found. Instead of destroying the astrolabe, she created this game to justify—to reinforce—what she believes she saw as a girl. It is the only explanation for this charade."

"Because if she had wanted to save my future," Etta said around the knot in her throat, "she would have told me to protect the astrolabe, not destroy it."

Her mother would have had her be the means of her own future's destruction, all the while lying about that being the only way to save it. The pain of it stole her breath.

When Etta was young, she had come to understand that loneliness had a pitch—that high whine of static that coated silence. Sometimes, she'd sit at her bedroom door and watch her mother paint in the living room, quiet and lovely. Cool and sharp. Etta would count the *wish, wish, wish* of the brushstrokes.

She stood in the silence, asking, *Do you see me?*

She played concert after concert to the empty seat beside Alice's, asking, *Can you hear me?*

As a child she went to her bed at night, leaving the covers near her feet, her light on, until her mother's bedroom door would squeak shut. Etta would cry the question into her pillow. *Do you care?*

All of her life, Etta had been quiet, and determined, and gifted, and caring, and patient, and so hopeful, even in the unbearable loneliness of her own home. Now she could barely breathe. She could not hear Alice, she could not find her way back to those memories, because then she'd have to see, she'd have to accept, that the one person who'd cared for her, about her, with her, was gone. She would have to see her life not as a seed sprouting into bloom after years of work, but like an orchid her mother had precisely clipped and watered just enough to survive.

"It's not true," she said.

But Henry only watched her, a hand rubbing his mouth and jaw. He looked as if there were something else he wanted to say, something that could possibly be worse, but he held it back.

It's not true, she whispered.

She knew she was crying too late to stop it.

"I don't—" Henry began, forcing his arms down to his side. His fists clenched, curling with each agonized word. "*Please*—I don't even . . . I don't even know how to comfort you." He repeated it, in wrenching disbelief. "I don't know how to comfort you. She did not even let me have that."

Etta felt herself dissolve into her own pain, pressing a fist against her throat to lock in her sob. The cruelty of this—the *viciousness*. How much her mother must have hated her to try to trick her into destroying her own life.

"As it turns out," she managed to say, "nothing about her has ever been real, except her indifference."

"Oh, Etta, *Etta*—" He shook his head, and whatever had held him back before was gone. The warmth of his fingers as they curled around her own reached her, even as she shook. "Etta, you're wanted, you're everything, don't you see? My God, it breaks my heart to see you like this. Tell me what I can do."

Henry's anger was *real*, and it was palpable, building a charge with each word he spoke, until Etta wasn't sure which of them would explode first. In some strange way, Etta was grateful he was there, that his fury was flaring, mirroring and building upon her own. It validated every doubt. It spoke to all of those times she'd cried herself to sleep, wondering if that would be the night her mother finally heard her, or if the silence would swallow that, too. Etta wasn't stupid, but like Henry had said, she'd been blinded by her own love, and the pointless pursuit of her mother's love.

And somehow the worst part of it wasn't how Etta had been used, but how Rose's plan for her had created collateral damage. *Nicholas.* What would he say to this—would he hate her, knowing that her family, not his, had ultimately been the cause of so much of his pain?

She was shaking, and tried to hide it by moving to the other side of the desk, sucking in enough air, smearing the tears from her face, until she found some calm undercurrent in herself to grasp.

"Can you tell me what's going on? I need to understand what happened. The last I knew, *your* men had nearly killed me and N—" She caught herself, because her feelings for Nicholas weren't something she wanted to share, not with this virtual stranger.

"And your . . . companion?" he supplied carefully, well aware of those feelings regardless.

"Partner," Etta continued. "And they stole the astrolabe and rode off into the sunset with it. The next thing I knew, I was waking up in another desert and another century. If these men aren't with you, where are they? And what happened?"

105

Henry sighed, rising back onto his feet. "I kept your identity and my interest in you secret from the others, and I regret it more than I can say. As for the rest, I realize you've been through a trial, but would you consider taking a walk outside with me? It's far easier to show you."

WINIFRED—WHO, IT SEEMED, HAD BEEN LISTENING AT THE door—handed her a pair of shoes as soon as Etta emerged from the office. By the time Henry appeared at her side, a light coat over his suit jacket, the woman had faded back down the shadows of the hallway like the ghoul she was.

"No coat?" he asked, eyeing her up and down.

"Darling Winifred didn't think I needed one, apparently," she said. One of the guards chuckled into his fist, earning him a swat across the chest from the other.

Henry looked mildly startled. "Your mother called her that as well."

"My mother met that woman and they both survived it?"

One corner of his mouth twitched, and the parts of her that were still raw, and awkward—and, worse—unsure, eased. "I never said they emerged unscathed."

"I always wondered how she got the scar on her chin," Etta said, trying to squeeze the smallest traces of humor from this.

"That was me, I'm afraid," Henry said. "We were rather ruthless fencing partners when we were much younger. It was another scar in her extensive collection, but, once she returned the favor"—he pointed to the pale, thin mark above his left brow—"the matter was settled."

Etta tried not to grimace at that. Blood for blood. How very Rose Linden.

The thought was drawn away by Henry placing his overcoat around her shoulders.

"Is that all right?" he asked. "The Octobers here are mild, it likely won't be too cold—"

It was the anxious look he gave her that made Etta keep the coat around her, clutching it closed between her hands. "Thanks."

"We'll be taking a quick walk down the street, Jenkins," Henry said, turning to the guard who'd laughed. The other man gave a curt nod, and when Etta and Henry started down the hallway, he and the other guard fell into step behind them. Etta turned, confused, only to be drawn back around by the offer of Henry's arm.

Rather than take the grand stairway down, he led her to a smaller staircase, one so thoroughly plain and serviceable that Etta assumed it was meant for staff. They made their way down two levels, emerging in a large, echoing entryway.

A portrait of a beautiful young woman, as regal as any queen in her velvet gown and diamonds, kept watch over the comings and goings of the foyer, lit by an enormous crystal chandelier that had somehow survived the quake by only molting a few of its feather-shaped ornaments.

Jenkins stood off to the side, next to the massive front door, and was soon joined by two other men, all roughly the same height, all with the same dark hair, some dusted with gray, others not. Etta stopped to examine the portrait for a moment, rubbing her sore shoulder.

"Are you in pain, Miss Hemlock? Would you like something for it?" Jenkins asked.

"Oh—um, no, thank you," Etta said, letting her hand fall. It did hurt, but she wasn't sure she wanted to be under the influence of any medication—she needed to be as focused as possible. "And it's actually Spencer, not Hemlock."

"You're a Hemlock through and through," Henry said with a faint chuckle. "Suffering in silence because of indomitable pride. Get her the medicine, Jenkins."

"That does sound familiar," Jenkins said with a wink. The friendliness of it, like a shared private joke, startled her all over again.

Henry offered her his arm again, but Etta breezed past him, still preoccupied with those six words. *You're a Hemlock through and through.* That would be easy, wouldn't it? To accept that, to give in to the comfort of fitting into those qualities, to have that place offered to her?

He removed two white tablets from a silver pillbox in his coat pocket.

"Aspirin," Jenkins reassured her with a small smile.

"I'm all right," she said, trying to keep the wariness out of her voice. "Really. Thank you."

Henry looked like he wanted to push the matter, but when he saw her face—which Etta was sure must have looked swollen and red after her crying jag—he decided against it.

"Shall we, gentlemen?"

Standing next to them, the resemblance between Henry and the others was overwhelming, so much so that Etta wondered if they were all related. All Hemlocks.

If they were security, were they also decoys? The thought moved through her mind like a lance. The four men, including Jenkins, stepped into a tight unit around her and Henry, cocooning them on all sides before they even stepped outside. Etta waited for them to step farther away, to break up the human shield as they stepped into the crisp night air, but they never did, even as they began down the steep path. Their movements had the practiced precision of a military maneuver, and she had to wonder what Henry was being shielded from.

But she already knew. *Ironwoods.* This man, just as much as her mother, was the sworn enemy of Cyrus Ironwood, and had been working to undermine him for decades.

They came to a turn in the road and stopped short. It was only then that Henry gave a small signal with his hands to send the other men back a few feet. They went with reluctant, shuffling feet.

"Now," he said, turning his attention back to her. "Tell me what you see."

Etta caught herself looking up at him again, studying the crooked bridge of his nose, the gruesome scar at the base of his left ear where it looked like someone had begun to forcibly cut it off. He'd attempted to tame his hair beneath his hat, but it was already rebelling, curling up to greet the moisture in the air.

She turned back to face the hills and streets that rolled out below her, easing down into the bay. "I see . . . suffering. Pockets of homes. Twisted buildings."

But on the whole, the damage—what her history texts had painted in broad, catastrophic strokes—was terrible, but not crushing. Frightening, but not terrifying.

"What you're seeing is a city which has taken a severe knocking with the quake, but has been spared from fire damage, which is what ultimately caused the bulk of the damage and deaths in the timeline you know," Henry explained, tucking his hands into his pockets. "But if you had come to this moment in Ironwood's timeline, there would have been almost nothing to see. That was how devastated it was, by one small change that rippled out to a much larger one."

This isn't Ironwood's timeline. Etta whirled back toward him. "What was it?"

"When Ironwood was pursuing his interests, or rather, the interests of his family's ancestral territory in the Americas, he altered the outcome of a war. The Russo-Japanese War. Are you familiar with it?"

Etta shook her head. "No—wait, that was before World War One, wasn't it? Over land disputes?"

"Over rival interests in Manchuria and Korea," he said. "When it was clear the Russians were beaten and riots at home were breaking out, Ironwood convinced Theodore Roosevelt to mediate the peace talks, rather than let the war proceed a few more months as it had in the original timeline. It cost far more Russian and Japanese lives, but it resulted in sweeping reforms in the former, and spared the lives of millions of Russians in World War One."

That was . . . impossible.

Like time travel, she thought grimly. And so was standing there, in an alternate version of the history she had grown up with. A passing breeze kicked a loose strand of Etta's hair up, forcing her to smooth it back. Instead of smoke and ash, the breeze brought with it the briny scent of the sea, the metallic breath of exhaust, and the simple stenches of humanity.

"But what does that have to do with an earthquake in San Francisco?" she asked.

Henry turned to face her more fully. "This is what I want you to understand, Etta. I sympathize with you, knowing that your future is no longer what you remember. I know that pain, feeling your life and friends and dreams are gone. All of us have had to come to terms with the fact that our loyalty is to time itself. It's our inheritance, our nation, our history. But the future you know is filled with strife and war; it is nothing like the world of peace that existed before Cyrus Ironwood decided to remake it."

Etta recognized that she was as much in mourning over her dreams of being a concert violinist as she was for Alice. She had slowly come around to the idea that there was something more for her in life, and that she could still play without the validation of crowds and success. But the idea of an entirely unfamiliar future would always remain overwhelming.

"Each change we make, big or small, ripples out in ways we cannot always predict, that we can almost never control," Henry continued. "A war in Russia spreads its vines throughout the years, touching individual lives, nudging them to different locations, shifting their choices, until one man, Dennis T. Sullivan, San Francisco's fire chief, is in the wrong place when the earthquake strikes, and he dies of his injuries, leaving inexperienced firemen to wield dynamite to create firebreaks. A woman wakes up a few hours earlier than she would have and decides to make breakfast for her family, causing one of the most devastating fires of the entire century."

"So . . . we're in . . ." Etta began, trying to wrap her mind around the words. "We're in the original timeline now? The men who took the astrolabe managed to change it back?"

Henry nodded, and, with that, changed her life as she had known it.

"We've been identifying potential linchpin moments in history for years—moments and people and decisions that have a huge impact when it comes to these ripples," he explained. "They tested our theory that the Russo-Japanese War was one, and altered the future from 1905 onward. Ironwood's focus was on the nineteenth and twentieth centuries, and, thank God, most of his changes prior to then were minor. There wasn't enough wealth at stake for him to care or make a major play before then."

"But, unfortunately . . . ?" Etta prompted, detecting the anxiety underscoring his words.

He gave a faint smile. "Unfortunately, we've heard reports that he's already dispatched his men to see about altering events back. If we don't move quickly, we'll lose this advantage."

"Move quickly to destroy the astrolabe, you mean," Etta clarified.

"My men who took it from you were immediately followed by Ironwood's men. One of them was, from the note we received, killed. The survivor is in hiding in Russia, still in possession of the astrolabe, waiting for us to rescue him," he said. "Tonight, I need to inform the others that the only way forward is with its destruction. The complete reversion of the timeline to what was meant to be. We cannot leave the astrolabe in play; if Ironwood ever got his hands on it, he'd open up passages to new years, inflict more crippling changes on humanity. He does not care how many people die, or suffer, so long as he and his line survive. He wants more and more and more, and yet all of these years have proven nothing will ever be enough."

Until he saved his beloved first wife from death. Until he had *everything*.

Etta drew his coat around her shoulders more tightly, trapping in the warmth.

Meant to be. He kept using that same phrase. "Do you believe in destiny, then? That something deserves to exist, just because it once was?"

"I believe in humanity, in peace, and the natural order of things," he said. "I believe that the only way to balance the power of what we can do is with sacrifice. Accepting that we cannot possess the things and people not meant for us, we cannot control every outcome; we cannot cheat death. Otherwise there's no meaning to any of it."

"There's one more thing I don't really understand," Etta said. "If my future changed, if my life isn't what it was, then wouldn't I have been prevented from going back in the first place? Wouldn't it have invalidated finding the astrolabe and losing it?"

The information was offered freely, patiently. Etta was so grateful, she almost smiled.

"We live outside time's natural laws; that's why you remember your old life, even as it no longer exists. But time has its own sentience in a way, and it despises inconsistencies. To avoid them, it maintains or restores as many of our actions as possible, even in the face of great change. So, in your future, you still travel back from when you did, but perhaps you weren't performing at a concert; perhaps you were only at the museum visiting."

And perhaps Alice might still be alive, her mind whispered.

That sweet spark of hope lit her from her scalp to her toes.

The astrolabe *had* to be destroyed. That was nonnegotiable to her. It was more power than any one person should have, by far, and she could sacrifice her future knowing that at least any future damage could be somewhat contained. But she liked this, what Henry claimed. That they thought not just about themselves, but of how their actions would affect the true victims of Ironwood's meddling: the regular people who were at the mercy of his whims and wants.

Her time, the future she'd grown up in, had come at the cost of untold lives and damage: not just to the travelers, but to the world. Returning the timeline to its original state spoke to the part of her that had struggled so badly with the notion that travelers *could* inflict positive change, but chose not to. It could be a return to a moral center, a new beginning to build stronger rules for the travelers to adhere to.

She needed to finish what she'd begun, and soon.

But . . . Nicholas.

Nicholas, who was waiting for her; who rose in her memory like the lavender sunrise stretched out before them. She let the thought of both wash over her, steady, brightening, beautiful.

I can spare him this. He never should have been involved in this mess to begin with. If she could keep him safely out of it, until the astrolabe was destroyed, maybe then she could begin to make up for the havoc her family had wrought on his life.

"Can I come with you?" she asked. The wind picked up around them, tugging at the coat, her hair, as if trying to move her more firmly onto this path. "To Russia?"

Henry looked as if he couldn't quite believe it. "You're sure? If you need a few days more of rest—"

"No, I need to see this for myself," she said. "Don't think about leaving me behind for 'my own good,' either."

"I wouldn't dream of it," he said, and it took Etta a moment to process that the unfamiliar tone in his voice was pride. She became just a tiny bit hungry to hear it again. "Let's go back, shall we?"

The guards formed their protective shell around them again, and they walked in companionable silence back up to the magnificent home that overlooked the city that had been spared by time. Inside, Etta started toward the stairs, but Henry nudged her to the left, into what looked to be a large, formal dining room. Piano music no longer sang out, but there was chatter and the heavy steps of people milling around.

Packing up, as it turned out. Several people attacked the last of the drinks and food left out on the tables. Others swept up any and all messes as men rolled up the sleeping pads and bedding at their feet; even more were laying out the contents of their packs, counting supplies or trading what they had with others.

Although many people were dressed in the severe style of the era, there were equally as many in a rainbow of silk or chiffon ball gowns and stately military uniforms. Women in the corner were helping one another arrange their hair in artful piles, every now and then reaching out to snag the few small children running loops around everyone's legs. Their laughter struck a chord in her, resonated even in her battered heart.

It was a liminal space, where dawn met night, and the past met the present. These people had gathered here to conduct their work in hiding, but, more than that, it was a secret, special place that created its own warmth and light, even as the fire was smothered and the candles were doused.

Etta tried to step back, but Henry led her forward. He did not have to say a word for silence to fall like a curtain.

Even the children turned to him, eyes wide, small pearly teeth flashing as they grinned. One held out an open palm, to the obvious, fond embarrassment of his mother. Beside her, Henry dug into his pockets, screwing his face up as if struggling to dig through all of the imaginary things there. A small wrapped piece of candy finally emerged, and the boy snatched it and ran back behind his mother's skirts with a shriek of giggles.

But not even that could distract the others from their fixation on Etta's face. The way panic gripped her entire chest made her feel like that little girl performing under the bright stage lights for the first time.

I'm not that girl anymore. Not after everything she'd faced.

"The similarities end with the face and hair," she managed to say, vaguely gesturing there with her hand.

There was a moment where the expressions of bald hostility turned to confusion. And then the woman, the same mother, began to laugh. The others around her caught the sound, relaxing into their own rueful chuckles. And like the timeline changes Henry had spoken of, the laughter rippled out, until the entire room settled into it.

"We have much to discuss tonight about our path forward," Henry said, placing a hand on her shoulder, "but would you all allow me the pleasure of introducing my daughter, Etta, to you?"

"Well, hey!" a man shouted from the back, cutting through the quiet din of surprise. "Another Hemlock to add to the ranks—it's high time for us to finally outnumber you Jacarandas for once! Congrats, old boy! And welcome, doll!"

Henry rolled his eyes but was smiling so hard he was nearly pink with it.

Once their surprise melted away, all that was left were the whistles and shouts that left Etta stunned in turn. The wave of women washed up to her, and warm hands clasped her own, touched her shoulder beneath Henry's coat, where the bandage was just visible. They were talking over each other, so fast Etta couldn't keep up with them.

"—kept you up there—"

"—was wondering where he'd gotten off to—"

"—aren't you a sight—"

But there was one cool voice that seemed to unfailingly climb over the others. Winifred came up behind them, touching Henry's shoulder. He turned away from the men who were slapping his back and giving him handshake after handshake.

"That creature you insist on working with is here to make her report," she informed him. "Would you like me to tell her to wait?"

Henry's brows rose. Interested. "No—no, I've been waiting for her report for days. Is she in the hall?"

The women were urging Etta deeper into the throng of Thorns, eagerly absorbing her, peppering the air with questions. She turned, searching for Henry's dark hair, and found him passing through the door, back into the hall.

With the morning light coming through the high windows, she could see the small figure waiting there in the entryway. Julian was out there as well, chattering away beside her. He gave her a playful punch to the shoulder, and whoever it was returned it in earnest, socking him hard enough in the solar plexus to send him staggering back, choking on his laughter.

As Henry approached, she pushed Julian aside altogether and straightened, flicking her long, jet-black braid back over her shoulder. She wore a cornflower-blue silk tunic buttoned at the throat, its wide sleeves embroidered with an intricate pattern. She tucked up her hands inside of the sleeves as Henry began to speak. Her loose matching trousers shone as she moved, heading toward the stairs. Just before she took the first step, the girl looked around Henry's shoulder into the room and caught Etta's gaze. Her lips parted, as if in disbelief. Etta wondered what the woman had that Henry wanted.

Julian hesitated at the door, watching the others, until one of the guards—Jenkins—shooed him away. Only the Ironwoods, it seemed, were unwelcome where the Thorns were concerned.

Etta turned back to the men and women around her and, for once, silenced the questions, the doubt that had chased her through the centuries. She fell deeper into the hands that reached out to greet her, and let herself find relief in their elation.

A family.

Meant to be, she thought. *This is what was meant to be.*

But in the back of her mind, there was a face: Nicholas.

Nicholas alone, the desert blowing hot and blinding around him.

I'm coming, she thought. *Stay alive. I'll find you.*

But not yet.

PRAGUE
1430

NINE

JULIAN HAD ONCE SAID SOMETHING TO HIM THAT STRUCK Nicholas now, as he breathed in the fog and cold mist: *All cities are jealous of Paris, but Prague is the envy of Paris.*

Tucked into the alcove of the building where the passage had released them, he had only been able to see the busy market in the open courtyard before him. As the weather turned and night crept in, the stalls rapidly emptied. Footsteps and cart wheels clattered over the cobblestones as all manner of people, in all manner of simple, colorful dress, fled the rain, carried off by surprised laughter and shouts.

Though he'd hoped his breeches and shirtsleeves would be unremarkable enough for him to pass among the century's occupants unnoticed, Nicholas was rather dismayed to find that it was not the case, unless he wanted to commit to the part of a peasant and rend his clothing. The men of this time wore doublets and jerkins, in the sort of style that made them appear to be strutting around with their chests puffed out like pigeons. Or, in the case of the paler fabrics, enormous eggs with limbs.

He turned to Sophia, only to find that she had shed her jacket, pulled the shirt out of the waist of her breeches, and affixed her belt over both, in a close approximation of a tunic. Perhaps not exactly correct, but perhaps not quite so *incorrect*, either. At least they'd both managed to keep their hose from ripping. Whatever small consolation that was.

Although he felt less aware of the color of his skin than he had in the eras they had passed through to arrive here, Nicholas now was struck by the first stirrings of doubt that the residents of the city might explain his presence away as a Moor or Turkish merchant. It was a blessing, then, to have the soaked, darkened city streets to themselves for a short time, and he meant to make the most of it.

Of course, that was before he stepped out from under their shelter and truly took stock of the place.

He understood what Julian had meant now. Rather than charge forward, Nicholas's feet came to a sudden, halting rebellion. Rain ran down his face in rivulets, soaking him as he studied the twin spires of a Gothic church. Around him, the sweet faces of the buildings stretched up into the low-slung clouds, the precise curves and angles of the gables and finials glowing in the odd light. At first look, it had all seemed rather simplistic in design, but he was almost delighted to find that the city defied him, that it refused to be absorbed in a single glance. The roads and paths away from the market curved into shadows, inviting mysteries. There was an unreal quality to the place, one that made it seem as though it had been someone's dream, imagined into stone and timber.

Sophia smacked the back of his head, knocking him out of his reverie.

"'We must make haste! We cannot delay!'" she said, in a mocking version of his voice. "So let's stand around and gawk where anyone can see us!"

Despite having sworn to himself that he wouldn't keep rising to her taunts, Nicholas felt himself bristle. "I was—"

"Good evening, sweet lady and kind sir."

Nicholas spun around, searching through the sheets of rain for the source of the small voice. A young blond boy dressed in a gold-and-ivory doublet and jerkin, his hose dampened by mud and rain, stood a few feet away, glowering at them. The feather on his jaunty little cap was wilted, and flopped as he tilted his head. "My mistress has invited you to take tea with her."

A hot cup of tea sounded like heaven itself, actually. But Sophia answered before Nicholas could accept. "We take wine, not tea."

He could have argued against that, very strongly, but the boy pouted in response and executed a smart little bow. Sophia smirked at Nicholas, just as he'd begun to suspect he'd missed something—some sort of code.

"If you and your . . . guest . . . would please follow me?"

Their golden child led them around the tower the passage had emptied into, and Nicholas was arrested by the sight of a large clock on its side layered with symbols, arms, charts. At first glance, the intricate layers of its face reminded him of nothing so much as the astrolabe.

Sophia retraced her steps back to him, her eye squinting at it. "Will you please take that ridiculous look off your face? It's an astronomical clock."

Which told him nothing other than that this, perhaps, was like a great geared astrolabe that also served the useful function of telling time, rather than corrupting it.

The boy continued on through the streets of Prague with the ease of a native, ignoring the architecture, the art embedded in the city's skin. Behind him, Nicholas was so absorbed in the wonders of the city that it took him longer than it might have otherwise to notice the peculiar thing unfolding around him.

He slowed his pace, wondering if it was his eyes, or . . . Nicholas *was* exhausted, practically dragging himself forward. But, still, he'd felt the sting of invisibility and dismissal far too many times to let this stand.

The next small cluster of men and women approached quickly, giving him another opportunity to investigate. But—*again*. He sucked in a breath, watching as the soldiers, the young woman, an elderly man, all stopped despite the rain, and turned their backs as he, Sophia, and the boy passed them.

"What are you huffing and puffing about?" Sophia asked. "You sound like a teakettle about to go off."

"We're being shunned," he said in a low voice, so the child wouldn't hear. "Or at least, our guide is."

Sophia's bewildered expression turned to one of muted surprise when he pointed it out to her, splashing through the puddles of the next narrow street. What confused him, truthfully, was that, despite their firm action, these people bore no signs of disgust, or even scorn. No obvious markers, such as sneers, or hateful, distrusting eyes. In fact, their expressions were as serene as marble statues, and once their party had passed, the men and women would turn back around and continue on their way. It made his skin prickle and tighten around his bones.

The boy glanced over his shoulder and must have caught his expression, for he said, "Don't be troubled, sir. They cannot help it."

Which meant . . . what, precisely? They were somehow being compelled? And in such perfect uniformity?

"Oh, I'd forgotten about this," Sophia said, waving away his attempts to engage her on this. "Some trickery to ensure there are no real witnesses. Grandfather—Ironwood—believes the Belladonna loaded everyone in this city with so much gold they don't dare breathe her name, let alone acknowledge her or her guests."

While money could buy a great deal, no matter the century, this seemed a step beyond mere coordinated cooperation. Nicholas crossed the short distance between himself and the nearest woman. She looked to be a servant, perhaps, as she was older and wore unadorned clothing. On closer inspection, the basket over her arm carried a small heap of vegetables, covered with a piece of burlap. She went impossibly still as Nicholas stepped closer to study her impassive face, and risked a faint tap between her shoulder blades.

The woman did not move, except to breathe. Not so much as a blink.

"You said she was not a witch," Nicholas whispered as he caught up to Sophia and the boy again. "You swore it!"

"She *isn't*," Sophia insisted, glancing back over her shoulder just as the woman shook herself, as if coming out of a deep sleep, and turned to continue on her way. Nicholas did not miss the rare flicker of uncertainty on her face as she admitted, "At least . . . I am reasonably certain she is not."

THE BOY BROUGHT THEM AT LAST TO A STREET OF STORIED mansions. Perhaps "small palaces" was a more apt description, each marrying different shades of colors and styles of stonemasonry. The homes announced themselves to passersby with doors that looked as though they could withstand battering rams if necessary, and windows from which candlelight and the gazes of servants fell softly over the three of them.

At the very end of the street, past the splendor of Prague's wealthy, lived a narrow little shop, which leaned so severely to the right on its haunches that the windows and door had been installed on a slant. Its front window was covered with a curtain, blocking the interior, and it bore no sign.

Nicholas reached up to touch Etta's earring on its leather cord and took a steadying breath. As he followed Sophia inside, the shop coughed up warm dust and the smell of rotting earth. Dozens of candles were scattered around the room like guiding stars. The dingy light, however, only served to make the shelves of bottles and jars, many cracked and half-full, seem filthier than the lace of spiderwebs connecting them.

Half of these same shelves had buckled and snapped, spilling their contents onto the floor, where they had been promptly forgotten. Wax from the candles was dripping onto the glass cases and chairs, many of which were torn or broken altogether. As much as he had longed to be in a place warm enough to begin drying out his clothes and thawing his blood, Nicholas's skin only felt an overwhelming itchiness amid the decay.

"Madam!" the boy called.

A crimson curtain behind the far counter rustled, and out from under the portrait of a doll-faced child came a young woman. Her hair was like a raven's wing: black, with a natural sheen that caught the candlelight, even without the gold-and-pearl netting that had been pinned to it. A heavy gold cross hung around her neck, dipping into the low bodice of her strawberry-pink silk gown—at odds with the filth that seemed to be steaming around her. Her face, with its too-large eyes and lips, was oddly arresting, so much so that Nicholas took a step toward her without meaning to. The thoughts that had been trying to sort themselves out went soft at the edges.

The woman received the boy warmly, leaning down to ghost a finger along the bridge of his nose, her smile as sweet as pure honey. He nodded at something she whispered in his ear and happily skipped off to a stool a short distance away, reclaiming a thin leather volume.

The woman glimmered in the candlelight as she smiled at them. Her skin, the gold, the beading and metallic thread shot through her gown—all called to him, shining and bold. The light caught her like flame on glass.

Nicholas leaned back against the pull of her, cocking his head to the side to better study her. There was something in the way she didn't move so much as flicker around, like the candles burning on the counter near her hands—something that made him question his eyes.

"See?" Sophia scoffed. "I told you you'd forget Linden soon enough."

He whirled on her, grasping for the words that only a moment before had been poised on the tip of his tongue. It wasn't that. Nicholas didn't feel a rush of attraction that set him back on his heels, the way he had with Etta, but . . . this was . . . it seemed closer to the flush that came with too much whiskey on a too-empty stomach. A sickness.

"Welcome," the woman said, in such a soft voice that Nicholas and Sophia took another step forward to hear her. The candles mimicked their movement, and, for just a moment, he was able to tear his eyes off the woman—the Belladonna—and notice that, in the middle of the stack of reeking, swollen tallow candles was one burning a sullen blood red.

"Welcome, weary travelers," she said again, this time with a smile that revealed beautifully white teeth, like seed pearls—something unheard-of for anyone in this era. "How may I assist you?"

This woman? This was the woman who had dueled with Cyrus Ironwood and won her independence from him? Perhaps this . . . beguiling charm . . . worked even on the stone-hearted.

"We've come to trade for information," Sophia said, leaning an arm and hip against the counter.

Nicholas glanced up at the slight vault of the ceiling, not quite a dome. Much of it was covered with a damp cloak of dust and mildew, browned by time, but here and there he could make out the strange, mystical symbols that bordered its edges. At the peak was a large silver crescent moon, half masked by the dark clouds painted around it.

"I possess many remarkable objects," the woman hedged. "And know of many more."

"Can we cut through this nonsense and get to the heart of this?" Sophia said. "I was made to believe that you know everything and everyone. If that isn't the case, we'll take our business somewhere else."

"Perhaps if you were to be more specific about what it is you're searching for?" The Belladonna's voice sounded as though it were being coaxed out of a violin.

"We're looking for information pertaining to, ah," Nicholas said, "travelers of a particular nature."

"Perhaps you could be a little less specific and a bit more cagey," Sophia muttered, shaking her head. "I'd *love* to be here to greet the next century."

A sound shuddered up from beneath the floorboards—a heaving, stomping sound that seemed to rattle even the timber beams overhead. A portrait of a benign, pale man tumbled from the nearby wall behind where the boy sat. It smashed out of its frame when its gilded corner struck the ground. The steps passed beneath them—Sophia straightened, tracking the sound with her eye. Nicholas kept a hand on the knife at his side.

"Who the devil is that?" he asked.

The woman smiled serenely. "I sell the finest of elixirs, sir. Perhaps I might interest you in a set for your pretty little wife at home?"

"That's not what he asked, you stupid cow—"

Sophia's words were cut short by the tremendous bang of the door behind her as it struck the wall, and the sudden appearance of a bundle of black-and-silver silk and netting. All of which didn't appear, so much as roll toward them with the force and menace of a thundercloud.

A woman nearly as tall as Nicholas strode forward. The bottom half of her face was hidden beneath a veil of black lace, but her eyes were a gleaming, almost feline yellow. Somehow, either by piercing or some art, three small pearls trailed down from the corner of each eye like tears. Her décolletage was modestly covered by a sheer panel of white fabric, but what Nicholas initially took for lace was anything but. The markings were the climbing, swirling lines of what appeared to be a tattoo. When she spun toward Sophia, Nicholas saw that her snow-white hair had been braided, intricately looped and knotted together.

"Who—?" The woman leaned toward Sophia, sniffing the air around her.

Sophia let out a small cry of surprise, swatting at her, but the woman had already moved on. Nicholas leaped back instinctively as she swung her attention toward him, subjecting him to the same sniffing. Truly, she sounded like a pig searching out a truffle, her teeth clattering behind the veil. He was dosed with her scent—that earthy undertone he had detected when they'd first entered the shop.

"Ma'am," he began, with as much composure as he could gather, "if you would be so good as to—"

She spun, carrying the same hint of damp soil and lavender away with her.

"Sir, please let me show you our latest arrivals," the woman behind the counter said, her smile never once faltering. The other woman glanced back, first at her, then the boy.

"Put her out." If the first woman sang her words, this one crushed them between her teeth.

The golden boy marked his place in his book and went over to the counter. He planted two hands on its dusty surface and jumped up, just high enough to blow out the bloodred candle Nicholas had noted before.

The Belladonna vanished, disappearing into the candle smoke that trailed up toward the groaning rafters.

That settled, the boy returned to his stool, picked up his book, and resumed his place in the story.

Sophia jumped forward, a wild expression on her face as she looked behind the counter for the woman—she met Nicholas's gaze when she looked up again and shook her head.

Disappeared. Gone.

Impossible.

He might have to accept that they were edging toward the shadows of the unnatural. Nicholas knew he would need to be on guard, and despite his shaky faith in a higher power, found himself thinking those words he'd heard Captain Hall say throughout his childhood: *God defend us.*

"How . . . ? Are . . . ?" Nicholas was not quite sure what he meant to ask.

The woman in black stormed back toward Sophia, who lifted a leather-bound volume off the floor and sent it flying toward the older woman's head, coming within inches of striking her.

The sniffing intensified, until finally the woman held out an arm, silvery black lace dripping from the end of the sleeve. "Come here to me, beastie."

Sophia took a rather large step back.

Before Nicholas could leap forward, the woman snatched Sophia by the arm and whirled her around, as if to swat her bottom. In one smooth movement, the woman pulled up the back of Sophia's shirt and pulled something out that had been tucked into the belt around the girl's waist.

For a moment Nicholas thought it might have been another trick of his eyes, because when her hand emerged it was holding a long, thin blade, but the end of it had been snapped off, leaving it a jagged claw. The base was adorned with a large ring, thin bands of silver weaving in and out of each other.

"Good God!" The words burst out of him as the woman held the pointed end up to her nose with one last, satisfied sniff. "You've been carrying *that* around this whole time?" he asked Sophia. "Where did you come across such a thing?"

Even as the words left his mouth, he knew. The body of the Linden guardian in Nassau, the one with the peculiarly small wound through his ear. She had reached the body first, and had somehow taken up the blade in the darkness of night. Without him ever noticing.

And she had held on to it for . . . what purpose, exactly? His guts clenched, picturing her expression of joy as she drove it through him while he slept.

Sophia refused to look in his direction. "How did you know I had it?"

The question was directed to the other woman—the true Belladonna, Nicholas suspected.

"The blood smells like the rotting intestines of a goat," the woman growled at her. "This will be payment enough for entry."

Holding it up to the candlelight, she studied something on the ring that Nicholas couldn't quite make out—it might have been the etching of a sun. Her breath made the veil over her mouth flutter.

"Payment?" Nicholas heard the disbelief in his voice.

"Yes, beastie. *Payment*. This is a place of business. Or did you expect me to offer you refreshments and the moon?"

"Is information part of the deal?" Sophia asked, eyeing her with her usual look of mistrust.

"It depends, of course, on what it is you wish to purchase," the Belladonna said. "I have been known to barter. From time to time. Boy, lock up the shop."

"Yes, madam," the boy said, brave enough to give her a petulant look for interrupting his reading again, but not brave enough to ignore the order.

"Children," the Belladonna huffed as she led Nicholas and Sophia to the door behind the counter. "The only thing they're good for is eating."

Sophia barked out a surprised laugh, but Nicholas wasn't quite convinced she was joking, given the casual way the woman had begun to twirl the blade with a shocking disregard for her fingers.

"She can follow me," the Belladonna said, gesturing to Sophia as she began down the dark stairs, "and to hell with you, you humorless sop. Oh—you'll want to hold your breath as you take the last few steps. If you faint, you roll down at your own peril."

"I beg your pardon?" Nicholas caught a hint of something vaguely putrid and found himself doing as asked.

The lower level seemed to be two flights down, lit only by the faint orange haze crawling up the steps from fires below. Nicholas had a vague memory of something Julian had told him—that there was a kind of underground city in parts of Prague where they'd been forced to build the streets and buildings up to avoid flooding. The overall impression he had was of climbing through a dark vein to reach the city's pale bones.

The light was coming from a fire in the corner of what looked to be some sort of workshop. The first small section they moved through contained mostly plants and herbs left to dry, as well as what looked to Nicholas like an area for blowing glass. They continued down the narrow, rough stone artery that connected that room to the next. At the very center of the room was a sort of circular stove, each layer stacked upon the next like the tiers of a dingy stone cake. Glass bottles ringed it like ornaments, many with long, hollow stems for pouring the liquids inside into another, simpler bottle below. As she passed by it, the Belladonna stooped to fan the small fire burning inside its base. Once past it, they were confronted with the sight of what looked to be a bell-shaped oven with small openings, as well as barrels, and mice scampering around them.

"Are you an alchemist?" Sophia asked, understanding the odd sight.

"Well spotted," the Belladonna deadpanned. "I dabble. You might consider the use of my youth elixir, beastie. You look old beyond your age."

Nicholas grabbed Sophia's shoulder before she could make good on the murder in her expression.

One last jaunt down another hall brought them to their destination: an even smaller, darker room. Its only occupant, save for them, was a painting that stood taller than himself, and wide enough to cover the entirety of the wall. Nicholas's eye was caught first by the glowing moon depicted in the dark, cloudy sky, and next, by the waves washing up onto a deserted, unknown shore.

"Now," the Belladonna said, "do not touch anything, do not look into any of the mirrors, do not sit on my chairs, and most of all, know that thieves will be dealt with in the manner of ancient justice."

Sophia gave a sarcastic salute, but Nicholas put a hand on the knife at his side.

With no further instructions or warnings, the Belladonna turned and stepped inside the painting.

UNKNOWN
Unknown

TEN

I
T WAS A PASSAGE, OF COURSE—AN ODDLY QUIET CREATURE
of a passage that sat just in front of the painted sky. The air shimmered
and distorted the peaceful image as the Belladonna passed through it,
and the usual drumming sounded off.

Both Nicholas and Sophia turned to look at one another
expectantly.

"Oh, no, we're here for you and your beautiful beloved, not me,"
she said. "You test the waters!"

"I only wished to ask if you knew where it led," Nicholas said
brusquely. "I always intended to go first."

She made a strangled sound of frustration, throwing her hands up.
"And subject me to a lifetime of shame and guilt because that witch
turns you into a pig and roasts you, before I can get through the passage to save your hide?" Sophia sniffed. "You'd like that, wouldn't you,
with all of your miserable, obnoxious honor."

"I would have to say most men wouldn't enjoy being transfigured
into a pig and eaten," he said. "But if something were to happen, it
might as well be to me. You have the better knowledge of where passages are located, and could continue on—"

Sophia rolled her eye and stuck out her hand. Nicholas stared at it, until Sophia let out a huff and grabbed his wrist, dragging them forward. The whole experience was so bewildering that Nicholas hardly took notice of the passage's usual stormy assault against his senses.

They were launched out of the passage at a run, their steps slowed only by the presence of a heavy Oriental rug and the ragged growl of a large white wolf, curled around the base of an imposing structure of iron that looked like it would better serve as a drawbridge than a desk.

Nicholas backed up as far as he could without brushing the passage, eyes skimming the space around them.

The room was small and without windows, but here and there were drapes slung down over the walls, and rows of glass bookshelves and cases, as red and rich as tides of blood. More alarming, however, was the lack of a door—at least a visible one. There was no indication of where or when they were. No telling sights or sounds. Beyond the dust and smell of age, the only scent he could detect was that same earthy one as before, heightened greatly.

Nicholas sent a wondering look up at the rows of dried herbs and flowers hanging low over their heads, pushing the bundles out of his way to better see the Belladonna. Before she sat behind her desk, she retrieved a jar of foul, bitter-smelling liquid from her shelf and dropped the dagger into it. The mixture bubbled over like a hellbroth.

Sophia took a step closer to the nearest case, where a heavy sword was displayed. The long, heavy blade was chipped and dull along its killing edge, but the gold hilt was pristine, embellished by two golden chimeras. While he marveled, Sophia's first instinct, naturally, was to lift the glass and make as though to take it out.

"If you touch that sword, I will use it to slice off your fingers, roast them, and feed them to Selene," the Belladonna informed her, not looking up from the glass she had dropped the blade into. Beside her on the floor, the wolf looked up from the bone it had been gnawing and gave a snort of confirmation. Nicholas looked away quickly, attempting to not identify it as a human femur.

"What sword is that?" Sophia asked, still eyeing it.

"Arthur's Caliburn," the Belladonna said.

"Excalibur?" Nicholas couldn't stop his brows from rising. A legendary sword—one that didn't exist. So far as he knew.

"How has someone not bought this off you?" Sophia asked. "Ironwood would probably love to use it to behead his most hated enemies. His murders could use a little poetry."

The Belladonna's veil rustled and crimped, as if she'd smiled at the word *Ironwood*.

She knows who we are, Nicholas thought with a growing sense of unease.

"One of my scavengers fished it out of a filthy lake for me," the Belladonna said. "However, I've never been able to prove the provenance of the object to your Grand Master's standards, and so it remains. Until it one day needs to be found. No, beastie, take that thought of stealing it from your mind—" Sophia's hand immediately lowered. "I'd hate for you to join my cadre of thieves."

Without lifting her eyes from Sophia, the Belladonna pointed to a large, drooping net hanging from the ceiling. It was filled with human skulls, all boiled and polished as smoothly as pearls from the sea. At the sight of it, Sophia scowled and moved on to examine the next case, which contained a line of eight bejeweled and gold-trimmed eggs of various sizes.

"Imperial Fabergé eggs, lately of Russia," the Belladonna said, pulling a grape from a nearby plate of them and popping it into her mouth. "I'm willing to bargain, if they're of interest. It's become damned difficult to auction them with the instability of that period."

Instability. Nicholas seized upon the word, storing the information away. Where there was instability, there were likely changes to the timeline.

"Maybe I should have let you go first," Sophia muttered to Nicholas, greedily eyeing a bowl of pristine apples that seemed oddly out of place. "I could be eating a fresh pork dinner right now."

"That does sound rather appealing, I must say," the Belladonna said, tossing a grape to the wolf, who snapped it out of the air. The animal gave a curious sniff in Sophia's direction, but lowered its head and resumed its watch over them. "There's King John's treasure in the corner over there, next to Cromwell's head, and a panel of the Bayeux Tapestry, if you've yet to finish wasting my time."

At her interested hum, Nicholas grabbed the scruff of Sophia's shirt, cutting off her path. "We've business here, mind you."

"Oliver Cromwell's head, though," Sophia said pitifully, as if this might convince him.

He stepped forward, winding through the rows of shelves that separated them from the desk. Sophia followed reluctantly, shaking off Nicholas's grip. To his complete and utter lack of surprise, there were no chairs for them to sit in. They presented themselves to the Belladonna like a mustering militia.

"Now," the woman said. "Tell me what it is Ironwood seeks, and I shall tell you my fee."

Sophia made a noise of disgust. "We're not here on the old man's business."

The woman settled back in her chair. "Are you not Sophia Elizabeth Ironwood, born in July of 1904, *lovingly*"—the word was impaled with sarcasm—"pulled from St. Mary's Orphanage in 1910 after you were caught pickpocketing for the third time—"

Sophia put her hands on her hips and said, "Well, they didn't catch me the other hundreds of times. Three is hardly a bad score."

Nicholas couldn't be sure why the other woman had said it, other than to awe them with her knowledge, or disarm Sophia.

Rescued, orphanage, pickpocketing.

Christ. Julian had vaguely mentioned to him in passing that Sophia had not had a lady's upbringing until Ironwood brought her into the family. But this . . . it went beyond humble origins. And as he himself knew, when you were forced to learn survival as a child, the instinct became etched into your soul.

The Belladonna smirked and her attention fell over him so heavily that Nicholas felt as though he'd gained another shadow.

"Everyone present knows of my origins; it's not necessary to reiterate them to prove some mysterious point. We've come because we wish for information," Nicholas said finally.

"Is that so?"

"We're looking for what the last common year is," Sophia explained. "To find someone orphaned by the shift, which I'm sure you are well aware of."

The Belladonna leaned forward, resting her arms against the desk. A quill fluttered in its cup, and two grapes escaped their plate to find freedom on the floor. She stroked the veil covering her mouth, the way a man would stroke a beard. "Indeed? That is certainly within my knowledge. Who is this person you seek?"

"It's Hen—" Sophia began, but Nicholas gave a curt shake of the head. He would rather not have the woman turn her eye onto Etta; the darkness of this place, the way it seemed alive with its own curiosity, made him want to protect her from this stranger's interest for as long as possible.

The older woman turned her gaze back toward Nicholas. The small silver bells sewn into her mass of hair tinkled.

"Well," the Belladonna continued, "your desperation reeks worse than your intriguing stench. You are clearly without earthly possessions, and neither of you was close enough to Ironwood to have new, useful secrets to trade. So perhaps our business has concluded before it began."

Sophia took a furious step forward, reaching for whatever sharp weapon she had strapped to her belt. The wolf jumped to its feet, baring its teeth as the girl came toward her, but Sophia growled back, glaring at the animal until its lips relaxed and its ears rose to their usual position.

Nicholas's heart began to beat back against the thoughts of *no* running through his mind. They had not traveled through centuries of swamps and storms to arrive at a denial. This search could be simple; they wouldn't have to chase down every passage in every century for a lead on Etta's whereabouts.

"Is there nothing else you want in exchange from us?"

In the silence, an idea seemed to shape itself from candlelight and shadow. Nicholas noted the moment it struck the Belladonna, how her hands laced together and her veil shifted, as if masking a smile.

"Many of my auctions are for items that are priceless. They defy valuation. As you may know, I select winning bids based on what they can offer me. A secret, or a favor they're willing to do. Here, we can negotiate—in exchange for the information you seek, I'll ask for a favor," the Belladonna said, her chair creaking as she leaned back. "It will be of my choosing, to be completed sometime in the future."

"I won't do anything . . ."—Nicholas struggled to find the right words—". . . scandalous. Immoral."

One eyebrow rose. "Goodness. What an imagination you have. By favor, I mean a task. Perhaps to find and retrieve something for me. Carry a message. Assist in my own travel. And so on."

That . . . did not sound entirely intolerable to him.

"So he has to serve you?" Sophia demanded. "No questions asked?"

"For a time, only insofar as it pertains to the task," the Belladonna said, flicking her long nails at the girl.

"Slavery," he said, the dull burn inside of his chest growing. *Intolerable.* He should have guessed this underhanded "business" of hers would strive to bind the wings of his soul.

"Nothing so foul," the Belladonna said, her voice sharp with offense. "It's indentured servitude, and only a day or two's worth. Your

138

task pays off your debt to me. Once our business is concluded, that bond will be broken."

Sophia grabbed his collar, yanking him down to her height and startling him out of his tangle of thoughts. "Forget this. We'll try the Jacarandas instead, like we planned."

And risk them not knowing? Risk running in circles long enough for this starting point to disappear? They'd failed to master time on this search, and now it was threatening to best them. Etta was hurt and alone, and the thought of taking a moment longer to debate this was intolerable. If anything, it was Sophia's infernal pride speaking for her again, her entitlement. Nicholas hadn't expected the answers to be handed to them. This was a business deal, and he had to believe that Rose Linden wouldn't send him into the jaws of a literal and figurative wolf. The woman's methods were patently ridiculous, but she was still his ally.

"Everyone has a master, whether you realize this or not," the Belladonna said. "Luckily, I am a benevolent one. Mostly."

How very bitter that truth was when swallowed. Some were bound by loyalty and vows, others by an obsession with wealth, and others were owned by other men through no fault of their own.

There was something else that Hall used to say—that life itself was uncertainty, and the only remedy to its madness was to act boldly. This was a risk, yes, but it was tied to a tantalizing reward. At least this was presented as a choice; at least he was retaining some measure of free will. Nicholas could tolerate this debt, so long as he felt the information he would be receiving was proportional to the work.

"There's no *we*," Nicholas told Sophia, detangling her fingers. "This is the answer."

Find Etta. Salvage her future. Fix those things he'd ruined.

And to one day live a life of his own making, be left to his own ends, whatever shape that might take now.

"You won't say what the task will be before we agree?"

The Belladonna's eyes narrowed, glancing toward a grandfather clock behind him. "I haven't yet decided. But you've thirty seconds to agree before the offer is rescinded and Selene escorts you out." She reached over and used one of her grotesque nails to tap the lip of the jar containing the thin silver weapon, marking the seconds.

Nicholas's instincts were murmuring in displeasure about the lack of time to weigh the costs of this. Perhaps if he could make the deal more tolerable, sweeter, he could find that boldness that good faith required . . .

"I have a single condition," he said, meeting the Belladonna's feline gaze. "Before I agree, I would like you to answer a different question first."

Are you in league with the devil? He shoved the thought aside. *Will you devour my soul like a tart?*

The Belladonna snorted, puncturing the silence that followed. "Yes. All right."

"Are the Thorns still in possession of the much-sought-after astrolabe, the one that used to belong to the Lindens?" Nicholas tried to be as specific as possible, so she could not twist her answer, or tell him the fate of a different astrolabe.

After a moment, with obvious reluctance, she said, "In the last report I received, yes, a Thorn was still in possession of the astrolabe." Her veil ruffled as she took in a breath, sucking it against her lips. "Earlier, you mentioned the Jacarandas—I do not suppose you mean Remus and Fitzhugh, the traitors?"

Sophia glanced over at Nicholas before asking, "So what if I did?"

"If you are hoping to find the Thorns, the group's last known location was in San Francisco, in 1906. They appear to be on the move, however," she added, "and I'm not entirely certain of where they'll settle next. And if *I* am not certain, those two toadstools have no hope of knowing, either."

Nicholas's brows rose. That was more information than he ever could have prayed for. He dared to test the limits of his luck by asking, "Do the Thorns have other times they frequent?"

"They do, but I'm certain they are investigating the changes to the timeline and will not be returning to any of those periods at present."

Nicholas felt the knotted muscles in his shoulder ease. He gave her a curt nod of thanks, feeling more secure in his decision to proceed now.

The metal desk creaked as the Belladonna leaned her weight onto it, but before she could speak, Selene let out a sharp whine.

A warning.

Through the wall to his right, Nicholas could have sworn he heard voices shouting the word *Revolyutzia!* in the instant before the room blurred like fogged-over glass and began shaking violently.

Thunder stole through the air, deafening and absolute. The jars and display cases rattled, heaps of glass smashing into each other as whole shelves collapsed. Sophia stumbled hard into the edge of the desk with a startled cry. Nicholas jerked backward, but caught himself in time to avoid the section of ceiling plaster that smashed near his feet.

"What the devil was that?" he demanded. A mortar strike?

More voices now: *"Za Revolyutzia!"*

The Belladonna shook the dust from her hair and gown not unlike Selene, and began to sniff inquisitively at the air. Satisfied with whatever she'd discovered, she glanced at the small silver watch pinned to her hip. "Calm yourself, beastie. This room has withstood any number of revolutions and riots. The only entrance is the passage. We are quite secure."

There were only a few moments of silence before the sound of heavy footfalls seeped through the walls, slashed through by the steady, racing sounds of shouts and gunfire. Voices were muddied, in a language he couldn't speak—*"Ochistite dvorets!"*

The Belladonna rose, her gaze sweeping around her room, breath hissing from her. She stooped to pick a small silver bell and rang it.

The longer it went without answer, the harder she rang it, until finally she heaved it at the passage. The young boy ducked as he entered, just missing a dead-on strike to the head.

"Clean up this mess," she told him. "And take an account of anything beyond repair."

The boy was sensible enough to wait until the woman looked away before sticking out his tongue.

"That's *another* year you owe me," she told him without taking her eyes off her desk. "Such ingratitude. And after I rescued you from my brother."

The already-pale child turned the shade of chalk. With a nod, he went back through the passage, setting off its usual thunderous roar, and returned a moment later with a broom and pan.

"Now, where were we?" the Belladonna said pleasantly, ignoring the irritated sweeps of the boy. "Oh, dear—"

She picked up one of the skulls that had fallen from the netting, stroking the curve of its empty eye sockets lovingly. "I was rather fond of her. She used to bring me daffodils."

"That was the timeline," Sophia interrupted, her voice hollow. "It shifted again."

Because someone used the astrolabe, or—? Nicholas had never experienced the sensation of time aligning from one version to a new one; by the time he'd begun to travel with Julian, it had settled into some stability under Ironwood's rule.

But the woman had mentioned revolutions, riots, implying that one might very well be happening outside of these walls. Could it be that the explosion they'd felt had been the actual cause of the change, and not someone acting in an earlier year?

Which meant . . . what, exactly, for Etta?

"We weren't orphaned," he said slowly, trying to reason this out on his own. "Are we in the last common year, then? Was that the change itself, and not just a ripple?"

"Yes. But if that's your attempt to get me to reveal our year and location, you will be sadly disappointed," the Belladonna said, "I shall neither confirm nor deny we are in a year after both of your birth years."

Meaning, by her sad attempt at a wink, they were.

"A change this large would impact the information we've discussed as part of the deal," Nicholas said. "To locate the person in question, we'd need to know this year as well as the prior change. To ascertain if she's been orphaned again, to this very year."

The Belladonna's jaw worked back and forth beneath her veil, eyes flashing. "All right, beastie. I suppose it's time to move this shop again, anyway. But know, my dear child, that you have asked and received far more of me than any man. I will not be pressed further."

"Understood. The transaction, then," Nicholas said, trying to clear the dust from his mouth and throat before he swallowed it. "How do we complete it?"

Nicholas had noticed in passing that she wore an abundance of gold and silver rings on each of her fingers. They stacked up past her knuckles, some as thin as veins, some seemingly as thick as the finger itself.

Now the Belladonna drew one off her ring finger and rose on creaking bones, shuffling through the fallen plaster and glass to the other side of the desk, carrying the whole room forward with her. Nicholas took the small gold band from her, surprised to find it so cold after being on her finger.

Under her gaze, he slid it onto the ring finger of his right hand, and waited. Not a permanent mark on his flesh, thank God, for he'd enough scars for a dozen men. But a sign of ownership all the same, however temporary.

Something inside of his heart began to sound in warning, like a ship's bell at the edge of a storm.

No. I have come this far, and there is still too much ahead to stop now.

"Our agreement is thus: a favor of my choosing for information on the last common year and the Thorns," the Belladonna said. "'I swear to abide by our agreement, or my life will be forfeit. That is my vow.' Repeat it."

He did, and no sooner did the word *vow* leave his lips than the ring seemed to flare with heat, tightening around his skin. Nicholas took a generous step back as he pulled away from the woman's clawlike grip. Not wanting to alarm Sophia, he clasped his hands behind his back and attempted to pull the damned thing off, or at least twist it to relieve the sudden pressure.

It did not move.

Selene retrieved her bone once more, her teeth clacking against its battered form. The Belladonna returned to her seat, sinking slowly into it.

Sophia leaned both hands onto the desk and said, "Let's have it, then."

The Belladonna's veil rustled again. How someone so old could have the laugh of a young girl, he would never know.

Horror was a beast of a thing. It devoured everything it encountered. Hope. Faith. Expectation. Nicholas felt a chill stinging along his spine.

"Ma'am . . . ?" he began, forcing his voice steady.

"Sweet beastie," she said, "for all of your talk, for all of your thinking you were clever enough to weight this deal in your favor, it never once occurred to you to specify that I needed to provide the information *before* you completed my favor. 'The future,' of course, can mean centuries or seconds, minutes or hours."

Nicholas gripped the edge of the desk so tightly he heard his own knuckles crack. "That is dishonorable—unconscionable!"

Sophia was more plainspoken. "You deceitful *witch*!"

The Belladonna's eyes were so harrowing, they nearly sent Nicholas's soul retreating from his body. "Such a thing to say."

"That is outrageous!" Sophia hissed. "They stole it from *me*! They beat me to take it—they left me with—"

She pressed the heel of her hand against her eye patch and swore again, spinning away, stalking back toward the passage.

"Hardly a tragic tale," the Belladonna called after her, "when it has created the woman you are now. You'll be of great help to him in this task. One eye will be enough."

Sophia stopped just for a moment, her posture rigid. "I don't need any eyes to tear you to shreds."

"You made it sound as though you weren't entirely certain what you would ask of me," Nicholas managed to get out between gritted teeth. *A deal is a deal.* He never, not for one solitary moment, would have agreed to this *favor* had he known it would eat up the one currency he didn't have: time.

"I've only just decided you were right for this particular one. It should not take you long, provided you are as industrious as I've heard."

Another faint stirring at his core. He squared his shoulders, meeting her delighted gaze.

"It's quite simple, really," the Belladonna said. "I would like for you to kill Cyrus Ironwood."

RUSSIA
1919

ELEVEN

IT OCCURRED TO ETTA THAT PERHAPS THE PASSAGE ITSELF wasn't cold; it was simply breathing out the frosty air of what lay on the other side of it.

She opened one eye slowly, half-amazed by the fact that she was still vertical. The passage had tossed them out at alarming speed after seeming to spin them head over heels, but . . . she'd *landed*. Landed solidly, as if she'd taken the jump out of it herself.

"There are you are," a voice said over the rattling moan of the passage. There was a slight pressure on her wrist, and the shallow daze ripped away, jolting her back into the moment. Etta forced herself to take smaller breaths, sipping at the freezing air, cooling her lungs and pounding temples. At their backs, a wave of pressure burst from the passage, and she didn't need to turn to know that the last two guards had finally come through it.

Etta swung her gaze around; when she'd traveled with Nicholas, she'd learned quickly enough that survival meant assessing her surroundings, determining the year, and figuring out how best to blend into the scenery. The lance of panic that went through her dissipated as her mind caught up to her instincts.

They had taken a passage on Russian Hill in San Francisco to

Russia itself, which struck her as too big of a coincidence to be an actual coincidence. Her mind would never truly accept this, how her heels could be crunching through loose gravel one moment, then sinking into the soft earth of a forest in the next. But trees sheltered them from all sides, their leaves shot through with fiery shades of red and gold, and the silence of this place made it feel more like a memory she rediscovered than a moment.

To her left, jutting out of the glassy surface of the crawling river, was a rock formation that looked like something out of a dark kingdom, its jagged height like the remnant of a small watchtower.

That same dark stone had been used to construct the breathtaking bridge that rose high over the water in an almost perfect arc. Its spine looked as thin as a finger from her vantage point. The way it was settled into the earth, becoming part of the mass of life around it, made her wonder if it wasn't just old, but ancient.

But what struck her most, what held her there in disbelief of its beauty, as the Thorns milled around, was the way the late-afternoon light reflected the image of the bridge into the water below.

"A perfect circle," Henry said from beside her. "Two halves meeting, for a time, as a whole."

Etta's brows furrowed at that show of romanticism, but Henry had already directed his attention to a pinched-faced Winifred, who was working her way through the mass of assembled guards. She'd changed into a fur coat, and a hat that looked like some sort of enormous, exotic flower was about to eat her face.

"Sir, all of the preparations have been made," she said. "He's expecting you for dinner this evening."

"He?" Etta asked, though she knew it was useless.

Winifred's eyes flicked over at Etta, at Henry's coat still wrapped around her shoulders. "I've procured a gown for her, if you'd like her to dine with you."

"Excellent," Henry said. "We'll stop by the others' hotel so that we can both change. I'm assuming you found an appropriate suit for me as well?"

"Of course," Winifred said. "It was the very first thing we did after we confirmed the alterations had taken hold."

"Any word from Kadir?"

The missing Thorn. Etta's focus sharpened on the woman's face, searching.

But Winifred shook her head, clearly troubled. "It's likely he's safe in the palace, and waiting for us to arrive."

"Why, Aunt, that almost sounded optimistic," Henry said with a knowing look to Etta.

"Otherwise," the woman finished, "he's dead and we'll only be in time to collect his remains."

"There it is," Jenkins murmured nearby. "Can always count on her to douse the light of hope."

Henry held out his arm to Etta, and once she'd taken it, they made their way toward the rough path that edged out from below the overgrowth of trees and bushes. Two of the guards jumped into place in front of him, leading the way. Etta found her feet naturally sinking into the footprints that already marked up the trail.

While not all of the Thorns had left San Francisco, an even dozen had gone ahead to make preparations for Henry's arrival. Julian, to her surprise, had been escorted out with them. She'd caught sight of him being half dragged onto the street, trying to hide the decanter of brandy inside of his coat.

"Where are we going?" she asked.

He glanced at her. "I hope you don't mind, but it's a surprise—oh, no, I promise, it's a welcome one. I simply want to see . . . I'd like to introduce you to a friend of mine, and an important place to my side of the family."

A parent who shared with their child. What a novel concept. "As long as it doesn't involve tigers. Or cobras."

"Pardon?" he said, startled.

Winifred swept into the conversation with her usual awareness and tact. "Far be it from me to tell you what to do, Henry, but I worry—the girl has hardly been trained, and the stakes of this dinner will be so high—let me at least work with her for a few days."

"There are no stakes. It is simply dinner with a friend," Henry said. "I need you to take charge of searching the various rooms for Kadir and the astrolabe."

The world darkened around them as the trees closed ranks over their heads and the sun continued its downward slide.

"What happens if he and the astrolabe aren't here?" Etta asked, her boots squelching loudly through the mud. "What then?"

"I haven't gotten past the prayer that he is here," Henry said. "I'm curious, though, what would you do in my position?"

"Do you care what I think?" Etta asked.

He seemed confused by the question. "Would I have asked otherwise? I want to know your thoughts."

Etta wanted to bask for a moment in the small, trembling warmth of that idea, but quickly stomped it down.

"The thoughts of a seventeen-year-old child," Winifred said. "Really, Henry."

But he wanted to know, and was plainly waiting. It made her feel . . .

Trusted.

When in her life had her mother ever stopped to ask her about her thoughts or feelings on something, without having already made the decision herself?

Even Nicholas. Even Nicholas had tried to take advantage of her trust, however halfhearted the attempt had been. He was overburdened with a guilty conscience, and was honorable in a way only the heroes of history and fiction seemed to be.

"Immediately start sniffing around any Ironwoods you can find," Etta said. "Set off more alterations—as many as you can manage at once."

Henry inclined his head toward her, considering this. "Ah. To lure Cyrus out with the astrolabe to fix them?"

Etta nodded. "Even if he didn't bring it out into the open, you'd still split the Ironwoods' attention. Meaning more chances to follow one of the Ironwoods back to wherever he's taken up and find the astrolabe there."

"Fortunately, we already have that information. He's bought back his old home in Manhattan, eighteenth century. We're having a damned time getting near to it with the British occupation, though." He let out a thoughtful hum. "I had considered using the Ironwood yearling to lure him out to more open ground. We simply don't have the manpower for what you're describing, though it's an excellent strategy otherwise."

"An excellent thought," Winifred said, picking up her pace to keep up with their long strides. "He has never brought anything to us to merit the kindness we've shown him. He's a leech."

"That's not entirely true," Henry said, with a fond look at Etta.

"That was pure luck," Winifred groused.

"Well, it was certainly fortunate," he agreed. "What did you make of him, Etta?"

"Julian?" she clarified, brushing a leaf from her hair. "He's . . ." *A brat, obnoxious, high on himself, rude.* ". . . an Ironwood."

"Was he untoward to you at all?" Henry asked carefully. "He's a shameless flirt, but I judged him to be fairly toothless. Many of the Thorns feel he's outstayed his welcome, and if it wasn't for the happy serendipity of finding you, I daresay I might agree."

"What do you mean, Julian's outstayed his welcome?" she asked.

"You've more questions than sense, child," Winifred muttered.

"He's no longer able to provide information about Ironwood that we don't already know," Henry said. "Ironwood has taken a few of our travelers prisoner over the years, and I had considered trading Julian for them."

"That's probably the thing he's most afraid of," Etta told Henry. "Ironwood might actually kill him."

A road emerged beyond the trees ahead of them. Within an instant of its appearance, streams of headlights swept over it, and two old-fashioned black cars rolled into place in front of the trees.

"You really think so?" Henry asked. "Everything is such a joke to him, I half expected his dalliance with us to be for amusement alone. Ironwood wouldn't kill his heir, not when he needs him."

"The astrolabe could be used to create new heirs, if he uses it to save his wife," she pointed out.

"That was your mother's theory, yes," Henry said. "And a likely one."

"Julian could have gone back to Ironwood at any point, especially when it became difficult to survive in hiding," she continued, working out her own thoughts on the matter. "Instead, he came to his grandfather's most hated enemy and betrayed him to you. He needed help, but he clearly felt like he needed protection, too. So I don't know if you should send him back to Ironwood, but you could at least use that same fear to get some last important details out of him that he might not give you otherwise."

He nearly beamed at her. Etta, again, had to fight the ridiculous glow her heart gave in response.

"Second most hated," Henry said. "I daresay that honor belongs to your mother, and she'd skin me for taking that from her."

Winifred let out a loud *harrumph* and released her hold on her nephew's arm, charging forward to the first of the cars. The driver barely had time to jump out and open the door for her.

"I might have a better use for him, if tonight turns out the way I imagine," Henry said as he wisely steered them toward the second car. He nodded to that driver. "Paul, how are the boys?"

Etta missed the man's answer as she ducked inside the car and slid across the seat. Henry joined her after a moment, removing his hat and gloves.

"All the logic of the Hemlocks, without the ruthlessness of the Lindens," he said, as he set both on the stretch of leather between them. The car dipped as one of the guards sat in the front beside the driver. "You'll do very well indeed."

As she settled into the warmth of the car and let it thaw her stiff skin, she passed his coat back to him. Henry folded it in his lap and turned his gaze out his window. Etta watched his face in its reflection, how the easy humor and brightness vanished like a flame blown out. He seemed to retreat into himself, leaving a look of severe contemplation as he touched the rose she hadn't noticed he'd tucked into his lapel.

And Etta could picture it so clearly then, how the reflection of the bridge had disappeared in the water, leaving one half to wait to see its other self again.

THE CITY DWELT IN DARKNESS. THE ROAR OF THE ENGINE swallowed every other sound from the world outside her window, those streets cloaked in the gray evening haze. Etta felt she was watching a kind of silent movie. As the car rolled down a huge main thoroughfare—"Nvesky Prospeckt," Henry explained—Etta had the sense they were slipping into St. Petersburg on the edge of someone's shadow: uninvited, unwanted.

The light slush covering the ground was nearly indistinguishable from the sludge of garbage that lined the street's gutters. The car jumped as it rolled over something—Etta craned her neck back, but saw only the tattered remains of a banner and two poles that were being dragged away by men in stark military uniforms. Her gaze followed their path to a courtyard where a bonfire raged. The cloth and wood were fed into it behind a wall of soldiers standing shoulder to shoulder, backlit by the flames. A few men and women lingered at the fringes of its glow, but the car sped by too quickly for Etta to see what they were trying to do besides stay warm.

The beautiful façades of the buildings that rolled by, with all of their glorious arches and domes, looked as though they'd been painted with jewels. It made the contrast of what was happening on the streets that much bleaker.

Etta leaned back against her seat, resenting the thick white fur coat Winifred had stuffed her into. The truth was, she burned with the desire to be herself, to see more clearly the points at which she and Henry might intersect. But dressed so grandly, wearing another creature's skin, and still feeling the burn of Winifred's crash course on period etiquette, she felt the pressure to let Etta slip away. To disappear into this false image of a lady.

Her dress was a thin, rose-pink silk sheath, cut straight and falling just above her ankles. The topmost layer was sheer, draping over her in scalloped tiers, each edged with the smallest bit of shimmering fringe.

Before they'd left the venue, Henry had handed her a pair of white gloves that stopped just above her elbow and a long strand of pearls, and had given Winifred some sort of diamond—hopefully crystal—barrette to affix in Etta's hair. After an hour-long struggle, the woman, with the help of two other maids, had managed to wrestle Etta's hair into something resembling finger waves, pinning the length of it up and under like a false bob. She'd be lucky not to find bald patches later that night when she finally got to take the pins out.

Etta wrung her hands in her lap, glancing around—at the driver, at Jenkins in the front passenger seat, at Henry. He had his gold pocket watch open again, but quickly snapped it shut. Etta caught a glimpse of the time: seven something. Way too early for there to be no other cars or carriages out on the street besides the ones that were parked, or those that looked more like tanks—clearly military. Here and there, a few scattered people moved by, ducking into shops or making their way home. It reminded her of the short time that she and Nicholas had spent in London during the Blitz; this scene had all the uneasiness of the last dying leaf on a branch, waiting to fall.

"Are we in the 1920s?" Etta asked, turning to look at Henry again. It was an obvious guess based on the cars, style of dress, and small touches of décor in the hotel.

He, however, had turned his head to look up at something the car was racing past—flagpoles?

"1919," Jenkins offered, turning to speak to her through the partition. "It's—"

"I thought the reforms had been passed," Henry said, with an edge of anger. Jenkins and the other guard seemed equally startled by it. "Why does the city look this way?"

They've already broken from the original timeline, Etta realized. In some way, big or small, the timeline had altered enough that Henry no longer fully recognized some of the parts in the century's great machine.

"Some socialist leader was imprisoned, caught red-handed in an assassination attempt on the minister of the interior," Jenkins explained. "A small alteration, not nearly enough to cause a ripple, only a headache for our preparations. Rumor has it there are some of the old Bolsheviks out working people up about it, hence the military presence. Give it a day and it'll pass."

"Bolsheviks," Henry muttered, pressing a hand to his forehead, "or Ironwoods?"

A single drop of sweat worked its way down the ridges of Etta's spine.

"This isn't the St. Petersburg you knew?" she pressed. "You seemed surprised by the state of the city."

"It's called Petrograd in this era," he corrected, with his usual gentleness. "I *am* surprised to see the state of it, knowing the reforms to improve lives across the country had passed. Whatever messes have been made, we'll clean them up while we're here."

The first tap against her window sounded like a rock kicked up from the road—it was the second hit that made her turn, just as a man launched himself out of the darkness of an alley and leaped over the sidewalk.

His arm craned back like a pitcher's, and Etta gasped, instinctively cringing as a bottle hurtled toward the car, smashing against her window. Another man, a woman, more, surged out from the city's cracks and crevices.

"Faster!" Henry barked, reaching into his jacket for a pistol.

"Trying!" the driver barked right back.

Another stone flew toward the web of cracks on her window, but she refused to be pulled down, to have her face pressed against the seat until she was nearly smothered by leather and flickering fear. Clattering, shattering, smashing. The whole car rocked with each hit.

Etta searched the buildings around them for more protestors. Up high, on top of a bakery, two cloaked shadows moved. As impossible as it was with the distance between the buildings, they seemed to easily make the flying leaps to keep pace with the car. There was a flash of silver, like a blade—

Or a gun.

This time, she yanked Henry back down with her as a gunshot—two—shattered her window, blowing shards of glass inside, over her head, along her back. Etta's whole body jumped at each blast, one hand pinned beneath her, the other rising to cover her right ear.

The men up front were slinging words and orders to each other over her head. Etta fought to breathe, to sit up again, but the heavy weight of Henry's arm kept her down until, finally, the shouting outside became muffled. The car wheezed and shuddered, but began to cruise faster.

She stayed in that same awkward position for the next ten minutes, until she felt the wheels of the car begin to slow. Henry released her, still swearing beneath his breath. Etta sat straight up, her vision black and spotty. She brushed small, sparkling pieces of glass from her coat and hair, watching, stunned, as they collected in her hand and lap like ice.

"Are you all right?"

Etta hadn't realized Henry was speaking to her until he gripped her shoulder, almost to the point of pain, and turned her toward him to begin inspecting her. There was a small cut above his left brow, but he seemed otherwise fine.

"My God," he was saying, "I'll kill them myself."

"I'm fine, I'm fine," Etta insisted. A cold wind blew up the back of her exposed neck through the opening in her window. "What was that all about?"

"Protestors," Jenkins said. "Damn it all! We should never have taken Nvesky Prospeckt. But the palace assured us it would be safe. Sir, believe me—"

"The people on the roof—" she tried to say.

Henry held up his hand, still breathing hard as the car rolled through a gate and came to a slow, shuddering stop.

Several figures in suits and nondescript uniforms flowed out of a nearby building's arched entryway. With a start, Etta opened the door and let herself out on unsteady feet, the glass spilling out around her feet, disappearing into the light smattering of snow. Her breath heated the air milk-white as she slowly tipped her face up.

They'd arrived at a building that was beyond imposing—*ornate* couldn't begin to capture its presence. It was almost Baroque, the way the pale green façade was trimmed with gold. The building itself was massive, stretching on as far as her eyes could see in both directions. Statues of women and saints watched from the roof above, dusted with the same sooty snow. It had to be the palace.

The second car with Winifred, Julian, and another guard zipped up behind them a moment later, skidding to a stop in a similar state of disarray. Winifred all but rode out of the automobile on a wave of her own fury, bellowing, "Those *beasts*!"

Julian was close behind, looking far less angry and far grayer in the face. He raised his brows in Etta's direction. *Bumpy ride?* he mouthed.

Etta's brow creased as she looked away, back toward Henry, who had deigned to let Jenkins brush the remaining pieces of glass from his coat. Then an elderly man was at her side, clucking and cooing at her, bowing in a way that made Etta take a startled step back. The Russian came too fast and furious for her to find the three words in the language she actually knew.

The whirling activity seemed to still somewhat as Henry stepped up behind her and followed her gaze upward. His face softened, the stern line of his mouth relaxing, as if seeing an old friend.

"Welcome," he said, "to the Winter Palace."

UNKNOWN
Unknown

TWELVE

NICHOLAS COULD NOT FIND THE WORDS TO ASK THE WOMAN to repeat herself, but she did it regardless, that same girlish laughter riding the ends of her words.

"Dare I ask the obvious question," Sophia said, oddly calm, "of why?"

"It's not your place to ask questions," the Belladonna said, never taking her eyes off Nicholas. "Only to obey. If you value your life, that is."

Nicholas's feet were rooted to the floor, but he felt his soul release and swing about the room, banging at the walls. In his life, he'd been made to feel the burn of humiliation and impotent rage many times, in many ways, by the world. But this—*this*. Unyielding anger choked him now. If he could have compelled himself to move, he would have slammed his fists against her great metal desk until he cracked it.

Around his neck, the thin leather cord that held Etta's earring felt like a wreath of bricks.

"What do you mean by that?" Sophia demanded. "Stop talking in riddles!"

She stormed forward, only to be brought up short by Selene.

And still, the Belladonna was watching him. Waiting for him.

"You . . ." he began, when his mind began to work again. "You expect me to kill my own kin? Can you begin to fathom what you're asking of me?"

He couldn't kill Ironwood. Desire and rational thought were at odds. Of course, he'd dreamt of it a thousand times, by a thousand different means, and woken less satisfied than he might have imagined, considering the tortures to which the man had subjected every person Nicholas loved. But when it was all distilled down—the torment, the fury, the desperation—the truth of the matter was laid bare: killing the old man would stain his soul and irrevocably bind them together, until Nicholas met his own reward and was forced to answer for it.

It was one thing to do violence in self-defense, but this was *murder*. Assassination. The thought alone left a taste like rust in his mouth.

"It's him or yourself," the Belladonna said. She snapped her fingers and the boy stopped pretending to sweep the same pile of glass and dried-out insects while eavesdropping. Nicholas turned just as he scampered back through the passage. "You'll come to find that I am the only one who can remove that ring, and the longer it stays on your finger, the more the poison inlaid in it will sap at your strength."

"I'll cut it off, then—cut the whole bloody hand off if I have to," he told her, reaching for the knife at his belt.

"Do it," she encouraged. "In fact, you may as well cut your wrists. Your weakened body will only absorb the poison more quickly. But of course, you're welcome to test the theory. It just strikes me that there's *someone* you wish to find first?"

She knows of Etta's existence. His blood seemed to turn to bile. The wave of nausea stole over him so quickly he was sure he was not going to be able to stay upright. *She knows of Etta.*

Witch. *Witch*. The illusions, the deceit, the cunning, and now . . . poison.

"Come now," she said, "would it be so terrible? Have you forgotten that he kept you as property? That you are the issue of a vile man who

164

forced himself upon a helpless woman? That he sold your mother to a man in Georgia who used her, who beat her, until the sickness finally freed her?"

Nicholas pressed a fist against his mouth, and would have turned his back to her to collect himself, had he trusted her not to stick a dagger through his back.

"He resides in the old house of your childhood," she said. "You haven't much time. He travels soon. I imagine I will see you back here soon as well."

"Madam," he said, "I will see you in hell."

There was a tugging on his arm, and he did not realize he was moving toward the passage until Sophia dug her nails through his shirt, into his skin. "Don't look back at her," she muttered, "don't give her that."

He did not. He held his breath as they stepped through the passage, and then released his scream into its thunder. The smell of the air changed as they emerged on the other side. That same stench of wet earth her clothing seemed to breathe out as she moved.

"Carter—wait—damn—!" She had to catch his arm to stop his path, swing him around to prompt his gaze. Nicholas had the oddest feeling that he was back on his deathbed, a fever wracking his brain. There was a haze about her, an unreal quality.

Fool—bloody fool! Christ!

Rose Linden had led him like a lamb to the slaughter, but he'd only himself to blame. He'd been rash, hadn't thought his calculations through, and now he was—

A slap across the face snapped his head to the left. Sophia raised her hand again, prepared to issue another blow.

"You looked like you were going to pass out," she explained. "And you're too bloody big for me to drag you."

"Thank you . . . my apologies . . . my . . . thanks . . ." He had no idea what he meant to say. But the hit had blown the dust off an old thought, one he hadn't dared to court in years.

Kill the old man and be free.

Of vows. Of guilt. Of this unbearable heaviness anchoring his heart to his guts— *No.* He'd sold his soul, but he wasn't about to damn it.

He held his hands to his face, trying to smother the bellow that tore out of him. The gold ring pressed a hot kiss to his cheek. Nicholas tried to yank it off again, with no luck.

He needed to find Etta, he wanted to find Etta, there was only Etta—

"Forget what the old bat said," Sophia said fiercely, her voice ringing like steel. "She doesn't have a hold on you. She only wants you to think she does. Show her you're above it! Show her you aren't afraid, damn it!"

"Are you saying that because you believe it," he asked bitterly, "or because you need Ironwood alive, so you can bring the astrolabe back to him?"

Sophia recoiled. It had been some time since he was on the receiving end of her murderous glare, and he was almost comforted by its familiarity. "You think I won't gut that man the first chance I get?"

"I think you're in this for your own ends," he told her. "I think a rather large part of you, the very same part that prevented you for years from lowering yourself into even conversation with me, loves seeing me bested by circumstances."

"*Of course* I'm in it to serve myself, you fool, and so are you!" she hissed. "We've derailed our search for the one thing that matters to find someone who ultimately really doesn't. But if you think I'd go back to the same family that wanted me just about as much as they wanted you, then you need to pull your head out of your ass before I do it for you!"

Orphanage. Pickpocketing. The past she'd kept hidden beneath the layers of silk and lace. She had worked hard to polish herself into something shining, gleaming, and what had it gotten her? Not the heir, or even being named it once the heir was gone.

As if he would ever let either of us truly forget our origins, he thought with a pang.

Anger, however, was easier to live inside than unwelcome sympathy. "Isn't that why you kept that blade hidden? Because you intended to use it?"

Her eyebrows flew up. "Is that what this is about? Yes, I picked that blade up when we were in Nassau. I might have told you about it, except I knew you wouldn't believe I hadn't had it on me the entire time. I just wanted to be able to study it without you snatching it away like I'm a child."

"You should have told me," he insisted.

"Because you've shown *me* so much trust? You've listened to me so well, such as ten bloody minutes ago, when I told you not to take that deal?" she said, throwing a finger in his face. "But you did take it, and now we have to live with it. So stop making that pitiful face and *buck up*. We'll go to Carthage, all right? Ironwood sends out notices about major changes to the timeline to all of the guardians and travelers posted throughout the centuries. By the time we arrive, the two Jacarandas will likely have the answer we need, or they can point us to someone who *can* tell us. Rose Linden can go take a long walk off a cliff and drag the Belladonna to hell with her!"

She'd mauled him with the truth—he had not, in fact, trusted her. Not even for a moment, because he'd been so certain she hadn't given him a reason to. They could not continue this way, but they could not seem to break out of this cycle of loathing, either.

"She said it'd be useless to talk to the Jacarandas—"

"And you *believe* her? After the trick she pulled?" Sophia pressed. "She told us all that nonsense about the Thorns to get us to trust her enough not to question the terms of the deal. Forget her. I'd rather travel to Carthage on a chance than believe *her* ever again."

She was right. If nothing else, they needed to leave this infernal place. Nicholas straightened, cracking his knuckles at his side to try to release the pressure that seemed ready to shoot from his hands.

This is shameful. I'm falling apart like a boy during his first boarding. Pull yourself together, man.

Nicholas passed through the alchemy workshop at a near run, and took the stairs two at a time. Sophia kept pace with him, plundering the depths of her extensive knowledge of profanities as she misjudged the distance of a step and fell forward, catching herself on her hands. She sprang up the last few steps, nearly spitting on Nicholas's offered hand. "I don't need your bloody help!"

"Then you won't have it," he shot back.

The golden-haired boy didn't look up from his book as they passed. With a chill that sank into his bones, Nicholas realized the woman was behind the counter again, the bloodred candle glowing beside her.

"Come again, your business is appreciated!" she sang out.

He and Sophia made matching rude gestures.

"Tell your mistress I'm coming back to skin that overgrown dog of hers," Sophia said to the boy, "and turn it into my next coat!"

He looked up, pale eyes shining with tears at the mere thought. "Selene?"

"All right, no, I won't," Sophia called back. "But tell her I said it!"

Nicholas chased his anger as he left the store, trying to master it before it mastered him. Rain rushed down the back of his neck, soaking him through in moments. He would have welcomed a bitter wind, anything to cool the monster of grief sweltering inside of him. Instead, the heat that started in his right hand, the ring finger, seemed to throb like a second heartbeat in his body. When he finally looked up, the city was lost to the fog, disappearing like the beautiful dream it was.

"Which way?" he asked Sophia. "How do we get to Carthage?"

"Follow me," she said, turning north.

And with no other choice obvious to him, he did.

———

Rather than waste weeks traveling by sea, Sophia charted a journey for them across the years and continents that involved a considerable amount of danger, but—blessedly—less vomit from her seasickness.

First, a journey back, yet again, to the swamps of Florida, and several hours of navigating murky waters and wasting coins to bribe the pitiful guardian punished with watching the passage there. That deposited them in Portugal, in what Sophia claimed was the thirteenth century. From there, they walked to yet another passage, this one leading to Germany in the tenth, and finally, after stealing a pair of horses and nearly bringing the wrath of a whole village down upon them, they found themselves in 1700, this time in Tarragona, in the region of Catalonia.

Of course, as seemed to be their lot, Nicholas and Sophia spent hours following the shoddy dirt roads on foot in the hope that her memory would serve them better than his own judgment. To pass the time, he tried to muster up what details he could about Carthage after years of the memories collecting dust. Perhaps the facts that remained would offer some protection against what might lie ahead.

Much of said knowledge had come from Hall, whose retention of maritime history remained relatively sharp, if slightly rusted by age and exposure to too much sun. The ancient city of Carthage, once Rome's great rival, lay in a supreme position on the northeast coast of Africa, with sea inlets to the north and south. Its immense wealth, without the flash of Rome's opulence, was owed to the fact that all ships passing in and out of the Mediterranean sailed through the gap between it and Sicily.

There had been three separate Punic Wars between Rome and Carthage; the one Hall recalled best, the second, had produced Hannibal, who had been a great favorite of Chase and Nicholas during the captain's post-supper tales. The ingenious general had sailed with an army of nearly a hundred thousand men and dozens of elephants, and together they'd torn open Spain and marched through the Alps to Italy. As boys, he and Chase had even attempted to re-create the crossing of the Rhône River by Hannibal's army, using discarded siding from Hall's ship as rafts, and rats in the place of elephants.

He tried to take some refuge in those lantern-lit memories, but the longer they walked, the easier it became to slip inside his darker thoughts and dwell there. Save for a few hares, they'd yet to encounter another living soul; while he'd taken careful count of the weapons Sophia had strapped to her body, he could no longer be sure there wasn't yet another knife hidden somewhere on her person—or that she wouldn't use it to strand him here and continue on without him. Or worse.

She cannot kill me without the nearby passage closing, he thought. How comforting.

The deception from the Belladonna had rattled him, but now he found himself regretting how easily he had trusted Sophia when she'd argued in favor of traveling to Carthage; he'd followed her to this spot, which might not lead them to Carthage at all, but a grisly death or yet another ruse.

Nicholas's hands curled into fists at his sides, bunching the already-tight muscles of his shoulders. He was useless as a traveler. Why couldn't he have pushed harder to learn the locations of the passages? Why did he have to place his trust back in an Ironwood, especially one who hated him with a force that could grind whole mountains to dust?

He was an able seaman, skilled in his trade, but here, he might as well have been one of those rats clinging to a poorly made raft.

"Who are these travelers?" he asked. "You said they were Jacarandas, and that they were being punished by the old man for something?"

"Remus and Fitzhugh Jacaranda," Sophia said. "They were both close friends of Ironwood's for decades, some of his most trusted advisors. Julian said the day he discovered they had defected to the Thorns, he went into such a rage that he burned all of their belongings, landholdings, and records. When they realized the Thorns weren't all they were cracked up to be, they tried to come crawling back to ask for forgiveness. Rather than kill them, he sent them to Carthage during the Roman siege as punishment to prove their loyalty. They're assigned to watch the passages there."

Roman siege. The Third Punic War, then.

"I'm sure it gave them plenty of time to consider their crimes," Nicholas said. "I can't imagine this is, or ever was, a popular destination for travel. What is there to observe?"

"Don't be ridiculous. The guardians and travelers assigned to watch passages aren't just there to track comings and goings in and out of them," Sophia said, to his surprise. "They ensure the passages remain stable and aren't in danger of collapsing."

Nicholas nodded. Julian had told him a passage became unstable— or collapsed—under two circumstances: with the death of a nearby traveler who was outside of their natural time, or, Ironwood believed, simply from overuse and age. As if they became worn-out and flimsy, like old fabric that had been turned too many times.

"More passages than ever have been collapsing and closing altogether," Sophia said, her profile outlined by the rough sea below. "That's why I believed him, you know. That he wanted the astrolabe to examine newly discovered passages, for their destinations and stability. I'm not *gullible*. I didn't believe everything he told me, and I didn't want everything he wanted."

Once the words were out, he saw her shoulders slump, as if relieved of the weight of them. He recalled his accusation in Prague, and wondered at how long she had let her temper simmer without exploding.

I know, he wanted to say. *No one who believed Ironwood so fully would have survived this long.*

He tried to picture her then, in her native time, in that orphanage. Small, filthy, and hungry enough to risk being caught stealing. That, at least, he understood. A child faced with the raw desperation of survival had it imprinted on their soul. They were never able to shake the sense that one day, everything good in their life might again vanish—not fully.

"Maybe that's the real reason he never made me heir." Her mouth twisted in a cruel little smile.

"He didn't make you heir because you're a woman and he's a bloody fool," Nicholas said. "And because there was Julian, in all of his shining glory."

Sophia glanced up, brows raised ever so slightly as she let out a *tsk*. "Speaking ill of the dead now, Carter?"

"He didn't—" Nicholas caught the word before it could escape.

"He didn't *what*?"

Damn it all.

He hadn't told her yet about the conversation he'd had with Rose about Julian likely surviving . . . not because she didn't deserve to know, but because Nicholas couldn't tell how she might react. While it might improve her view of him, it might just as easily throw off the uneasy balance between them they'd managed to obtain. No need to rock a boat already struggling in stormy waters.

Sophia seemed to be careening from unpredictable highs to surly lows, her moods like errant breezes, and he needed her steady and focused on finding Etta, not changing her mind and disappearing to search out Julian—it was callous of him, he knew this, and hideously selfish. It took him buffeting his heart with years of memories of her vile insults and cutting dismissals before the notion sat well with him.

The end here justified the deceitful means. He could lie, if Etta was there to later absolve him of the guilt of it. There could be no side trips to find Julian or learn where he might have been all of these years, or even what might have become of him in the meantime. If he knew his half brother at all, he had commandeered some palatial island retreat to hide away in. Julian always landed right side up.

"'Shining glory,'" she muttered. "How can you not see it? He never liked Julian. Hated everything Julian loved. Gambling and drinking and painting. Wasn't shy about telling him how worthless he was on any given day. He was a resounding disappointment, no matter what he did."

Nicholas's brow furrowed. He'd known the old man hadn't outwardly mourned the "loss" of his heir, but he'd assumed that was because any sign of weakness, any crack in his veneer, would have been taken as an invitation to his enemies to try and seize his throne. That, and his heart had calcified long ago. "Was it truly as bad as all that?"

"Worse, probably. Ironwood was ashamed and plagued by him. He was *convinced* Julian would ruin his empire. If Julian hadn't died . . ."

"What?"

"He probably would have done it himself," she finished slowly, eyes forward.

"And yet, you didn't believe us when we told you in Palmyra he desired new heirs," Nicholas said coolly.

For once, Sophia had no response to that.

"Was he a disappointment to you?" he countered. He'd always wondered about this: Julian chased every skirt he saw, knowing Sophia was at home, waiting for their wedding day. He'd spoken of his intended with a kind of affection that, having met and known Etta, Nicholas saw now wasn't the sweet fire of love so much as the cool balm of friendship. But Sophia had mourned him—genuinely mourned, with all the black crepe and seclusion it required.

"His *death* was the disappointment," she said. "You letting him *fall off the side of a mountain* was a disappointment."

"So now you believe it was an accident after all?" Nicholas challenged. "I didn't push him?"

She cast him a pitying look that made his soul heat and itch. "I can see now that you don't have what it takes to pull off a murder. There's no iron in you. If you *had* done it, you'd still be on that mountain, weeping about it."

Nicholas opened his mouth and barely caught the words. *I'm more Ironwood than you are.*

An icy current swept through his blood, and he let out a low, bitter laugh at himself. Did he really have so much pride that he'd use his hated heritage to argue that he wasn't as soft as she believed?

"He was my best friend," she said. "My *only* friend. I'm not going to apologize for being furious with you for what happened, because his life mattered to me. But . . . it wasn't what you had with Linden. If I'd had a choice, if there'd been any other way to get a modicum of respect in that family, I wouldn't have . . ."

"Become betrothed to Julian?" he finished.

"Nor any man." Her eye bored into him in the beat of silence that followed, daring him to say something about it. "I have always preferred the company of women, regardless of history's views of it. The rare exception being your idiot beloved, who can eat rocks and choke for all I care."

Nicholas, as it stood, did not have an opinion or prejudice about any of this, other than to think the feeling she'd described was likely mutual on Etta's part.

"Have a care," he said, with a light warning in his voice. "My beloved is not by any means an idiot, but she has been known to have a rather vicious backhand."

"I'm not . . . I'm not without a heart," he heard Sophia say, her chin raised, eyes straight ahead. "I'm *not.* I just don't have the luxury of being soft. I am trying to survive."

The same as you, his mind finished for her. Life had offered them both poison—different, bitter variations of it, but poison all the same. He reached up, rubbing a hand over the curve of his scalp.

"You don't have to trust me," she told him, eyes shifting away. "Just trust my anger. I would rather die than let that old man have everything he wants. He needs to know what it feels like to want something forever out of his reach."

Nicholas nodded. He could manage that much. She'd made excuses about needing his help to disappear once the astrolabe was found in their initial bargain, but he had a far easier time trusting revenge as her motivation. But there was something about the way she held herself, tugging at her ear, that made him wonder what was being left unsaid.

Sophia walked faster, moving ahead of him on the path, dodging his questioning look entirely.

Their destination rose into view on the cliffside. The crumbling remains of the Roman amphitheater, stacks of stone slabs left to manage the weather and world the best they could, looked ghostly under the bone-white touch of the moon. Beyond them was the sea, its endless glistening, thrashing darkness. He wondered, given the strategic position, if the Romans had held this land to watch for, and ward off, the Carthaginians in ancient times.

"I think it's just this way," Sophia said. "Remind me to nick a harmonica if we ever find ourselves past the eighteenth century again. Finding the passage by resonance would make this bloody mess a great deal easier."

They ventured down the steps, the seats, toward the main stage at the center of it all. Dust flew up around Nicholas's feet, staining his damp shoes, filling his lungs. He squinted into the dark, but the only indication the passage was nearby was a faint tremor that crawled along his skin.

"I'll check this way," he called to Sophia, who was walking the perimeter of the amphitheater above him.

Nicholas turned to make his way down the next set of steps, which seemed to lead into some sort of partly collapsed pathway or room beneath the section of seats.

"I'll take the lower level, if you search—"

He walked into a shivering patch of air—and walked face-first into a cold, crushing pressure that stole the breath from his lungs and seemed to wrench his heart clear out of his chest.

———

175

Before his mind made sense of what had happened, before his body seemed to wake to the fact that he'd stumbled onto the passage, he was drowning—salt water rushed into his lungs as he gasped in alarm, choking him. Water—water—he was caught in a rolling current, feet over head, feet over head, tumbling—

Nicholas kicked his legs to break out of the riptide, his mind so disordered his vision blackened like tar. He couldn't find the surface of the water—it was all darkness, darkness and the moaning drum of the passage, which made the water around him beat with a frantic rhythm.

Do not panic, get ahold of yourself—bloody hell—bloody passage—

And bloody Sophia, as well, for not so much as alerting him to the fact that some madman had hidden the passage underwater.

Salt water turned his eyes raw, but he kept them open against the burn. His entire chest ached with the need for air. He wasn't going to drown, damn it all. But it was night, and without a good glow from the moon or fire, it was nearly impossible to tell up from down. He forced himself to stay still, feeling for the current. Just as he was about to start swimming in the natural direction his body wanted to float, there was a burst of movement beneath him, almost like an undertow, as the passage exploded back to life and Sophia shot out of it. He reached down, gripped whatever part of her he could, and began to kick wildly in a direction he hoped was *up*.

Nicholas broke through the surface of the dark water with a rattling gasp, one hand clawing at the sky, as if he could haul himself up into the cool air. Sophia made a sound like a furious bird of prey as she followed, and Nicholas realized after the fact that he had drawn her up by her hair.

"Terribly—terribly sorry," he managed to get out, his voice ragged from the water he'd choked down. "Forgive—"

"Quiet!" she snapped back. "Do you want them to find us? *Swim!*"

"Where?"

"*Anywhere!*"

Nicholas blinked, willing his eyes to adjust to the darkness. The water around them shook and waved in a peculiar, unnatural way. The *clang-clang-clang* he'd merely assigned to the passage was louder now and far more varied in speed and intensity, to the point where, at last, he knew more than one person was hammering and banging along.

Recognition sliced through him, a searing blade of alarm. It was the sound of something being built, of blades being hammered. It was a sound of war.

Above even that persistent clanging was a creaking sound, the moans of wood being strained and pestered by waves—a sound as familiar to him as his own skin. *Ships.*

Nicholas turned. A large circular arcade, almost coliseum-like, stretched around them, interspersed with columns that reached up high into the night sky, giving it the unified look of a portico. The sight was made all the more impressive by the ships berthed between them, waiting to be launched.

They were of a design unlike any he'd ever seen outside of etchings, with a smaller draft and almost flat across the deck like a barge.

He swam forward a bit toward the closest one, docked between the nearest two pillars of the arcade, his eyes roving over the openings for dozens upon dozens of oars. At the front, glaring back at him like a fiend, were two brightly painted eyes, and an enormous bronze piece at the bow, which, he imagined, would tear another ship apart when it was rammed—

He was yanked back by his collar before he could swim closer.

"Would you stop making eyes at that bloody ship? It's a *siege*," Sophia grated at him. "If they catch us, they won't just kill us; they'll make a whole show of it. Use our decapitated bodies to boost morale."

Right. Yes. Siege. According to Hall, Rome had laid siege to its great rival Carthage for years, ultimately pillaging and razing the city to the ground and killing hundreds of thousands of its occupants. Depending on the timing of their trip, they might very well be eyewitnesses, if they did not get on with their business.

Wonderful.

Adrenaline flooded into Nicholas, warming his cold limbs, lighting up his mind and sharpening his thoughts. Behind them, at the very center of the arcade, was a mountain of a structure, a kind of watchtower constructed in four layers that grew smaller as it reached the top. The lowest layer, with all of its arches and columns breaking up the ship sheds, also seemed to serve as a dry dock—there were several skeletal frames of ships waiting to be completed.

But it was the highest level that intrigued Nicholas, that turned his heart cold in his chest. There, he could see torches—the shadowy outlines of men standing guard.

"Follow me," Sophia said, taking a long, confident stroke toward a bridge that connected the watchtower to the entrance of the city. This time, he was the one to snatch her back, pressing a finger to his lips at her look of outrage and splashing.

This wasn't a mere harbor—it was a *military* harbor, likely making it one of the best-protected and most -watched locations in the whole city. As a preventative measure, there would be few places they could use to slip inside of the city, and all would be defended.

He swiveled his head in the opposite direction. If Hall's stories had been true . . . Nicholas's eyes finally began to see through the veil of darkness, and—there it was. There wasn't just one harbor in ancient Carthage, but *two*. One military, one merchant.

Nicholas had no doubt that the Romans had it well blockaded by now, but what mattered was that the merchant harbor would be far more open to the city. Merchants would need a way to bring their goods into the markets and conduct their trade.

Without wasting breath on explanations, he dropped beneath the cold waves and began to swim, his body taking to the water in long strokes. Nicholas came up for air only when necessary, and only slowly, to avoid splashing. Every few strokes, Sophia's hand would brush his leg or foot, reassuring him she was still there. He kicked his way beneath the iron chain gate, the moonlight just strong enough to give him a glance of it as he swam beneath.

He hadn't realized, until his stomach cramped and his limbs went as hollow as straw with effort, how long it had been since he'd last eaten, since he'd given them any sort of rest. How long he *and* Sophia had gone without more than a few bites of bread. The next time he broke through the surface for a breath, he made it a point to curb his nerves and stop to ensure Sophia was still keeping pace.

He waited.

The water in the harbor shoved at his back, rocking him, splashing into his eyes and nose as he kept low to the surface and waited for Sophia's dark head to pop up again. Unlike its military counterpart, this harbor kept to a long, rectangular shape, allowing a few scattered ships to dock along it lengthwise, like fingers. Several shadowy figures moved steadily along the water's edge, occasionally crossing paths as they moved in opposite directions.

A light patrol, then; the harbor was large enough that he felt confident all they needed to do was wait a few more moments, until the closest soldier moved out of sight. As he'd suspected, there were several low limestone buildings constructed along the harbor, their faces darkened by night. Those would be the warehouses used for storing goods. Some things never changed with time.

What he *hadn't* expected was to find Sophia ahead, already climbing up from the water onto the docks. He watched in growing disbelief and, frankly, mild outrage, as she snaked her way toward the entrance of one of the warehouses, up behind one of the guards posted there with his back turned. She leaped onto his back, smothering him with one hand against his mouth and an arm banded over his throat. When another man emerged from the nearby warehouse, she pounced on him and did the same.

By the time Nicholas had climbed out of the water and ducked over to her, she'd already stripped the men of their tunics and shoes, as well as their swords. Nicholas accepted his with a pointed look of disapproval.

"Can you attempt to keep up?" she groused, turning her back to allow him to change.

"I will endeavor to do my best," he said dryly, quickly tugging off his wet clothes and pulling on the soldier's uniform with expediency as Sophia did the same. He bundled everything, including his soaking shoes, into his travel satchel. "Now where—"

A shadow melted away from the wall of the warehouse behind her, tucked into that very same pocket of blindness that had bedeviled her before.

"Move," he breathed. *"Move!"*

But Sophia had, it seemed, already read the fear in his features, and she threw herself to the ground, just as a sword blade sang through the air, coming within a hair of scalping her. The sword instead slammed into the building, embedding itself so deeply, the attacker abandoned it in favor of another.

A curved dagger that stretched from the man's finger like a claw.

THIRTEEN

A LANCE OF PAIN SLASHED ACROSS HIS SHOULDER BLADES. Nicholas was thrown forward by the force of the unseen hit, his breath exploding out of him. He whirled to see the last glimpse of a long spear disappear into the nearby water. Blackness threatened to swallow his vision as he rolled closer to the nearest building's wall, trying to find cover from above.

Sophia— He searched her out, fuming and fearful. A hard gust of air and a grunt had him flying back, narrowly avoiding a new hooded figure as he slammed his sword down hard enough onto the stones for the blade to spark. It was close enough for him to see his own startled reflection in its surface.

Hell and damnation.

Nicholas ripped his own knife from his belt, parrying the swipe the first attacker took with the clawlike dagger. His forearm throbbed as it absorbed the shock of the blow, and he couldn't pull back far or fast enough to avoid the bite of its tip at his chin. The cloak the man wore smelled of salt and sweat, and looked to have been cut from the night sky. It was only because the moon shone from so high above them that he could make out the embroidery stitched along its edges, the swirling pattern of what looked to be vines, or the powerful rays of a hundred small suns.

His attacker's foot lashed out, hooking behind his knee, taking advantage of Nicholas's unsteady balance and exhaustion. He crashed to the ground hard enough to see the lights of heaven behind his eyelids. As he tried to push himself off the ground, his right arm seemed to fill with white-hot needles and collapsed beneath him, aching.

A sickening thump struck the ground to his right, but Nicholas didn't dare take his eyes off his attacker except to throw himself back onto his feet. His mind locked into the elaborate dance of death—strike, block, swipe, jab—the heat beneath his skin growing as he leaned into the fight. He allowed the towering man to back him up closer to Sophia, where she was now bending to retrieve her own knife from the neck of the shuddering body on the ground.

These attackers were all the same: black in the cloak, silver in the claw.

What the devil is this?

The attacker missed slicing the tip of Nicholas's nose off, but clobbered him with a blow under the chin. Hard enough to knock that thought, and his brain, loose. Seeing double now, he couldn't tell which of the split forms was the man, so he took a broad swipe at both. The claw lashed out, slicing up his arm, nearly puncturing his wrist. Closer, he saw the paleness of the man's skin, the waxy quality of it, as if he had known nothing but night itself.

The attacker stumbled suddenly with a lurch and a gasp. Behind him, Sophia wrenched her knife out from where she'd jabbed it between his shoulder blades. Nicholas raised his wrist, but his arm still felt peculiar, heavier than it ought to have been, so slow that his next slash was blocked by heavy dark leather gauntlets. The attacker righted himself, keeping his claw on Nicholas and his blade on Sophia.

"You must be joking," she said, eye white as a pearl in the dark.

He was not. If the man had split himself down his center and become two, he couldn't have been any more effective than he was then, with his attention divided between them. Nicholas struck, Sophia struck, and he threw them back again and again. Nicholas felt every ounce of pent-up fury crest over his final bit of restraint. A last gasp of strength surged into his body, and, beneath it all, a single, cool thought.

Lure him in.

He feinted left, letting the man's next hit knock the knife from his hand, letting him crowd closer. Sensing easy prey, the attacker moved in for the kill. The claw ripped the air in two, skimming over his throat as he leaned back.

Sophia slammed her blade into the base of his skull. The attacker's hood was thrown back as he fell to the ground, his long, pale hair stained with bubbling blood.

The air heaved in and out of Nicholas, his lungs screaming for mercy as the red haze disappeared from his vision and that most basic instinct—to kill or be killed—abandoned him. He wiped his face with his sleeve, ignoring the way his hands shook.

"That was . . ." he began at the same time that Sophia said, "It's the same weapon, isn't it?"

Trying to rub away the prickling pain from his right arm, he glanced down, searching for a wound that might explain the slash of hot pain that stretched across the back of his hand. But there was nothing, not even a cut.

A word hissed through his mind, unbidden. *Poison.*

Impossible. If anything, he'd strained a muscle or given himself a sprain. This would resolve itself, with nothing so nefarious to blame.

But the sensation did not disappear. It worsened. There'd been longer and harder battles fought for his life that had left him feeling nowhere near the level of exhaustion overtaking him now, like a sudden illness. Nicholas coughed up dust he'd inhaled and spat out a wad of blood, retrieving the satchel from where it had fallen some distance away. The hollowness at his core spread as he checked to make sure the string with Etta's earring was still around his neck, still safe. He clutched it in his left fist, as his right felt nearly too numb now to move.

Not good. Nicholas glanced down at the ring again, and forced himself to look away before his thoughts sank him any deeper into worry.

"Come on, we need to get rid of the bodies before—" Sophia interrupted herself midsentence, her gaze shooting up toward the warehouse above.

But Nicholas had seen the shadows first—five of them, fluttering around like ravens, jumping between the buildings with animalistic ease. Nicholas took her arm and forced himself into a run, moments before the first arrow cleaved through the air over their heads.

He looked up in time to see another shadow on a nearby roof. With the lingering traces of his composure, he hefted a large stone and threw it as hard as he could. It startled their attacker long enough for Nicholas to drag them under the cover of the nearby building's overhang. But the pounding steps behind them didn't cease, nor did the realization that they were running without any particular destination in mind.

Better to be like rats, he thought, and try to confuse a pursuing cat by taking as labyrinthine a path as possible. It was just a matter of finding the right hole to disappear into.

"Who are they?" Sophia gasped out.

The Belladonna's men? The rogue idea cut up through the rest. She had taken particular interest in getting the claw back, hadn't she? She might have overheard where they were going and taken action after his refusal to serve her.

"I'm reasonably sure we should not stay to find out," he told her, craning his neck just far enough to check for the shadowy figures on the roof. Seeing nothing but the clouds and stars, he motioned for her to follow, and picked up his punishing pace again.

The whole of the city reeked as though it had been boiling in its own waste for a month. It felt like climbing into a festering wound. Unwashed bodies, living and near-dead, blocked their path no matter which street they turned onto, sleeping scant inches away from rotting garbage—or, in a few sorry instances, using the rotting garbage as a kind of pillow against the unforgiving stone streets.

Sparks flew up, scattering across the night, as they passed a blacksmith busy beating a sword into submission despite the late hour. Feeling the unwanted prickling in his right hand again, he switched his knife to his left, and he kept his head down as they passed, only glancing at the pile of metal goods waiting to be melted down and re-formed, and the pile of finished, somewhat crude weapons waiting to be picked up and taken to battle.

There was a sliver of space between his workshop and the next building, an alleyway that curved around. He led Sophia into it, giving them a moment's reprieve to catch their breaths.

"I think we've lost them—"

Sophia had cursed them with that. A darkly cloaked woman burst out of the streams of fabric that had been draped over lines to dry, like a wraith.

Without a second thought, Sophia tossed Nicholas the soldier's blade she'd been carrying and, catching it, he whirled back, smashing the hilt against the attacker's throat, stunning her. While she gasped, Sophia seemed to flow in, cutting the woman across her face with her knife. The moment the attacker hit the ground, pressing her hands against the flowing blood with a howl, they were running again.

The city curved before them like a question mark, laid out like a maze within a puzzle. Pale, sturdy limestone buildings leaned against their close neighbors, and lines of them stretched as far and wide as Nicholas's eyes could see, culminating on a hill at the city's heart. The homes rose not just two stories, but usually six or seven, as if the city had one day decided the best course was to grow up, rather than out. Much like, he thought with a sad sort of smile, the way Etta had described her Manhattan.

At the next small lane they approached, Sophia stopped, blocking him.

"Let's go a different way," she whispered quickly.

Nicholas held his ground as he felt Sophia pull at his shoulder, searching for what had upset her—and, with a shudder, located it. Stretched across the stone, curled up on his side as still and pale as a seashell, was a child. On closer inspection Nicholas saw that his eyes remained open, unblinking, that his skin was dotted with scabbed-over sores. He followed the line of the boy's desperately thin arm. His fingers were still hooked around a slender hand hanging out of the bottom of a pile of bodies, already at the mercy of flies and vermin.

He kicked a rat away before it could reach the boy, his stomach rioting. The only reason he didn't cast up his accounts was because there was nothing left in his stomach to lose. Sophia heaved once, twice, pressing the back of her hand against her mouth, and looked away.

"There's disease here," he said unnecessarily. "We'd better make quick work of this. Try not to touch anything or anyone."

Sophia nodded, wiping her hands against the tunic she'd taken from the unconscious soldier.

As they approached a low hill and the stately structures atop it, the stench of the city was tempered by smoke. But rather than masking the excrement and sickness, it drew out a different flavor of it. History, as it was, stank of disease and desperation, fire and ash. The slightly damp quality of the air made Nicholas feel as though it were seeping inside of his skin, as though he would carry the proof of his visit here forever. And in the distance, the infernal clanging carried on unseen out in the dark water.

Where the Romans are lying in wait . . . Building something? Manufacturing the tools of Carthage's destruction? The sound was incessant, without beginning or end, and Nicholas wondered how long it had been carrying on for. If the people of this city had been forced to listen to it each day and night, like the heavy steps of a predator edging ever closer.

A rattling up ahead drew his feet up short; both he and Sophia pressed themselves against the nearest wall, their backs flush against it.

He had only just closed his dry eyes, rubbing at the crust forming on them, trying not to dwell on the hopelessness of it all, when a familiar scent hit his nose. Swinging around, Nicholas cast about for the direction the breeze was blowing from. And there it was, just to the east of where they stood. Warm, fresh animal excrement.

"I think there's a stable near enough," he told Sophia, already picking up his steps, trying to fight the urge to run when his suspicions were confirmed. A long, two-level building was up ahead, with piles of dried grass tucked up against the back wall. There, stalls had been formed from arches, not unlike the ship sheds in the harbor, which opened to a kind of courtyard. Nicholas crouched low, trying to massage the burning sensation in his right arm away as he crept forward, using the tents and draped fabric for cover.

A lone soldier stood guard at what looked to be a side entrance, leaning back against the heavy iron door. Nicholas glanced at Sophia, who had caught up and crouched beside him. At her nod, he slipped out into the night's shadows, casting one last glance around to ensure there was no one else watching.

He decided he liked these soft sandals the men of Carthage wore—they made sneaking up on a soul far easier than the leather shoes of his own era. By the time the soldier startled fully out of his light doze, Nicholas already had his arm hooked around the man's throat.

The soldier smelled of sweat and sweet wine, and his breath exploded out of him with a spray of spittle. He thrashed, kicking his legs out and around, clawing so deeply into Nicholas's arm that he wondered if the marks would scar. With the slightest bit more pressure, the man passed out. Despite being nearly a full foot taller, Nicholas struggled to get a grip on his weight—it was like holding an unwieldy sack of warm water, limbs spilling and flopping around as he dragged him.

Sophia rushed forward, feeling for the ring of iron keys hooked to the man's armor. Her hands shook, either from exhaustion or excitement, as she tried each of the six in turn.

"Hurry!" he whispered.

"Hah!" she breathed out when the right key slid into the crude lock. She shoved the door open with her shoulder, and showed an enviable amount of patience in holding it open long enough to allow him to drag the soldier inside the stable's warm darkness.

Nicholas dropped him behind several barrels, stopping only long enough to use the sword to crack the wood and see if there was water or wine inside.

Wine. Sophia doubled back to help herself to a mouthful of it and would have tried to gulp another if Nicholas hadn't taken his turn. The sourness exploded across his tongue, but it wet his dry mouth and aching throat.

A few candles held on to their faint glow, casting shallow pools of light along the path leading to the front of the animal stalls. Nicholas balked a moment at their size, wondering how many horses they were keeping in each to require them to be that large. The walls were covered with bright paint—in the low light, he could just make out the soldiers, the scenes of ferocious battle. Nicholas felt his feet slow to a stop, and was leaning in to study the legions of soldiers depicted, when the sudden sound of heavy steps rained down over them.

There was something awake up there. Dust drifted from the ceiling with the movement, marking a path.

Sophia's gaze shot toward the other end of the stalls, where another door, this one likely leading upstairs, stood closed. He waited a beat of silence more, his body drumming with adrenaline, but no one emerged. He waved Sophia forward.

"Let's find the storeroom," he whispered. "If it looks like oats or barley, take it, even if it's from the horses' feed bins."

Sophia nodded and took off at a fast clip. She swung her attention up toward a stall in the middle of the long line. The candlelight caught the angle of her face as she looked up, then up again—first in surprise, and then in pure wonder.

Nicholas doubled his pace, catching up to her in a few short strides. "What's the matter—?"

He stumbled back against the wall in alarm.

A long, leathery gray trunk snaked out from between the stall bars, coming within inches of Sophia's face. The elephant watched them, interest flickering in its dark eyes. Its ears flapped against its neck like butterfly wings as it made a small trumpeting sound. Nicholas had never seen an elephant before—only etchings and sailors' descriptions—and he found it almost impossible to look away. He leaned forward, only to fall back again when its ivory tusks banged loudly against the stall door.

"They use elephants in war," Sophia muttered, her voice as soft as he'd ever heard it, her fingers brushing the trunk. It seemed to tickle the loose pieces of her hair. "Sorry about this, my handsome fellow."

She reached between the bars and carefully, with a touch as soft as a flower petal, unlatched the door.

"Sophia!" Nicholas whispered. Scraping up the remains of her trampled body from under an eight-foot-tall beast hadn't been included in his plans for the evening. "Stop this!"

Sophia held out a hand and eased her body into the stall. The elephant shuffled its heavy body back a step, giving her enough room to slip inside the stall and crouch in front of the large food trough, half-full of what looked to Nicholas to be grain and grass. Sophia took up her small bag and began to stuff handfuls of the raw food in it, before motioning for him to pass his bag over.

"Here." She filled it, then threw his bag back to him. "Let's get moving."

He caught it easily, turning back toward the door. Sophia gave the beast's flank one last pat before she shut its stall. Eyes scanning the ground, the walls, for anything that might be of use, Nicholas had nearly missed the one thing that *wasn't* present.

The guard.

He gripped Sophia's arm and brought a hand to her mouth, muffling her protests. Nicholas nodded to the spot where they'd left the unconscious man and felt her suck in a small gasp of surprise. Pulling away, he moved back to the entrance and put his eye back to the door's lock, peering out into the darkness.

There was movement outside—shadows gliding against one another, fading in and out of the night. Sweat broke out at the base of Nicholas's skull, his mouth shaping into a silent warning as a nearby guard was knocked out in an instant, crumpling to the ground; shadows swept in around him, covering him, dragging him away.

Hiding the evidence.

Not killing him, so as to avoid changing the timeline? He and Sophia had played a dangerous game in how careless they'd become, risking change after change to ensure their own survival. These . . . travelers? These *warriors*, men and women, were decidedly *not* careless.

Nicholas strained his ears to catch the murmuring on the other side. Once his eyes adjusted well enough to the darkness, he was able to count four figures of varying stature, all sweeping toward the door like a high tide. It might have been the thrumming fear in his mind playing an unwelcome trick, but he could have sworn the ring on his finger grew warmer with each step closer they took.

Sophia pointed up, but Nicholas shook his head, competing thoughts racing to best one another. There might be more soldiers on the second level, and to get out of the stables, their ultimate goal, they would need to jump onto a nearby building—but none were near enough, and all were taller. He didn't fancy breaking his neck after nearly being drowned and stabbed already in one night.

In battle, you could fight a foe head-on until both of your ships were in splinters around you. But, when outmaneuvered, there was always the potent combination of creating a distraction of some sort and escaping at full speed, hopefully with the wind on your side.

His idea was almost absurd. In spite of everything that had occurred, or perhaps because of it, Nicholas felt a grim smile touch his lips. It hadn't made sense to him why they would store wine here in the stables, other than to hide it from the people outside who desperately needed it. But what if the wine wasn't for men at all, but for the elephants?

They'd pour it down the elephant's throats, see, Hall had told him and Chase, miming the gulping. *Get them good and primed. The wine would send them into a rage, enough to trample any men who stood in their way.*

Nicholas ducked down, peering one last time through the lock to see if the men had moved. As if they'd somehow heard him, one of the men—the one nearest to the door—shouted something. Sophia clucked her tongue, likely at the viciousness that coated the nonsensical words.

"I have a thought," Nicholas told her. "About what to do—"

"Is this a thought that's going to get us murdered, our heads smashed under an elephant's foot, poisoned, et cetera?"

He gave her an exasperated look that Sophia shrugged off as she took his place at the door. "Keep watch for a moment—make sure they aren't planning to storm their way in."

She gave a sloppy salute and leaned down to peer through the lock. "What are you on about, Carter—?"

He took the sword and swung down, cracking open each of the wine barrels in turn.

"Are you *deranged*?" Sophia whispered, jumping to her feet.

He took her by the arm again and launched them at a run back toward the nearest elephant's stall. Before Sophia had time to question him, Nicholas unlatched the door and dragged it open.

The elephant didn't move.

There was a sliver of a second in which he was furious with himself for wasting good drink. Then, as the air thickened with the smell of the wine, the elephant let out a deafening trumpet, as if alerting the others, and all but charged out of the stall. Sophia leaped back with a cry of alarm, even as Nicholas attempted to shield them with the stall door. The animal must have weighed well over a thousand pounds. The whole building quaked as it galloped toward the pooling wine.

"My God," Sophia said. "That's an animal with his priorities straight."

"Come *along*," Nicholas insisted, waving her after him.

There were two more elephants stamping and hollering to be let out, their enormous ears flapping like a ship's colors. Nicholas leaned back, away from one of the trunks that was feeling down his front, as if trying to hurry him along, as he worked the door open.

The third elephant, larger than even the first had been, had no patience at all—he rammed his way out of the stall, his tusks tossing the barrier to the side. Sophia dove out of the way, narrowly missing the door as it smashed back onto the stone floor.

Somewhere, beyond the gray mountains of their leathery hides, the main door burst open and the shadowy attackers attempted to rush inside—attempted, because the nearest elephant lifted its head from the wine and trumpeted a warning that would have made the dead turn in their graves. The two in front had a moment to fall back before the elephant reared up, scraping the ceiling with its tusks, and forced its way out through the door, stampeding into the night.

"What now?" Sophia asked, righting her eye patch.

Nicholas pointed to the side of the nearest stall, which led into an open-air exercise or training courtyard. Hopefully there would be a way back into the city through it as well. He hoisted his full bag, switching shoulders, as he entered the stall. The soft grass padding it seemed to eat his footsteps, but it didn't matter—three drunk elephants were enough of a distraction for their pursuers.

Nicholas edged around the nearest wall, tucking himself between two tall structures, out of sight from the street. A moment later, Sophia followed. He leaned his head back against the stone, looking down at her, brows raised. She returned the look. "Elephants. That was a first. Not bad, Carter."

He inclined his head, accepting the rare compliment. He wasn't such a fool to think it would be the first of many; fighting had a way of bringing even the unlikeliest of allies together. Once the haze of excitement wore off, they'd be back to circling one another like half-starved sharks.

And their brief alliance would devour itself.

"We need to find the Jacarandas," Sophia whispered. "Now. I don't want them to catch wind of anything strange and guess there might be travelers here before we have a chance to come forward."

"All right," he said. "How do you propose we—?"

The clawlike blade caught the light of a nearby torch from above, casting a glow on Sophia's dark hair. Nicholas shoved her as hard as he could, but not nearly soon enough to prevent her from taking a kick to the face as a cloaked attacker leaped down from the roof of the building behind them.

"You just can't take no for an answer, can you?" Sophia growled, clutching her cheek.

The fall should have broken his legs, but the man rose, pushing his hood back just enough for Nicholas to see the gleam of his bald head, his pointed features. It was a man well within the prime of his life—a life that had sliced his face into a quilt of scars.

"Give it to me," he rasped out. "I will spare the woman. Give it to me—"

The tip of an arrow sprouted from the center of the man's throat. The spill of blood from the wound left him sucking at the air, his claw clicking against the arrow's crude metal tip. The fear that had coiled so thickly around Nicholas's chest did not release—not when Sophia staggered up to her feet; not when the frail old man in a homespun tunic stepped out of the night, his bow still in hand.

"Come now," he said, his voice frayed with fear. "The Shadows feed on the night, and they will not stop until they consume us all."

PETROGRAD
1919

FOURTEEN

It was a strange kind of procession that wound its way through the entrance of the Winter Palace. Henry led the small flock of them, talking quietly with an elderly man with a bowed back—some sort of courier. Etta studied the two of them from under her lashes, listening to their muted Russian. A long, seemingly unending red carpet stretched out before them, running along the tile and stonework like an invitation into the palace's hidden heart.

The cold and shock finally began to thaw out of her. Etta was surprised to find that the palace was well heated despite its immense size, to the point where she shrugged out of her absurd coat and let one of the men in suits take it off her hands.

Behind her, Julian was whistling a faint tune just loudly enough to be annoying. Winifred remained behind him, complaining to the Thorn guards about their "shocking lack of foresight" in the route they'd had the party take. Those men, behind even her, kept slowing their pace, as if trying to build more distance between themselves and the mouth spewing venom at them.

"Is there a way to shut her off? Some hidden switch?"

Etta didn't turn back or even acknowledge Julian. He was forced to lengthen his strides to keep pace with her. When the sleeve of his formal dinner jacket brushed her arm and she took a generous step away, he gave her an amused look.

"The last girl I chased at least gave me a kiss for my trouble," he said in a low voice, sparing a quick look at Henry's back.

"Do you often accept kisses from *deranged* girls?" Etta asked.

His mouth twisted. "Don't be sore about that, kiddo. For a second it really looked like you were ready to engage in mortal combat. It was just self-preservation."

More like wounded pride, she thought. He hadn't expected her to try to fight her way out of that room in San Francisco, never mind back him into a corner.

"So what do you make of all this?" he asked. "The changes, I mean. I've only ever known the world Grandfather created, which I'm guessing is the same for you?"

She looked ahead, breathing in the faintly perfumed air, drinking in the sights around her. It didn't feel real—she knew that this wasn't her timeline—but she had expected *something* about it to register as different to her senses, like seeing the world in a mirror's reflection. This was a glimpse of what Henry and the others had lost. What the world itself had lost.

But instead of appreciating it, all Etta could think of was the last time she had been in Russia, for the International Tchaikovsky Competition. With Alice. Competing. Winning it all. The *Times* article. "Classical Music's Best-Kept Secret."

All of it had melted away from her life like the snow in the palace's courtyard, leaving her nothing but pockets of glistening memories that felt like they could disappear completely at any time.

My future isn't the real future, she reminded herself. *It only existed because of one man's greed.*

Etta shook off the thought, reaching up to smooth back a loose strand of hair. Julian walked with the easy nonchalance of someone who had no idea he was being led into the mouth of a wolf. And that soft part of her she had hated so much, the one that now set her apart from her mother, ached a little at the thought. Standing in Ironwood's presence for less than an hour had been a triumph of courage. She could only imagine what growing up with the man had been like.

"You know . . ." she began, "you'll be able to pay him some compliments about it directly. Soon, if I had to guess."

"Pay him some . . ." Julian's words trailed off at the exact moment his eyes widened slightly. He turned away from her, coughing into his fist. "Please. You think . . . that is, I'm sure you think you're warning me, but I already know. Of course I do. My best skill is knowing when to leave a party before the fun's gone."

"I'm sure that's been incredibly useful—"

"Etta?" She looked up to find Henry had stopped and was extending his arm to her. "May I escort you in?"

With one last glance at Julian, she crossed that last bit of distance and took Henry's arm. The courier moved ahead, signaling to the two guards posted at an imposing set of doors to open them. As they stepped into the next room, Etta felt unsteady on her small heels.

"Have they found your man yet?" she asked. "Kadir?"

Henry shook his head, but gave her hand a reassuring pat. "He mentioned in his note that if he did not feel it safe to stay, he would hide the astrolabe somewhere in the palace. It may take days of searching yet, but I haven't any doubt we'll find it here as he promised. The others will begin their search immediately, but I'd like you to meet an old friend of mine first. There are a few things I need to discuss with him to secure this timeline."

The ceiling stretched high above, a dome beautifully painted in the colors of sky and earth, framed—of course—with gold. The black-and-white-checked tile was a quiet design touch compared to the stone figurines of women and angels carved into the arches where the gray granite columns met the roof. Around them, two layers of windows brought in a flood of moonlight to aid the glowing golden sconces. The walls were a pristine white where they weren't covered with panels of silk or art or gold, most of those embellished to within an inch of their lives with meticulously crafted vines, leaves, and flowers.

The party went up one staircase; on the next landing, steps led left and right, winding up to the same high point overlooking the room.

"This is the Jordan Staircase," Henry said by way of explanation. "Impressive, isn't it?"

"I don't know," Etta said. "I think it could do with a touch more gold."

"More gold—" He turned toward her, brows furrowed, before his face broke into a wide smile. "Oh. Sarcasm. That's a *most* unattractive trait in a young lady, you know."

"Yes, sarcasm; one of the many services I have to offer," Etta said, her voice even more dry, "along with driving Winifred insane."

He gave her a knowing look. "She'll soften, given time."

"The way a fruit softens as it rots away?" she guessed.

He struggled to summon a stern look. "That was unkind."

But not untrue.

They walked for seemingly forever, until Etta, an experienced city walker, felt like she might want to sit down and take her shoes off, just to spare her toes the agony of being pinched for a few minutes. The rooms blurred together in a rainbow stream—edged, of course, with gold. Blue rooms. Green rooms. Red rooms. Great halls with chandeliers the size of modern trucks. Ballrooms waiting to be filled with flowers and dancers. Parquet floors whose swirling designs were made up of a dozen types of wood. Marble floors so very glossy Etta could see her reflection as she moved over them.

And still, it took another ten minutes before a crisply dressed servant met them at the base of another grand staircase and said, in accented English, "He'll see you in his study before dinner. Shall I show your guests into a drawing room?"

"I think we all shall wait—" Winifred began.

"I'll be bringing this young lady with me," Henry said. "The rest are to have free range of the rooms to conduct their search."

Etta's gaze slid over to Julian's, just as Winifred drew herself to her full height with a huff and curled a thin hand over his shoulder.

Don't leave me, he mouthed as the woman dragged him away, following another servant back down the hall. Jenkins moved to follow Henry and Etta, but was waved off.

"Sir—" he began.

"We're safe here," Henry reassured him. "Lock the Ironwood child in a room and go see to the search. Inform Julian that if he throws a temper tantrum or breaks anything, we'll certainly break something of his."

Jenkins nodded, but didn't look especially pleased as he retreated.

The servant opened the door and went inside, but Henry held Etta back a moment.

"This friend of mine is neither a guardian nor a traveler, though he knows of our existence," Henry said, his voice barely above a whisper. "I ask that you not share the details of the timeline you grew up with, as it might frighten him into acting rashly."

Etta nodded and reached up again, pushing a rogue strand of hair back out of her face. Sophia had told her, in no uncertain terms, that to reveal what they could do to any non-traveler brought layers upon layers of consequences. She was surprised Henry was taking the risk at all.

Dark wood paneling surrounded them on all sides, making the awkwardly shaped room seem almost coffinlike. It was so aggressively masculine in its bold lines, the air drenched in wood polish and tobacco, that Etta wondered if the room ever received female visitors. Bookcases, most with glass doors, ran along the edge of the room, broken up in places by small oval portraits of men in military uniform. Around a corner, Etta saw a grand piano peeking out. At the center stood an impressive desk covered with picture frames of all shapes and sizes. She didn't notice the man sitting behind it, a book open under the glow of a brass desk lamp, until he lifted a tumbler of alcohol to his lips.

"Your Imperial Majesty, Mister Henry Hemlock and Miss Henrietta Hemlock."

Imperial Majesty.

The words dripped through her mind, slow as syrup.

As in . . . the tsar.

All at once she understood the warning that Henry had given her, not to speak of the timeline she'd grown up in. Because this man, who stood only an inch taller than her, with neatly combed brown hair and piercing blue eyes, should have been dead a year ago, along with his whole family.

"Thank you, that will be all," Tsar Nicholas II said, dismissing the servant, who gave one last swift bow on his way out.

"Nicky," Henry said simply, and it was Etta's turn to be stunned as he favored the other man with a true, warm smile.

His friend. A friend he hadn't saved, or hadn't been able to; one who'd been murdered, along with his family, as a new regime had risen to power in his country. Etta's hands felt cold and damp inside of her gloves.

This was what it meant to form attachments to people outside of their small, insular world of travelers, Etta realized. They were at the mercy of the timeline. Saving them was no guarantee that events wouldn't change for the worse, but to live with the knowledge of their deaths . . .

Etta glanced at Henry again, took in the way he rubbed a hand over his face, fought to keep his expression from slipping. A sharp jolt of pain went straight through her heart. She knew this feeling. She knew this exact brand of painful elation. Seeing a younger Alice had changed her perception of death entirely, forced her to recognize that time wasn't a straight line. As long as she—as long as any of them—could travel, they wouldn't be constrained by the natural boundaries of life and death.

And this was what truly set the Thorns apart from the Ironwoods; the old man only saw humanity as tools to carve and hone his vision of what the world should be. But here, in the way Henry had to press a hand to his face to mask his relief, was a kind of love; a compassion for messy, flawed humanity. A wish to spare this life, just as they had struggled to spare the lives of San Francisco's many fortunate strangers.

The thought made Etta eager to leave, to join the other Thorns combing the rooms for the astrolabe.

All of this could be over in a night. *Less* than that.

"Oh, dear," the tsar said with a faint laugh, extending a hand toward him. "I can't imagine what's about to happen to me to provoke that sort of reaction from you."

His English was better than hers, somehow crisp and smooth all at once, with a refined edge.

"No, it's only—" Henry cleared his throat and laughed. He took the tsar's hand, releasing Etta to clasp it with his other one. "I was only thinking it's been so very long. Will you do me the honor of allowing me to introduce my daughter, Henrietta?"

"Daughter!" The tsar came around the desk, grinning. "You never said! What a charming beauty she is."

Henry nodded. "And wit to match."

The tsar smiled. "Of course. Intellect and charm."

"It's . . ." Etta realized she should be doing something—something like curtseying—and did an awkward sort of bob at the knees. "It's incredible to meet you."

Because, honestly, what else could she say? It was incredible, absurd, and more than a little alarming.

"The pleasure is, of course, all mine." The tsar turned his attention back toward Henry, repeating that same stunned exclamation, "*Daughter!* I wish you had sent word. I would have brought my own with me from Tsarkoye Selo. As it was, I hardly had time to travel into the city myself."

"Please forgive my abhorrent rudeness on the matter. We made an unexpected trip here, as you might have gathered. And, regretfully, I only recently became reacquainted with Henrietta after a number of years apart," Henry explained. "We've been making up for lost time."

The tsar's lips twisted into an ironic smile. "It seems odd to me that your kind can 'lose' time when you stand to gain so much from it. Please—sit, sit, and tell me, how have you been, my old friend? What news from your own war?"

Oh my God. The knowledge that he was well aware of their world, and had directly benefited from his association with it, made Etta shift uncomfortably. This was the very first lesson of their world Sophia had given her. How chillingly serious the other girl had been when she'd said, if nothing else, they couldn't reveal themselves or what they could do. They couldn't share news of the future with the past, save the dead from their fates, or even break character.

The passivity of it had infuriated her, but to see the effects of breaking those rules now, even in the service of something good, was a little frightening.

Etta found herself in a stiff-backed chair without ever remembering sitting down. Henry settled into the chair beside hers. The tsar reclaimed his own.

"It continues," Henry said. "I take it you became acquainted with two of my men?"

The tsar sat back in his seat, his hands folded over his chest, his initial pleasure dimmed. "I think perhaps you already know the answer to that."

Henry tried for a smile. "Are you furious with me, then, Nicky?"

"I was many things," the tsar said. "Defeated soundly by the once-inferior Japan. Humiliated in the eyes of my cousins and peers the world over. Chastised by the poorest of this country for the conditions they were subjected to. Sickened by the Duma taking more and more power, mine by birthright."

Etta tried to fight her cringe as the man's voice grew hoarse. "Betrayed by former allies. Humbled by the notion that I have failed to maintain the power of my father and his father before him. But *alive*. The tsar. My country struggles, as all do in the face of great change, but the reforms you encouraged have been a boon, including the cessation of pogroms against the Jews, which I would never have believed."

"The recent disturbances . . ." Henry began, looking troubled.

"Already tidied up," the tsar finished. "I will find a way to soothe the ruffled feathers."

"I'm certain of it. But what of the treaties?"

"Breaking them came more easily than I might have imagined, with France aiding the revolutionaries, who were misguided in thinking one less monarchy would better the world. It was a simple thing to stand against political assassinations, given the history of my family. Serbia was a sacrifice, but one that kept us from the war."

The First World War, Etta thought, straightening. Russia had lost millions of soldiers; the badly managed effort, the poor conditions at home, and the machinations of other governments had all led to the ousting of the tsar, and his own eventual assassination.

"I hated you. Bitterly, I'm afraid, for countless years," the tsar said. "I cursed you with every breath. But I trusted you and prayed on each decision. Your family has been the steward of mine for many generations, the caretaker of this land for longer than even the Romanovs."

As in . . . guiding their choices? Etta wondered. *Advising them on the right ones to make?*

How was that any different than what the Ironwoods were doing?

"I thought you were against interfering in the timeline?" Etta asked Henry, however rude they might think her for interrupting.

"Oh, no, Etta, it's not quite like that," he said, quickly. "We worked very diligently to protect the timeline from the changes other families were making, especially as they pertained to ruining the fortunes of this part of the world."

"That is true," the tsar said. "They have never bowed to the demands of my family for more information, for ways to overcome our enemies. They have been protectors, not puppeteers."

Settled somewhat, Etta nodded. Henry turned back to the tsar.

"The Germans no longer had quite as much interest in your rule, did they," Henry said knowingly, "once they considered you humiliated after the war with Japan. Did they even bother with Lenin?"

The tsar shook his head. "And now they are quite busy, as is the rest of the world, with pulling themselves back together after their own humiliation. Your traveler war seems to be the only one which cannot find its end."

Henry smiled. "We might surprise you yet. Did one of my men indicate they would be hiding something in the palace during their visit in 1905? Do you recall?"

The tsar stroked his mustache. "I'm afraid not. They were harried and bloodied, in no state to do anything but hand off your letter. The guards were reluctant to let them in to see me. They were given food and rooms to rest, but by dinner they had fled again. I'll have one of the maids show you to their rooms after dinner—you'll stay and dine with me, won't you? Your men will be busy searching. There are fifteen hundred rooms here, you'll recall."

And how many hundreds of hiding places in each? Impatience stirred in her. *We'll be searching for days.*

"Where is your foe now? I'm not sure I've ever seen you look quite so relaxed."

"My spies have Ironwood safely ensconced in an earlier century, in Manhattan. His men are far too distracted by the changes in America to focus on you and your country."

"I'm glad to hear it," the tsar said, showing what Etta thought was admirable restraint in not pushing for more details. The man took only what was offered, though he probably had ways and means of demanding more. He reached back for his glass and held it up in Henry's direction.

"Yes, thank you," Henry said as the tsar crossed the room to a small cabinet, where a crystal decanter was stored.

"I'll take one, too," Etta said before she could stop herself. The tsar laughed as he poured out the liquor into the two glasses, but Etta wasn't joking. She could have used the liquid courage to prop her nerves up. Her back only straightened as the tsar passed the glass to Henry and resumed his former position.

"Tell me about yourself, my dear," he said. "I'm afraid you've got me at a disadvantage, as you likely know more about me than even I do."

Etta swallowed again, feeling Henry's gaze bore into the side of her head.

"Well," she began, "I grew up with my mother in New York City some time past, ah, now."

The tsar raised his glass to Henry. "For your own protection, I'm sure. A wise choice, my friend. There are times I wish I had done it myself. But continue, child."

"I'm not sure there's anything else all that interesting," Etta said, then added, "beyond the obvious, I mean. I've recently begun to travel. I do play the violin, too."

"A fine pursuit!"

"The tsar is a great lover of music," Henry explained, visibly relaxing. "You should know, Your Imperial Majesty, that Henrietta has quite undersold herself. She's exceedingly talented and has won numerous international competitions for her skill."

Etta turned toward him, her heart in an absolute riot—because, for a minute, he'd sounded like he was *bragging* about her.

To the last tsar of Russia.

"Brilliant," the tsar said. "You'll play for me, won't you?"

"I—yes—what?" Etta blinked.

"She's got Tchaikovsky in her repertoire," Henry continued.

"I do, but—"

"The violin concerto, no doubt," the tsar said, crossing the room in several quick strides. He retrieved a small case from where it was tucked beneath the piano.

That looks like—

A violin case.

"Oh," Etta said, feeling rather stupid. "You meant right now."

The tsar's smile fell somewhat as he set the case down on his desk. "I shouldn't have presumed you'd feel comfortable—"

"No, I'm happy to," she said. The usual tingle of stage fright was gone, swept off by an overpowering sense of longing—for the instrument, for the music. Weeks had passed since the concert at the Met, and Etta hadn't gone longer than two days without playing since she was five years old. The anticipation hit her like a drug, and she was shaking with it.

"Wonderful. It will send us to dinner on a pleasing note. Henry, you'll accompany her, won't you?"

Henry stood, too, ignoring Etta's look of surprise. Accompany her—the violin concerto was generally played with a full orchestra, but there was, of course, a reduction for a simple violin and piano duet. Sure enough, Henry was moving toward the piano, trailed by the tsar. He took a seat at its bench.

"Perhaps just the first movement," he suggested. "Unless you'd prefer the second?"

"Yes—I mean, of course. The first movement is fine." Etta realized that she was still standing by the tsar's desk, stunned and trembling with nerves, and quickly moved to join them. She accepted the violin, taking a moment to simply feel the slight weight of it in her hands, to let her palm run down the graceful neck, along the striped grain of the wood.

There was a single moment when she debated the propriety of taking off her gloves, but went for it regardless, needing to feel the instrument against her fingertips. She tossed the long lengths of silk over the back of the nearest chair. If the tsar was scandalized, he didn't show it, merely wetting his mustache as he took another deep sip of his drink.

Henry pushed back his sleeves, giving himself more freedom of movement. Etta wondered if he was truly planning to play without any sheet music, and felt a swell of admiration despite herself.

"When you're ready," he said.

She drew the instrument up, tucking it beneath her chin. She'd played this piece any number of times, the last of which being the competition in Moscow; Alice had never favored it all that much, despite its dominance in their world, and loved to repeat an early review of the concerto that claimed to play it was to "beat the violin black-and-blue." She only hoped she remembered it well enough to do it justice, and not humiliate herself in front of her . . . in front of her father again, like she had at the Met concert.

Her left shoulder stung with the effort of keeping the instrument up, but Etta pushed past the strain, forced her hands to stop shaking, and drew the bow against the strings. She nodded to Henry, who made his gentle entrance into the piece on the piano, launching them into the music.

And that was how Etta found herself playing Tchaikovsky's Violin Concerto in the early twentieth century for Tsar Nicholas II.

The piece wasn't just hard, it was devilishly difficult, to the point that Etta wondered if Henry hadn't suggested it because of Tchaikovsky's obvious ties to Russia, but because he wanted to showcase her skills in the flashiest way possible.

But from the first note, it was like learning to breathe again—the simple relief of hearing the music, using that part of her mind and heart. The tactile presence of the violin swept her away as she began, gliding into the gorgeous framework Henry established, announcing the piece's main theme.

The first movement of the concerto built and built, adding a theme, repeating the main theme, creating variations that grew more athletic. The runs became faster, reaching an amazing cadenza that made Etta's heart feel like it would burst from the joy of it.

Her eyes flicked over to Henry, watching his own eyes slide shut, as if imagining each phrase as he carved it out on the keys. An expression of pure, unself-conscious joy.

This is where it came from, she thought in wonder. *I inherited it.*

And that was what she would still have, now that she had altered the course of her life. No concerts, or competitions, or debuts—simple joy. And, much like seeing how Henry had nudged the timeline to reveal its secrets, it wasn't bad; it was *different*. It was a new, sweeter future to match the world's.

When it was over, Etta reluctantly lowered the violin, and let the world back in.

The tsar clapped, rising to his feet. "Wonderful! Absolutely wonderful, the two of you. Perhaps we won't discuss business after, but will simply play—"

There was a faint knock at the door, and the same servant that had escorted them in stepped back inside at the tsar's command to enter.

"Ah, of course. Every dream ends. That will be dinner, then," he said, retrieving the violin from Etta.

AS THEY WALKED TO DINNER, TRAILING THE TSAR, HENRY whispered, "You've got an odd look on your face. Is something the matter?"

"No, I just . . ." Etta lifted her gaze off the plush carpet and looked at the man ahead of them. "It surprised me—that he's just a normal person. That he's a *real* person, I mean, not just words on paper or a photograph. And *nice*."

Even with the infinite possibilities of time travel, Etta hadn't truly considered that she might *meet* someone famous or noteworthy. She and Nicholas had kept to themselves, avoiding the people around them as much as possible, and she'd assumed it was the same with other travelers, too. All her life, she'd thought of these historical figures as still lifes, to be studied through a layer of distance and glass like precious objects in a museum.

Henry snorted. "He's real, all right. And as fallible as any of us uncrowned mortals. He is rather nice to his friends, but of course, there have been many versions of his life that have seen him oppressive, cruel to those of other beliefs, foolish, and even blind to the needs of his most vulnerable subjects. You could say it was because he came to power too soon, before he was ready; because he picked poor advisors; or that it was a collision of unfortunate events. But I've seen it, time and time again: he cannot stop the march of a future that no longer has a place for him and his family."

"He's killed in this original timeline, too?" Etta whispered.

Henry rubbed a gloved hand over his forehead, considering his answer. "His death . . . it's inevitable. The events leading up to it grew worse and worse with Ironwood's interferences and alterations, but it has happened, and it will happen; only this time, it must play out the way it was intended a year from now."

He took a deep breath. "You remember what I told you before, that we must accept it, we must be ready to sacrifice what we have in order to see to the well-being of the whole? When I was younger, I came up with so many scenarios, so many different plans of how to save him, this one life, and still keep the timeline intact. But the pattern is undeniable. He is taken again and again; we are separated again and again. That is why I believe that certain things are destined; I can see the patterns, and cannot deny the repetition and the greater purpose they are trying to serve. At least in this timeline, I can be content in knowing the rest of his family will only go into exile."

A tremor of sadness in the words, but also resignation. "Etta . . . I wish I could spare you this, but it is inevitable that you, too, will be asked to relinquish something. You will see the pattern, too."

Etta tightened her grip on his arm, giving him a reassuring squeeze. In truth, she didn't know how to comfort him, or what to say, but she was grateful beyond words that he could see his friend again, even if it was for the last time. She would have shattered every rule the travelers had ever imposed if it meant being able to throw herself into Nicholas's arms and feel his steady heartbeat murmuring beneath her cheek.

As much as he presented himself to the world with a grin and an infectious laugh, every now and then Etta caught a glimpse of the part of himself that Henry tried to hide. It complicated her perception of him, made her want to study him that much more closely. She'd had a hard time seeing how her mother, who was so cold and sharp at times that she could cut without a single word, had ever found herself entangled with someone who acted as though laughing and smiling were as necessary to him as oxygen. But now Etta had seen the embattled parts of him; she'd witnessed that irresistible quality he had that made him a friend of tsars and Thorns alike.

"Henrietta . . . *Etta*," he corrected himself. Her heart gave a twist at his gentle tone. "You play exceptionally well. My compliments to Alice. I don't think she'd mind my saying that you surpass even her skill."

He'd heard Alice play at some point. She smiled sadly. It helped, somehow, to know that someone else remembered the way Alice had made her violin sing.

"Thank you," Etta said. "How long have you played the piano?"

"Nearly my whole life," Henry said. "From before I was tall enough to reach the pedals."

Etta nodded, her fingers pressing against his sleeve. "It must be hard to find time to play. What with all the traveling. Hiding. Scheming."

"Not as hard as you might think," he said. "I *make* time. It's true that altering timelines or events is a kind of creation, but there are always consequences, good or bad. Music is something I can create that is neither. It simply is the meeting of the composer's mind with my heart. Oh, dear—" He laughed. "Don't tell anyone I said that. It's rather maudlin, even for me."

Etta smiled. It had made perfect sense to her.

"Why do you play?" he asked her. "Not just play—why would you want to make it your life?"

Etta had been asked this question so many times over the years—by Alice, by reporters, by other performers—and had asked it of herself even more often. Every answer had been a reprise of the same practiced refrain. And yet here, with Henry, she felt safe enough to admit the other truths, the ones she had pushed so far back in her heart they'd begun to rust. The ones she hadn't even shared with Nicholas.

"I wanted to find something that would make Mom proud of me. Something I could excel at," she told him. "But some part of me thought that if I was out there performing, if everyone knew my name, I might reach my father or his family. They might recognize me. They'd hear my music and want to come find me. Know me." She let out a deep breath. "It's stupid, I know."

Up ahead, the tsar had slowed to greet Winifred and Jenkins near yet another of the palace's elaborate doors. Their voices carried down the hall, punctuated by polite laughter.

Just as Winifred turned to make her way over to them, Henry looked away, thumbing at his eye. When he looked back at her, nearly stricken, she wasn't sure what to do, other than tighten her hold on his arm.

They were still feeling around each other's edges. Trying to learn the same étude, each trial bringing them closer and closer to learning the skills of caring for the other.

"I heard you, Etta," he said softly. "I heard you."

CARTHAGE
148 B.C.

FIFTEEN

THE MAN IN THE DARKNESS STEPPED CLOSER, HIS FOOTSTEPS muffled by nearby insects and a cloud of disturbed birds launching into the night sky.

"That's quite far enough," Nicholas said, raising the sword so that its tip rested at the man's throat.

His eyes bulged at the implicit threat, but he did as he was told. Nicholas took careful stock of him. He was stooped at the shoulders, like a man who'd spent his life out in the fields, toiling over a plow. His red tunic was threadbare, nearly as weathered as the deep-set wrinkles in his ragged, dark skin. All of this was offset by a shock of white hair; his thick beard and brows looked as though they'd been left out to gather frost.

"What business do you have here, travelers?" the man demanded. "How did you find us?"

What Nicholas could see of the man's legs looked thin, almost knobby-kneed, and that general unsteadiness likely accounted for his slight limp and his reliance on a tall walking stick.

"My name is Nicholas Carter," he said. "We've come to trade information, nothing more."

"No, child, all you've done is bring the Shadows, disturb our peace," he said hoarsely, his gaze darting around the courtyard, as if expecting to find someone else there.

There was that word again, *Shadows*, and always whispered, as if to avoid summoning them.

Sophia snorted at the word *peace*. "It's not about Ironwood. We want a true trade—we have information we could share, but we've also got *food*"—she held up her sack of elephant feed—"food we'd be willing to part with for answers to a few questions that would stay between us. Which one are you, Remus or Fitzhugh?"

"Remus." The old man muttered something else to himself, one hand rubbing the other as he looped the bow over his shoulder. His gaze drifted away, his breath coming in quick, urgent bursts.

"Sir? Time is of the essence in this matter," Nicholas tried. The man leaped back as if struck.

"All right, yes, come with me," he said, voice strained. "Yes, follow me. Quickly now. It will be all right."

"We'll see about that," Sophia said, and her words leeched the rest of the color from the man's face.

His senses were piqued, his attention snared and drawn back toward the stables. Voices were rising, and the sound of the elephants' cries had ceased altogether. It seemed their diversion had run its course.

"It is lucky you survived," the man told them as they moved through the night, "but far luckier indeed that you did not cause a change to the timeline with that elephant stunt."

Fair point. Nicholas knew that his luck was bound to run out, but having received so little of it in his life, he was willing to push on to find its limits. Still, he couldn't release the last few tremors of doubt as he followed the man's unsteady steps any more than he could take his eyes from him. It was unfair, perhaps, given that the man had saved them when he could just as easily have left them to die on the attacker's blade, but he couldn't change his nature in a night.

"Ease up and unclench, will you?" Sophia muttered, taking notice.

"He's ancient. And he'll have a pot to boil whatever it is we just stole from the elephants."

"You're thinking with your stomach, not with your head," he sniped back quietly.

"Didn't you catch what he said about the *Shadows*?" she whispered. "He knows who they are—"

Remus spun around, his voice low. "For the love of Christ, do you want someone to hear you speaking another language and assume you've snuck in? I won't be saving you then, believe you me!"

Nicholas and Sophia kept their mouths shut. A good thing, because as they rounded onto the next street, Nicholas had to take a generous step back to avoid crossing into the path of several women heading the opposite way, toward the homes they had passed, where candles were lit and waiting for them. The ladies' dresses were longer and somehow more elegantly draped than the simple tunics of the men, their gauzy hems swirling around their sandaled feet. One nodded as Nicholas passed her, with dark hair shorn shorter than even Sophia's.

"Lice?" Sophia asked Remus cautiously, once they were clear of the street and onto a far smaller and quieter one.

He shook his head. "They cut their hair to give to the soldiers for their bows. Do you know nothing, child?"

Sophia made an insolent face behind his back.

"Why would they need to?" Nicholas asked. "I thought they were renowned for their military?"

"They are a fierce people," Remus said, his voice sounding steadier the farther they walked from the city's center, away from anyone who might overhear them. "Every man, woman, and child is or will be armed and expected to fight. Each home is a fortress in and of itself. They are rebuilding their arsenal."

"What happened to their original weapons?" Nicholas asked.

"When the Romans landed on these shores, they demanded hostages and the whole of the city's arms, which they were given. But that was not enough—they wished for the complete surrender of the city. The Carthaginians defied them, taunted them, even tortured Roman prisoners in full sight of the Roman army. And so it goes."

"The Romans are building something out in the harbor, aren't they?"

Remus gave him an exasperated look. "A mole, yes."

As he'd suspected—moles were massive structures, built from rock, stone, or wood, to be used as a kind of pier or breakwater. In this instance, it would seal up all of the warships he'd seen in the military harbor.

As the sun started to climb, they began their ascent up the hill toward the citadel that overlooked the harbor—Byrsa, the old man called it.

Nicholas kept his head down as they moved; the men and women here wouldn't be alarmed or find his dark skin particularly noteworthy, but he knew from long experience that men were unlikely to remember someone who didn't meet their gaze. His sandals shuffled along the worn stone, his thoughts dwindling to merely *left, right, left, right,* to order himself to keep going. He didn't look up until he was met with the sight of feet less than half the size of his own, bare and covered in cuts and sores.

The dark-skinned boy stepped aside quickly, allowing Remus, who was building speed like a churning storm, to hobble past. Sophia slid around Nicholas, shooting him an irritated look as she continued on ahead.

The boy couldn't have been more than eight or nine, Nicholas decided—too small, and wasted to the very bone. His tunic hung off his shoulders in tatters, knotted here and there in awkward lumps to keep it on him. The boy met his gaze from beneath his mass of matted hair. His dark eyes were bold with pride, in absolute defiance of his dismal state.

Nicholas knew that look well; the pride meant going hungry in silence, rather than lowering oneself to asking for charity, to begging. He'd been the same way, even as a slave, even once he was freed by the kindness of the Halls. If the captain hadn't force-fed him the first few nights, Nicholas wouldn't have eaten at all.

You've the pride of Lucifer, Hall had informed him. *It's the only thing that family gave you, and believe me, you don't need that inheritance.* Unbidden, his mind drew up the image of the child he and Sophia had seen earlier in the night, dead and wasted away from disease and hunger, left in the street like a common animal.

Nicholas gave the boy a tentative smile and lifted his bag from his shoulder, carefully removing the few things he might need from it, leaving only the food. The leather bag's design was simple enough to pass for something created in this time—and he doubted the boy would take care to notice it much at all. Careful not to say anything, he held it out toward him.

The boy stared at him, and Nicholas knew the moment he'd understood the gift. He snatched the strap of the bag from Nicholas's hands. Nicholas let out a faint laugh, but as he turned away, a small hand caught his wrist, forcing him to turn back around. The boy's fingers disappeared inside of his shirt, and he tugged off a thin strand of leather Nicholas hadn't noticed before. Dangling from it was a small pendant, just smaller than Nicholas's little finger. The boy held it up, gazing at him with fierce, dark eyes until Nicholas took it.

A trade, then. Nicholas nodded in thanks, and the boy turned and ran, never once looking back. He studied the unexpected gift, holding it up to the light. It was a face—glass that had been painted or colored somehow, and shaped to resemble a man with a curling row of hair, dark brows, large eyes, and a rather magnificent beard that extended from his chin in ringlets. An amulet, perhaps?

He shifted the objects he'd retrieved from his bag in his arms, and, with enough care that his hands shook from it, slid the glass bead onto the leather cord around his neck, next to Etta's earring.

221

"*Carter!*" Sophia barked.

Nicholas's long legs devoured the distance between him and Sophia and Remus, who had watched the exchange with suspicious eyes. He didn't look back—didn't want to give the boy the opportunity to refuse his gift.

Stay alive, he thought. *Stay alive. Escape.*

"You are *ridiculous,*" Sophia said in a low voice. "How *will* you continue to play the hero if you don't eat?"

"I'll find something else," he said. *I've gone longer without.*

Hunger was tolerable. The alternative was to be haunted by those eyes, by the bitterest sort of regret that wouldn't ever dissolve, no matter how much sweetness the years brought. It wasn't a weakness to have those thoughts, to feel that need to help another, to save lives. It made one *human.* He couldn't help but think that the travelers had fallen too deep into the practice of being silent witnesses. It drained the empathy from them, allowed them to build a wall of glass between themselves and suffering.

Sophia looked at him, making a strained sound. "All you're doing is prolonging the inevitable. Isn't it better to go this way than suffer what the Romans have in store for him?"

I'm not heartless, she'd said. And so she wasn't. Their hearts were made of different fibers, and perhaps her heart was more durable for that sort of decision than his own.

He was too exhausted to argue with her. Sophia's feet, much like his own, were dragging across the stones. Even her words lacked their usual venom and conviction.

"Is Fitzhugh at home now?" Nicholas asked the old man instead.

Remus shook his head. "No. My husband's a physician, you see. He is out making his rounds to visit the ill. It was left to me to investigate who came through the passage."

"You heard it from all the way up here?" Nicholas asked, glancing back over his shoulder at the city spread out below. The pale hue of the limestone was all the more breathtaking in the early morning with the tint of violet spread over it.

He'd lost the sound of the passage as they'd slipped further into the city. All he could hear now was the distant banging of the blacksmiths, who had woken with the dawn.

"We're near the other passage," Remus said. "It resonates with its brother in the water. Dreadful noise, but useful in knowing when to expect company."

Nicholas nodded.

"Satisfied, detective?" Sophia asked. "Might we try for a bit of shutting up now? Tonight's given me a crashing headache."

Remus's pace slowed as they reached the next door. He turned one last time to press his fingers against his lips before pushing it open. It creaked painfully, scraping the uneven stone. Nicholas ducked beneath the low arch and stepped into a small, shady courtyard, one hand on the hilt of his sword.

"This way," Remus whispered. Nicholas cast one last look around, searching for any potential entrances. Piles of bows, swords, shields, and spears rested beside brooms and other simple household tools, waiting. A prickle of anxiety fizzed in his blood; there was one way in, yes, which meant it would be easier to keep watch for trouble, but it also meant there was only one way out if trouble did actually arrive.

The three of them went up a steep stack of steps to the second level, where a second door waited. Remus cast one last nervous glance around before opening it and ushering them inside.

The smell of earth and greens had bled into the dry air, giving the open room a musty, medicinal smell that instantly put Nicholas back in a place of unease. Physicians in his time were often no better than butchers, their tools as dull as their skills.

On the left side of the room was a bed pressed against the wall, with strands of greens left to dry over it. The opposite wall was dedicated to Fitzhugh's work—more drying herbs and plants, along with small vials and ceramic pots, a grinding stone, and a rudimentary scale. Across the room, below the windows, was a carefully arranged living area; there was a low table, a rug to cover the polished stone floor, a chair, and pillows on which to sit. At the center of it all was a hearth, with a pot boiling over, spitting bubbling water into the hissing fire below.

It was a comfortable home, but nothing like he would have expected for two travelers. To their credit, at least there were no outward hints that they weren't native to this era—most travelers, as he'd seen even with Etta's great-grandfather, couldn't resist the temptation to cobble together small stashes of trinkets and souvenirs. Instead, there were just a few small statues and stone figurines of foreign, ancient gods.

"We can eat and discuss whatever it is you're here for after I finish my rest, and you've had some yourself," Remus said, sitting on the bed and removing his battered shoes. "At a decent hour."

"Time is not on our side," Nicholas began, even as Sophia made herself a small bed from the pillows near the hearth and table.

"When is it ever, my lad," the man said, as the feather mattress and rope frame settled beneath him. "When is it ever?"

"How can you be sure the attackers will not bother us?" Nicholas asked. "That they haven't tracked us here?"

"They move in darkness," the man said, blowing out the candle on the table beside the bed. "We are safe. For now."

Nicholas released his frustration in a harsh breath, but found a place to stretch out on the rug. The uneven ground beneath him was as unforgiving as it was in every other century he'd recently visited. He took the opportunity to assess his aches and cuts, as well as the new, hot spikes of pain in his right hand. Holding it up, he examined the pattern etched into the ring in the soft morning light.

He tried tugging it off again.

Failed.

With another snort, he crossed his arms and turned his back to the wall, closing his dry eyes. But he did not sleep. His mind did not relent in trying to chase the ghost of Etta's face, remembering how sweetly her body had curved against his own. Nor did it allow him to ignore the familiar pressure of someone's gaze taking the measure of him.

But hours later, when Nicholas finally turned over to confirm his suspicions of being observed, Remus had dipped deeply into his dreams, and the only thing that moved beyond the door was the lonely wind.

HOURS LATER, AS THE SUN SWEPT INTO THE ROOM AND THE fire warmed its confines, Nicholas propped himself up against the table on the floor and attempted to stay awake. Or at least alert. Sophia, who had slept without a second thought, drummed her fingers on the low table, impatient for the man to finish brewing his tea and cooking the oats.

"Here you are," Remus said, offering a cup of the former to Sophia, wincing as the hot tea splashed out of the small wooden cup and onto his trembling hands. Without any sort of prompting, he pressed another cup into Nicholas's hands, turning back to fill one of his own.

"We need to agree to secrecy, before we begin," Nicholas said. "What we discuss here cannot leave this room."

Remus's brows rose. "Who do you think I would tell, beyond Fitzhugh? We don't exactly receive guests, and even if we wanted to, Cyrus has forbidden contact. I cannot contact my Jacaranda family any more than Fitz could his immediate Ironwood family. He would have us killed for disobeying his explicit orders."

Nicholas should have known that—he himself had been exiled, confined to his natural time. But the man's words did not sound promising for the information they needed.

"Let's get on with this business, then, my new friends," Remus said. "Ask me your questions. I have a few of my own."

Sophia blew on her cup of tea, then took a deep gulp. Her face screwed up, lips puckering. "Why does it taste like I'm drinking dirt?"

225

"It's *green tea*," Remus said indignantly. "It tastes of the pure earth. It's not readily available in this era and continent, so have some respect for my hospitality."

"Whatever you say."

Nicholas had always been one for coffee over tea, the bitterest, darkest coffee available, but he was willing to try any sort of stimulant to keep his thoughts sharp.

He raised his own cup to his mouth, letting it wet his lips. It smelled of wet grass, and what taste he got was sour, not at all fortifying or refreshing. Setting it on the ground beside him, he leaned forward against the table. "We're hoping to discover the last common years of the two most recent timeline shifts. Have you received any notices about them?"

The man looked stunned. "Oh, I'm afraid you've gravely overestimated how much contact we have with the outside world. In case it wasn't clear: none. We don't receive notices from the messengers anymore because we are not allowed to travel, and therefore any dangers the shifts present don't affect us. We've been trapped in this era for *years*, with no communication—no food, no assurances we'll ever be allowed to leave."

Damn it all, Nicholas thought, weary and frustrated down to his soul. But of course.

"You were stupid enough to think he'd forgive you if you came back groveling," Sophia said, one brow arched.

"I wished he'd just gone and executed us then, with all the others. The bastard put us here because he knew it would be our tomb, and that we'd think every day of what we did to spite him, and regret it," Remus said. "Now, Fitz and I only regret the cowardice of leaving the Thorns. It was rough living, especially when it seemed as if Ironwood had massacred half their ranks. But tell me—with everything going on, is he sufficiently distracted now for Fitz and I to make our leave to another era undetected? He told us there were men posted at the entrances to both passages to ensure we could not leave."

"There was no one at the one we came through," Sophia admitted. "Did you really not even check? Ever?"

"No. His rage is absolute, and we were foolish enough to think we might earn our forgiveness eventually, with good service to him." Remus laughed darkly. "What a fool I've been. Well, no more. Fitz and I will accompany you to the other passage out of the city when he returns. We'll disappear this time."

Nicholas approved of the manner in which the old man's words vibrated with fuming resentment. Rubbing his tingling hand, he watched Remus for any signs of deceit, and found only the portrait of a man hardened by the bitter taste of disappointment.

"I thought for sure you came because of the work I'd done on the Shadows—the research Cyrus had me conduct," Remus said, rising to stir the oats. Testing their consistency, he scooped out two steaming bowls to serve to his guests. "Ancient traveler lore, yes, I can assist you with. It's very likely the only thing I'm good for these days. The rest is beyond my sight and knowledge."

Nicholas was momentarily distracted by how hard he had to grip the wooden spoon in his hand to feel it. Batting down the fear pawing at his heart, he turned the whole of his attention to the food. The oats were plain and burned his tongue, but Nicholas was sure neither he nor Sophia had ever consumed a meal with more speed.

"Is there anyone who might be willing to help us discover the last common year without it getting back to Ironwood?" Nicholas asked, setting his empty bowl aside.

Remus considered this. "Most of his large alterations were made in the nineteenth and twentieth centuries. You might try asking a guardian named Isabella Moore, in Boston. Ironwood had her son killed around the same time Fitzhugh and I left to join the Thorns, and I know her to be well connected, but with no love of the man. Try her any time after 1916 and before 1940."

Another lead. Which might go just as far as this one did in answering their question: nowhere. He forced his good hand to release the edge of the table he'd been gripping.

"What did you mean when you said you thought we were coming because of the . . . Shadows?" Sophia asked, blowing on the surface of her tea before taking a deep gulp of it. "What do you know of them?"

Remus looked offended when she let out what was either a small hiccup, belch, or some charming combination of the two.

"First, I think you ought to be honest about what you're truly searching for," he said, "for I've only ever known them to hunt one thing: the astrolabe."

Nicholas felt the skin on the back of his neck start to crawl. Even Sophia choked on the last sip of her tea.

"Surprised?" Remus said. "Cyrus never changes, not even in the most dangerous of times. But then of course, knowledge is power—all the more reason for him to hoard the truth about its history and nature."

That, Nicholas could not dispute. "And you know of it how?"

"Before Ironwood did away with the position, I was a record-keeper for the families for longer than you've been alive," Remus explained. "I know things that would slow the blood in your veins. It's one of the reasons he was so irate that we left, you see. He did not want anyone else to have that knowledge, least of all Henry Hemlock. But he cannot execute me, either, for the old records were burned and I might have one last detail or piece of knowledge he needs. I know that, to create a passage, legend holds that you must have the astrolabe, but you must also have something from the time and year you wish to go. I know the songs all others have forgotten."

Sophia gave Nicholas a nod, confirming all of these things.

"What do you know of alchemy?" Remus began. "Of its principles?"

"I know it's a load of garbage," Sophia said. "Outdated hogwash that has spurred on countless pitiful idiots to waste their time trying to turn lead to gold, look for a cure for all ailments, and find a way toward immortality."

"Sophia," Nicholas said, his tone warning. He didn't want to scold her, but he wanted to get what information they could and leave this place as quickly as possible.

"You've covered some of it, yes, but the principles of alchemy extend far beyond the tangible. You might say that it is the search for understanding about the true nature of life, and how energy can be manipulated: a careful study of the beautiful mysteries of life, death, and perhaps resurrection. 'As above, so below, as within, so without, as the universe, so the soul.'"

That might explain some of the odd symbols he had seen in the Belladonna's store and workshop, then. It was as much a belief system as a craft or profession.

"There once lived a man who achieved this perfect knowledge by broadening his understanding of how *immortality* might be accomplished—what better way to conquer life than to destroy that which limits it?"

"Time," Nicholas finished. "You mean to say . . ."

"This man, the originator of our line," Remus continued, "harnessed these energies, transmuted them into something new, something tied to the earthly influence of his own blood. It was contained within a device, a key that allowed him to control it. Three copies of this master key were made for his three children, but each copy was weaker than the next. His children fought viciously for control of the original version, each with what they thought was the true path for it, until one day, two of the children turned on the youngest, who they felt was the alchemist's favorite. When the alchemist attempted to intervene, both he and the youngest child were killed in the fray."

"There's the Ironwood in them," Sophia muttered.

"In the chaos, the master key was stolen by a fourth child, an illegitimate bastard, a by-blow of some poor wench."

Sophia straightened at that, her top lip peeling back in a snarl at the word *bastard*. And, for the first time in a long while, Nicholas realized he had never quite considered her own parentage in this context—the same context as his own.

"Having lived and worked in the shadows of his legitimate brothers and sister, having been the alchemist's apprentice, he knew how to harness the power of the master key—the master astrolabe—and he knew well that the others would never let him possess it. And so the apprentice ran for centuries, weaving in and out of time until his trail became too muddied for the others to follow with the lesser astrolabes," Remus said. "Years passed, and he began to release his fears, fathering families across the continents. But the continued use of the astrolabe had altered the composition of his body, with curious results. His life was extended a century beyond what was natural, and the children he sired inherited the ability to travel through the passages he had created without needing to be in possession of the astrolabe. Almost as if, by using it, he had absorbed some of its essence into himself, and had become an extension of it. The same proved true of his remaining half siblings, and the eldest finally succeeded in finding his bastard brother, by then old and decrepit, and killing him."

"How, if their lives were prolonged?" Sophia asked.

"Their lives were prolonged and they aged and aged and aged, but only so long as they were not unnaturally interrupted by, say, foul murder," Remus said. "Though our bloodlines have been diluted, and we no longer live beyond the normal years of men, some small spark of the astrolabe remains, allowing us to travel."

Nicholas shook his head. The talk of alchemy, this kind of immortality outside of heaven, was almost too heathen to believe.

And yet . . . he thought again grimly.

There was a kernel of pure, primal truth in Remus's tale—fear, even more so than greed, was a powerful motivator, especially when coupled with the determination to survive. However the story may have been embellished, there was some validity to it.

"The daughter fell to history's mercy, and no record of her remains, other than that her elder brother stole her astrolabe and used it in some unnatural way. The record is unclear, only that the copies disappeared. There is only one left now—the master astrolabe—and, if Cyrus's wild beliefs are true, the eldest son still hunts for it."

"I thought each of the four families had their own astrolabe?" Nicholas said. The Lindens, then, had held the master copy in their family for generations.

"Perhaps they possessed them for a time, but all were stolen back. The eldest son has quite the force behind him—travelers taken from their families, who have had their lives stolen and shaped to serve only him. For lack of a better, proper term, they were noted only as Shadows in our histories." Nicholas's mouth tightened at that, a small flinch that Remus caught. The old man chuckled before he continued. "I can sense the disbelief in you both. I realize how it all sounds, of course."

"Like bullshit you're trying to sell us," Sophia snarled.

"There are things in our forgotten history that are so ancient, one must search for the few clues embedded in our lore, our shared nightmares. Generations ago, the old records vault was burned in what was said to be the fault of a single candle, and now, so little proof remains of the alchemist and the Shadows that many travelers simply refuse to believe in their existence. Missing children are explained away as having been orphaned by the timeline, or that they simply wandered off into passages, never to be seen again. The mind can dream up any number of explanations for dark things, of course."

Nicholas shook his head, rubbing at his eyes once more. "What is the role these Shadows play, then?"

"It is said they work on behalf of the alchemist's surviving son, carrying out his wishes and stealing traveler children to continue a

231

cycle of service to him and his mission to find the master astrolabe," Remus said, as if this were not absurd. "Though their story itself has been lost, and fewer and fewer children are lost, the fear is still taught to traveler children to this very day, however unwittingly. Tell me, girl, that you don't recall the old song: *From the shadows they come, to give you a fright . . .*"

Sophia surprised Nicholas by easily finishing the rhyme. *"From the shadows they come, to steal you this night."* She looked unimpressed, to say the least. "You don't need to shill bad poetry."

"Finish it, girl," Remus said. "How does the rhyme end?"

She gazed at the man in defiance, but softly sang, *"Mind the hour, mind the date . . . and find that path which does not run straight."*

"These Shadows are the ones who hunt you now," Remus said. "The shadows of his glorious sun. They will stop at nothing to prevent you from taking possession of the astrolabe, should you find it. Your paths have crossed, unfortunately, and now there is no way to disentangle them."

"Is there really nothing to be done about it?" Nicholas asked. "You read nothing else about their methods in your time as a record-keeper?"

The old man shrugged the question away as he stood and went back to the hearth, this time for his own meal. In the silence that followed, he was absorbed in the simple, hypnotic task of stirring, and stirring, and stirring. A spark of instinct began to tug at Nicholas's ear, begging an audience.

Sophia, in deep contemplation of this information, pressed her face into her hands, breathing deeply. But Nicholas felt too anxious to remain seated, too full of absurd stories to sit idly by. He began to do laps around the cramped room, stopping occasionally to study a small piece of decorative tile, a bust, small wooden boxes. One of which yielded a solid, rectangular object wrapped in burlap: a harmonica.

It was one of those painful moments when need was at odds with morality. His fingers ran over the cool, shining surface, and he leaned over, far enough to see the reflection of his haggard face. He'd stolen as a child—scraps of food, affection, his own freedom for a time—and the thought of doing so now stirred a poisonous self-loathing inside of him. Nicholas shut the box and turned to the spot where Fitzhugh Jacaranda ground his medicines and did whatever it was physicians or ship surgeons or healers did when they weren't pulling rotten teeth or sawing off limbs.

Below the wooden bench, tucked nearly out of sight, was a stiff, cylindrical leather bag with a long strap, its drawstring opening just wide enough to look into. Glancing back to ensure the man was busy with the pot on the hearth, he nudged it open the rest of the way with his toe. It was filled to the brim, nearly spilling over with sachets, neatly wound bandages, and those same small vials he saw on the table. Beneath that was a layer of tools, primed and ready for use.

That nagging feeling was back, until realization lit Nicholas's mind like a blast of gunpowder, blowing him back off his feet. Studying the man out of the corner of his eye, he forced his voice to remain even, and took a deep breath before asking, "Why, if Fitzhugh is making his rounds as a healer, has he left his bag here?"

Remus stopped stirring, his shoulders bunching up as he froze in place. Nicholas's heart made the dive from his chest to the very pit of his stomach, and his hand came to rest on the hilt of his sword.

In the breath of silence that passed between them, Remus reached for one of the nearby knives, his hand shaking as it closed around the hilt and he brandished it.

"Don't run. You'll only make it worse for yourself," Remus said. "And you won't get far at all."

PETROGRAD
1919

SIXTEEN

ETTA WAS MISTAKEN IN ASSUMING THE "SMALL DINING Room" would bear some sort of resemblance to the simple dining room you'd find in any house—slightly worn furniture, a floor scuffed by chairs and feet, a few personal touches here and there. Instead, it was a miniature version of the grander rooms they'd passed on the way in, with one chandelier instead of five, six, or seven.

There was almost too much to absorb at once—Etta saw her stunned reflection in the mirror that hung over the small fireplace, just past the gold clock and candelabras artfully arranged on the mantel.

Etta was led to a seat two over from the tsar, beside Henry, who sat at his right. Winifred, preening, sat to the tsar's left, and beside her was Jenkins, who seemed as much at a loss as Etta over what to do with himself. Missing were the other Thorn bodyguard and Julian, who, despite being invited to the palace, was not welcome in the tsar's company. She thought that wise, given the havoc his grandfather had brought to this side of the world in the other timeline.

A footman pulled out her yellow-silk-covered chair for her, guiding it back in once she'd settled into place. Now that she was sitting, the arrangement of the table seemed egalitarian—the tsar could easily look at and speak to everyone around him. It did have the trappings of some kind of a family dinner in that way, at least.

And then, the elaborate dance that was their meal began. Soup was spooned into Etta's bowl, and small meat pies were placed on one of the plates. Etta's eyes slid over to Henry, watching him watch the tsar. Once he began eating, so did Henry, and, for that matter, so did Etta. With gusto. She'd had a bit of bread in San Francisco, and a little fruit at the hotel where they'd changed, but nothing as filling as the rich, creamy soup, or as warm as the meat pies.

"Tell me," Henry said into the silence, "how does your wife fare, Your Imperial Majesty? She was unwell during my last visit, and I regret I wasn't able to see her."

"She's much improved, thank you," the tsar said. "She is enjoying life outside of Petrograd, and it gives me pleasure to see her so content."

"Indeed," Henry said. "I'm glad to hear it."

As he finished his course, Henry set his cutlery on the plate and his hands in his lap. Within seconds, one of the waiters was there to clear. Winifred did the same, and like magic—or at least a well-rehearsed stage production—another waiter swept in.

Etta did the same, and was still surprised by the speed at which her bowl and small plate were taken, and by the sudden realization that each diner had his or her own waiter to serve them. The tsar's, even more surprisingly, was an older gentleman, who seemed to bow beneath the weight of his heavy tray. Etta watched in sympathy as the tsar subtly helped steady the waiter's trembling arm when he refilled his wineglass.

Winifred's and Jenkins's waiters exchanged a glance over the table at the sight, young and robust compared to Etta's own waiter, who looked as if he was on the verge of being ill. He was pale-faced and sweating profusely at the brow as he carried another tray out.

The next course was fish, *Dviena sterlet* in champagne sauce, for which Winifred went into such overblown raptures that Etta felt embarrassed to be sitting at the same table as her. Next came chicken in a richly flavored sauce she couldn't identify, and, because that wasn't enough meat, a course of ham. Each was served with a different kind of wine; there was so much of it that Winifred looked ready for a nap, and Etta herself had to switch to mineral water to keep from sliding out of her chair.

Some pirate, she thought. *Can't even handle a few glasses of wine.*

Etta was still picking at her ham when the tsar finished his plate. Another apparent rule: when the tsar was finished, so were you, regardless of whether or not you were still eating. Etta lost her plate with the fork still in her mouth.

"Peach compote, my favorite!" Winifred crooned as the next batch of small plates was brought out. Jellies, ice cream, compotes—Etta was afraid that if she ate even one more bite she might be sick. Her waiter might *actually* have been sick. His hands shook as he set the last of the plates down in front of her, shook so badly that the porcelain clattered against the table. Etta could have sworn she felt a drop of sweat hit her bare neck. She turned toward Henry, to find his narrowed eyes already tracking the progress of Etta's waiter as he made his way back around the table. Etta felt a jump in her pulse like a staccato note.

"I remembered as much," the tsar said. "I'm sure they had quite the time finding peaches during this season, but it's worth it to see the smile on your face."

Etta's waiter had left the room at last, and a new waiter swept in, moving to the sideboard. He lifted a wine bottle out of an ice bucket. It looked no different than any of the others, with the tsar's monogram and the imperial insignia, but as he turned back to the table, he held it by its neck, not its base.

"You are too kind," Winifred said. "I'm sure it was—"

Jenkins lurched up out of his seat. *"Iron—"*

One minute Etta was seated; the next she was falling back, knocked over by the force of Henry's arm as it smashed across her chest. In the sliver of an instant before she hit the ground, she saw the waiter raise the bottle of wine and send it sailing down onto the table, between the tsar and Winifred. Just before the glass shattered, two words tore from the man's throat.

"Za Revolyutziu!"

The whole of Henry's weight drove into her, knocking the breath from her as he covered her. The walls and ceiling above her seemed to run with colors, as if washed with rain. Time trembled, thundering with the force of the oncoming change. And with an eardrum-piercing roar, the air exploded into a tidal wave of fire, and the floor disappeared beneath them.

CARTHAGE
148 B.C.

SEVENTEEN

THE FIRELIGHT CAUGHT THE LONG BLADE OF REMUS Jacaranda's knife as he held it between them, but the man's face was in shadow. The only sound in the room beyond the popping fire was Nicholas's harsh breathing.

Finally Remus said, his voice small and quaking, "You have to understand. . . . There is nowhere we can go. . . . This is the only way."

"The only way to *what*?" Nicholas demanded. His eyes slid over to Sophia, who was still sitting at the table, her head in her hands. He hissed at her, "Get up, will you?"

"To survive. None of us can survive without Cyrus's protection, without kin or kindness. There is nowhere we can go that he will not find us, that the Thorns will not try to kill us for betraying them, too. We need him. I need him to *trust* me again—"

"*Sophia,*" Nicholas hissed. "We're leaving."

"It's a sign of how much he wants you," Remus said, trying to straighten his hunched shoulders, "that a runner came even to *us* to promise a bounty. This is our way back to his good graces."

"All of those things you said before, about being free, escaping him—why can't that be true? Why not leave with us now?"

"It will not work, it will not work. . . ." The weakness, that pathetic

243

quality to the old man, had made Nicholas dismiss the threat of him so easily, knowing he could be overpowered with ease. Twice now, he'd been tricked. Hatred scorched his heart. There truly was no end to the villainy travelers possessed. Each was more self-serving than the next.

"So Fitzhugh has gone to bring back the cavalry, has he?"

Damn his eyes. He and Sophia wouldn't make it back to the passage in the water, but he might be able to find the other one the man had spoken of, if she would just—

Nicholas turned toward her at the sound of the first, retching gasp. Sophia jerked back from the table with a rattling cough, her hands seeming to spasm against the wood.

"What's the matter?" Nicholas asked her. "Sophia?"

"Can't—" she gasped out, "can't feel—legs—"

Nicholas spun toward the man, drawing his sword so quickly, it sang as it sliced the air. "What have you done?"

Remus smiled, backlit by the hearth.

"Did you know," he began, his voice brittle, "that the clans of the families united under the names of trees because they thought it was a clever way of symbolizing their reach into the future, and their roots winding deep into the past? Ironwood, Jacaranda, Linden . . . I've always thought that the Hemlocks picked their name not for the tree, however, but for the flowering plant."

"You—" Sophia choked out.

Nicholas stilled, hollowed by his words. The flowering plant. But then, that was . . .

Holy God.

"That's right," Remus said, smiling. "The Hemlocks are poison itself, and they inflict their terror in the same manner as the *tea* you drank. They identify what it is you desire, lure you in with promises of trust and respect, only to trick you into doing their bidding, into believing their lies about the timeline."

Sophia turned to Nicholas, her face etched with naked terror. That

244

alone set his blood to boiling. For someone so unacquainted with fear to have that expression—he was sure it would be seared on his memory forever. Both hands were clawing at the muscles of her legs, as if trying to work the feeling back into them by force.

"You won't be able to return now, will you?" Remus sneered at her. "I've put myself beyond your reach, and you matter so little to this world that the timeline has not even shifted to account for your impending death."

Nicholas came down on the man like a thunderbolt, forcing him up against the hearth, close enough for his tunic to smolder and for the stench of burned hair to pierce the air. Remus's smile faltered, his eyes flaring.

"You didn't . . ."

"Drink your nasty concoction?" Nicholas sneered. "No, I did not, sir."

Remus slashed wildly with his knife, catching Nicholas across the back of his sword hand and nicking his jaw. He slammed the man against the wall, hard enough this time to knock the breath from his lungs and the knife from his fingers. It clattered to the ground, and Nicholas kicked it into the hearth.

The old man's face scrunched up mockingly, as if daring Nicholas to push him into the flames as well. Nicholas's hand knotted in the front of the man's tunic, giving him a warning shake. "Is there an antidote? Tell me, damn you!"

The bulk of his fury wasn't even directed at Remus Jacaranda— Nicholas could have punched himself for missing the signals, the clues. Even when he'd noticed the other man stalling, he hadn't pinned any sort of purpose to it.

"You'll find out soon enough," Remus said, eyes sliding over to Sophia, who was twisting around on the ground, struggling to rise onto her feet. "You were fools to come here—"

Nicholas smashed the hilt of the sword against the man's temple, knocking him clear into unconsciousness. He barely managed to keep his grip on him, yanking him forward out of the flames and letting his prone form slam to the ground.

The fool you *are,* Nicholas thought, *if you think for one second that Ironwood will ever show you mercy.*

"Nic—Cart—"

He spun back toward Sophia, kneeling beside her. Her hand lashed out; he caught it, giving what he hoped was a reassuring squeeze. What did he know about hemlock, other than that it had killed Socrates? "Do you know any sort of antidote?"

Her face was distorted by pain and panic, but she still managed to give him an incredulous look.

Damn. Who would know how to help her? They couldn't stay here in Carthage; they didn't speak the language, they didn't know how to find another physician, and it would be too easy for them to be tracked.

A crack of thunder cut through the clear morning sky; Nicholas jerked at the drumming beat that muffled the crackling pops of the fire, rivaling the sound of the Romans hammering out in the harbor. The other passage.

No time, he thought, *no time—*

He dove toward the ground, scooping up his possessions and stuffing them into Sophia's bag, looping it over his shoulder. He turned back to see her struggling to compose her face and failing.

"Pardon me," he said, bending down to scoop her up off the ground. One of her hands came up, smacking him in the face in protest. "I wasn't aware you walking out of here on your own was still an option, but if you think you can fly out on pride alone, by all means . . ."

She went very still.

"I thought not."

He rose onto unsteady feet, his vision blacking out as the blood left his head. He wasted precious seconds waiting for his exhausted body

246

to steady before carrying her to the door. Her skin had gone the sickly shade of a fish left too long out of water, and her trembling hands . . .

Medicine. Surely they wouldn't have made the poison without an antidote? Surely there was something here if Fitzhugh Jacaranda truly was a healer? Surely?

Nicholas carried her over to the worktable, setting her down only long enough to pick up the man's bag and cinch the opening closed. He had them to the door in two quick strides when he doubled back to the chest, where he'd seen the small wooden box. With a huff, he plucked the harmonica out of its bindings and slid it into Sophia's bag. They wouldn't need it now, not with the passage bellowing loud enough for all of creation to hear, but he couldn't trust the future to bring the next one to him so easily.

He kicked the door open, shifting Sophia from his arms to over his shoulder. She hit him weakly in protest.

"Be easier to run—" The words died in his throat. From his vantage point on the second story of the building, he could see over the courtyard's wall into the street below.

Four figures were shouldering quickly through the milling crowds—four men, in a sea of women and children. The one leading the way at the front wore a faded blue tunic, his head ringed with blond, strawlike hair, clearly older than the rest. He looked to be in danger of being trampled by the men charging up behind him. Their "tunics" were poor imitations of togas, with sheets likely stripped off a nearby bed in a hurry—worse, their hair was still parted and slicked down in the style of the nineteenth or twentieth century. One even had a dark, neatly trimmed mustache like a slug above his upper lip.

It was a surprising lack of planning by a group of Ironwoods, who usually prided themselves on prudence and an overabundance of caution to avoid tampering with the Grand Master's timeline.

Not for the first time, Nicholas wondered what price Ironwood had put on his life. Most travelers wouldn't risk the old man's wrath, or throw away decades of conditioning and training, for anything less than a tidy sum. He felt a foolish swell of pride at that.

"It's just up here," he heard the old man in front—Fitzhugh?—say.

"Your tip better be good, old man—" groused the traveler behind him. Miles Ironwood, of course. The last time he'd seen the man, Miles had been ordered by Ironwood to pummel him with his fists for Julian's death. What a charming reunion this would be.

No time.

"Who . . . ?" Sophia asked.

"Miles Ironwood," he said.

"Always . . . wanted to . . . stab him."

"Well, here's your opportunity," he said. "Don't die before you give me the pleasure of watching you do it."

The house had the same problem the city did: if the Ironwoods were coming through the courtyard, then he and Sophia had run out of exits. Unless . . .

Nicholas made for the stairs that led up to the next level, and the next one after that. Sophia went alarmingly slack against his shoulder. "Sophia? *Sophia!*"

"Hey!" The shout rose from the street, cutting through the din of voices. *"Carter!"*

His legs burned as he raced up the uneven stairs, Sophia bouncing against his shoulder, his whole body quaking with the effort of keeping them upright. Third story, fourth, fifth—he nearly lost his footing as they reached the roof, momentarily distracted by the heavy pounding of steps behind him. He swung them both around, scanning the roofs around him for the nearest one to jump to.

His breathing was so labored, tearing in and out of him, that he didn't hear the whistle of the arrow at all—only felt the pain of it slamming into his shoulder. Nicholas staggered forward, knocked off-balance by the force of the blow.

"Carter, stop!" one of the men shouted. "You'll only make it worse for yourself!"

Make it worse how? As far as he was concerned, these men would only be taking him back to Ironwood one way: dead. And he still had too much to accomplish before he'd ever let that happen.

He still had to find Etta.

Nicholas dug deep into the well of his strength, moving to the far end of the roof, trying to judge whether or not the distance would be too great to throw Sophia, when he heard a sharp whistle.

It took him a moment to locate the source: a small, dark-robed figure, crouched on the roof just beyond the one he'd been studying, waving him forward. His heart surged with the hope that it was Rose, that he might finally achieve the dream of strangling her for this mess she'd tossed them all into—but he wasn't, to his surprise, disappointed to realize that the mystery figure was Li Min. If the choice was between Ironwood's men and a thief who was at least clever enough to find them a way out of Carthage . . . well, the choice was rather simple.

"Apologies," he told Sophia as he slid her down off his shoulder.

"—what—"

He tossed her like a basket, wincing as she struck the solid roof. He reached back, gritting his teeth, and snapped off the long end of the arrow, ignoring the warmth soaking through his tunic. There was only about a yard of distance between the two buildings, and he crossed it without trouble. Li Min met him there, kneeling to help him pick Sophia back up.

"Ma'am, are you here to help for your own mysterious reasons, or are you here to kill her for stealing your money?" he asked, his face serious. "Because I haven't the time for the latter, and your competition is arriving shortly."

Li Min looked up from her study of Sophia's ashen face. "What has she been given?"

"Hemlock." Saying the word aloud made the immense danger of it tangible, gave the threat new life.

"Quickly, then," Li Min said. "We haven't much time."

Out of other options, his body fast approaching that murky line of uselessness, Nicholas followed her over to the next roof.

"Drop," she told him, eyes flickering to something just over his shoulder.

He barely had time to take a knee before she flung a small knife from the depths of her hooded cloak, striking the first man at the dead center of his heart. The weight of his body sent the others tumbling back down the stairs. The one who managed to remain on his feet found another knife lodged directly in his throat.

Nicholas turned back to Li Min, only to find her already making her way down the stairs winding around the back of the building.

"This way, this way," she called. "Keep up!"

"Keep up, she says," he muttered, trying to pick up his pace without sending both himself and Sophia into a tragic tumble.

Li Min was incredibly light on her feet, not difficult for her diminutive size; still, he felt like an inelegant beast lurching along behind her. He was beginning to lose feeling in his left arm, where he felt the tip of the arrow scraping against the bone. Nicholas couldn't focus on that thought without feeling like he was about to retch; instead, he turned what remained of his drifting attention to maintaining his grip on Sophia. The voices shouting in English were still so close, tearing through the unpleasant stillness of the besieged city.

He was grateful when his feet were back on solid ground, but there was no time to stop and clear the darkness edging into his vision. His eyes tracked Li Min as she wove in and out of the startled crowds around her like a dolphin leaping through waves. Someone—a woman—put a concerned hand on his arm as he passed, but Nicholas brushed it off and kept going, his stomach tightening as they continued up the hill to the buildings crowning the Byrsa.

250

Just before they reached the apex of the hill, Li Min took a sharp turn and ducked between the last two homes, kicking open a gate that stood in her way. There, just beyond a shaft of light pouring into the narrow alley, was the shimmering entrance to the passage.

As if sensing them, the pitch of its voice grew higher. Nicholas felt himself faltering, choking on dust and the metallic tang of blood, but he gave himself one last shove forward and felt himself vanish like a passing breeze.

PETROGRAD
1919

EIGHTEEN

ALICE HAD TOLD ETTA ONCE THAT IN ORDER TO BECOME A
concert violinist, she would need to protect four things above all else:
her heart, from criticism; her mind, from dullness; her hands, so she
would never falter in eking out the notes; and her ears, so that she
could always judge the quality of the sound she was producing.

But in that moment, Etta couldn't hear anything over the sharp,
painful ringing that jabbed like knives into her head. The weight of the
world pressed down on her chest and shoulders, smothering her next
few breaths.

She forced her eyes open, gagging on the thick air.

The cloud of smoke masked everything, creating a dreamlike haze,
even as fire raced up the silk panels hanging from the wall, scorching
the plaster. The chandelier above the table had shattered, glass raining
down like ice on the wreckage below. And the table . . . the table and
a section of the floor beneath it had caved in, leaving a jagged, gaping
hole. Etta's eyes stung as she blinked, searching for the others through
the embers rising up.

They were gone—the tsar, Winifred, Jenkins. The waiter. They'd
gotten out, then—rescuers had already taken them to get help—

No.

A chill of sudden certainty crept over her, stifling the scream in her throat.

No.

They hadn't gotten out. There would have been no time to move away from the blast. Which meant that . . .

They fell through the floor. Or they . . . their bodies had . . . the blast . . .

Etta gagged again, her chest too tight to breathe. There was a stabbing in her side that seemed to drive deeper and deeper each time she shifted, trying to push the crushing weight off her chest and bring air into her lungs. One hand was pinned beneath her back, the other between her chest and the warm mass on top of her.

Henry.

"Henry . . ." Etta felt the word leave her throat, but couldn't hear it above the ringing in her ears. *"Henry! Henry!"*

He'd managed to throw himself over her, covering her almost completely. Her heart began to ricochet around her rib cage, beating so fast, so hard, she was terrified it might burst.

His face was turned away from her, one arm drawn up over it protectively. But he wasn't moving. *He wasn't moving.*

Etta dragged her hand out from where it was trapped between them, her still-healing shoulder screaming in protest. Without the benefit of her hearing, with the smoke still churning around them like waves, Etta felt like she was moving underwater, watching the distorted images of life beyond the surface. Her hand flopped around, touching the exposed, raw skin of Henry's back; he'd been burned by the blast. She began to tremble as she felt up his neck, searching for a pulse.

Don't die, don't die, please—

It took her a moment to sort her own shaking from the faint murmur beneath his skin, but it was there. He was alive, if just barely.

With as much care and strength as she could muster, she rolled his weight off her, just enough to slide out from beneath him, but not enough to flip him onto his scalded back. The stench of burned flesh and hair made the bile rise again in her throat. She had to press a fist against her mouth to keep from retching when she looked over and saw what remained of Winifred. *Oh my God, oh my God—*

Iron—Jenkins had shouted *Iron*, unable to finish the word, to fully name the assassin. *Ironwood.* The waiter, the *assassin*, had shouted a word she hadn't been able to make out, but she'd recognized the moment when the timeline had shifted again.

Henry had been right—Cyrus Ironwood *had* sent agents out to push the timeline back to his version . . . but this wasn't what had happened in the timeline she had grown up in. This couldn't be Ironwood's timeline. Which would make it . . . a new one?

Her hatred made it feel as though her whole soul had caught fire.

The floor beneath her feet was still crumbling; she felt a section of it collapse and realized she'd lost both shoes in the explosion. It wasn't safe—Etta felt a wave of panic swelling, threatening to wash away whatever rational thoughts she had left as she surveyed the room. Its bright, glorious colors and shining gold had been replaced by shards of glass, splashes of blood and cinders.

She was alive. She had to stay alive. She had to—just breathe—just get out—

The ringing was so piercing that she could think of nothing else. She reached down on unsteady legs and got her arms under Henry's, circling around his chest. The open wounds on his back oozed blood onto her dress, and the mere touch was enough to make him groan; Etta felt the vibration move through his body.

The jagged mouth of the floor revealed the smoldering room below. The fragments of metal and wood that had flown like shrapnel sliced through her stockings, lacerating her heels and ankles. She winced as Henry's long legs butted and bobbed helplessly against the ground. The only way she could move him was through sharp, short surges of strength, and she could already feel herself fading when a door appeared through the smoke. It had been left open, a tray of food overturned nearby.

The smoke had already drifted into the hall, but Etta felt herself take her first real breath as she put Henry down, carefully laying him out on the plush carpet. She knelt, searching his face again for signs of life. He'd cracked his forehead against something—a knot had formed on his right temple, and blood continued to trickle down his cheek.

She should have surged up onto her feet and started to run back the way they had come through the palace, but Etta found herself rooted there, unable to move when parts of her felt like they were fading.

She'd only just found him, and now . . .

Etta choked on an unwelcome sob, unwilling to release that last bit of control she had over herself until she could *think*.

What would it have been like, she wondered, to stay with the Thorns? Her mind played scene after scene, waltzing through the possibilities. To be with a father who wouldn't use her, who appreciated her talent, who explained their way of life, who showed some sliver of interest in her beyond some task he was saving her for in the future. To strike back against Ironwood until his grip on their kind dissolved into memory. To find Nicholas, and bring him to a group that might appreciate and respect him the way he deserved. To see the whole of time, the scale of everything her beautiful world could offer. . . .

"Etta."

With the piercing whine in her ears from the explosion, Etta would never be certain if she'd actually heard her mother, or imagined her voice the instant she felt the deadening weight of Rose's presence. She turned slowly, and a moment later her mother took shape in the smoke.

When she'd been taken by Ironwood, drawn into his net of deception, Etta would have done anything to see her mother and have her explain what was truly happening. But now she knew, and it had come only through loss and the most devastating of betrayals. Staring at

Rose now, truly seeing her, Etta wondered how she had ever missed the tremor just below the surface of cold calculation Rose projected. As if the wild delusions skimmed just beneath her skin.

She would be here now for a reason. Rose *always* had a reason.

"Did you do this?" she demanded, shouting to hear herself.

Her mother wore man's pants tucked into tall boots and a loose white shirt. Her long blond hair was braided back away from her bruised left eye and right cheek. Etta's heart gave an involuntary clench at the sight, before she let the anger back in to harden it. At Etta's question she flinched.

That's right, Etta thought, *I know what you're capable of. What you want.*

Her gaze lowered from Etta's face to Henry's and she took a step back, as if only seeing him now. When she came closer, making as if to kneel, Etta felt the last of her self-control snap. "Do *not* touch him!"

"All right, all right, darling." Rose's face looked strained as she spoke loudly, holding out her hand. The other strayed to the gun at her side. "You need to come with me now."

God, how Etta had prayed for this exact moment—how desperate she had been for any sign that her mother was alive and coming for her.

A sign that she wanted me.

"Henrietta," Rose said, her voice scalding. "You don't know what's coming, what's been chasing me for years! I've kept them off your trail for weeks, from the moment you were taken, but the Shadows—!"

Shadows. Etta let her lip curl back in disgust. That last, small hope in her that Henry had been wrong, that they'd jumped to the wrong conclusion, turned to dust.

Beneath her hands, Henry shifted, and Etta grabbed him by his lapel as if she could hold him there, conscious. As a child, she had always hidden her tears from her mother, too aware of how little patience Rose had for them, but she didn't care now—not when Henry's eyes opened. They moved from her face to Rose's.

Her mother's hands went slack at her side. Neither moved, but Etta felt his heartbeat as it began to drum harder and harder against his ribs. She leaned down, straining to hear him. "Come . . . to finish me off, Rosie?"

Her mother's face was stone. She stood, unflinching, even as her voice iced over.

"You never understood. You never believed me—"

"I understood . . . me . . ." he rasped out. "But Rosie . . . *Alice?* Why . . . *why* did she have to die?"

Alice.

"Etta, she'll protect you . . . go now—" He clutched her hand, trying to get her to look at him.

Alice.

Rose's face appeared in front of her own, still speaking loudly, urgently, "I can explain as we go, but—"

Alice.

Etta stepped back, out of her mother's reach.

She'd been taken and manipulated and shot and nearly lost her hearing for *Rose*. Everything Etta had ever done had been to earn a smile, squeeze a measure of respect, from *her*. She'd made excuses for her mother time and time again, even as the material she was using to build those protests dwindled down.

Etta turned, gripping her elbows, trying to fold in on herself. Disappear.

She killed Alice.

Had she watched Etta go through the passage with Sophia? Had she *smiled*, knowing she'd won that round, too? All Rose had to do was pretend to believe in her, just one time, and Etta had let her shape her future.

She left Alice to die alone.

Her eyes pricked with shame and a humiliation that would not quiet. She'd been so proud of herself, so defiant, so ready to *show* everyone in this hidden world that Rose's daughter could be just as strong and sharp and cunning as the woman herself. But she wasn't Rose's daughter—she was her tool. Years spent fighting for her love, her praise, for some kind of acknowledgment . . .

"You—" she choked out. She pressed a hand to her eyes, felt the fat, hot tears spill over her fingers. *Look up,* Etta ordered herself. *Look and see who she is. Who she's always been.* "It was you—"

Rose met her gaze. Defiant.

Denying nothing.

It was Alice's face now that she saw, freckled and young, in the uniform that brought her so much pride; in her apartment on the Upper East Side, smiling as Etta learned her first scales; upturned in the audience, as she watched Etta perform from the front row. Her *life.*

I was raised by a stranger. The words roared through her mind, barbed and scalding. *I never meant anything more than what I could do for her.*

Maybe this was the reason her mother hadn't told her about their hidden world, about her father—because she knew Etta's soft heart would twine her together with the Thorns, and she would lose the best hope she had of seeing this fantasy through.

No more.

Alice, the woman who had raised her, who had given her love, attention, focus, everything of herself—Alice had been her true mother, and *this* was the woman who had taken her from Etta. *Murdered her.*

She straightened at the sound of pounding feet, and looked up in time to see two figures in black cloaks race down the edges of the hallway, long, curved daggers in their hands. Rose spun, swore viciously, and without a second's hesitation raised her gun and fired. The attacker on the right dove into a marble table to avoid it, but Rose fired again, and this time did not miss. Her aim, as always, was perfect.

Until she ran out of bullets. She fired again at the other attacker, but the gun clicked in her hand, the chamber empty.

Henry watched, riveted, still trying to summon his strength to rise. His mouth was moving, he was saying something, but Etta couldn't hear anything over the sound of her own furious heartbeat, the static of the blast.

Rose threw the gun aside and charged the remaining attacker, slamming him to the ground. When she rose to her feet again, the man sprang up as well, his blade arcing up as if to pierce beneath her chin.

Etta kept her focus on the soldiers charging down the hall, the footmen that rushed in behind them. By the time they were within reach of the dining room, Rose had already run past her, shoving her aside as the attacker leaped forward to follow.

The impact of slamming into the wall jarred the grief from Etta's mind, leaving nothing but pristine, pure hate. Fury would have to be enough to carry her for now.

"Etta—" Henry was trying to sit up, choking on his own breath. She could barely hear him over the ringing in her ears, as he was surrounded and lifted by four of the soldiers. One tried to grab her, but she slipped away again and again, pulling out of their reach. "Listen—listen to me—!"

This has to end. If her mother had started this, then Etta, the only other living Linden, would take the responsibility of righting it. Any doubt she'd had was gone now, blasted away. The original timeline had to be restored. It was the only hope she had of salvaging everything, possibly even the lives that had been taken.

The choice was offered to her. It should have been frightening, the weight of it, but as Etta shook off the past, the unbearable questions and the uncertainty, it freed her instead.

She looked at Henry and made a promise. "I'm going to finish this."

"No—*no!*"

She tore herself away from Henry, from the soldiers, and bolted down the wide hall, until only a trail of bloody footsteps on the carpet was proof she had ever been there at all.

Reaching down, Etta gripped where the hem of her dress was torn, ripping it further to give her legs a better range of movement. She made a sharp left around the next corner. Her ears had begun to pop and crackle in a way that frightened her, but the ringing was fading enough to give her a warning.

Her feet slid to such a sudden stop that the Oriental runner bunched beneath them. Dozens, maybe even hundreds of people were charging down the narrow hall toward her, chanting, shouting in fragmented Russian—*"Ochistite dvorets!"*—over and over and over. The man in front held a bloodred flag in one hand and a gun in the other. Behind him, a variety of tools and weapons were waving in the air.

They're taking the palace, clearing it out. Etta struggled for her next breath, limping heavily. Ironwood's plan here went beyond mere assassination. No doubt his men had been here all along, sowing the seeds of discontent, greasing the revolutionaries' wheels before setting them on a path toward violence. Had he known Henry would come with the other Thorns? Had he ordered them to wait for his arrival?

She turned and doubled back the way she had come, taking a left rather than a right. Etta couldn't stop herself from looking back over her shoulder one last time. But she could not make anything out through the heavy cover of smoke.

A hand reached out, snatching her arm. Etta felt a shriek tear out of her throat as she was yanked off-balance and dragged through a doorway. She kicked, clawing at whoever had grabbed her. The door slammed shut and she was slammed up against it, knocking the breath out of her again and smearing black over her vision.

"—ta, what's happening? *Etta!*"

She jerked away from the hands holding her in place, rubbing at her eyes.

"What . . . that . . . can . . . me . . . ?" The words were broken up by the pulsing in her eardrums. Etta looked up, surprised to find Julian's face tight with worry as he touched the side of her cheek, his fingers pulling away red with blood.

"Explosion!" She had to shout the word to hear it herself. Julian cringed, nodding.

"Thought as much."

Etta pulled away from him, going for the door again. *"Attackers!"*

He said something that might have been "revolt" or "revolting."

"Run," she told him.

"Where are you going?" he shouted back, finally loud enough for her to understand.

"Search the palace—find astrolabe—"

"It's not here!" He grabbed her shoulders, turning her back toward him. "They found his body—stuffed in a bloody wardrobe, no astrolabe in sight. They were going to tell your father after dinner—"

If Etta had taken a knife and stabbed it deep into her belly, it would have been less painful than this. He'd killed his enemy; he'd taken what he wanted most. Her mind shaved down each of her wild thoughts, until only facts remained: *Ironwood has it. Need to find Ironwood. Need to finish this.*

Julian opened his mouth to say something else, but Etta pressed her finger to her lips and opened the door a crack, peering out of it. There was a dull roar coming from down the hall, but she couldn't pick out any one word. Satisfied that the men and women who'd flooded the palace were heading toward the dining room, Etta grabbed Julian's arm and pulled them both back outside.

Even before she began to run, she felt him dig in his heels, resisting. Etta sent him an incredulous look over her shoulder, which was met, to her surprise, with genuine fear. Julian seemed flummoxed by what was happening—at least until a man at the edge of the crowd turned and shouted something at them that made the others turn as well. Then survival instincts kicked in, and suddenly he was the one running, the one dragging her.

Etta wasn't sure it mattered whether or not he knew where he was going. The palace was large enough for anyone to get lost on a good day, with countless halls and rooms and closets to duck into. But that didn't seem to be the plan. Etta looked back again, just in time to see a man raise a gun. The bullet slammed into the face of a golden angel statue, splintering off the cap of its skull.

"Cripes!" Julian yelped.

How did anyone ever find their way out of this place without help? She blew the loose hair out of her face, trying to assess her options. They needed an exit, any sort of exit—a door, a window that could be smashed, a sewage pipe, she didn't care, as long as it was in the opposite direction from the mob. Neither did Julian, who had taken to running blindly forward, his arm thrown up over his head like that could somehow protect him.

There were hallways that served as large arteries to the palace, but those seemed to be clogged with soldiers, staff trying to flee, and the plainclothes people who'd come storming in from the outside. Right now, the only thing guiding Etta's steps was silence; she found herself searching for it beneath the throbbing and whistling in her ears, reaching for some part of the palace that was still, that hadn't been engulfed by the fury pouring through its gilded veins like acid.

Revolution. Her mind spun the word out, with all of the disaster and destruction and promise it encompassed. In a different year, in a different form, but revolution all the same, this time stirred up by the Ironwoods.

She drew them around a corner and, in the next instant, felt a blow to her chin, a knee to her leg. The breath wheezed out of her, and when she finally inhaled, dazed and on the floor, there was the smell of laundry and starch. A young girl, a maid, was sprawled out on the floor in front of them, her uniform ripped at the skirt and slightly askew from where she'd slammed into Etta.

Julian had managed to stay upright and say something to the maid in halting Russian. The maid pointed, her whole arm shaking, toward a door at the end of the hallway.

The maid took the opportunity to scamper off, picking up her small valise and all but running down the hall in the opposite direction, her blond braid streaming out behind her. It was the last clear sight Etta had before the electric lamps around them surged with brightness, and, with a hiss, flashed out completely, leaving a few scattered candles in sconces to light a hall bigger than Etta's whole apartment building in Manhattan.

"Well, that was bloody ominous. She said to go this way," Julian told her, jerking a thumb up ahead, to where the small hall dead-ended at the nondescript door Etta had seen before.

"You speak Russian?" Etta asked as they began to run again.

"Er, just barely. She either said this was some sort of inner servant hall, or their quarters, so I guess we'll be in for a surprise, won't we?" Excitement bubbled out of him, giving him a slightly breathless quality.

The door flew open then; the sudden light momentarily blinded Etta, who threw up an arm to shield her eyes. The silhouette of a man appeared in the doorway, a box-shaped flashlight in his hands—it wasn't until he made a noise of surprise and turned the light away that Etta saw it was one of the men who had met them outside, still wearing the palace's ornate livery. He adjusted his grip on the light so they could see him press a finger to his lips and wave them forward.

Etta and Julian exchanged a look.

"What are the chances . . ." he began.

". . . we're about to be murdered?" Etta finished as they made their way forward. "The better question is, what do you have on you to defend yourself?"

"Um . . . besides you? Did I need something else?" he whispered. "You won't let them take us alive, will you, kiddo?"

At any other moment Etta might have laughed, but the truth of it landed hard: there was only so much Julian could do to contribute to their survival. If it came down to it, she *would* be the one fighting. And she had no doubt that if things went badly, he'd leave her to deal with the mess.

But she *also* knew that if anyone was going to help them get back to the passage in the woods, it would be him.

In exchange for something else, I'm sure, she thought grimly. Not for the first time, she felt her heart crimp at the thought of how much easier this would be, how much safer she would feel, if it were Nicholas at her back. Even if neither of them knew where to go or how to find the passages, there would have been an equality between them. The thought of putting herself in the hands of a born-*and*-raised Ironwood again, even temporarily, made her feel sick to her stomach.

"Come, come, this way—" the man said in heavily accented English. "This way—"

Julian's pace eased off long before Etta's; she reached the man first, her fingers curled into fists at her side, trying to read his face in the darkness. The man studied her with open horror. "Is he dead?"

Etta hesitated before nodding. The man closed his eyes, turned his face upward to steal a calming breath. Then he stood at his full height and pressed the handle of the flashlight into her hands.

"Follow this hall to the end," he said haltingly. "There is a window left open. Go *now.*"

"Wait a tick—" Julian started, but the man pushed past them both, and went the opposite way.

"All right," Julian said after a beat of silence. "Have to admit, I'm still waiting for the firing squad to spring up and take us out, Romanov-style."

"That is *not* funny," Etta said sharply, stalking down the hall.

"Lighten up, Linden-Hemlock-Spencer," he whispered back, jogging to catch up to her. The inner hall muffled the chaos outside of it, but only just. The gunfire was endless, blurring into thunder. "Maybe we should just hide—stay here until the trouble passes?"

"Until someone finds us and finishes us off?" Etta said, catching the first hint of the open window's freezing draft curling toward them. *The way they probably grabbed Henry.* Every time she blinked, the explosion seemed to set off again behind her eyes, blinding, disorienting, incinerating her from the inside out.

Did I really leave him?

With a start, she realized she was crying.

Did I leave him there to die?

"Come now, old girl, it's not as bad as all that," Julian said. "We'll be fine. I can get us out of here in a jiff. There's a passage at the Imperial Academy of Arts, just across the Neva River. How do you feel about sunlight and warmth and a charming lack of Gatling guns?"

NINETEEN

FROST COVERED THE WINDOW; AT SOME POINT, THE DARK sky had begun spitting down snow. Some of it had blown inside through a small crack, leaving a mess on the floor. A few different sets of footprints were already pressed into the slush, leading away from the window—clearly, others had taken the chance to leave.

Outside, she heard that same phrase being chanted in the distance: *"Ochistite dvorets!"*

Etta got her hands under the window and tugged it up high enough to slip through. The chill cut straight through her flimsy dress and the silk slip beneath, but it was a good sort of cold—it lifted the mental fog, sharpening her thoughts.

"Up you go," Julian said, offering his hands to hoist her up. Etta ignored him and pulled herself through, despite the pain that lanced through her shoulder and bare feet at the impact on the hard stone path below. Julian landed just as roughly behind her.

The palace sat close to the river, separated only by a small street and embankment. There was no one around them that she could see, but Julian heard something. He reached over, switching off her flashlight, and held out an arm to keep her in place as a car raced down the road, slinging mud and slush up into the air. Julian let out a noise of protest as it splattered onto the front of his otherwise pristine trousers.

Etta scanned the street and river for any way across both. There seemed to be a bridge in the distance, but between it and them was a mass of humanity making its way down the street. She wasn't about to stick around and see if the marchers were soldiers or more of St. Petersburg's—Petrograd's—unhappy population.

Julian darted across the street to the embankment, leaning over the wall. He shouted something down—Etta saw his mouth moving, even if she couldn't make out his words. The fact that her hearing hadn't fully come back, that she was still drowning beneath that same piercing whine, threatened to sink her with fear.

Etta limped over to him, peering through the darkness to see what was below—a boatman, as it turned out, in one of three rowboats tied up to the small dock, smoking as if he didn't have a care in the world. The trail of smoke curled up toward them, a wriggling wisp of white.

Julian's face was outraged when he looked at her. "He wants over seven thousand rubles to use one of his damned boats. Said the other servants were willing to pay for him to ferry them. I don't have that kind of money, do you?"

After everything that had happened over the course of the last hour, Etta felt a strange, unnatural calm settle over her. Improvised explosives were a problem. Fleeing a furious mob was a problem. Greedy boatmen were not.

"May I have the flashlight?" she asked, holding out her hand.

He passed it to her, but tried to tug it back at the last second. "What are you planning? You've got that deranged look in your eye—"

Etta yanked it out of his hand and sidled up over the wall, then down the short hill that brought her to the wooden dock.

"English?" she called out.

The boatman stood up, stepping out of the boat, a leering smile on his face. His eyes skimmed over the place where the strap of her dress had ripped, exposing one shoulder. "Little English for little lady."

Etta mentally gagged as she returned his smile with one of her own and said, in what she hoped was a sweet tone, "Yes, little lady in desperate need of help. Will you be a hero and help a girl out?"

"You're *flirting* with him?" Julian called down in disbelief.

"Where?" the man asked, smirking.

Etta glanced across the wide stretch of the river, to where another imperial-looking building loomed. She pointed, and the man turned his head to follow the line of her arm, her finger—

Etta slammed the flashlight into his skull, blowing him back into the boat, where he collapsed, unmoving. Stunned, but still breathing.

"Good God, Linden-Hemlock-whoever-you-are!" Julian called, stumbling down the hill.

Etta threw the broken remains of the flashlight into the nearest boat, and reached down to untie the boat the man had fallen into, letting it drift into the patches of ice on the Neva. She thought about apologizing, but then decided that moment that she just didn't care.

A pirate wouldn't apologize or thank him. A pirate would just *take*. And if she had to shut off some crucial, feeling part of herself to survive this and find her way back to the real pirate in her life, she would.

She heard Nicholas's voice whisper in her ear, a protesting, *Legal pirate, thank you,* and for an instant allowed the small, sad laugh to bubble up in her chest.

Julian gave her a look that told her exactly what he thought about that laugh.

"Spencer," she told him. "My last name is *Spencer.*"

Etta quickly stepped down into the boat, feeling it wobble beneath her feet. It steadied with the added weight of Julian, allowing her to easily reach up and unknot the line anchoring it to the dock. They drifted out toward the clumps of ice forming in the river's slow waters, and for a moment they both looked at each other expectantly.

"I would row," Etta told him, "except my shoulder is killing me and I can barely move my arm—so maybe you could try contributing to this escape?"

"Of course," he said quickly, not meeting her gaze. "I was just waiting to see if you'd be stubborn enough to attempt it yourself."

Julian picked up the oars, got them on either side of the boat, and then lifted them up and down in the water, doing little more than splashing. Etta stared at him; she was freezing, tired, shaken, and on the verge of reaching over to strangle him for even trying to make a joke at a time like this. But he kept doing it, his brow wrinkled, as if confounded about why the boat was slowly turning in a circle and not moving across the water as expected.

"Are you serious?" she asked him in disbelief. "You don't know how to *row a boat*?"

His shoulders set against her words. "I'll have you know, Nick was always there to do it when the situation called for it."

Etta felt her jaw tighten to the point of pain as she held out her hands. He hesitated a moment before passing the heavy oars over. With a movement that made her shoulder protest pitifully, she got the boat turned around, her back to the other bank, and made the first long stroke. Those days with Alice rowing by the Loeb Boathouse in Central Park had been for something more than enjoyment after all.

Julian released a relieved sigh, leaning back to look up at the snow falling on them. No matter what he did, he always seemed to be posing and waiting for someone to compliment him on it.

"You're rather handy, Linden-Hemlock-Spencer," he said. "That was some brilliant teamwork, if I do say so myself."

"I'm not sure you know what that word means," Etta managed, her teeth clenched. She tried to mine the small bit of gold out of this situation—she was alive, and the rowing was at least warming her stiff muscles—but she could already feel the rising urge to take one of the oars and whack Julian into the freezing water.

"You're the brawn, I'm the brains, kiddo," he told her. "You don't need my help with this."

Etta was beginning to think that the real reason he'd gone to the Thorns was that he was at least self-aware enough to know he wouldn't be able to survive on his own.

"Call me kiddo again . . ." She felt the words growl out of her throat, too low for her to even hear over the splash of water and the painful ringing.

"Your ears still giving you a spot of trouble?" he asked. "It's a good sign you can hear at all—it means it might heal completely. Lesser explosions have destroyed people's eardrums, from what I understand."

Etta grunted, putting the full force of her anxiety into the next pull of the oars. Beethoven could compose and play instruments when he was mostly deaf. But she wasn't Beethoven, and the thought of never hearing music again left her feeling as if her chest had been hollowed out.

Stop thinking, just row.

"What happened at dinner, exactly?" Julian asked. "One minute I was being berated by the Thorn guard for innocently inquiring about his mother's species, and the next, the whole place started rocking on its bones."

Etta looked down at her lap, avoiding his gaze. She might as well tell him—though it seemed unlikely, Julian might have the answer to the question that had been nagging at her since she'd been jolted back into consciousness.

"We had . . . we had just started the last course, when one of the waiters brought out a wine bottle to serve the tsar. He shouted something and slammed it down onto the table. The next thing I knew, I was on the ground and half the floor was gone. Henry was hurt badly, and the others . . ."

Julian's brows shot up. "Was there liquid in the bottle?"

She nodded, pulling the next stroke.

"Based on the year, it was probably nitroglycerine. It explodes on impact. Very volatile. Even Grandfather didn't like using the stuff." His expression turned thoughtful. "How on God's green earth did you manage to survive that?"

A good question. "Jenkins—the other guard, I mean—he jumped on it, I think, just before it hit the table. And Henry, he . . ."

I left him there to die.

I left him.

Etta wiped the sweat from her forehead with her tattered sleeve. "It was an Ironwood—both Jenkins and Henry recognized him. But he shouted something before he threw down the explosive—" She tried to repeat it the best she could.

"*Revolyutzia*, maybe? That's *revolution*," Julian said, his voice oddly quiet. "Pretending to play the part of a revolutionary for the assassination. Evil, Grandpops, but rather elegant. There is a rather unfortunate tradition of tsars being assassinated, so no one would question it."

Etta took a breath, trying to wipe the blood from her face against her shoulder. Her stiff knees ached as she tried to stretch them out in the cramped boat. "So we're back to your grandfather's timeline?"

"Hell if I know, kid," Julian said, briskly rubbing his arms to try to bring some warmth back into them. "I don't intend to find out, and neither should you. Your opportunity to escape has presented itself, and you are hereby invited to join me in Bora Bora for as long as it takes them to sort this out."

Etta dragged the oars through the dark water again. "I'm not going to Bora Bora."

"Oh? I wasn't aware that this escape involved a real plan, but do share."

"If the Thorn, Kadir, was found dead, it means your grandfather got to the astrolabe, which means I need to find him," Etta said, explaining it to him slowly, as if he were a small child. His mouth twitched, trying to hide a smile. "As far as I know, he's still in 1776, in New York. How do I get back there from this point?"

"No," Julian said, throwing his hands up in the air. "*No.* Because this is absurd. You should just come with me. This doesn't have to be on your shoulders. You don't need the weight of it—it'll just smother you. Come with me to Bora Bora and let the devils have their hell."

"It's always that easy for you, isn't it?" Etta said, shaking her head. "Let everyone else risk their lives to try to fix what your grandfather has done. Don't take any responsibility for your family."

He gave her a pitying look that set her teeth on edge. "Christ, you sound like Nick, with all of this talk of *responsibility.* Morality is a bore, kiddo. And if you think any one person can stop Grandfather, you're mistaken. He was born out of a cloud of sulfur and his bones are brimstone."

"Imagine what you could accomplish with your life," she said, "if you weren't so damn afraid all the time."

The gentle thud of the broken ice against their boat and the splash of the oars in the water was the only conversation for several moments.

Julian let out a dramatic sigh and dipped a hand into his jacket, pulling out a small leather notebook.

"I suppose I'm going to have to be the lesser person in this situation and allow you to take the title of bigger," he said, thumbing through the pages. It must have been his traveler's journal, with notations of where and when he'd been, so he didn't cross paths with an older or younger version of himself.

"Here we are," he said. "There are three passages in this year and city. The one we're headed to will take us to Alexandria, 203 A.D. From there, there's a passage through the Vatican, and from there, you can connect to New York in . . . 1939. Little Italy, on Mulberry and Grand."

Etta's grip on the oars tightened. "How does that help me?"

"You'll just need to get to where Whitehall Dock used to be. There's a passage to 1776, in Boston," he said. "That's the most direct route to that year."

She could find a way from Boston to Manhattan. If nothing else, she could turn herself over to the Ironwood guardian who would inevitably be watching the passage, and let him or her bring her to Ironwood for her punishment.

"Why is everyone still banging on about that damn astrolabe?" Julian complained. "It's always been more trouble than it's worth. No one is ever satisfied with life, are they? What more does he have to sacrifice at this point? He's gone and killed his entire family over it."

"I had it. . . ." She could hear the pain in her voice. "But it was taken by the Thorns—the ones who went missing. It's my responsibility to find it and finish what I started."

"Why? The timeline's already changed again, and it'll only get worse from here."

Etta leaned forward. "You're sure it changed?"

"You didn't feel it?" Julian shook his head. "I suppose not. It's not that different from the pressure of an explosion. The whole world blurs for a moment, and the sound is deafening. It's unmistakable. Whatever this new timeline is, it's bound to be bad."

"More reason to find the astrolabe," Etta said, through gritted teeth. "And destroy it in order to reset it back to its original state."

Julian wore a strange expression. "Is Grandpops's timeline really that bad? I wasn't around to see the original one, and neither were you. Who's to say he didn't improve on a few things?"

Etta shook her head. This was the trouble with meddling at all— who decided what was considered more peaceful, or improved? A benefit to one part of the world might be a detriment to the other. You could stop a war, and it might inadvertently cause another. You could change the outcome of a battle, and it would just be the other side who experienced the losses.

"It doesn't matter. No one should have tampered with it in the first place, least of all Cyrus Ironwood." And even though she already knew what his answer would be, she tried anyway: "You could help me . . . find Nicholas and Sophia and the rest of your family. Apologize for tricking them into grieving for you."

"Appealing to a sense of honor only works if a person *has* one," Julian informed her. "I'll go with you as far as the Vatican, but—"

She heard the crack of the gunshot and its echo as the bullet slammed into the water, sending up a spray of freezing water at them and rocking the boat. Both Etta and Julian ducked instinctively.

The next bullet splashed down on the other side of the boat.

"Can't you row any faster?" Julian complained.

"Can you try *helping*?" she fired back, but Julian had already turned around to shout something at them in Russian.

The next shot from the embankment hit the rim of the boat, splintering it so close to his hand that Julian yelped in alarm, and made as if to dive into the freezing river. Through the curtain of snow, Etta could just barely make out the men gathered there, one of whom was climbing down toward the other boat.

"Why are they chasing us?" he complained.

"*Thorn!*" one of them bellowed in an American accent. *An Ironwood.* "Come back at once and you will be shown a measure of mercy!"

Julian groaned, sinking back against the boat in dismay. Etta's arms worked faster, the oars beating at the water as the other embankment finally came within a few dozen yards.

"It's just not fair. How did you get us into this mess? What kind of bad-luck charm are you?"

"Can you *please shut up*?" she snapped. "Reach for the embankment when you can and pull us in—"

The next two gunshots splintered the floating ice, spraying water across her face. Etta's heart felt like it was about to unhook from her chest and pass up her throat. Rather than wait for Julian, she used one of the oars to catch the lip of the embankment and pull them over to it.

She felt the slice of a bullet across the back of her exposed neck before she heard it explode through the air. Etta gasped in shock more than pain.

Don't think about it don't think about it don't think—hard to ignore a literal brush with death, but Etta slithered up onto the snow-dusted embankment, trying to get her bearings. She clung to her last shreds of focus, swinging her gaze around. Most of the embankment's walls were high—too high to climb up from the water. But just in front of the building—which she hoped was the Imperial Academy of Arts that Julian had mentioned—were steps that led down to the water's edge, guarded by two enormous stone sphinxes facing inward, as if squaring off against each other.

"Don't leave me!" Julian called after her, still crouched in the boat. A shot zinged off the stone embankment, forcing Etta's attention up toward the group of rowboats moving toward them, shining flashlights across the dark ice and water.

"They'll kill me," he told her in a rush, struggling to reach the embankment again. "That's why I never came back—Grandfather didn't want me for his heir, and he would have killed me—"

She wasn't surprised by Julian's admission, but she also didn't have time for it.

"Come on," she said, stretching a hand out toward him. Her shoulder was on fire, her ears felt like fireworks had been set off inside them, and her whole body was trembling from the cold; but, digging deeper, she found the last burst of strength she needed to grip his hand and draw the boat forward again. Julian scrambled up onto the embankment, lying as flat as he could across from her—so close that Etta could smell the alcohol on his breath.

"What do we do?" he asked.

"You said you were the brains!" she snapped. "Where's the passage?"

"The statues—do you see them? The right sphinx, just at the base."

The air around its enormous stand did seem to be shimmering, but

Etta had chalked that up to shock and exhaustion—and had chalked up the faint drumming buzz in the air, as if it were electrified, to her ears coming back around.

"Then we run," she told him. It was a short distance, maybe five feet. Granted, that would be five feet of opportunity to be shot dead, but she liked those odds. Before Julian could launch his newest protest, and before she could give herself time to think about where in the world the passage might open up, Etta pushed onto her feet and ran as hard as she could. She brought her hands up just in case he was wrong, and she was about to slam headfirst into immoveable stone.

"Stop! This is your last warning—!"

Etta didn't hear the rest. She dove into the wild heartbeat of the passage and felt the pressure of its touch tear at her skin and tattered dress. The dark chaos made her feel like she was spinning head over feet, until it shoved her out with a final, shuddering gasp.

Inertia carried her forward into a skidding stop. Her feet slid against rough stone, and she swung her gaze back over her shoulder. A small sphinx, identical to the one that had brought her here, gazed out over a glistening white city and an enormous bay that had turned pink with the sunset.

Julian shot out through the passage behind her, snatching her arm and forcing them both back into a run.

They dashed around the statue and made their way down a broad avenue. The moon-bright limestone columns and steps led up to buildings that looked more like temples than homes or places of business. Etta dragged in air that was completely void of gasoline, but brimmed with hints of life—just animal sweat, human waste, and a touch of brine that could only come from being close to the sea. As they kept to the darkness, she caught sight of a distant lighthouse between the next two buildings she passed, its bright, watchful eye sweeping over the harbor below it.

"How much farther?" Etta gasped out.

"We're following this big avenue down until we find a rather handsome temple called the Caesareum. We're looking for two enormous red marble obelisks."

They found them. Her heart felt like it was about to tear out of her chest by the time they reached the passage, and they sped through it into further darkness.

Julian slid to a stop on the stone floor, nearly crashing into a row of prayer candles that had carelessly been left to illuminate what appeared to be a church nave. Etta turned, her eyes sweeping over the altar's shadowed cross, then back out at the rows of pews that spread like ribs between the confines of the walls. They were alone, finally.

"Come on," he said. "I'll get you to your passage."

She nodded, rubbing her hands over her face. *The Vatican.*

But this wasn't the Vatican she remembered visiting with Alice. It lacked the heartrending works of art and the sweeping grandeur that conspired to make the visitor feel as insignificant in the face of God as the dust on their shoes. It was almost humble. "What year?"

"Fourteen ninety-something," he said with a vague gesture as they reached the doors. Pressing an ear against them, he was satisfied by whatever he did or didn't hear, and dragged the heavy doors open just enough for them to slip into the hall.

The torchlights blazed on the walls alongside them. Etta tried, failed, to calculate the hour. She reached back to rub her neck, but only felt what wasn't there. *Where—?*

The chain she had used to carry her mother's earring had slipped down the front of her dress and caught on the beadwork, but the earring itself was gone.

Etta couldn't stop the panic that writhed in her as she looked around the floor for it. *Why do I care?* She'd used the earrings as proof of her mom's belief in her, to steady her when she was afraid. The mere thought of what it represented should have sickened her.

And yet . . . it didn't. Not entirely.

Alice, she reminded herself, *she killed Alice—*

"What's the matter?" Julian whispered, doubling back when he realized she wasn't behind him.

She looked up. "Nothing. Where to now?"

He opened his mouth, eyes narrowing, but thought better of it. They walked in silence, Etta trailing a step behind him as she tried to pull the pieces of herself back together, to forge them into new armor.

Julian stopped, backing up a few steps. "Wait—" He looked at his journal, checking something. "Ah. This is my stop. Yours is three doors down, just at the entrance to the apartments."

He pushed the door to the small chapel open.

"Are you not coming with me?" Etta asked. "You could do real good."

He threw her one last smirk over his shoulder. "Where's the fun in that, when I could go to Florence instead?"

She blew out a harsh breath from her nose and let her expression tell him what she thought of that. The idea of him slipping away from facing the consequences of his actions sparked that same helpless anger she'd felt while listening to Nicholas confess his pain and shame and doubt over what had happened on the mountain.

"Godspeed, Linden-Hemlock-Spencer," he said, stepping into the small chapel. "Here is my final benediction: wherever your road takes you, may it never cross with Grandfather's."

She heard the passage's tempestuous language bang on through the wall.

"A-hole," Etta muttered, blowing her hair out of her eyes. She had turned to continue down the hall when a sound like a gunshot bit the silence. Something heavy smacked into the door with a grunt of pain.

She fumbled with the latch and opened it. Julian spilled out at her feet, blinking up at her. After a moment, he pressed his hands against his face and let out a frustrated holler.

"What . . . just happened?" Etta asked, alarmed.

He pushed himself upright and began the impossible work of patting down his unruly hair. "I got *bounced* out of the passage. Crossed paths with myself. Some version of me is already there."

Whoa. "Didn't you check your notebook?"

"I *did*," Julian said, smacking a hand against the stone. "Which means it's the future me, and I haven't gone yet. Damn!"

Etta stared. "Does this . . . happen a lot?"

"To me more than others, apparently. Once or twice it's kept me out of a bad scrape, but I cannot even begin to explain how obnoxious it is to be babysat and scolded by your future conscience. I can't believe Future Me is such a . . . a *wurp*. A chuffing bluenose!"

What he was saying seemed possible and impossible all at once—but it was time travel, and the usual rules never did apply.

"You're sure you didn't just get completely drunk and forget to note your visit?" Etta asked, leaning over him.

"I love that you know me so well, Linden-Hemlock-Spencer, but I assure you, no. Say what you will about changing the timeline, but my whole life has been a lesson in self-fulfillment. I can't know what's ahead, but Future Me knows what's behind, and he's a humorless fool about letting me have my fun."

To her, it sounded like Julian's future self was pretty skilled in keeping himself alive, but Etta kept her mouth shut and moved away, so he could stand up and brush himself off.

"Maybe Future Julian wants you to be a better person?" she suggested.

He pulled a horrified face.

"All right, kid, let's go to the Big Apple, then. We'll split up in Little Italy. I've a hankering for good pasta, anyway," he whispered as he stood. "Oh boy, 1939 means that my old nanny will be there—she retired to her natural time once she was finished with me and Soph. I like to think we were the ultimate cosmic test, and she didn't dare risk getting worse little demons—"

"Shhh," Etta begged, her head pounding, as they walked. "Shh . . ."

"I wonder what the old bird is up to? I could give her the fright of her life and drop in," Julian said, his voice low. "You know, I think I'll do just that. She can keep a secret, especially now that Grandfather no longer controls her purse strings. Or I'll just play it off as past Julian, rather than present Julian. . . . Hmm . . ."

Etta gave up and let him talk, let him fill her head with his memories until they pushed away her own painful ones for a time. She tried to bring up Nicholas's face, to imagine finding him after she saw this mess through to its end, but seeing its bold lines, the curve of his contemplative smile, brought no relief—it only made her feel desperately alone.

THE PASSAGE SHOVED THEM OUT TOGETHER, SENDING JULIAN to his knees and throwing Etta on top of him. Black ringed her vision at the jarring impact, and it took her longer than she would have liked to recover enough to stand.

"That was a definite *ouch*," Julian said, staggering up. "You sure your head isn't made out of marble?"

Etta held her throbbing arm close to her chest, waiting until the pain passed before saying, "Sorry."

They'd landed in the middle of a rocky, fog-smothered path. Etta could hardly see a few inches in front of her, let alone take in what was supposed to have been the city's skyline.

"Manhattan, huh?" she said, turning to Julian with an arched brow. "What was that about having excellent records?"

But Julian was rooted to the spot, one hand twisting the front of his shirt.

"No, Etta," he said. "This *is* New York City."

"In prehistoric times?"

The terrain was wild—craggy hills shadowed by thick, silky fog. Etta could just make out the shape of other mounds in the distance. Someone nearby had lit a fire; the smell of charred wood bloomed in the air.

The silence breathed thickly around them, as if trying to get her attention. To tell her something. *Listen.*

"Maybe we took the wrong passage out of the Vatican?" she suggested.

"No," Julian said, the word harsher now. He still hadn't moved. *"This is New York."*

Etta was about to shake him when a breeze stirred the fog, swirled it. The muddied shapes, which had clearly been hills and rough terrain, were now sloping piles of brick and stone, the warped frames of buildings and burned-out bodies of cars. The frost near her feet wasn't frost at all, but shattered glass. Flecks of white flurried around her, and for one stupid, insane second, Etta thought, *Snow. It's snowing.*

But the only thing falling around them was ash.

VATICAN CITY
1499

TWENTY

THE DARKNESS NEVER LIFTED.

For a single terrifying moment, Nicholas was certain he, too, had somehow lost vision in one or both of his eyes. The blackness was absolute; the air breathed around him, thick enough to slice into ribbons. Already unsteady from exhaustion and—*Christ*—blood loss, he landed hard enough on his knees to nearly bite off his own tongue. Sophia almost slipped out of his arms. He gripped the back of her tunic for purchase, avoiding her cold, slick skin.

"Sophia?" he said, his voice echoing back to him threefold. "Sophia? Can you hear me?"

Silence.

Stillness.

The touch of death, he thought.

The hairs on his body prickled to attention as panic surged through him, and he shook her gently, trying to provoke any sort of cutting word. "Sophia!"

"Give her to me," Li Min said, forcing the matter. He should have fought her, he should have argued with her for propriety's sake, but there wasn't the time, and he hadn't the strength. Sophia was inches taller than her, but the other young woman easily arranged her on her back and carried her forward quickly, her steps light. Nicholas was horrified that, even with the additional weight gone, his limbs dragged as if he were deep in his cups.

Pounding steps . . . or perhaps his own heart. No—there was another sound underscoring it, one that pierced his awareness. Someone was dragging a blade against stone, and he felt it, he felt it as if the sword or knife were scraping at his own bones.

"There's nowhere you can hide that we won't find you!" Miles Ironwood. "Come out now, Carter, and I'll let you choose how you'd like to die."

The other men laughed in response to Miles's threat. Nicholas barely managed to catch his tongue before he shouted something back.

"Blade or barrel, blade or barrel," Miles sang out. "I don't think you want the old man to choose for you. Blade or barrel, what'll it be, Carter? My knife or gun at your throat?"

Li Min muttered something he was sure was an oath.

"This way!" Her voice floated to him through the darkness, bounced between whatever walls were around them, cutting through even the passage's groaning.

"Where—?" He coughed, trying to clear the tightness in his throat. "Where are you?"

It was so dark—so very, very dark and still. There wasn't a hint of starlight or moonlight to warm the air with their glow, and there was no wind stirring against his skin. The utter stillness of this place was devastating. Terrifying. There did not seem to be a beginning or end to it.

"Get *up*!" Li Min sounded nearly breathless.

Where are we? A cellar of some sort? Holy Christ, why hadn't he even thought to ask before he'd gone charging through the passage?

Get ahold of yourself. Nicholas was nearly frenzied with the need to seize some sort of control, some understanding, over what was happening.

Over the scraping and footfalls, there was a snick of sound, and a small spark of light floated like a firefly a few yards in front of him. His mind reached through its tangled mass of chaos for the word. *Match.*

Li Min had lit a match. She drew it close to her face, illuminating the stark lines of concern etched there.

"She's not . . ." he tried to tell her. "I can't . . ."

"We haven't much time—stand *up*, Nicholas Carter. If you cannot, then I will carry you both."

His legs bobbed like a newborn calf's, but Nicholas, seemingly by the grace of God alone, got his feet under him. His eyes had adjusted to the darkness well enough to see the stark lines of the narrow walkway, the walls that opened here and there in doorless entryways.

In this state, he couldn't think and walk at the same time, so he shut off the valve to his thoughts and followed each prick of light that the girl lit, until finally they veered off the main walkway, and into what looked like . . .

A mausoleum.

It was one in a string of three that shared walls. Li Min had stepped through the nearest, her hand brushing a small engraving of a leaf, nearly hidden by the fading fresco of men. Nicholas stepped down into the structure, carefully balancing as loose stones bit into the thin soles of his sandals.

"Is she alive?" he whispered, but Li Min ignored the question. Sophia hadn't said a word since they'd made their way through the passage, and he could no longer feel to ensure her chest was rising and falling. He could barely see her in this impenetrable darkness.

You cannot die, he thought, the words searing and unyielding. *You owe me a debt.*

Etta's terrified face, the moment before she disappeared, cut through his mind. What would happen if Sophia died? The passage they'd come through would likely collapse—but would she disappear, the way Etta and Julian had when they'd been caught in a wrinkle and tossed through time?

I need your help. Desperation turned his stomach hollow. *I cannot do this without your assistance. Do not die, do not die, do not die—*

Li Min blew out her match just as the passage began to make itself known again, beating out a warning against the stale air.

Reinforcements. Nicholas clenched his jaw, struggling with the pain in his shoulder, the way it leeched at his strength.

Li Min grunted in the darkness, adjusting Sophia's weight. "This way."

From what he'd seen before the light went out, there was nowhere else to go. Nothing to do but hide and hope and pray.

"Must be up in the Basilica by now—"

"—split up, see if we can find a light—"

The voices were thrown between the walls, allowed to volley back and forth, to meet the passage's calls blow for blow.

"This way!" Li Min's voice became more urgent.

She struck one last match. Nicholas felt himself balk—first at the sight of the open sarcophagus at the center of the mausoleum, and again as Li Min all but shouldered him toward the stairs that had been hidden beneath its lid and silently urged him down into a darkness deeper than sleep.

The quick steps of the Ironwoods were pounding down like rain, growing in speed and strength. Nicholas couldn't question it. He had to *move.*

The sensation of descending into a tomb, into a maze of graves and stones, made him feel as if Death himself had one hand around his throat, his bony fingers bruising. Nicholas stopped, poised at the edge of the steps. What small sliver of light Li Min's match had provided disappeared as the girl set Sophia down and pulled the lid shut over them.

For the first time in a long, long while—since he'd been a child, since his mother had told him to climb into that cupboard and *stay hidden* until it was safe to come out—Nicholas felt his throat tighten to the point of choking. His mouth had gone so dry, it felt as if he were breathing ash in and out of his lungs. Every sense was dampened; what innate sense of direction he possessed was stripped away, leaving him with only touch to feel his way down the last of the steps.

"'Through me you enter into a city of woes,'" he muttered, half-delirious. "'Through me you enter into eternal pain . . . through me you enter the population of loss. . . .'"

"'Abandon all hope, you who enter here,'" Li Min whispered, just above his ear. "Dante. How original."

Nicholas grunted back, his feet finding flat ground, and his forehead the disastrously low ceiling. His forehead cracked against some sort of stone support, igniting the aches and agony he'd managed to push aside. That was it for him—his body simply ran out of whatever means it had of continuing on. He drooped like a slack sail.

Distantly, he heard Li Min set Sophia down and race back up the steps to pull the cover back over them.

Nicholas fell onto his knees, his strength draining as quickly as the blood from the arrow wound. His limbs shook from the strain of their run, from carrying Sophia's slight weight for as long as he had, and he fought to stay conscious. Inching forward, even just a foot, felt like a Herculean task. A beast that would not be slaughtered.

And then . . . there was light. It spilled out from a gas lantern in Li Min's hands, illuminating the mosaics on the floor and the peeling frescos dancing on the walls around them. She was rummaging through a small bundle of wares in the corner: blankets, pots, a ruthless-looking dagger, and a leather sack of something he hoped was food.

This was her hiding place, her stash—or someone else's stash that she'd taken advantage of. He watched as Li Min spread the blanket out over the ground, snapping it to shake the dust free.

Nicholas felt himself take his first deep breath in hours.

Li Min drew her lantern closer and unknotted the laces of her hooded cloak to drape over Sophia's shivering form. She wore an

291

approximation of the longer draped dresses he'd seen on the women of Carthage, her hair braided into a crown around her head. She worked silently, her fingers pressing along a point on Sophia's neck. Then she leaned forward, an ear to Sophia's chest.

"Is . . . is she dead?" Nicholas asked, voice hoarse.

Li Min sat back. Shook her head. "She lives. Barely."

"I brought—" Nicholas fumbled with the physician's bag, yanking it over his head and passing it to her. "I brought this—do you know anything of medicine? Of poison?"

She snatched the leather bag and began sorting through its contents, lining up each sachet, small bottle, and pressed herb on the ground beside her. She stopped now and then to sniff one or dab a drop of liquid on her tongue.

"Sit her up," Li Min commanded at last, seizing one of the small bottles and uncorking it. "Hold her jaw open with care, or else you'll break it."

He rolled his stiffening shoulder back, trying to loosen it into use, and felt a trickle of fresh blood race down the curve of his spine. His thoughts took on a flickering quality that set off a clanging bell inside of his skull.

Still, he did as Li Min asked, sitting Sophia's slack body up and tilting her head back. He used his index finger and thumb to nudge her jaw open wide enough for Li Min to pour whatever was in the bottle down Sophia's throat. She measured it out, sip by sip, her free hand stroking Sophia's face sweetly, like a delicate spring rain.

"What—what is that?" he demanded. "Won't she choke—?"

Sophia had been nothing but deadweight from the moment he'd carried her out of the house in Carthage, but she'd at least had her usual barbed edges and venom. Over the course of ten, fifteen minutes, it had all bled away, leaving nothing but a husk of bones and skin. But now she returned to life, seemingly all at once: retching, gagging, and then casting up her accounts all over him with a wet, putrid splatter.

Her eyes remained closed, but he could feel her breathing more steadily now, the puffs of it warming the air between them.

"Dear *God*—" he said in alarm, pounding on her back to help her clear her throat. The smell—the *smell*—

"Something to help her get the vile poison out of her," Li Min said, finally answering his earlier questions.

"Thank you," he said, wiping his chin against the shoulder of his tunic, "for that timely warning."

"Lay her back," Li Min said, sitting back on her heels. "She needs to rest now. Some of the poison has been absorbed by her body, but we may have luck on our side yet. The Thorn's intention wasn't to kill her. Ironwood's bounty specifies he wants you both alive, or else the payment will be forfeit."

Nicholas didn't realize his sword hadn't made the journey with them until he tried reaching for it. His fingers had to settle for a broken shard of stone, some crumbled section of the statue behind them. "Is that the reason you've come, then? You caught wind of the bounty and knew where to find us?"

Li Min snorted, smoothing Sophia's hair out of her face. "I came to ensure I might be able to claim my end of our bargain. The bounty is a handsome windfall from the gods, but the Ironwoods can rot."

"I warn you—" Nicholas blinked, trying to clear the spots floating in his vision. "I warn you that we won't . . . we won't be taken."

Li Min ignored him, taking Sophia's hand. She spoke to the other young woman firmly, leaning over her as if to drag her spirit back, should it try to escape. And with time, those same words became embroidered with soft pleading, though their meaning couldn't penetrate the fog growing in his mind.

"That's not—" Nicholas tried to push up onto his feet, but the world swung wild and unhinged around him, knocking him back into place. "Won't be . . . taken . . ."

The ring on his hand burned as he felt his body betray him.

Nicholas slumped back to the ground, fighting the way the light faded around him, gently receding in waves until there was nothing left of the world but blissful emptiness.

NICHOLAS WOKE TO A SHARP COMPLAINT FROM HIS LEFT shoulder, a badgering, insistent sting that dragged him forward again each time he tried to slip back into the darkness.

He was flat on his stomach, the side of his face pressed against the ridges of the mosaic beneath him. By the time his vision cleared and the cotton stuffing inside his skull was plucked out, Nicholas had the very disturbing realization that someone was stabbing him repeatedly and quite literally in the back.

"You—" His attempt to surge off the ground was met with firm resistance; a hand easily pushed him back down.

"Be still while I finish," the voice growled back. "Unless you'd like me to accidentally sew your neck to your shoulder? It might improve your looks."

Li Min. His gaze pivoted; from his vantage point, he could just see Sophia, still stretched out on the ground. The tiny bottles, herbs, and medicines had been stowed in the bag again, but now Li Min was rummaging through it for something else, muttering to herself. When she returned, her touch was as rough and uncaring as it had been before.

"Did you . . . give me something . . . to make me pass out?" he asked, teeth gritted. He'd had at least a dozen slashes stitched up in his career at sea, and the feeling of being sewn back together like a doll never improved.

Li Min leaned forward, so he had a clear view of her face as she raised a dark brow. "No. You are weak and faltering—not only in body, it would appear, but in judgment."

He followed her gaze to where his hand was splayed out against the dirt. The ring looked like a tattoo in the darkness.

"Nonsense," he said, even as the band burned, tightened. The wave of nausea that passed through him momentarily stole the feeling from his lower half. Nicholas jerked, bucking like a horse.

"Settle yourself," Li Min ordered. "Activity will only make her poison work faster. I might ask what you traded this favor for, but I already know. You were a fool, but you are even more foolish to avoid the terms of your contract. What was her task?"

"Murder," he muttered.

"Ah," was her reply. "A life for a life, then."

"You might have . . . warned us," he said, letting the bitterness bleed into his voice.

"I never thought you foolish enough to go through with it," she said simply.

"Foolish," he agreed, "and desperate. Where are we?"

She continued her work. "The Necropolis of the Vatican. 1499."

He rubbed at his eyes, clearing the dust and grime. He'd been right, then, to feel as though they were descending through the levels of hell to the dark heart of the earth.

There was another sarcophagus flush against the far wall, and he wondered idly if they'd moved the poor occupant from his rest upstairs to this . . . chamber. More importantly, he wondered who "they" were.

"Is this . . . your hiding place?" he asked. If nothing else, talking was a distraction.

"Yes. It belongs to a particular line of my family—the Hemlock clan, I should say." Li Min pressed a hand flat against his bare back, holding him steady. The last surge of pain was short, at least—she knotted the thread she'd used to patch the wound in his shoulder and gave him a pitying pat on the head.

He wasn't feeling up to it, but he forced himself to sit up regardless, hating the disadvantage the prostrate position had put him in. The Ironwoods and Lindens had secret homes and hoards—he shouldn't have been surprised to find the same of the Hemlock family.

Li Min made another of her disapproving noises, pushing him back

295

down. "This was used as a place to amass treasure and documents until it was forgotten. Someone sold me its secrets for a price."

"Seems a rather inconvenient hiding place for you," he noted, rubbing the back of his neck. To have to go through the hassle of Carthage to arrive here . . .

"It's abandoned in every era, up until the twentieth century. And there are many, many passages in the Papal City, as you know. Three in this year alone."

He didn't, but Nicholas nodded nonetheless. "What is your plan, if not to bring us back to Ironwood?"

"She's unconscious, and you're as weak as a lamb," Li Min reminded him. "You've trusted me thus far. I do wish to receive recompense for the gold that was stolen from me, but I am curious about this mission of yours. How it ties to the many threads that are reverberating throughout time."

"We've already spent it. Your gold. There's nothing left, and we've nothing else to trade you."

"You've that gold." She pointed to the leather string tied around his neck—Etta's earring. "That is not *nothing*."

His hand closed over the earring and the glass pendant. "If you think about touching this, you will lose more than a hand."

Li Min looked doubtful at that, her dark brows lifting in pity.

"You can have this," he said hopefully, holding up the hand with the ring. Sensation had fully returned to it; his arm felt unusually stiff, but cooperated as he tested its range of movement. Perhaps he had simply torn a muscle, as he'd originally believed.

"I'd have to cut it off, which would only kill you faster," she informed him.

Hell and damnation. That confirmed the Belladonna's warning.

"Where did you come by that amulet?" she asked after a moment, pointing to the large bead he'd been given.

"A boy gave it to me," he said.

"A stranger?"

"Yes, what of it?"

She shrugged. "Nothing. Everything. He wished you protection and good fortune. It has value. Do not part with it for anything less than your life."

"If it's so valuable, then why don't you take it to cancel our debt?"

"It is not the object that holds power, but the intention behind it. The wish made when it changed hands. I could no more steal that than I could take the light from the stars."

Something in her words rattled him to his core. *I shouldn't have accepted it.* Who needed protection more than that child?

"I suppose you see yourself as 'protection and good fortune,'" he said, wiping the sweat from his face.

"How you wish to see me is your choice," she said. "For now, you should know that I am your only chance of survival."

Neither friend nor foe, it seemed. More a temporary ally, the way Sophia had ultimately come to fit into his life. Nicholas looked around again, drawing his knees to his chest. "As long as we don't run out of air, this will be a suitable hiding place."

"It is convenient, too," she said idly. "If you die, I can leave you down here."

"If Sophia dies, you mean," he said, surprised at the tightening in his throat.

Li Min shook her head. "She will not die. Too stubborn. Too much left unfinished. It's *you* I fear for. Huffing and puffing like a locomotive over a minor flesh wound."

"A *minor*—" Nicholas fought his wince. To knot the tattered remains of his pride, he added, "I've seen myself through far worse than this."

Li Min made a disbelieving sound at the back of her throat. "Running from Ironwoods?"

"Ship boardings," he said. "My—" Nicholas paused, then continued. "My adoptive . . . father, he is a captain."

How strange that he'd never referred to Hall that way aloud. It was always "the captain" or "the man who raised me." But for all his hesitance to put that label to it in his own era, Nicholas had always known the truth in his heart. As a grown man and an officer on Hall's ship, he hadn't wanted the others to feel he was receiving preferential treatment, or that he hadn't earned his position there. As a child, some part of him had feared that Hall might face judgment if Nicholas went around telling that to other, less . . . *forward-thinking* people of their century.

What a poisonous thing it was, to distance himself from a man he loved, a man who had cared for him, for fear of what others might think.

He craned his neck back to find Li Min's dark eyes studying him. When she didn't break her gaze, he realized he hadn't finished his thought. "Fought off pirates for years on voyages, and then became a legal one at the outbreak of the war. Sorry, the American War for Independence. There's been quite a number of them, hasn't there?"

"Pirate?" Li Min said with disbelief. "No chance."

"And what do you know of it?" Nicholas said, trying to straighten his shoulders.

He felt her shrug. "It's not an insult. I only mean to say you'd hesitate before cutting off a man's head to steal his gold teeth. It's not a qualm you're allowed in that line of work."

Fair point. "Spent a lot of time with pirates, have you?"

To his surprise, she said, "Yes. I served under Ching Shih for ten years, from . . . the time I was a child."

"Who the devil is that?" Nicholas asked curiously.

"A pirate unrivaled," Li Min said. "There is no greater one in all of history."

"When did he live? Or she?"

She seemed appeased by this, her gaze softening slightly.

"Ching Shih bridged the eighteenth and nineteenth centuries. She

298

was born in 1775. Tens of thousands came under her command, and she beat back whole empires."

That partly explained why he hadn't recognized her name; that and the biases of the West had likely prevented her legend from spreading past the Pacific. "What became of her?"

"She successfully negotiated her retirement."

"Impressive," he said, because it *was*. More than glory or infamy, successful pirates were those who survived the endeavor and didn't drown, hang, or rot in prison. He stored the story away, to save for Etta.

"Have you always known you were a traveler?" he asked. "How did you get mixed up in all of this?"

"I have always known. I inherited the skill from my mother, who had once been captive under Ching Shih. When I . . . when the time came, I sought Ching Shih out to learn from her. To manifest my strength." Li Min shifted, rising onto her knees and then her feet. "And now I answer only to myself."

"That's something," he said, hoping he didn't sound as bitter as he feared. "I've spent my whole life trying and failing to reach that place."

For the first time since crossing paths with her, Li Min's expression softened. "It's not so easy for some. I should know—I've felt the grinding of the world as it has worked against me. The worth is in the fight, not the conquest. Do not give up."

"I don't intend to," he said.

"But something stands in your way . . . ?"

"Things are . . . rather complicated at the moment."

"Complicated how?" she asked.

"My life has taken me down a path I did not expect," he said, dodging the root of her question. "I have come so far. But the path ahead of me, the one I know I should take, is at odds with the one my heart believes is right. What's the value of my life if I sacrifice my soul?" How much easier it was to admit such things to a stranger, and how well she

299

listened as he continued on, his story flowing from him as simply as if he'd cut a vein and let it bleed out.

Nicholas would carve a path through hell itself to find Etta and finish answering the question of what their life would be together. That was the only certainty on which he could hang his hope. But there were too many factors beyond his control now, and he felt himself drifting further and further from all of those shining possibilities which had been a safe harbor for his heart.

In his life, he had been a slave to man, and now he grew more and more certain that he had allowed himself to become a slave to death. There was no way to break this chain that bound him to the Belladonna without staining his soul; in killing a man, he would murder his own honor and decency.

Li Min considered his story carefully, as if turning over each word to examine it and see what might be hidden beneath it.

"I understand. There is the journey you make through the world— the one that aches and sings. We come together with others to make our way and survive its trials," she said. "But we are, all of us, also way- farers on a greater journey, this one without end, each of us searching for the answers to the unspoken questions of our hearts. Take comfort, as I have, in knowing that, while we must travel it alone, this journey rewards goodness, and will prove that the things which are denied to us in life will never create a cage for our souls."

Nicholas closed his eyes, drawing the damp, cool air into his chest, easing the fire there.

"I will return shortly with food and clothing," she said. "If you leave this spot, you will be lost forever to the darkness of this place. I will not find you, not even to bury your rotting carcass. Do we have an understanding?"

"We do, ma'am," he said.

"Keep watch over her," Li Min said. "Her color is returning, but it will be some time before she regains use of her legs. She will be frightened upon waking."

"And you think I'm the best one to comfort her?" Nicholas scoffed. Sophia would rather accept the tender ministrations of a rabid dog over him.

Li Min seemed genuinely confused by this. "But . . . you don't care for her? Why, then, did you fight so hard to save her?"

Is that what he had done—fight for her? Nicholas had felt himself stumbling again and again. Half of his rage had been aimed at Remus Jacaranda; the other half had been reserved for himself. Not just for ignoring his own instincts, but because . . . because . . .

I nearly let someone die under my protection.

"I require her assistance," he said. "She owes a debt to me."

Sophia made a faint sound, a whistle of a breath between her teeth. Nicholas dragged himself closer, his hand straying down to her wrist to feel for her pulse. It felt steadier than before, and her breathing was no longer labored. The yellow light of the lantern warmed her skin from its former pallid, marblelike state, and he was surprised to find it reassuring.

I'm glad, he thought, the words jolting him to the core. *I'm glad she's not dead.*

He'd wished for nothing so much as that in the moments after Etta had disappeared, after Sophia's betrayal. If she'd been standing before him then, he would have reached out and strangled her.

Nicholas tore his gaze away, studying the shape of his shadow on the opposite wall.

"I wasn't going with them. . . ."

The voice was so faint, he might have marked it as another unnatural breeze. Sophia's eyes were closed, but he could see her lips moving.

"Don't speak," he told her, gently laying a hand on her shoulder. "Save your strength. You'll be well again soon."

"I wasn't . . . going with them . . . wouldn't have . . ." Sophia swallowed hard. "Wouldn't have gone to the Thorns."

"When?" he asked. "In Palmyra?"

Her eyes cracked open and she winced at the light. "I heard . . . what Etta was saying. What you were saying. About Grandfather. The timeline. I went to steal it back from the Thorns. I would have . . . I would have come back with it. Instead . . . *humiliated*."

"Just rest," he told her. "We are safe here."

"That's why . . . it's my fault . . . my eye—"

Nicholas straightened. "You mean to tell me you went with the Thorns to steal the astrolabe back from them? *That's* why they beat you?"

"And because . . . I'm an Ironwood . . . They thought I was . . . *his*." She looked at him from under her dark lashes, her eye patch flipped up to reveal the hollow socket beneath. After a moment, Sophia nodded. "Kill them. Will . . . kill them both . . . kill them . . . all. . . ."

It had never made sense to him that she had been so savagely beaten when she'd been a willing participant in the betrayal, riding off with the Thorns. But because of her nature, it had been easy to brush aside and dismiss. Sophia had an unusually potent talent for bringing out the absolute worst in the people around her, and it had drawn out his own ugly, heartless suspicions. He'd dismissed his doubts with the cruel assumption that she'd said something, done something, to provoke their ire—as if *anyone* could deserve that fate.

Li Min had been so quiet on the stairs that it wasn't until she released a low, pained sigh that he noticed her again. She was at the edge of the lantern's light, but the bleakness of her expression lent itself to the darkness.

But she said nothing as she continued climbing. Nicholas reached for the handle of the old, rusted lantern. "Don't you need this?"

Her voice floated back down to him, soft as a memory. "I have always found my way in the dark."

Li Min shouldered the weight of the heavy stone cover, pushing it aside. A small chill raced down the steps and made a home inside of the tomb in those few moments before the lid was shut again.

He took hold of Etta's earring between his fingers again and worried the metal hoop between his fingers, rolling it back and forth.

"If I . . . die . . . *sorry.*" Sophia's voice wasn't even a shadow of a whisper, but he heard her well. He understood.

"Don't be ridiculous," he told her, mimicking her prim tone. "It's as I told you before, in Damascus. You are not allowed to die."

Her answer was silence.

We are, all of us, on our own journeys. . . .

Sophia would never be privy to the journey he had undertaken since childhood, to find that freedom denied to him. But as much as Etta was his heart's helpmate, Sophia was the sword at his side on the expedition he undertook now. From this moment on, for as long as their paths were aligned, she would have his trust and his blade to rely on.

Nicholas leaned back against the nearest wall, the stone cold against his overheated, sore skin, and closed his eyes. For a moment, he merely breathed in. Out. Believed, didn't. Trusted, didn't. Doubted, didn't. Rode the tides of his emotions, the way he and Chase used to float on their backs in open water, watching the sky. And in that way, in a city of the dead, he finally slept as the dead did: undreaming, and unburdened.

TWENTY-ONE

THERE WERE CERTAIN KINDS OF EXHAUSTION THAT LINGERED like a drug in the body, making even the simplest tasks, like lifting one's head from the ground, feel impossible. Nicholas's mind seemed to be in combat with the needs of his body. He startled awake, and felt as though he were locked inside a drunken stupor. Soft voices drifted over to where he remained on the ground, curled around his throbbing right hand. The lantern had been dimmed and his eyesight was blurred, but he made out Li Min's shape leaning against the wall, Sophia's head in her lap.

". . . is this quite necessary?"

"Very," he heard Sophia say. "I am very delicate at the moment, you see."

"I do see," Li Min said dryly. "*Delicate* is most certainly a word I would use to describe you, what with how you flee from weapons and faint upon seeing a drop of blood."

"I haven't the slightest idea as to what you're implying," Sophia said primly. "I might die yet."

"Oh, dear," Li Min whispered. "However can I prevent this?"

Sophia seemed to consider it, then lifted her hand from where it

304

had been draped across her chest. "You ought to check my pulse again. Make sure you count it for . . . a few minutes."

He drifted away again to the sound of Li Min softly counting *one, two, three, four . . .*

The next time he woke, it was to screams.

They came to him from a great distance, muffled but ripe with agony. In the moment it took his mind to shake off sleep, the voices seemed to transform into a living, breathing thing. Nicholas surged up off the floor, knocking his head against the low ceiling and sending a spray of plaster dust down over his body.

"Shh!"

Sophia was awake and sitting upright, having positioned herself against the wall. Her dark eye fixed on him as she struggled to hold up a half-eaten loaf of bread. Nicholas accepted it with ravenous relief, tearing off a chunk for himself. He chewed and swallowed absently, his attention shifting from the much-needed food to the small figure at the base of the stairs.

With the sword Nicholas had taken in Carthage in one hand, a dagger in the other, Li Min kept one foot braced on the bottom step and her eyes fixed upward, toward the entrance.

"What is that?" he whispered, coming to stand beside her. The screams tore at his nerves; his hands curled at his sides, slick with sweat. "*Who* is that?"

Surely not . . . the Ironwoods?

"We are being hunted," Li Min said. Her eyes looked black in the low light. "Eat and put on the clothing I've brought you. We will not be leaving in the near future, but when we do move, it will be quickly."

Nicholas ignored her, taking two steps up to better hear the fighting outside—the wet sound of flesh and the piercing yelps somehow permeated even the thickest of stone tombs. "What—*who*—is out there? You know, don't you?"

Li Min wiped the sweat from her brow, glancing back at Sophia.

With a start, Nicholas saw that Sophia had already changed into a plain white shirt and fawn-colored breeches, and had busied herself with trying to lace up a leather waistcoat. Two pairs of scuffed black boots had been tossed onto another pile of clothing at the center of the room—his, he assumed. The Chinese girl wore a billowy white shirt as well, only she had found thin hose for herself, and a red pleated doublet to be layered over both and secured in place with a heavy leather belt. They would all be traveling as men, then.

"For the love of God, tell us whatever you know," he said. *"Please."*

"You wouldn't believe it," she murmured. "If it is what I think . . ."

"I *believe* we are possibly about to be savagely killed, so the time for thoughtful hesitance has sadly passed," Nicholas said. "Do you know who they are?"

"I do. They have been hunting you for as long as I've tracked you. They left a trail of bodies behind them—guardians and travelers alike—all dead, the same as that Linden man in Nassau."

Nicholas's whole body stilled.

"There is an evil here that reeks of age and decay," Li Min said, turning to look at him. "They will not stop until they have what they're looking for."

"And how do you know that?" Sophia demanded. "Did you use your nose for that as well?"

"I know," Li Min said quietly, cradling each word as if afraid to release them, "because I used to be one of them."

"Pardon?" Sophia said mildly.

"There is not enough time to explain," Li Min said. "They are the Shadows nurtured by the Ancient One. Stolen from their families as children, their humanity ripped from them with bloody training and manipulation. They are here for one purpose alone: to serve him. To find what he seeks above all else."

Sophia scrabbled along the ground until she found the knife she usually kept tucked into her low boots. She swung it out toward Li Min.

"No," Li Min said, kneeling before her again, letting the tip of the blade press against her heart. "I escaped as a child. My mother was a guardian, as was my sister. I was born able to travel, so the Shadows took me to fill their ranks and murdered my family. Witnesses to their existence dig their own graves, you see."

"Then how did you escape?" Sophia asked, still not lowering the blade.

"I was always the smallest, the weakest," Li Min said quietly. "The Ancient One felt I was undeserving of the privilege of serving him. One night, when the elder Shadows were teaching night stalking, I was chosen to serve as prey. As bait. Whoever killed me would receive his radiant blessings."

Nicholas reeled back in horror.

"But it was a moonless night," Li Min said, the words tumbling out of her. "I slipped away. They never found me again. They have not, at least, until now."

I sought Ching Shih out to learn from her, she had said. *To manifest my strength.*

"It's all true, then," Nicholas said, fighting not to touch the ring on his hand, to ignore the way it scalded him deep down, at the seat of his soul. *"From the shadows they come, to give you a fright. . . .* Why does this . . . why does this . . . Ancient One, you said? Why does he want the astrolabe?"

"Because he believes that he will be granted complete immortality if he consumes its power; he will be impervious to harm and time's ravages," she said. "He has prolonged his life by taking the power of the copies, but they were not nearly enough to sate him. He fills the heads of the Shadows with promises that they, too, will live forever and inherit the world. They are acolytes as much as they are his servants."

Sophia shook her head, as if she could fling the story away. "No. *No.*

That Jacaranda was full of it. Alchemists? Hogwash and horsefeathers!"

But Nicholas was nodding, rubbing his face. Forcing himself to accept this, the way Etta would, in order to move on.

"You believe me?" Li Min asked. "Truly?"

He met her gaze in the low light. It was the first time he had detected true vulnerability in her voice. A hopefulness threaded with disbelief. "It aligns with what we already knew, and you've no reason to lie to us. But I imagine few would believe it without this evidence in front of them. Have you never spoken of this before, then?"

She tossed her braid back over her shoulder again, the corners of her mouth slanting down. "I did not think—as you said, the story is impossible to believe for anyone who has not lived it. One cannot go about prattling on about Shadows and immortality and such and be hired for delicate jobs, you see."

"I do see," Nicholas said, understanding better now why she worked as a mercenary, rather than inside the fold of the Thorns and Ironwoods. A secret was easiest kept by one, or none.

"It's all true," Li Min said. "And if we cannot escape, then we will never leave this place."

The tortured cries died to whimpers. Li Min placed a finger to her lips. Nicholas held his breath, reaching for a weapon on his tunic's belt that was no longer there. He looked to Li Min, who blatantly ignored him, keeping both weapons in her hands and lowering into a defensive stance. But then his attention was drawn upward again, toward the entrance to the tomb.

They sounded as any man's footsteps would in a careful approach. It was only when that same scratching began, that long, continuous drag of sound, that Nicholas realized they weren't hearing anything at all—not through so many layers of old stone. They were *feeling* the vibrations of the movements. Plaster shook loose from the ceiling, and he wondered, with a sickening twist of his stomach, what could be so heavy as to have caused that.

"Li Min," he whispered. "Do they use a peculiar kind of weapon—a long, thin blade like a claw?"

"Yes," she breathed out. "They receive it upon their initiation. So you *have* seen them for yourselves."

They had. They'd struggled blow for blow against them in Carthage, without ever realizing it. His hand reached up and closed around the small amulet and Etta's earring. The shaking worsened, thunder crackling through the walls, making it sound as though whoever these travelers—these Shadows—were, they were in the tomb beside them.

This is hell, he thought, *or all the devils have escaped.*

The light around him dampened as Sophia reached over and dimmed the lantern.

If they died down here, who would be the last of them to bear witness to the others' screams?

Cease this at once! he barked at himself. My God, he was becoming prone to theatrics in a way that would have made Chase weep with pride. A heap of good that would do him. He'd fight, as he always had. He'd give Sophia and Li Min the opportunity to escape, and then he would follow. He would not die down here in the dark when there was a future to claim.

Nicholas could not say how much time passed before muffled voices began to bleed through the walls. He spoke French and Spanish, as well as passable Italian, owing to his time mixing with other sailors in ports. He could speak and read Latin and a touch of Greek, thanks to the patience of Mrs. Hall, but this was simply too low to make out.

Li Min cocked her head toward the door, her face twisting in concentration. For the first time in their short acquaintance, he saw a tremor of helplessness run through her expression, and a lingering flare of hope he didn't know had died out.

There was a moment of silence before another sound began to drift through the air, curling against his skin, making his every hair stand at attention. It seemed so out of place that his mind had trouble placing it:

Laughter.

Sophia pressed a hand against her mouth. Nicholas's skin felt as though it might actually retreat from his bones.

The steps grew softer. The vibrations settled from quakes to shivers to nothing at all. He and Li Min exchanged one last look before he released the tension that had wound up his system. He took a deep breath, expanding his lungs and chest until both ached.

"Change," Li Min told him. "Quickly. We will need to leave before they think to return."

Nicholas nodded, moving back to the pile of clothes. "Do you require assistance with your boots?" he asked Sophia. Her arms and hands were moving again, but he had yet to see the same of her legs and feet.

She drew in a sharp breath and, with great effort and an enormous swallowing of pride, nodded.

"I will do it," Li Min said, brushing his hands away. He glanced at Sophia, ensuring she was comfortable with this, before picking up the breeches and sliding them on. They were undersized, which might have been a comment on how Li Min viewed him, but was more likely a matter of what was available—what she could steal or purchase without incurring any notice.

She herself wore a heavy cloak that served to blot her out of sight. He hadn't considered before how strange it was to have a slight advantage over someone else, in spite of the disadvantages the world had foisted upon him. A dark-skinned man in the Papal City, especially one in simple clothing, would not be nearly as remarkable as a young Chinese woman.

The boots were also small, but tolerable. He turned his back to the others for a moment, changed out of the soiled tunic, and slipped the soft linen shirt on, tucking it into the breeches. He left his own doublet unlaced, ignoring how short it was on his frame. No one would be allowed to see him long enough to question it; and, well, the world had a way of ignoring its poor and simple.

He ran a hand over his face, the rasp of whiskers growing in. "If we should need to fight . . ."

"Aim for their skulls, throats, or along their sides just below the rib cage where the seams of their chest plates can be cut," Li Min said. "We are safer disappearing."

"Is there a passage nearby?"

"Two upstairs," Sophia said. "I can guide us. Help me up, will you?" She reached an arm out. Nicholas and Li Min both moved to her side, but he arrived first, gripping her by the wrist and pulling her upright— and, as it turned out, forward. Her legs gave out and she gasped in alarm.

Nicholas caught her easily enough. "Do you have any sensation in them yet?"

Sophia nodded, clearing her throat and blinking, until finally her gaze hardened again. "I might . . . need help. Just for a little while longer."

"I'm amenable to that," he told her. His shoulder was aching from the stitches Li Min had put in, but he felt stronger just having rested. His right arm, the one that had plagued him in Carthage, protested in pain as it absorbed some of Sophia's weight, but he tossed that concern aside.

"You won't tell a soul of this, not even Linden," Sophia said. "And you'll carry me on your back, not as some sort of damsel, otherwise I'll cast up my accounts in disgust."

"Naturally," Nicholas said.

"Not a *word*," she grumbled.

"Not on my life," he promised.

Behind them, Li Min was gathering up their bags, pushing her dark cloak back to loop them over her shoulders.

"You're actually coming?" Sophia asked. "And helping us? It would be so easy to leave us as bait and escape."

"I may be a mercenary, but I'm not a beast, nor am I an imbecile. I cannot fight them alone. He cannot protect either of you that way, or quickly escape," she said, "not without dropping you first. And you are incapable of running or fighting should it happen."

"I wouldn't drop her," he said, just as Sophia snarled, "I've never run from a fight in my life!"

"If we are *leaving*," Li Min said, talking over both of them, "then let us *leave* this place. I know the way up into St. Peter's Basilica."

"The lantern—" Nicholas began.

"No; we move in darkness, as they do," Li Min said, taking the first few steps up. "Quickly; quickly."

As it turned out, he did have to set Sophia down to help Li Min lift the cover off the sarcophagus. Almost immediately, the stink of fresh, hot blood assaulted his senses. He heard Sophia gag behind him, her arms tightening around his neck as he bent to pick her up again.

"Do you hear that?" she whispered. When he didn't respond, she put his head between her hands and turned it to the right.

Drip . . . drip . . . drip . . .

The air was cool down here, too dry for condensation. A shudder rolled through him, prickling at his scalp, cutting down his spine. Li Min stood off to the side of the grave, her weapons raised, looking up—up to where Miles Ironwood's body had been stuffed into one of the tomb's alcoves, his unblinking eyes glowing in the dark. Rivulets of blood raced down the wall to the body of a second man, his body contorted as if his back was broken.

"Holy God . . ." Sophia breathed out. Nicholas swung back toward Li Min just in time to see the glint of silver, the dark shape that swung down toward the girl's face.

"Li—!" he began, but the girl was already moving, the shorter of her two swords spinning out, catching the arm with a sickening *thwack*. A gasp split the air as the Shadow flew back and Li Min stooped for something on the ground. When she stood up again, she threw the longer blade his way, only to have Sophia grab it out of the air and slice at the Shadows behind them; he felt the reverberations as she struck something solid.

"Who's there?" she bellowed near his ear. "Show yourselves! Show yourselves, you bloody cowards!"

He could see it now—see *them*. They were a shade darker than the air, until one, a young man with a startlingly pale face, looked up at him from beneath his hood. Nicholas felt himself dissected by the piercing gaze, cut down to his marrow. He took an involuntary step back as ice flooded his system, the backs of his knees bumping into the sarcophagus.

In one smooth movement, he pulled the sword out of Sophia's hand and lunged forward, stabbing into the Shadow's throat as Li Min had instructed. A hand lashed out, and he had to jump and twist onto the sarcophagus's lid to avoid being skewered by the claw.

Sophia released her grip on his shoulders, slamming back against the edge of the sarcophagus. She reached over and pulled the knife off his belt, bracing herself as if to take a blow. Li Min let out a ferocious cry and dove toward the other Shadow, a woman with a shock of red hair. She swung her blade around, swirling the disturbed dust as she spun with it, swinging down to try to take off the Shadow's head. The other woman was too fast, parrying with a kick hard enough to throw Li Min back a step, but not hard enough to stop her. Rage steamed off the Chinese woman, searing the air, hollowing her cheeks as she opened her mouth and let out another roar.

The furious clanging of their blades should have woken the dead.

A blade lanced down through the darkness, forcing him to drop to the ground to prevent it biting into the juncture of his neck and shoulder. Nicholas lashed a leg out, trying to upend the Shadow, but the man jumped to a nearly inhuman height, flipping back down to catch Nicholas in the face with the full force of his body.

A thousand stars burst behind his eyelids and he was momentarily blinded by the flashing of them. Sophia's shout made him turn just as the Shadow's claw would have pierced the inner part of his ear. It caught him over his cheek instead. Nicholas slipped in the pools of blood on the floor, unable to get his feet beneath him.

Damn it all, get up, get up—

He had fought a hundred battles at sea, fended off pirates and boardings. He'd avoided knives to his belly and axes to his neck and he had *survived*; even the fighters hardened by the sea, he'd survived. But the best-trained of those men were raging, dumb animals compared to this Shadow, who seemed to anticipate his blows before Nicholas decided to try for them.

Etta— He took a vicious punch to his chest, and felt ribs crack. *Etta—*

He tried to imagine her the way she had been on the *Ardent*, when she'd appeared in the haze of battle; he tried to use that image, like a prayer for strength, to drive his next hit. Yet, when his mind's eye drew the memory forward, the scene was cracked between the jaws of darkness. Her screams suddenly silenced, the blood running in rivulets over her face. The clean slice of a claw through her ear.

Her body as pale and still as the marble angels that surrounded them.

He surged up from the ground, knocking the Shadow back. The attacker made as if to lunge forward, but halted, dropping to a knee and howling in pain. Behind him, Sophia had slipped to the ground and cut the tendon of his ankle. Nicholas seized the opportunity at the same moment she did, each of them slicing toward the Shadow's neck.

The body fell to the ground.

Another screech of metal on metal brought Nicholas back around to where Li Min was using her arms, every trembling ounce of strength in her body, to turn the Shadow's long claw back onto the woman's body, piercing the soft flesh of her neck.

"I am . . . forever . . ." the woman gasped out.

"You are dead," Li Min corrected, and finished her.

"As are you," came another voice. Nicholas whirled back toward the entrance of the tomb, his sword following the path of another Shadow as he stepped inside. Two more fell in line behind him. "Little lost one. Do you remember me, as I remember you?"

He knew she didn't mean to, that it was likely the way the man's voice licked at the air like a snake's tongue, but she stepped back, just that small bit. Her hands gripped her dagger hard enough for him to hear her knuckles crack.

Though he knew she would likely despise it, Nicholas felt a fierce surge of protectiveness for the young girl stolen from her family and brought into their darkness, and the young woman who stood before him now, having survived it.

The entirety of his right hand lost sensation, and then the rest of his arm. Nicholas barely caught the sword with his weaker left hand, his gaze narrowing on them, as his heart beat a vicious tattoo of fear.

"Li Min," Nicholas said quietly. "Take her and go. I'll catch up to you."

"No—" Sophia began as Li Min knelt beside her. "Wait, are you—"

"I have the astrolabe," Nicholas told the Shadows. "Who will fight me for it?"

The flash of Sophia's white shirt at the edge of his vision told him, if nothing else, that they had gotten out of the cramped space. One of the Shadows broke off to pursue them, only to be summoned back by the flick of the first man's hand.

Nicholas raised his sword, swallowing the blood in his mouth. *I will live.* It was not a question, but a necessity. He only needed to create a path to the entrance of the mausoleum, and then he could lose them in the darkness.

The Shadow in front matched his stance, letting the hood fall away from his face.

A voice in the darkness began to whisper, to pulse, to growl. The Shadows recoiled at the sound of it. Two ducked back through the entrance, vanishing with a soft patter of footsteps.

"Liar," the Shadow said, lingering just a moment more before pulling his hood up and following their path. Nicholas staggered forward, using the walls to support himself as he moved. If the Shadows had gone left, he would go right, and hope it might lead him to Li Min and Sophia. To the Basilica.

But from the depths of the city of the dead, a voice rang out, as brittle and airy as the plaster dust that swirled around him. *"Child of time."*

The words scored down his heart, tugged his attention back. He turned, clutching his numb arm to his chest. And though his tired mind was prone to tricks, and his heart weary of them, he could have sworn he saw another figure standing there. The long, pale cloak clasped around his neck flowed down the line of his back, curling at his feet like a cat. It gave his bearing a forceful regality that made Nicholas wish he could summon the strength to turn away again. The distance seemed to close between them, though neither of them moved, and Nicholas saw that his profile was as faultless as if it had been painted by a master's hand. All at once, the ring on his finger began to sing its song of pain, flaring as the man turned his head more fully, his gaze dropping to it. It was only then, when he caught the whole of the man's countenance, that Nicholas saw that his features were like that of a demon—like that of Death himself.

He turned and ran as if hell burned behind him.

TWENTY-TWO

IT SURPRISED HIM SOMEHOW THAT A CITY OF THE DEAD would be arranged like an actual city, but here he was, running down dark, winding streets that split the rows of tombs and structures into a grid. When, at last, his feet found the edge of a set of stairs, he realized he'd begun to climb toward the surface. He was grateful for the challenge of the steps, the warmth that crept into the air as he rose up through the layers of earth and carved stone, and nearly wept at the first sighting of fat candles perched along the wall of a narrow hallway. It meant he was near the end.

He was even more grateful to find that Sophia and Li Min were already there, waiting for him.

"What took you so long?" Sophia demanded from where she sat on the ground. "Damn you for sending us away!"

Nicholas looked at her as though she'd declared herself recently hatched from an egg. He wiped the stinging line of blood from his cheek, only to find that he was still clutching the sword. His right arm hung uselessly at his side, and he forced himself to quell his fear at the realization, so as not to frighten them. "I worried for you, too, Sophia."

"Ugh," she said, crossing her arms and turning away. "I knew you'd be revoltingly sentimental about this."

"Forgive the presumptions I made about your character on our first meeting," Li Min said. "I see the sort of person you are now."

"Yeah, a bleeding *idiot*," Sophia muttered.

"Are you hurt?" Li Min asked. "Beyond what we can see?"

The smell of warm wax coated the air, clearing the lingering touch of decay in his throat and lungs. Nicholas turned back to see if there was a way of barring the door behind them—there was. He slid the latch into place, fully ignoring the voice that told him it wouldn't be enough.

"I saw something," he told them, instead of answering her. "I need to know . . . I need to understand what it was."

"You saw *him*. The Ancient One," Li Min said, as if his face alone had revealed it. "He allowed you to live?"

In that moment, when he'd met the man's gaze . . . there was no other way to describe it, save to say that Nicholas had felt acutely aware of his own years, how they might fit inside the man's palm.

"He called them—the Shadows—away," Nicholas said. "I haven't the faintest notion as to why."

"I did not know he was capable of mercy." He did not, for one moment, enjoy the flash of fear he saw trespass on Li Min's face. She continued in a hurry. "Something more is at play here. Where is it that you hope to go? Are you still hoping to find the last common year?" She swiped the back of her hand against her forehead, smudging the blood and dust there. Her hands were covered in liquid so dark, it almost looked black.

Blood, he realized. That was the travelers' blood. In the rush of their fight and flight, he'd neglected to spare more than one horrified second thinking of the Ironwood travelers who had been killed and left for them to find. Their lives had been reduced to splatters of gore, and they'd become nothing more than a way to taunt the next victims. These Shadows could have done the same to any of them, and that put their odds of surviving this in rather stark terms.

"Yes," he told her. "Did you learn what it was?"

"1905," she said, with a look that hinted that she had known the whole time. He was too ravaged by pain and apprehension to care much in that moment. "We can take the passage upstairs, the one that leads to Florence. From there, it will be a voyage, but it should not take more than a few days—"

"What the hell is wrong with your arm?" Sophia interrupted. Without preamble, she reached up, gripping his right wrist and using it to haul herself, at last, to her feet.

Nicholas looked away. "It is only sore—"

"You haven't moved it once!" He could see that Sophia had dug her nails into his hand, but could not feel it. "What—you mean it's the ring?"

Her voice was rising in pitch, and she looked as if she wanted nothing more than to pull the arm out of its socket and beat him senseless with it.

"The Belladonna's poison," Li Min said, taking a turn at lifting his arm and turning it to and fro, as if reading a map. "If you do not complete her task, it will eventually travel to your heart and cause it to seize in the same way. What did she ask of you?"

"To kill Ironwood," Sophia said, before he could.

"But why?" Li Min asked, her tone hushed.

"Have you *met* him?"

"Enough," Nicholas said. "We can discuss it along the way to 1905."

"Yes, please," Sophia said.

Li Min drew the hood up over her ears, obscuring most of her face from view. "Niceties don't suit you."

They suit almost the entirety of the world, Nicholas managed to think, not say.

"This way, then." Li Min urged them forward again, her cape fluttering down the hall.

"You need to do this," Sophia ordered him as they followed. "You

319

can't trade your life for the old man's. It's not worth it. Half the world would throw you a parade for it."

"Like you'll kill the men who harmed you?" he asked.

She turned, staring straight ahead, her jaw set. "That's different. *I* won't die if I never find those roaches. If you won't do it, I will. The day Cyrus Ironwood gets what he wants is the day my corpse is lowered into its grave."

Ironwoods, he thought, shaking his head. Always so eager to shed their own blood.

"What happens when the old man is gone?" he asked. "Will you step up as heir? Expect the other families to fall in line behind you?"

"All I care about is wiping that smear of shite off the face of this earth, and salting the ground that grew him," she snapped. "Whatever becomes of the families when he's gone is up for someone else to decide. I want no part of any of this anymore."

She wants to be free of this. The one person he saw as being an emblem of everything the family stood for wanted nothing more to do with it. Remarkable.

Li Min slowed as they reached the next imposing door, pressing her ear against the rough, dark wood. She glanced back, nodding to Nicholas, then pushed the door open, revealing a set of steps that spiraled up out of sight.

Nicholas started forward, only to stop again at the sound of a voice floating down to them. He drew Sophia back into the shadows of the nearest wall, his mind trying to spin up possible explanations for what they were doing down there—to be caught now, and in their bloodied appearance—

A light moved along the stone wall of the stairwell, marking the man's progress. He appeared sooner than expected, an older gentleman in robes whose pleasant face went slack with surprise.

"We are—" Sophia shifted smoothly into Latin. *"We have come to pay our respects—"*

Li Min's arm lashed out, thumping the priest on the head with the flat of her sword. Nicholas barely managed to step forward to catch him in time as he wilted to the ground.

"Too slow," she said to Nicholas's incredulous look. "Time to move."

"She was right about one thing," Sophia said as she passed him. "You're no pirate, Saint Nicholas. Where's that ruthless edge that lets you hack sailors apart on ships?"

"Affronted by this lack of honor," he told her.

She must have rolled her eye. "Hang honor before it hangs you."

Li Min, at least, seemed to know where they were going. It took Nicholas some time, however, to even realize that they'd entered St. Peter's Basilica and were walking its quiet halls. Sophia had referred to it as the "old" St. Peter's, and he saw the truth of that immediately. This structure had none of the grandeur he'd witnessed when he and Julian had visited it in search of the astrolabe—but that had been, what, the twentieth century? He'd been struck mute by the masters of art who graced its ceilings and walls; it had collected treasures and grandeur over time, the way a traveler family would. This iteration was simple, with stark lines and angles that lacked both a sense of gravity and permanence. Still, it was by no means as humble as the Anglican churches in the colonies, which seemed to pride themselves on being as plain and grim as possible.

He glanced up as they passed by a large chapel, its door open just enough to catch the glimmer of rows of candlelight. Beside him, Sophia kept her gaze down, her pace as labored as his own. Nicholas was so deep in his own thoughts that he did not notice when she drifted a few steps behind him, stopping.

"Good *lord*, Carter," Sophia whispered. "You've been mooning over this damned thing for a bloody month, and *now* you just drop it willy-nilly?"

Sophia held up a familiar gold earring, its small leaves and blue stone shivering with the breeze. Nicholas's hand flew to the leather cord around his neck, his heart slamming up from his chest into his throat.

Hell and damnation—

But the talisman and the earring were still there, secure. He felt the slight weight in his hand. So how . . . ?

A drumming began in his chest, spreading out and out and out through his blood until he couldn't quite feel his fingers.

"Surely it's not the same," Li Min said, taking it from Sophia. "Look—"

But when placed side by side in his hand, they were almost identical, to the best of an artist's skill and capability. They were a pair. They were . . .

Etta.

Nicholas tore away from the others, stumbling back toward the chapel, running down the length of it, finding nothing and no one. He returned to the hall, wild with disbelief and hope, searching for any other hint of her—anything that might tell him where she had gone. Dust stung his eyes, blurring his vision. It choked him, filling his lungs, wringing the last gasps of air out of him. The desperation was intolerable, but he couldn't let it go, not yet—

"Etta?" he called, his voice as loud as he dared. "Etta, where are you?"

"Oh God," he heard Sophia say. "This is painful to watch. Make him stop. Please."

It was Li Min's face that brought his frantic searching to a halt. The carefully constructed cipher cracked as she bit her lip, her eyes darting to the side. "Surely you are not referring to Henrietta Hemlock?"

"Hemlock?" Sophia said, holding up a hand. "Wait—"

"Henrietta, the daughter of Henry Hemlock—"

"Etta Spencer," Nicholas said impatiently. "Her mother is Rose Linden, and, yes, Rose told me Hemlock is Etta's father."

"Why didn't you tell *me* that?" Sophia asked. "You didn't think it was relevant that the leader of *the Thorns* procreated with the beast that is Rose Linden? My God, this explains so much. *So* much."

Li Min could not look at him. Her jaw worked silently, her hands clenching at her sides. Nicholas felt his stomach roll in revolt, and he'd stepped into a trap, and there was no way to free himself from the painful, searing cage of hope. "Do you know where she is? That's who we've been trying to find. She was orphaned, to the last common year—"

She closed her eyes, releasing the breath trapped inside of her. "I do. I am . . . truly sorry. Your search ends here, for she is dead."

NEW YORK CITY
1939

TWENTY-THREE

Etta was not sure how long she stood rooted to that same spot. Terror had such a firm grip on her that it could have pulled the skin off her bones. Julian ventured forward a few steps, waving the soot and ash out of the way as best he could. Revealing only more soot and ash.

"There's . . . there's *nothing*," he said, turning back to her. "How is that possible? The buildings, the people . . ."

He wasn't wrong; as far as the eye could see through the smoke—which turned out to be very far, without the hindrance of buildings crowding the park's boundaries—there was nothing beyond the husks of what had once been. If the air cleared, Etta knew she'd at least be able to see the East River. She had thought the destruction of the San Francisco earthquake had been absolute, but this . . . this was . . .

"Oh my God," she said, pressing a hand against her mouth.

She'd been right. This was a third, alternate timeline—it hadn't reverted back to Ironwood's timeline like he must have intended with the assassination. He'd grasped burning, dangerous threads of history and knotted them into something far more sinister. Something unrecognizable.

There's nothing left.

She lowered herself to her knees, suddenly unable to support her own weight.

"What could cause this?" Julian asked. "Shelling? Aerial bombings?"

"I don't know," she said. "I don't know—we need to—we need to go—"

If it was something worse, like a nuclear weapon, then they'd already exposed themselves to harmful radiation. The thought pushed Etta back off the ground, dried the tears that were beginning to form in her eyes.

But when she turned to tell Julian, something else caught her eye—the sweep of headlights cutting through the thick smoke, brushing over them.

"Survivors, call out," a voice crackled over a speaker, broken up by either emotion or the technology. *"Help is on the way. Survivors . . . call out if you can. . . ."*

"Come on," Etta said, turning back to the passage. "We need to go!"

Julian shook his head. "No—Nan—I'm going to find her—"

Etta's words caught in her throat. If she'd been in the city, there was very likely nothing left to find. But before they could protest, the headlights found them again, and an engine revved as it raced toward them. Before the vehicle had fully stopped, a man in a full black jumpsuit and gas mask—something that closely resembled what Etta knew as a hazmat suit—leaped out of the back of a Jeep and rushed toward them.

"My *God*! My God, what are you doing here?" The man's voice was muffled by his oxygen mask. "How did you survive?"

"That, chap," Julian managed to get out, "is an excellent question."

ETTA KNEW THAT SHE SHOULD HAVE STEERED THEM BACK through the passage, but some part of her wanted to know—wanted to see for herself—what had become of her city.

She should have considered what that would do to her heart. After a while, she stopped looking out at the devastation as the military-issue Jeep bounced through the smoldering wreckage, and cupped her hands over her eyes.

This isn't right, this isn't right. . . . None of this was right. This timeline . . .

A medic riding with them had given them both oxygen masks, which cleared her head somewhat. Etta winced as he swiped antiseptic over the cut on her arm again, and then turned to the slash across her forehead.

"Say . . ." Julian said, his voice trembling slightly as he leaned forward to speak to the driver. "They figure out who to pin this on yet? We've been a bit, uh, out of it. Trapped in that basement, you know?"

Julian Ironwood: worthless at paddling a boat, but quick with a lie.

"I'll say," the driver called back. "The Central Powers proudly took credit for their handiwork. Made sure to hit Los Angeles and Washington, too, just to drive the message home."

Etta had to close her eyes and breathe deeply, just to keep from vomiting.

"Never seen anything like the flash when this hit. Millions, just—" The man trailed off.

Gone, Etta's mind finished.

It was light enough outside that once they approached the Hudson, heading toward what the men had described as a medical camp and survivor meeting point in New Jersey, Etta could see the dark outline of a bicycle and a man against one of the last standing walls. Almost as if they had disappeared and left their shadows behind.

"Paris and London are still standing, but it's only a matter of time," the medic said bitterly. "This was to warn us off joining them in their fight, I bet. They knew Roosevelt was thinking about sending aid or troops over to the Brits—that they've been gearing up for a fight. So the Central Powers declared war on us."

"This isn't war," the driver said. "This is hell. They knew we'd jump in first chance we got, and so they crippled us. They showed us who's boss."

Etta didn't ask about the government, about the other cities. And she didn't ask Julian about how they would get back to that passage, or what other ones they could reach in this year. Exhaustion swept over her. It stole whatever spark of fight she had left. She closed her eyes on her ruined city.

"Almost done, honey," the medic said. Under any other circumstances she would have hated the endearment, but she was feeling battered, and the man had a grandfatherly quality that reminded her of Oskar, Alice's husband. "You'll need to find a doctor to stitch up your arm when we get there, you hear me?"

Etta couldn't muster the strength to nod.

Where would she even start? How could anyone fix *this*?

Anywhere, she thought, and *with everything I have.*

THE MEDICAL CAMP WAS SET UP IN ELIZABETH, NEW JERSEY. Far enough from the blast site in the center of Manhattan to be out of immediate danger, but still close enough to be shrouded in toxic clouds of fumes and dust. To get there, they'd had to drive by cleared fields where the bodies of victims had been brought, some covered with tarps, others not. Etta's breath was harsh in her ears, and she couldn't seem to let go of the image of their twisted shapes, the way the charring had left them looking almost hollow. As much as she felt like she had to be a witness to these atrocities, that she owed it to them to form a memory of their wasted lives, Etta didn't protest when the medic leaned over and covered her eyes.

"You don't have to see this," he said. "It's all right."

But she did.

I did this, she thought. By letting the astrolabe slip away, she was responsible; the thought left her trembling so hard that the same medic had her lie down across the seat to administer an IV.

330

By listening to the radio in the Jeep, Etta learned the following: the attacks had happened five days ago; the secretary of labor was now the president of the United States, as he'd had the good fortune to be on vacation outside of the District when the bombs struck; and there'd been no decision on whether or not to make peace or declare war.

"Is there a registry?" Julian asked. "A list of survivors from the city?"

"Not yet," was all they were told. "You'll see."

And they did see. The old warehouse that had been converted into an emergency medical facility was wrapped around twice with a line of people waiting to get inside. Many of them—in fact, most—were African American. They, too, made up the bulk of those coming in and out of the tents that had been set up along the nearby streets. Their rudimentary bandages looked like basic first aid, not actual treatment.

"Why are there two lines?" Julian asked, sounding as dazed as Etta felt. She turned to see what he was staring at. Two separate booths, both with the Red Cross's symbol, both handing out the same parcels of food. But there were two very distinct lines: one for white people, the other for blacks.

Etta fought the scream that tore up through her. The whole city was in ruins, millions of people were likely dead, and they still followed this hollow, cruel tradition, as if it accomplished *anything* other than humiliation.

"You know why," she told him. Julian was an Ironwood; he traveled extensively; he had been educated about the history his father had created; and he was acting like none of that was true. Somehow, it only infuriated her more.

"But *why*?" he repeated, his voice hollow.

"Come on, you two," one of the soldiers said.

"What about the rest of them?" Julian asked as they were walked right past the line waiting to get into the warehouse.

"Waiting for blood from one of the black blood banks in Philadelphia," the soldier said, as if it weren't a completely insane statement. *Blood is blood is blood is blood.* The only thing that mattered was type. This was an emergency, an utter disaster, and still—*this.*

Calm down, she told herself. *Calm down.* . . . She crossed her arms over her chest to keep from tearing the world apart around them in a rage of devastation. *My city. These people* . . . Etta choked on the bile that rose, and it was only by pressing the back of her hand against her mouth that she kept from throwing up until she was truly as hollow and empty as she felt.

"What are we doing here?" Etta whispered as the men led her and Julian toward the warehouse. "We can't stay, you know that."

He shook his head, turning back to look at the faces of the people at the door, waiting to get in. "There are open beds. Why are they outside if there are open beds?"

"They'll be treated when the rest of the staff from Kenney Hospital arrive," the medic said, speaking slowly, as if Julian were a child. "This way."

The medic relinquished them to a bleary-eyed doctor, who ushered them over to sit on a cot. The man began to examine the cuts and burns on Etta's arms and hands without so much as a word. A nurse with strawberry-blond hair eventually wandered over with a pail of water and a rag.

Julian stared at a man two cots over, quietly weeping into his hat.

"Let me help you there, sugar," the nurse said, and cleaned away the grime and blood Etta had been carrying with her since St. Petersburg. "It's all right to cry. It's better if you do."

I can't. Something cold had locked around her core, so that she didn't even register the doctor stitching a particularly bad cut without anesthesia. She didn't register Julian scooting to the edge of the cot so that the nurse could lift Etta's legs up, laying her out on the cot.

Etta watched, in some strange state between sleeping and wakefulness, as the doctors, nurses, servicemen, and families of the injured moved between the cots and curtains that divided the enormous space into makeshift rooms.

"Will you stop with this—" A nearby voice was rising, flustered. "I don't need to be examined."

"Madam, you do—if you'll let me continue, I won't be but a moment—"

"Can you not understand me?" the woman said, her voice dripping with a venomous mix of fear and tension. "I don't *want* you to touch me."

Etta opened her eyes, craning her neck to see what was happening. The doctor who had stitched her up went right to the other, badgered doctor's side. A black doctor.

"I'll finish here, Stevens," the other man said. "The next shift will start soon. I'm sure they need your assistance more outside."

"*Why*—" Julian had been so quiet, she'd assumed he'd gone and wandered off. "Why are there empty beds, when there are people outside?"

He wasn't speaking to the doctors; he wasn't speaking to the nurses, or the patients, or any one person in particular. There was a manic edge to his tone that drew eyes, nervous glances.

"I want you to tell me *why*—"

"The same reason," Etta murmured, "you never truly trained your half brother. The same reason he had to sign a contract just to travel. The same reason," she continued, "no one ever acknowledged him as being a member of your family."

Julian turned on her. "That's not true! That's not! You have no idea—"

She wondered if his privilege had made him blind to others' suffering in his travels, or if maybe it took something of this magnitude to shatter that shield of self-righteousness that being white and male and wealthy had always provided him with. Etta didn't doubt for a second that, as the heir, he might have been protected from harsher years so as to keep him alive, but she also didn't doubt that Julian had never been able to see further than a foot in front of him when it came to other people.

Or maybe he'd treated traveling as all of the other Ironwoods seemed to; they disconnected themselves from decency time and time again to play the parts each era demanded of them. They had seen so much, they must have become desensitized to it—the way she could watch a film, see characters suffer, but never fully invest in their lives because of the emotional distance. Because it never truly felt real; not in a visceral way.

This kind of destruction was what traveling did to people—not the travelers themselves, but their victims, the common people who could not feel the sands of history shifting around them before they were smothered.

Julian's hands were limp at his side, turned slightly toward the room, as if he could weigh the odds of life or death for each person stretched out on a cot. He had closed his eyes; his breathing was shallow, his face screwed up. *Powerless.*

"Remember this," she told him. "How you feel right now."

What it felt like to move through the world without power, at the mercy of things bigger than you. Unable, even if just for an hour, to control one's life. How Nicholas had felt for years, before he'd taken all of that strength she loved so much about him and pulled himself up, out, back to the sea.

Etta turned her face against the rough fabric of the cot and focused on nothing beyond her own breathing, fighting back the sweep of shame and anger.

I have to finish this. A single man, on Ironwood's orders, had set this disaster in motion. The blast from the explosion hadn't just killed the tsar; its effects had rippled out, exactly as Henry had said, cutting through millions upon millions of innocent lives. For the first time in her life, Etta felt *lethal*.

"We need to leave," she told Julian. "We have to find your grandfather. He has the astrolabe. We can still fix this."

Julian shook his head, rubbing his hands over his face. "I can't go back—I *can't*."

"The survivor rosters have gone up," she heard a soft voice say. "I'll take you to them, if you'd like. They only account for this field hospital. We should have others by the evening."

Out of the corner of her eye she saw a nurse leading Julian toward the entrance, where a man was hammering up handwritten lists on large sheets of butcher paper. Those who could rise from their cots did so, swarming that small space. The line outside began to push forward as well, surging toward the sheets in a tangle of arms and legs, until everyone was nearly climbing over each other to get a better look.

By the time she saw Julian again, almost twenty minutes later, the same nurse was by his side again, leading him toward an area in the far back of the warehouse that had been sectioned off by sterile white curtains.

Etta pushed herself up and followed, bracing herself for this next hit. Either his old nanny was alive, or he was being drawn back to identify a body. She caught the tail end of the nurse's instructions as she came up behind Julian.

". . . need to wear a mask and try not to touch her—the burns are exceedingly painful."

"I understand," Julian said, accepting both gloves and a face mask from the young woman. Her tidy uniform seemed at odds with the barely managed chaos of the place; she cast them both a sympathetic look before falling back.

Etta accepted her own set and pulled them on. *She survived.* What a small, precious miracle.

"They say she doesn't have long," Julian told her, with an odd, forced lightness. Etta knew this feeling, too, of overcompensating to rise above the pain in order to function. "The air way out in Brooklyn was so hot it damaged her lungs."

Etta put a hand on his arm. "I'm so sorry."

He lifted a shoulder in a shrug. "I'd like to ask her a few things, if she can answer. But mostly . . . I think I . . ."

Julian never finished his thought. He took a deep breath, smoothed his hair back, and stepped through the curtain.

Inside, about a dozen or so beds were arranged in a U shape around a central station, where two nurses were cutting bandages and measuring out medicine. The lights from the lanterns were kept dim, but the shadows didn't hide the heavily bandaged figures on each of the beds, the blistered patches of exposed, unnaturally gleaming skin.

Julian paced toward the far right end, counting under his breath. Finally, he found the one he was looking for, and Etta saw him straighten to his full height as he moved to the small wooden stool beside the cot. He moved the basin of water onto the floor and reached for the hand of the woman on the bed.

Etta hung back, unsure whether or not she was meant to be listening or watching. The woman seemed less bandaged than the others, but wore a bulky oxygen mask. Her face was as pink as the inside of a seashell, and her eyebrows were entirely gone, as were patches of her gray hair.

With utmost care, Julian stroked the back of her hand, careful to avoid the IV line. Within a moment, the woman turned her head toward him, her eyelids inching open. Etta knew the precise moment she saw him and made the connection, because her free hand floated up to pull down her oxygen mask, and those same blue eyes went wide.

"You're . . ."

"Hullo, Nan," Julian said, his voice painfully light. "Gave me a bit of hell trying to track you down in this mess."

Her mouth moved, but it was a long while before words emerged.

"I thought I might be . . . I thought I might have passed. But . . . you're not you, not from before—?"

Etta wasn't sure what she was asking, exactly. Julian just responded with one of his infuriating shrugs.

"Before I supposedly plummeted to my untimely death? It's all right. It was only a bit of play. I never did go splat. You know how I love my games."

Even in her condition, the woman, a guardian, knew to be wary of revealing his fate to a traveler—however false a fate it might have been. She blinked almost owlishly at him.

"I thought . . . I thought so. You've the look of a man now. You've grown so well." As if the whole scene wasn't awful enough, the woman began to cry. Etta began the slow process of backing away without being noticed. "I'd always hoped to see you . . . one last time . . . that you'd come to visit me when I was older, so I could see you . . . smile again."

Etta's heart stretched to the point of ripping at the unbridled emotion in the old woman's voice.

"A fair bet, that. You've always known, Nan, there's no getting rid of me," Julian told her. "What did you say? Luck of the devil, lives of a cat? I'm only sorry I didn't come sooner."

The eyebrows had been singed from her face, but Etta imagined them lifting at that, just by the way her eyes took on a sudden glint. "Thank the good Lord you didn't. Or else you'd . . . be . . ."

Dead. Dying. Incinerated.

Gone.

Etta's stomach turned, and she looked away, toward the heavy, dark curtain covering the shattered window. The movement must have finally caught the old woman's attention, because Etta felt the pressure of her gaze like a chain jerking her head back up.

"My God—*Rose*—"

Etta jumped at the viciousness of the woman's tone, less amused now to see yet another person all but cross themselves at a reminder of her mother.

"No, Nan," Julian said, pressing her gently down onto the bed. "This is her daughter. Etta, this is the great Octavia Ironwood."

This didn't seem to improve the woman's opinion in the slightest. Her breathing had become labored, to the point where even Julian shot a panicked look at a nearby oxygen tank. Etta took another step back, wondering if she should leave—Julian's old nanny was so fragile right now, any sort of disturbance seemed capable of shattering what strength she had left.

"I never thought . . . I'd see you with the likes of a Linden, and *her* daughter, no less," the woman coughed, hacking up something wet from her lungs. Julian's face softened; he reached for a rag and a bowl of warm water from the nearby stand and dabbed the blood from the corner of her lips.

"Don't . . . bother yourself. . . ."

"It's no bother at all," he told her. "Just returning the favor for all the times you did it for me as a little prat."

"You were never a prat," Octavia told him, her voice severe despite the whistle of air in and out of her chest. "You were *trying*. You tested. But you were never"—she cut her eyes at Etta—"stupid."

That one stung, Etta had to admit. Initially, hearing things like that had made Etta think of her mother like one of the paintings Rose restored at the Met—its true image obscured by layers of age and grime. Now, she wore the truth like a badge of shame. "You tried your best raising me," Julian was saying, "but you know me—all style, no sense. I was bound to run with a rougher set sooner or later."

The burned half of the woman's face pulled into an agonizing smile. Etta couldn't tell the difference between her choking and laughter.

"You're a little love," she informed him. "I might like you . . . even better . . . if you could find me a drink of the good stuff."

"I'll bring you a whole bottle of Scotch," he vowed, "if I have to go to Scotland and bring it back, still cold from the distillery."

"Tell me what's . . . what's happened," she said. "This wasn't what was meant to be."

Julian began to explain what had happened, quietly, quickly.

"There's a lot to be said about Cyrus Ironwood," Octavia began. "There's . . . much to be ashamed of. How he treats—how he treats his own family, for one. He was so hard on you . . . for not being what he meant you to be. For not fixing . . . your father."

Etta's hands curled around her biceps, squeezing the muscles. Nicholas and Julian's father, Augustus, had been a vile piece of work; Etta had to wonder if *he* was what Cyrus had "meant for" Julian to be.

The shadow that passed over Julian's face lifted again as the woman's eyes flickered over to him, then to the room's other sleeping occupants. She spoke so softly, Etta had to move closer to her bed to hear. "There is . . . madness in him. Oh, don't look so surprised. Those of us . . . those of us closest to him have watched him step closer . . . closer . . . to the fire. But he did create a world better than what had . . . come before. None of this . . . none of this should have happened. But Rose Linden—she and her outcasts could never accept it."

"This wasn't part of the original timeline?" Julian clarified, just as softly. "I didn't think so, but I couldn't be sure. There were so many changes when Grandfather went to war with the families."

"No," Octavia said. "I wouldn't have stayed. I wouldn't have . . . let children . . . let anyone die . . . I wouldn't have let this happen."

Etta's heart froze in her chest, seizing painfully. If Octavia thought—*believed*—that she could have prevented this, or at least saved herself, then that meant . . .

She'd had it wrong. Etta had assumed that guardians, unlike travelers, wouldn't be able to recognize when the timeline shifted—that they would simply be carried forward, their lives and memories adjusted, blissfully unaware that their lives had ever been different. But that wasn't the case at all. The Ironwood guardians, in service to the old man, would know how things were meant to play out. If they survived the changes, they would *know* the timeline had been altered, and live out its consequences. Etta was almost breathless with the unspeakable cruelty of it. These people were born into this hidden world, yet were as much at its mercy as a normal man or woman. Only, they would know when something was lost, and when there was a reason to be afraid.

"I know, Nan," Julian said, cupping her hand between his. "You would have saved the whole damn city if you knew."

"You didn't know, either . . . so why . . . why come?" Octavia asked, turning her head to better look at him.

"Because I needed to find out a few things," Julian said, lying just a little, "and you're the only person I trust."

Another painful smile as her burned skin pulled beneath her bandages. "Tell me. But—*she* goes."

"Nan," Julian cajoled. "Etta's not like her mother. She wasn't even told she was one of us until last month. If you hold her mother against her, you'll have to hold my father against me."

"Her mother *was* the reason for your father's change . . . for his cruelty. She created it in him—"

"Let's not—" Julian cut her off, then cringed. "She didn't make him who he was, she only released what was already inside of him, waiting to be let out. Let's just . . . I only meant that we're trying to find out what's been happening with the family. Grandfather has been trying to track down his old obsession again, and now we need to find him."

The candlelight drew deep shadows across Julian's face as he leaned forward, searching Octavia's face. He shifted uncomfortably, and the creaking of the chair cut through the murmur of life and death in the makeshift ward.

She won't talk until I leave, Etta realized. But she wasn't about to step outside and rely solely on Julian relaying the complete picture to her.

"Easy, Nan," Julian said. "This one's all right. Vetted her myself, otherwise I wouldn't have brought her to you."

She clearly had some doubts about his judgment, but let this pass.

"Be careful . . . won't you? He's been . . . traveling again. Came here only days ago . . . called a family meeting. Don't let him . . . find you," Octavia said, fixing her gaze back on Julian.

"Him?" Julian repeated. "Grandpops? Why? The old man moves once every two decades at best."

"If I tell you . . ." Octavia blew out a long, wheezing sigh. "What trouble . . . will you find yourself in?"

"The good kind," Julian promised her. "The kind that makes you proud of me, even as you put me in the naughty corner."

The sound that came out of her must have been a laugh, though it was painful to hear. "There's . . . an auction. Came through . . . the family lines. He came to take . . . the gold from his vault here. Buy-in."

"An auction?" Julian repeated, glancing at Etta. "Did he say what for?"

"Is there anything else . . . he could want . . . so desperately?"

The astrolabe.

"He doesn't already have it?" Etta asked. Who had taken it from Kadir in the palace, then?

Julian must have had a similar thought, but arrived at an actual guess. "The Belladonna. I should have known the blasted thing would turn up with her. She must have sent one of her minions to steal it, or one of Grandpop's men went rogue and brought it to her for a fee. Do you know the location of the auction? The year?"

Octavia shook her head, and Etta felt herself deflate. The old woman grabbed Julian's hand, holding him in place. "Leave . . . go back. As far . . . back as you can."

"I've got a few things to do first," he told her, "but I will. In time."

"No—Julian, the Shadows—even guardians hear whispers of such—of such things—*murders*—"

341

"Shadows?" Julian's brow creased. "Are you trying to be funny with me, Nan?"

Despite her condition, she leveled him with a look perfected by years as a nanny.

"You also told me my hair was going to fall out if I didn't stop eating sweets, so forgive me if I doubt the story about the creatures who snatch naughty traveler children in the night."

"What are you talking about?" Etta asked, looking between them.

"You know, the one your mother gently traumatized you with from a young age—about people who live in shadows and steal little traveler children who don't follow the rules?" He rubbed at the stubble on his chin, and Etta wondered why everything he ever did made it seem like he was posing. "Huh. You don't know. Oh! Right. Your terror of a mother kept everything secret, et cetera. Have to say, this is the first time I've been jealous of you. *From the shadows they come . . .*"

It was only because he had mentioned her mother. It was only because the memory of the Winter Palace was still so close to the surface, blooming with renewed pain every few minutes. It was only because of those things that Rose's words circled back to her then, and tentatively linked with what Julian said.

"You can say if I'm telling it wrong," he told Octavia. "But there's this old story, about a group that lives in the shadows and takes traveler children who stray from their families. I always thought it was made up to explain how kids got left behind in time periods or were orphaned. Is that not the case?"

"Killers—" Octavia let out a brutal cough, bringing blood to her lips. Julian leaned forward, gently dabbing them with the wet cloth.

"Easy now," he told her.

"Murderers . . . the whole lot of them," Octavia said. "We knew of them . . . Cyrus—he wants the same thing that—that they do. Destroyed all records of them. Never wanted . . . anyone to know about them . . . otherwise, they'd be too frightened . . . to help him search for it."

It. The astrolabe.

You don't know what's coming, what's been chasing me for years, her mother had said. *I've kept them off your trail for weeks, from the moment you were taken, but the Shadows—*

But the Shadows . . .

What had Henry told her about Rose's delusions? That she'd become afraid of the darkness, that the delusion of the radiant man who'd haunted her had sent Shadows out after her?

"What do they look like?" she asked. Rose's attention in the palace had been drawn away by attackers in black. She'd assumed they were Ironwoods, even palace guards, but—her mind was moving too quickly, strumming through possibilities. There was one more piece to this, something that would weave the truth together. It couldn't be as simple as . . . no, it wasn't.

Henry wasn't wrong. Her mother needed help. She was a *murderer* who'd killed a member of her own family—her best and only friend.

"Don't . . . know," Octavia said. "I don't—just stay *away*—"

"All right, it's all right," Julian said, glancing at Etta.

But the Shadows . . .

What's been chasing me for years . . .

Octavia's chest began to rise and fall, fluttering shallowly. When the old woman turned to him again, it was with a wide-eyed desperation, with wretched, gasping breaths. Julian stood from his stool, and Etta thought for one infuriating second that he was about to bolt for the exit—but he only slipped that same tattered notebook out of the fold of his clothing. He retrieved the stubby pencil secured to the back cover with string. The leather was so soft, the journal fell open on the bed, revealing an unfinished sketch of a street.

He's an artist. Etta had forgotten that, somehow. Or maybe she'd just never been willing to see him as anything other than a coward and a flirt, because it would have been another complication when her entire world had become a series of them. If he had been one of her mother's paintings, one of those at the Met she had worked so hard to restore, peeling back layers of age and patches, Etta wondered how bright his colors might be beneath.

"Do you remember the old house, Nan? The one we lived in just off the park, up on Sixtieth?" he asked her. His right hand held hers, but his left was already sketching on a blank page.

"With the . . . with the . . ."

"The columns and marble and carriage entry," he continued softly. "Our little palace. Remember how I slid down the banister and cracked my head on the ground?"

She nodded. "Blood. Amelia . . . fainting. Butler moaning about . . . the damned vase . . ."

"That's what you remember," he told her. "What I remember is this."

He held up the rough sketch for her to see, but the cover blocked it from Etta's sight. It wasn't meant for her, anyway.

"I remember you scooping me up, holding me, telling me that it would be all right, and that you were there and always would be, to take care of me," Julian whispered.

Octavia touched the page with her finger. "Beautiful . . ."

"That's right. I had a proper, beautiful life, thanks to you." He kissed her bandaged hand. "And now I'll do the same for you."

"Don't do . . . anything . . . foolish. . . ."

"Nan," he said, fighting for his smile. "You can bet on it."

THE WOMAN SLIPPED INTO SLEEP AND ETTA MOVED AWAY, leaving Julian to keep vigil. Her head felt empty of real thought, even as her heart was clogged with everything threatening to burst out of it. What surprised her most, though, was the jealousy, burning just beneath the pity and fear.

He gets to be with her.

Julian would be there for Octavia when she died. Etta didn't think she had much time left at all, but she knew with certainty that Julian would not leave her. It was more than she'd been able to give to Alice.

Henry had stayed with Alice.

And who had stayed with Henry?

Etta lost track of time, walking between the rows of cots, trying not to notice the new openings in the beds. It didn't feel like nearly enough hours before Julian emerged and came straight toward her, shooting through the rows of the dead and dying like a fiery arrow. He took her arm and drew her forward, stopping only long enough to lift a pile of plain gray trousers and white shirts—the same thing the nurses had changed most of the wounded into.

"Here," he said, motioning her toward a screen. "Change here."

Etta slipped behind it, watching his silhouette move against the white fabric, pacing. "What happened . . . ?"

She let her dress fall to the ground and tugged on the soft, oversize clothing.

"Nan's finally at peace," he told her quietly, coming closer. "I was waiting for it . . . for the timeline to shift. To be flung out of here. But it never came. And then I tried to remember—I tried to remember if any change had ever been caused by a guardian dying, or if time just sees them the way Grandfather does: disposable."

"And?"

"And I couldn't. I couldn't. It feels like it should have shifted the whole world. A traveler can do one thing outside of his time and the whole of it can shift. I don't like that—that it makes it seem like she wasn't important." He was talking quickly, almost too quickly for Etta's tired mind to keep up with. "All done?"

Etta stepped out from behind the screen and let him pass her to start changing.

"Julian," she said gently. "Are you all right? Take a minute if you have to. . . ."

"I don't think we have a minute, do you?" he said. "There's an

Ironwood message drop in this year just a ways upstate. The Belladonna will have flooded the drops with invitations to the auction, just to get as many bidders as possible. We can start looking there."

"Who is the Belladonna?" Etta asked.

"She's a collector and an agent of sale for rare artifacts," he said, pulling his new shirt over his head. "There's going to be a buy-in amount in gold we'll need to provide, but the bidding is done by submitting offers of secrets and favors. We just need to get inside, and then we can do whatever it is you think we're supposed to be doing."

"Destroying the astrolabe," Etta said.

Julian leaned out from behind the screen. "Destroying it—what good is that going to accomplish? Shouldn't we use it to try to save these people?"

One of the first things she'd learned about life as a traveler was that you couldn't save the dead, not without consequences. But whatever fate the original timeline had intended for these people, this wasn't it.

"It'll reset everything," she explained. "Bring it back to the original timeline. The one we knew . . . it'll be gone."

Julian turned away from surveying the cots, the weeping men and women by the survivor boards, and glanced back at her over his shoulder. "Then let's go."

VATICAN CITY
1499

TWENTY-FOUR

Nicholas felt himself nod.

Nod as if to say, *Yes, I expected this. I accept this.* Because in truth, some part of him had. This was fate's delight. To give him what he desired, or what he had not known he desired, only to viciously snatch it back again, just when it seemed as if he might seize it.

"What?" he heard Sophia say. *"How?"*

"A notice went out to all of the travelers and guardians," Li Min said, struggling with each word, like her throat threatened to choke on them. She dug into her bag, retrieving a small slip of paper, and passed it to Sophia.

"'Henry Hemlock demands satisfaction from Cyrus Ironwood for the unspeakably cruel murder of his daughter, Henrietta, who has lately passed into eternity from wounds sustained from an attack by his guardians, while she was already weakened'—oh my God. Date and place of death is listed as October 2, 1905, Texas."

Something like bile or fire was rising in his throat. He couldn't speak. Nicholas felt parts of himself begin to close off, as if to deny entry again to that now-familiar pain.

I wasn't fast enough.

I couldn't reach you.

I only wanted to save you.

The cathedral of hope in his heart, which he'd carefully crafted each day since he and Etta had been torn apart, burned down to its foundations of desperation and despair.

Oh God. *Oh God.*

"Carter," Li Min said. "I think perhaps we should continue through the passage, find a place to sit, and take some water, yes?"

He shook his head, straining to get away from her. He began to stalk down the hall again, reaching for doors, tearing them open. It couldn't be right. Her earring was *here.* Hemlock must have been mistaken. He would have felt it, wouldn't he? He would have felt the world crash down upon itself if she'd passed on. The bell of his spirit would have been silenced. "She's—"

She had been dead, nearly the whole time he'd been searching for her.

He had been chasing a ghost. A memory. No.

No.

Sophia stood there watching him, letting the death notice slip from her fingers. Li Min finally caught his arm, and this time she didn't let him shake her off. "I know what it is you think, but consider the possibilities."

"They said she died in Texas, two days after she disappeared, but then—then, how is her earring here?" he demanded.

Li Min's response was as infuriatingly calm as always. "Someone might have taken the earring from her, or traded her for it. Or this earring, this version of it, might be from a past time in her mother's life, before she ever gave them to her daughter. It might have been you, in the future, who returned here."

Her words dripped through him one by one, poisoning that last small hope moving beneath his skin. He did not know Etta's father from Adam, but he knew Li Min now. He trusted Li Min.

His stomach rioted. He raised his hand, pressing his fist against his mouth. Time travel. Bloody impossible, bloody unmerciful, bloody befuddling time travel.

Why had he ever accepted Ironwood's job? Why hadn't he just *listened* to Hall when he'd advised Nicholas to steer as far away from the family as he was able? Why hadn't the sea been enough for him? He never should have allowed himself to be drawn back into this web. It was only ever going to catch him, wrap around his throat until it strangled him.

But it wouldn't have stopped Ironwood.

He still would have stolen Etta out of her time. She would have been sent on the search alone. Nothing, and no one, was ever going to stop Ironwood until he had the astrolabe, and everything he'd ever desired.

"She's not here," he rasped out, trying to grasp the meaning of those words.

Li Min nodded.

"She . . ." Nicholas forced himself to say, ". . . was most likely never here at all."

Sophia looked away. Pride warred with humiliation in him, before both were sunk by a devastation that left him breathless. It stole the years of experience he'd collected in steeling himself to the world, took even that small measure of dignity he'd eked out from his existence. And what was left inside him was that same pain he'd felt as a child, alone in the dark cupboard of the Ironwood house in New York, waiting for some signal of when he was allowed to step outside of it.

"Thank you," he told Li Min. "I apologize . . . I am . . . not myself . . . I do believe . . ."

"Will you find her mother, then, to tell her?" Li Min asked. "This Rose Linden?"

"No. I'm almost certain she already knows," Nicholas said. Perhaps that was, in the end, why she had never come.

"If she'd taken her revenge we'd know by now," Sophia said. "That bit of news would travel quickly in our circle."

A light shone from down the hallway, marking the path of someone coming toward them. Sophia took his limp arm and pulled him toward the door they had stopped outside of. On instinct, he tried to drag his feet, as if another search might turn up a different result. Li Min lifted a candle from the wall and opened the door, then latched it behind them.

Nicholas knew the *Pietà* the moment he saw it, though it caught him off guard to find it in such a small side chapel. The Carrara marble was flawless, glowing like warm moonlight. The Virgin Mary, her face too young to be holding the body of an adult son, was a mysterious contradiction of sweetness and grief.

Love. Sacrifice. Release. An endless, eternal story—no, this traveler war wasn't anything so pure. This was a story of revenge. Of families who'd warred so long that no one could remember who'd instigated the fights in the first place. An Ironwood had killed Lindens, and a Linden had caused the death of Ironwood heirs, and so the Ironwoods claimed the life of the Linden heir. The awful symmetry of it all did not stop with only those two families. There must have been hundreds, thousands of stories like it over the years. It was a cycle that he himself had been caught in.

Staring at the woman's serene stone face, with Sophia and Li Min whispering behind him, Nicholas felt as still and quiet as if he'd become the eye of a hurricane. In the candlelight, it was so very easy to imagine Mrs. Hall's face, warmed by the fireplace as she read to him and Chase from the Bible, as she did every night. *Never take your own revenge, beloved, but leave room for the wrath of God. . . .*

But God had had His chance to pass judgment on the evil that lived in Cyrus Ironwood's heart, and had failed to act. Nicholas, for the first time in his life, questioned His judgment, because it was neither true, nor righteous, nor acceptable.

It's left to me.

"I require a path," he said. "Back to 1776."

Li Min and Sophia ceased their conversation.

"Look, Carter," Sophia began. "I know how you feel—"

"Do you now?" he said coldly. "How would you feel, then, to know that Julian survived his fall and wasn't ever lost to you or any of us?"

He was surprised how easily the words flowed out of him after being held inside for so long. Some part of him recognized how unfeeling it was to drop it on Sophia's head like an anchor, but Nicholas found himself beyond caring. If anything, he felt his hurt should be catching. There was more than enough to be shared by the parties present.

Sophia turned toward him, her lips parting.

"I was mistaken in how I interpreted that moment on the cliff. Rose Linden was the one to correct my misunderstanding. He was orphaned by a timeline shift, and never returned to us. I apologize for not telling you sooner," he said, his bloody guilt getting the better of him, her single dark eye burning with the intensity of its gaze. "Initially, before you told me the truth of your heart, I thought if you knew he might be alive, you'd want to find him and restore your engagement. Find forgiveness with Ironwood. And then it was only a matter of not wanting you to be distracted."

That earned him a hard fist to the cheek, blowing him sideways.

"What I always *wanted* was respect!" she growled out. "Shame on me for thinking I might have found some of that in your regard. Shame on me for ever being so *stupid*."

"You're not—"

"I nearly got myself killed helping you—not because I owe it to you, but because I want to find the men who attacked me. I want to take from them what they took from me, and even our score. I want Grandfather's rule to crumble, I want to watch it pulverized to dust, and see everything he loves ripped away from him," Sophia seethed. "Why would I ever search out someone who abandoned me? Someone who had no regard for *any* of us, who ran because he's too much of a damn coward to stand up to his family!"

353

"I know that now," he said. "I'm sorry. But it felt like too much of a risk—I—"

"Needed to use me?" Sophia said. "To go after *your* person, to achieve your ends? My *desire* was to be heir, which might have gotten me treated like a whole person, not fodder for marriage. Julian was my friend. I cared—*care*—about him. But I decided in that desert, before you ever found me, that what I really wanted was the freedom to do as I pleased, with whomever I pleased. I wanted to move as freely as the wind, and not be called back into port against my will. *That* is power. Do you understand?"

He nodded, his throat tight. "Beyond measure."

Their conversation had drawn the attention of someone outside the chapel. There was a pounding on the door, a muffled voice that called out a question. Li Min whirled back toward Nicholas.

"If you mean to complete the Belladonna's task," she said, "then I will be your guide."

"No." It was a terrible thing, and he wanted them far from it. "I need to see this through myself."

She shook her head. "You will need someone to dig your grave, for even if you finish with the old man, the journey to that moment will end you."

Sophia let out a harsh breath, crossing her arms.

"This is my path now," he told her, using his left hand to lift his right, to show her the ring. "I am dead regardless. If I don't kill him, the poison will take me; if I'm not quick enough arriving there, the poison will take me. If I succeed, at least there will be one fewer evil in the world."

At least this way, I might yet live long enough to return to Hall and die at sea.

The pounding on the door grew louder, as if someone was throwing their weight against it.

"You're not leaving us behind to sweep up your mess after you,"

Sophia snarled, pulling him toward the shivering air of the passage. "You'd just better pray I don't kill you first myself."

THEY PASSED THROUGH A SERIES OF PASSAGES COBBLED together from their combined memories, leading, at various points, to a rather treacherous section of the Australian outback, a pristine glacier, and the most dire year of the Middle Ages that Austria had to offer, with countless small insignificant connections between each. When they encountered anyone, he and Li Min shrouded themselves, letting Sophia speak in the rare instances speaking was necessary.

Nicholas wondered several times over the course of this journey if a man could feel so hollow as to become invisible, or if people only saw what they expected to see—which, in the case of their situation, was not a Chinese woman or a black man. In any case, the silence suited him well enough. It was easier to keep his mind still and focused on the days ticking down.

On the night of the sixteenth, a few miles from the last passage on the outskirts of Mexico City, Nicholas began to sense Li Min and Sophia slowing, eating away at his own pace. Out of the corner of his eye, he saw the young women exchange a look; not wanting to confront it, he dug his heels into his horse's side to urge it forward. Before the mare could work herself back up to a gallop, a small hand lashed out and ripped the reins from his hands.

"What the *devil*—?"

"You will do what you have now attempted three times—you will ride that animal until it collapses and dies beneath you," Li Min told him sternly, pulling the reins further out of his reach. "I do not intend to share my horse. Do you, Sophia?"

"Certainly not."

"I have not—" he began.

"We haven't slept in two days, Carter," Sophia interrupted.

Surely not. "We stopped a night ago."

355

"*No.* That was Austria. That scenic little spot you picked by the rancid moat. I'm sure one of us picked up the Black Death as a parting gift."

Christ. She was right.

"Let's move off the road. Camp for a few hours," Li Min suggested.

Revolt surged inside of him, and must have been clear from his expression, because Sophia turned her horse and led them off the worn road and onto the lush, green earth. Somehow, Nicholas had always pictured this part of the world as entirely desert. But even this late in the year, there was life and vegetation sweeping up from their valley to the peaks of the mountains around them.

He counted the paces under his breath, from the road to where Sophia decided was far enough to drop her saddlebags, and decided it was two hundred paces too far.

He could go ahead. Let them rest and catch up to him later.

Before he could devise a course of action, Li Min led his horse forward toward the others and began to unhook its harness.

He breathed sharply out of his nose, but finally dismounted. "I'll hunt."

Shooting something sounded marvelous, now that he had gunpowder again. He could not shoot with his right arm, useless as it was, but he wasn't a terrible shot with his left.

"Li Min is already going," Sophia said, from where she was laying out the bedding. He turned, then turned again, surprised to find Li Min's small form retreating into the distance. "You can find the firewood and kindling."

"All right. But I'll cook."

Sophia made a face he didn't understand.

"And water?"

"We're fine for now," she said, tossing away the wide-brimmed hat she'd found abandoned on the road. "*Go.* Before your expression finally does *me* in. For someone out for cold-blooded revenge, you've got the look of a sad, sorry bastard about you."

356

Somehow, he didn't doubt it. Nicholas gave her an ironic little bow before setting about the task in front of him. Li Min had not returned by the time they had started the fire and brought the little pot they'd acquired to boil. Rather than try to talk to a stone-faced Sophia, Nicholas slid his right arm from the sling Li Min had knotted for him and lay down with his back to the fire.

His eyes felt too gritty to shut, but he tried. He tried relaxing his body against the unyielding dirt, and he tried to clear the swirl of dark thoughts rising up inside of him before they pulled him under. One hand dipped inside his loose tunic and closed around the string of leather. When he felt brave enough, he opened his eyes to study the bead in the image of a man and Etta's earring.

He was seized by a compulsion he didn't understand. He yanked hard on the cord, trying to rip it off by force, then reached back to fumble with the knot.

"By doing that, you'll only feed the fire of regret that burns in you," Li Min said from nearby, having returned from her hunt. "Not extinguish it."

His hand relaxed, but didn't fall away. Nicholas shoved himself up off the ground, intent on cooking now that she had returned.

"This reminds me of a tale," Li Min said casually, before he could fully stand. She sat between him and the fire, casting a long shadow over him. "Would you care to hear it?"

Not precisely, but he grunted, knowing she would tell it regardless.

"It goes as follows. Many, many years ago, Emperor Yan had a daughter, Nüwa. She was as lovely and elegant as a crane, but stubborn as an ox. More than anything, she loved to swim, and often chose the East Sea for its wild beauty. I think you understand the impulse, no?"

He only seemed to be capable of grunting. His chest was too tight to manage actual words.

"But tragedy struck. One day while swimming, she drowned. Her will, however, was strong, and she would not give in, not completely.

She broke the surface of the water and transformed into a Jingwei bird—have you seen one? They are quite striking. A gray beak, red claws? Well, regardless, she sought out her vengeance for drowning. Every day she flew to gather stones and sticks from the Western Mountains and dropped them into the East Sea. Her desire was to fill it, to prevent others from drowning. She never rested in her task. She continues to this day."

He turned over fully, when it was clear her story was at an end. "Then it was an impossible task. What meaning am I supposed to derive from this?"

Li Min shrugged. "You may make anything of it you wish, Carter. The purpose of that tale was to distract you long enough for dinner to be served, and that has not been an impossible task after all."

Nicholas sat up straight, outrage burning through the gray haze around his mind. "I told you I would do it!" What good was he if he couldn't contribute his share of work?

"This may come as a surprise to you, but I don't actually prefer my meat shriveled and charred so far beyond recognition I mistake it for old firewood," Sophia told him, turning the skinned rabbits over on the spit.

"That's how you know it's cooked!"

Both women gave him their variations of a pitying look. His stomach rumbling, he took his share of the meat with a reluctance that could only come from pride. When he finished, he accepted Li Min's suggestion that he rest first, and take the later watch. On his bedding once more, he turned his back to the fire, resting his head on his arm and staring out at the dark mountains. He drifted to sleep, ignoring the warm grip of the gold band around his small finger.

A *clang* cut through the darkness, followed quickly by another.

"—better, better, but do not lean in so much as you thrust—no! To your left! Yes!"

Nicholas fumbled his way back to awareness, unsure whether he was hearing Li Min's voice or dreaming it. Turning onto his back, he looked toward the fire, watching as two slight, shadowy figures sparred with swords.

"It's *useless*," Sophia said. "I'll never get it right, not really."

"You've done it perfectly, as well as you have everything else I've shown you tonight," Li Min said, a smile in her voice. "You move through the world like a cat, all silk and sinew. Soon you'll be better than me, and then I'll really need to watch my gold."

"No chance of that," Sophia said after a moment. Frustration edged into the words.

"You are a superb fighter," Li Min said, settling on the ground and resting her sword across her legs.

After a moment, Sophia lowered herself to her knees, placing her weapon down on a nearby blanket. "It's just . . . I used to be better, before this."

She gestured absently to her eye patch.

"Ah," Li Min said.

"The world looks different," Sophia said. "At first I thought it was only my imagination, self-pity, what have you. But the truth is, the shadows and highlights have peeled back. Colors seem flat. And my perception of how near or far something is from me is occasionally a little off. But the biggest problem is the blind spot."

He closed his eyes, sighing. He'd expected as much, and felt rightly worse for not trying to help her overcome it in any way he could. Whether or not she would have accepted his help was debatable, but he should have *tried*, dammit.

"Stand up, I'll show you something," Li Min said. There was a shuffle of fabric and feet in the dirt as Sophia did. "Assume your usual stance."

When Sophia slid her left leg back, angling her right half forward, Li Min clucked her tongue and reversed it, her fingers gliding along

Sophia's skin, clasping, just for a moment, around her small wrist. "Fighting is all angles, yes? Altering your stance so your good eye is set back might help; however, I think you'd feel most comfortable switching back and forth quickly, like this—"

Li Min danced from side to side, quick and light on her feet as she circled Sophia, constantly adjusting her stance so her left eye, which she had shut to demonstrate this to Sophia, was never in front for long.

"It looks like you're dancing," Sophia said, voicing Nicholas's own awe. After a moment, she attempted to replicate the movement. Her face fell at her initial clumsiness, but soon she seemed to match Li Min step for step. And she was *smiling*.

"It feels a little ridiculous," Sophia admitted, as they returned to the blanket and relinquished her blade again.

"You've not had time to become used to it," Li Min said, placing a soft hand on Sophia's wrist. "It will get better with time. You should know that there are countless stories of warriors who've borne a similar injury and overcome it. One general from my land was said to have been shot in the eye with an arrow. Rather than crumble, he pulled the arrow out, and ate the eye off it."

"That's disgusting, even for me," Sophia said, laughing. "And you know it's far more likely he did crumble and scream like a child. But who can blame him?"

"There is no doubt in my mind about that," Li Min said, and for a while, they seemed content to play a game of trying to avoid the other catching their gaze. The slow drift of fingers across the blanket, easing closer and closer with each soft breath.

He was about to close his eyes and turn again to give them privacy when Li Min said, "There is still such a shadow on your face. What is troubling you?"

Rather than pull away, Sophia slid her hand lightly up along the other girl's arm, drawing her loose sleeve up to touch her pale skin.

360

She leaned forward, so close that, for a moment, Nicholas was sure she might rest her forehead against Li Min's shoulder. "Did you mean what you said, about seeking revenge? That there's no way to survive it?"

A deep sigh. "After I escaped the Shadows, I wanted nothing more than to grow strong enough to return and butcher them, as they had done my mother and my sister. It was enough to sustain me for years. I fed on the anger, bathed in fury, prayed with malice. But one morning, a woman on my ship asked me what I would make of my life after I had taken my revenge for their lives. I had not pictured anything beyond it. To me, it was a destination, and I had let it become a final chapter in my story. That realization made me decide the best revenge of all was to not willingly squander my gift of survival, but to live with the strength I had fought for and won."

"But—" Sophia began, struggling to master her voice. "How do you live with it—the anger? The shame?"

Shame. Nicholas felt something rise and lodge in his throat.

Li Min's hand stilled from where she had raised it, hovering just above Sophia's tangled dark hair.

"No matter how hard I try," Sophia continued, "I can't forget it. It never leaves me. Its hands are hot around my neck."

"Because one moment in life does not define a person," Li Min said. "Without mistakes and misjudgments we would stagnate. It is no shameful thing to be beaten when outnumbered, not when you were brave enough to try. Nor is a scar or injury something to despair over, for it is a mark that you were strong enough to survive."

"But it's beyond me. The mistake didn't end with me." Sophia turned her head in Nicholas's direction, as if trying to see whether he was still asleep. "I feel . . . we were in no way friends, but I feel sore about Linden. Responsible for what happened to her. His sad bastard face isn't helping matters, either."

"That's understandable," Li Min said, an odd quality to her voice.

Her free hand cupped around Sophia's, turning her palm up to rest in her own. She did not speak again until Sophia looked up and met her gaze. "But she had made her own decisions that brought her to that point."

Had she? As far as Nicholas saw, Etta had never had a true choice from the moment Sophia Ironwood had entered her life.

"I mostly just worry about what will happen to *him*," Sophia said. "Before, I wouldn't have believed him capable of taking his vengeance out on Ironwood. Now I'm not so sure."

Him.

Me.

Nicholas shifted on the ground, wishing he could use his right arm to brace himself.

Li Min nodded. "Earlier, I wanted to give him comfort, tell him that after the first death, there is no other. She has returned to the cradle of her ancestors, who shield her and protect her. But you can only say such things to people willing to hear them. He's not there yet."

It was like a hot blade sliding between his ribs. Nicholas pressed the back of his hand against his mouth.

"But what matters is what *he* believes, and he seems to be suffering not only a loss, but a questioning of faith and his path forward as well."

"That seems to be going around these days," Sophia said.

"It occurs to me that, while losing your eye has partially hindered your sight, the experience has allowed you to see through the lies you were raised to believe. You may go anywhere you like, so long as you take care, and you may be whoever you set your heart to be. There is true power in that, as you said to Carter before. Some of us are not so lucky—please do not take this for granted."

"I won't." Sophia shifted, turning so she could brace a hand against the ground, trapping Li Min's legs between her arm and the rest of Sophia's body. She leaned forward, studying Li Min's face as closely as Li Min examined her own. When she spoke again, the words were in that secret language between them, husky and low. The fire popped, devouring itself, and the small sound was enough of a distraction for Li Min to tear her gaze away, turning her head toward the distant city.

"You have been a good . . . *friend*," Sophia said, softly. "Thank you."

Li Min shook her head, rising out of the other young woman's grasp. "I am not your friend, *nǚ shén*, nor will I ever be in the way I want. I cannot be anything but what I am. Take care with your heart."

"You don't have to be alone, you know," Sophia said. "You don't have to keep making that choice. You talk about wearing the past with honor, but yours hounds you. You let it. You cannot let yourself accept that people would believe you. Help you."

"You know nothing," Li Min said, without a hint of anger. It was only frustration that wound itself through her words, an unmistakable ache.

It was a few moments later, as Li Min's steps came toward him, that they both heard Sophia say, "And you should know, I wouldn't go anywhere the two of you couldn't follow."

NEW YORK CITY
1776

TWENTY-FIVE

THEY WATCHED THE WEALTHIEST OF THE CITY'S REMAINING gentlemen strutting like peacocks, and the ladies in all of their silk and pearls stepping off carriages and washing up the steps of the brick house before them, as if carried on a wave of high spirits and laughter.

Perched two roofs over, embracing the darkness of a new moon, Nicholas leaned forward as much as he dared, counting the latest batch of officers coming up the street. He might have thought them on patrol with the other regulars he'd seen, save for the inordinate number of decorations they'd lavished on themselves. It was a time of war, but the city had been occupied for months with little trouble, and the high polish of their boots, as if hardly used, seemed to prove that point. Their ceremonial swords caught the glow emanating from the three stories of windows. As the door opened for the guests, time and time again, it gave the effect of the sun rising over the streets.

"I can't believe the bastard is throwing a *ball*," Sophia snarled.

"He has to keep up appearances in this era, if only to maintain his timeline," Nicholas said. The hollow mouth at the center of his chest widened. It devoured the black mood in which he'd arrived in his natural era, devoured his anger, his pain, and now his heart. There was a freedom in this, too, in relinquishing decorum and manners, and giving himself over to the chill spreading through his veins.

The people on the streets below were going about their merry little evening, untethered by worry or fear. Those who weren't entering the frivolities were making their way down the street, to one of the theaters putting on a production that evening.

I never took her to a play.

One more thought to feed the hollowness. He could not bear to think of her now, not on the cusp of doing something so vicious. Etta believed so doggedly in the good in him—that he was honorable, a man of merit and esteem. What would she see now, looking down at him? He was unrecognizable even to himself.

Li Min had been still for so long, wrapped in that impenetrably dark cloak of hers, that Nicholas might have forgotten she was there at all if she hadn't turned to look at him. He was beginning to suspect—and accept—that she was the sort who could measure, swallow, and digest a man and his mettle with a single look. Rather than feeling frustrated or startled by her merciless insight, he was almost relieved by not having to explain himself or attempt to put a name to the storm raging inside of him.

"Do not fight it," she told him. "It will help you. Anger is simple. Anger will move you, if you find yourself faltering. If you cannot avoid the darkness, you must force yourself through it."

Li Min held out something in front of him—a dagger, made of what looked like ivory. He took it from her gingerly, examining the dragon's head carved into its hilt. The curved blade smiled in his palm.

"I'm a better shot," he told her, trying to give it back.

"You can't use a flintlock," she said, pushing it back toward him. "Even with the music, someone is bound to hear."

Fair point. He accepted the dagger again, testing its weight and the feel of the hilt in his hand. The knife he'd been carrying was dull by most weapons' standards, and while it had accomplished what he'd demanded of it, a sharpened, well-made blade would make a better tool for . . .

Assassination. Nicholas rolled his shoulders back.

"Know a little something about this, do you?" he asked.

"After I escaped the darkness, before I was able to secure many types of jobs," Li Min told him, "I had just one."

He looked at her again, but her expression was blank.

"He is not a man, Carter, but a beast," she said. "Do not waste your time on his heart. Slit his throat before he can say a word."

It wasn't Nicholas's first time killing a man—the abhorrent pride in him wanted to inform of her of that. It was, however, his first time killing a man when not in defense of his own life, and that was a difficult thing to reconcile with his soul. Each second that passed seemed to grind him down to his raw, fraught essence. Now and then, he felt bewildered by the notion that he was here again, that it had come to this. This journey had begun here, in this very city, with a choice.

With a young woman.

He tucked the dagger into his belt, reaching up to touch the pendant and Etta's earring beneath his shirt. *Let the ends justify the means.*

"Thank you," he told Li Min. She had been a stranger mere days before. Now she was attempting to comfort him, when what he needed most was a voice of reason beyond the berating one in his mind. He would never forget it.

"That's the minuet," Sophia whispered, crawling back over the slight slant in the roof. "Do you want to wait until they're a few more dances in?"

Ironwood's balls always began with a minuet, during which he danced with a lady of his choosing. The focus of all of the attendees would be on the dancers congregated on the first floor of the old house, gliding around the card tables, trays of food, and hothouse flowers.

Even Ironwood's bevy of guards might be distracted long enough for Nicholas to make his entrance on the third floor.

He shook his head. The time was now, or he'd never muster the strength.

THE HOMES ALONG QUEEN STREET—SPARED BY THE FIRE TO the west of Broad Way—were tall, proud creatures that might have been transplanted from the streets of London's gentry. The old Ironwood house, by virtue of the man's ego, was a rose among daisies, his own palace from which to rule an empire of centuries. Its endless series of windows, and the natural attention it drew, of course, made it damned hard to creep up on if one made one's approach from the street.

Rope, tied to the chimney of the neighboring house, tossed with a hastily procured grappling hook onto Ironwood's roof, made the task easier—but only just. Without the use of his right hand, Nicholas had to hook his right arm and both legs over the rope, and inch forward with an agonizing, awkward slowness. Sophia followed at a determined pace, and he found his expectations disappointed when Li Min didn't walk across the rope like a cat, but deigned to cross it like a mere mortal.

The rope was cut free, a section falling slack against the neighboring house. The remaining length was tied to Ironwood's chimney. Li Min used it to walk down the back of the house and then along its walls, passing between the windows with practiced ease. Suddenly, Nicholas had no problem seeing her at home on a pirate ship.

She disappeared from their sight, but he heard her negotiating a window below them.

"Rather handy, isn't she?" Sophia said with clear appreciation, leaning over the edge of the roof to watch her at work. Nicholas gripped the back of her dark jacket to keep her from tumbling off the ledge.

A tug on the rope told him it was safe to descend, but Sophia, who was to keep watch, stopped him. She seemed to be struggling to speak; her mouth twisted as though she'd tasted something bitter.

"You'll be all right . . . won't you?" she asked after a long moment.

"I'll be quick, at least," he said.

"Seems unfair," she said as he began to edge down, gripping the rough rope. "He deserves a worse end than you'll be able to give him."

"If something happens—"

Sophia gripped him by the collar of his shirt. "Nothing is going to *happen*."

Nicholas nodded. "Understood, ma'am."

Sophia used the rope to ease him down just enough for Nicholas to swing his legs forward through the open window. Li Min reached out, pulling him the rest of the way through the frame.

His memory of the house's layout had served him well, after all. Li Min took a candle from the wall of the servants' staircase, leaning around the landing to ensure no one was coming. Though they were inside the house now, the staircase was so insulated, set so far apart from the house's grandeur, that even the lively music seemed muted.

It was remarkable, he thought, how swiftly memory could cut a man. It was the air, the way it seemed to sour in his lungs, the familiar creaks of the floor, that upset his stomach. This was a house in which all things were eventually extinguished, even hope. Whatever composure he'd summoned took a lashing as he stood there; for a moment, he was too tense to think about moving, too afraid that he might see his mother's ghost walking up the stairs toward him.

Nicholas felt Li Min's eyes on his face, trying to take the measure of his response. He didn't turn toward her. The bile in the back of his throat stung and burned, but he swallowed it, ashamed that standing within this house's walls was enough for his past to begin nipping and tearing at his resolve.

He had thought he'd known hatred, but he had not realized it lived in this place like a fine coat of dust. The familiarity of it was devastating; in all the many ways he had changed, the house hadn't. Even now, the shadows seemed to grasp at him, pulling at his skin, as if to remind him, *You belong to me. You will always belong to me.*

It would always claim a piece of him he would never have back.

I need to leave this place. Finish what he had come to do, and leave.

"Signal if you need assistance," Li Min said. "If his death causes any of us to be orphaned, find your way back to Nassau in this year. We will regroup."

He nodded, sliding the dagger she'd given him out of his belt. He couldn't think of the consequences of this just yet. The passage they'd come through, to the north of the city, would likely collapse—but what else might? For decades, time had revolved around Ironwood himself, and there was no way to predict what might happen once the center of that control collapsed.

He began to climb the stairs. They were shorter than he remembered, but spoke to him each time he put his weight on them, reminding him why he was there, what he needed to do. For the first time, he was glad he had a blade instead of a flintlock. Perhaps he'd give the old man a cut for every year he'd stolen from her life.

Etta.

Ironwood never liked to see his servants and slaves unless they were performing a specific task in a particular room. Each floor had a narrow servants' hallway built into it, connecting to the hidden staircase, and each bedroom of this floor had a door disguised as part of the wall.

Nicholas was careful, achingly careful, and waited at the top of the stairs for any sign of a servant. But the entire house was occupied with seeing to the needs of the men and women below; he would need to enter the old man's bedchambers and wait. If time had been an ally and not an enemy, he might have waited until the man was asleep and do it then, but the wasted hours would only provide more opportunity for his own body to fail him. Even now, he felt as if his head were stuffed with feathers; his vision was blurring at the corners. It had to be now. Once the task was completed, Sophia would drop a rope down from the roof for him to escape by.

It was simple, but even simple plans were prone to unexpected disasters.

Nicholas navigated forward, ignoring the squeaks and rough brushes of the mice scampering past his ankles. From the other side of the wall, he heard two men—guards—muttering to each other about the amount of food they'd eaten, and knew the next door would be the one he was looking for.

After a moment to ensure he couldn't hear anyone inside, he put his hand on the latch. Lifted it. The door swung open, surprisingly silent, given its weight. Nicholas took a steadying breath. His eyes were drawn to the crackling fire at the far end of the room, hidden by a large red velvet chair.

This room, too, had been resurrected to its previous life, when Ironwood had first owned it. Nicholas remembered the patterned rug, smugly imported from across the world. The forbidden leather-bound volumes that lined a small bookshelf had tormented him with their unknowable words. Even the bed seemed to have been carved out of his memory, with its plain white linens and tall posts strung with toile curtains.

He shut the door softly, still gripping the dagger in his hand as he moved across the room. The rhythmic pounding of feet and clapping from the dancers below broke up the silence, their voices dulled to a low rumble as they passed up through the cracks in the floors.

It seemed to him that the best, and possibly only, place to hide was behind the screen in the corner. Even the bed was too low to the ground to slip beneath and wait. Nicholas crossed the room, softening his steps, but was caught by the sudden, sweet smell of tobacco.

He stilled.

Nicholas had initially dismissed the smoke as escaping from the fireplace; as he stepped past the chair, he saw how deeply mistaken he was.

Ironwood's fine dress coat lay over his lap like a blanket, despite the old man's position directly in front of the fire. Under Nicholas's gaze, his grandfather relinquished the powdered wig he'd been toying with to the carpet, where it kicked up a small white cloud.

The man kept his attention on the small book in his lap, his hooded eyelids masking his expression. The way the firelight brightened his round face gave him unmerited warmth, and almost masked the way his cheeks seemed to hang like jowls. One of his fingers rubbed at the notched tip of his chin.

"'—But there's a tree, of many, one, / A single field which I have look'd upon, / Both of them speak of something that is gone,'" the old man read. "'The pansy at my feet / Doth the same tale repeat: / Whither is fled the visionary gleam? / Where is it now, the glory and the dream?'"

Nicholas remained as still as stonework, as if he'd been run through the heart with a blade. His every last thought fled.

"Wordsworth," he explained, setting the small volume aside. "I find I don't have the patience for merrymaking these days, but there is comfort in reading."

He rose to his feet and laid his coat over the chair. Nicholas took an instinctive step back, both at the suddenness of the movement and the weary tone of Ironwood's voice. The old man brushed past Nicholas as if he weren't holding a dagger in his hand, and moved toward the corner of the room where he kept his whiskey.

Move, Nicholas ordered himself as the man poured two glasses. *Move, damn you!*

Without a word, Ironwood offered one glass to Nicholas, and, when he didn't take it, drank it down himself in one swift gulp.

"How does this house speak to you, I wonder?"

That jostled Nicholas out of his stunned silence. It was impossible for the old man to know his thoughts—he recognized this—but the other implication seemed worse; their minds followed similar tracks. Their hearts spoke the same language.

"It speaks to me of regret," Ironwood said, pressing the rim of his glass to his temple. And this was the precise moment Nicholas began to feel the hair prickle on the back of his neck; for Cyrus Ironwood was a great many things, but none of them were maudlin or sentimental.

Drunk? Nicholas wondered, fingers tightening around the hilt of the dagger. He'd seen the man drink three bottles of wine himself and remain sober enough to take business meetings. In fact, Nicholas had always assumed it was a carefully cultivated skill, this tolerance for alcohol, meant to disarm rivals and potential business partners who hadn't a prayer of keeping up.

Every aim, every word, every action from this man was meant to disarm his opponent. This false sentimentality was surely the weapon he'd picked to rattle Nicholas, and, all at once, he was furious with himself for falling for it.

"I wasn't aware," he heard himself say, "that you were acquainted with a feeling like *regret*."

"Ah," Ironwood said, saluting him with his glass. "And yet, I've regrets enough to paper the walls of this house."

He finally looked at Nicholas, studying him in the room's relative darkness. "From the moment you entered, I wondered why—I have always known there would be a *when*, but the *why* of it, that was the mystery. Because of your status when you lived in this house? Because your mother received Augustus's unwanted attentions and was sold away? Because you felt slighted by the family? Because you broke our contract, and knew that this was the only way out of it? Or is it, Samuel, simply for the satisfaction?"

Nicholas knew by the gleam in the man's eye, by the use of his birth name, that he'd laid out all of these strikes the way a chef would lay out his knives, debating which one was best to use to make a cut.

"Or . . . is it because you've come to take revenge for *her*?"

Nicholas swung the dagger around, tracking the man's movements. Rather than go toward the chest of drawers or his bedside table, he went toward the trunk at the foot of his bed.

"*No,*" Nicholas said, knowing full well that he could be hiding a flintlock or rifle in it. "Take a step back."

"Of course," the man said, with mocking graciousness. "If you'll retrieve the package inside. I have, after all, been keeping it for you."

Nicholas recognized this bait for what it was, but he was disarmed by the man's demeanor. Ironwood was never more truthful than when he was trying to inflict a mortal wound on another person's heart.

Keeping his eye on Ironwood, keeping his dagger out, Nicholas bent to retrieve a flat parcel, wrapped in parchment and tied with string. It looked as if it had come a great distance, whether that was miles or years.

"Go on, open it," Ironwood said, clasping his hands behind his back.

And, God help him, Nicholas did. He tore into the paper with one hand. Even before he saw the fabric—the sheer *gömlek*, the emerald *chirka*—he smelled jasmine; he smelled the soap-sweet scent of her skin.

And he smelled blood.

The feeling in his hands was gone. His pulse began to pound at his temples. So much blood, the fabric was stiff with it. It flaked off as he ran his fingers across the delicate embroidery, moving along the seams of the jacket until they snagged at the ragged hole at the shoulder, where she'd been shot.

"A guardian sent these to me weeks ago," Ironwood said. "As proof of Etta Spencer's death. Her father claimed her body, but I thought you might want the reminder of her personal effects."

This is what remains. . . .

Memory would fade from him, her footprints would be washed away—this was all he was to have of Etta Spencer now.

"You did this. . . ." He breathed out, his gaze snapping up. "*You—*"

"Yes," Ironwood said, his face drawn, as if—as if he *cared*. As if he felt *sorry* for this. Nicholas's fury overwhelmed him, and he slashed out with the dagger, catching the man across the chest. Ironwood leaned back in time to avoid being gutted, but a gash of red extending from his shoulder to his hip began to ooze. Nicholas felt frantic, sloppy, like he was damn near to clawing his own face off to try to release the boiling anger and grief. He did not want to collapse onto his knees. He did not want to scream himself hoarse.

"All because you want one blasted thing, when you already have *everything*! You aren't satisfied with the destruction you wrought; you need the tool that will make it complete," Nicholas seethed, knowing full well that the man's guards would be coming in, that they'd kill him where he stood. And yet, Ironwood didn't move, didn't taunt, didn't defend himself.

Kill him—just finish him! his mind was bellowing, but he couldn't move from that spot.

"What you feel now," Ironwood said, "I have felt every day of my life, for forty years."

"Don't say another word," Nicholas said. "You know *nothing* of me or what I feel. *Nothing.*"

"Don't I?" Ironwood said carefully, glancing over at the portrait by his bedside. Minerva. His first wife. "I can see how badly you wish to stick that dagger in my heart, and I cannot blame you."

"You don't have a heart," Nicholas snarled. "If you did, you never would have dragged Etta into any of this. She wouldn't be—"

He couldn't bring himself to finish, coward that he was.

"And if Rose Linden hadn't betrayed us and hidden the astrolabe, if her parents hadn't fought as hard as the rest of us to control the timeline, if our ancestors had never used the astrolabes to begin with—do you see how futile this line of reasoning is, Nicholas? We can live in the past, but we cannot dwell there," Ironwood said. "What you cannot seem to grasp is that the astrolabe isn't a tool of *destruction*, it is one of *healing*. It can right wrongs. Save lives."

Save her.

He had not even considered that. How was it possible he had never once considered that by waiting out a year, he might travel back to the

377

spot where she was to die, and save her, before the Ironwood men had a chance to reach her? That he could find a way to prevent Etta from being taken?

"You would risk," Nicholas began, "orphaning countless travelers, shifting the timeline, for your own selfishness."

"For love," Ironwood corrected. "For *her*."

There was nothing ironic in his tone, or even condescending. Nicholas shook his head in disbelief, his chest bursting at its seams with dark, humorless laughter. As if this man had any inkling of what that word entailed, the scale of it.

But he hated the softer part of him, the one that whispered, over and over, *Forty years. Forty years. Forty years.*

Forty years of *this* feeling. This unbearable tightness, of being caught in a cage of helpless rage and grief.

Because some part of Nicholas was listening. Some part of him heard the truth in the old man's words, and was reaching, grasping for the solution presented to him. Nicholas had the oddest feeling that he was back on his deathbed, a fever wracking his brain. There was a haze about the man, an unreal quality.

"You seem to believe that I am blind to my own faults," Ironwood said. "But I *improved* the world. I did my part to fix it, after years of fighting between the families. I brought us stability and order, and brought the worst of the travelers to heel. As long as the astrolabe is in play, we will never have peace."

"Is that why you let your sons die?" Nicholas asked sardonically.

The man rasped a hand over his chin, his shoulders sagging. "I have been asked to sacrifice so much, and I have come so far, and still . . . still we die out, like an inferior species. I wonder from time to time what my life would have been like, had I not been tasked with this role. I think I might have been a merchant, a sailor. You've felt it, too, haven't you? How vast the world is, when you cannot see anything but water on the horizon?"

"Stop it," Nicholas said. "I know what it is you're doing—"

"The moment I knew you had that inclination, that you were a natural . . . I recognized myself in you," Ironwood said. "My father. *His* father. All forged in the same fire. And when you fought so hard to leave our family's service, I knew for certain; for a true Ironwood cannot bear stagnation, or to be held against his will. You made your brother seem like nothing more than a yearling. He never had the grit he needed to manage the family—that grit which has kept me searching for the astrolabe all these long years. That which brought you here tonight."

Nicholas startled at the word *brother.* As long as he had known the man, he had never heard him use that phrase, without qualifications.

"I am nothing like you," Nicholas said. The old man rose to his full height, looking him in the eye.

"You have not yet lived a full life," he said. "You have not accumulated the triumphs and the sorrows. When you are my age, you will look back and see a stranger, and then all you will have to your name will be your convictions."

He believes he has done right by us all, Nicholas realized. There was nothing false or scheming about his words. He had spent years as a child cowering in the servants' hall and shrinking back at the sight of the man as he strode through the house. Like a soldier, his swinging fists always seemed to enter the room first.

In his youth, when he traveled with Julian, he had seen a calculating emperor who demanded tribute from his followers and tribulation from his enemies. And now he saw . . . an inverse of himself. A warning of what might come from rationalizing the lapse of his own morals, compromising his deepest values with the false promises of *just this once* and *never again.*

"You are my true heir," Ironwood said. "You alone. I was a fool for squandering your potential for so many years. We can begin again. I am not as young as I once was, and there are so many now who would betray me. I need your assistance in certain tasks, as a guard, as my eyes in places I cannot be."

I cannot kill him. Sophia and Li Min were right, but their reasoning was flawed. To give over to the baser instincts of revenge would hand the old man a victory; it would undo Nicholas utterly, splinter him more and more with each year. He could not damn himself with this. There was nothing so important as being free from this man, his poisonous words and bloody legacy. If that meant his own death, then at least he might escape this man's pull that way, and deny him an heir.

His grip on the dagger tightened, until he felt the dragon on its hilt imprinting its shape into his skin, lending its ferocity.

"You say these things like you know where to find the astrolabe," Nicholas said.

"I do. It's found its way into the Witch of Prague's hands," the old man said. "I received the invite to the Belladonna's auction only yesterday. We only need to bid now and it's ours—I have far more secrets to tempt her than anyone else who may come."

The words swept over Nicholas's skin like fire, blistering through the layers of muscle and bone. The Witch of Prague, indeed. What a fool he'd been. If he'd known at the beginning of their appointment that she was the original bad penny, he would have parsed her words more carefully. *In the last report I received, yes, a Thorn was still in possession of the astrolabe. . . .*

So precisely phrased. If he hadn't been blinded by his own desperation he might have been able to dissect what she didn't say. *In the last report.* Not *presently.*

The woman was a fearsome creature, choosing and evaluating her words with the mind a jeweler would pay to buying precious stones. Loathsome, of course, but there was no denying her cunning; if it hadn't been for the fact that she'd poisoned him, he might even respect her for it, just that small bit. No wonder she had survived Ironwood's rule. She was that rare, dark thing that thrived by tricking the light into passing over it, that fed only on shadows and deceit.

"You need time to think on this, I know," Ironwood said. "But we haven't any. You—I must tell you something, and it cannot be shared outside of this room. I will not have panic in our ranks, and I know logic prevails for you as it does for me."

Our. Our ranks. Of course, to Ironwood, Nicholas's acceptance was a given.

"I've had a great rival for the astrolabe these many years—"

"The Thorns," Nicholas said, interrupting him.

"No," the old man said. "He who has no name, but has lived generations. I believe him to be one of the original time travelers, for there has never been record of him apart from legend. He has found the other copies of the astrolabe, drained them of their power. He cannot have this one, too."

Nicholas, again, listened to the tale of the alchemist and his children, forcing his face to remain as stone. On his hand, the ring burned.

"Why does this . . . Ancient One seek it?" Nicholas asked at the end. "And why should it matter beyond your personal gain that he take it?"

Ironwood lowered himself onto his bed, staring into the fire. "There is an incantation, a spell of sorts, I'm sure of it, that bleeds the power of the astrolabes and feeds him, extending his life beyond its natural years. But it must destroy the astrolabe itself, leave it as an empty shell. And that cannot happen."

"Why is that?" This was in line with what Remus Jacaranda had explained to them, but there was a thread of worry in the old man's voice now that made him wonder if there was something more to this. Something worse.

"Because, if the legends passed down within our family hold true," he said, "destroying the astrolabe will not just revert the timeline back to its original state . . . but it will also return every traveler to their natural time, and seal the passages forever."

The dagger slipped from Nicholas's hand. His mind was adrift in the storm of possibilities that tore through it.

He lies. He lies with every breath. He wants you to help him. He will do anything to have it.

But the fear—the slick, sweaty coating of it over the old man's words—*that* painted a portrait of truth, because if there was one thing the old man had never been in Nicholas's eyes, it was afraid. Or vulnerable.

Late at night, while at sea, Hall would sometimes wake Chase and Nicholas and bring them up on deck to learn to read the stars and navigate by them. Once, while he'd been stretched on his back, the sails flapping sweetly above them, the sea rolling beneath them, he'd seen a star fall from the sky, scorching the air with its speed and brilliance.

His next thought occurred to him in much the same way. *He does not want the astrolabe destroyed, because it would dismantle the traveler life. It would ruin him. Break his rule.*

It wasn't enough to take this man's life. This was the problem with these traveler families, their history. Another cruel man or woman would step up their own savagery to fill the void he left behind, and they would all be thrown into further chaos. Better to end this, once and for all—to spare the families, the world, the kind of grief he felt now.

And then I can rest. He could die knowing that he had finally broken the last chain binding him to this man. But Etta . . .

Love. Sacrifice. Release.

He could not save her and still destroy Ironwood. Even if he had the time to steal the astrolabe and escape—the shallow flutter of his heart, the labor it took to stay on his feet, spoke the truth: if he did not kill Ironwood, he was not long for this world.

And he would not kill Ironwood.

This was all he could do, and still live as he chose. It would be a good death, an honorable one. And, in this way, he could tolerate the surrender.

He would see them again. His mother. Friends lost at sea. *Etta.*

Wait for me, wait for me, wait for me. He would follow, as he had before, into the unknown; into whatever adventure awaited them there.

The man began to pace, his hands clasped behind his back. His words ebbed and flowed, disappearing into nonsensical muttering as Ironwood worked through his plan. If he had stripped out of his attire, Nicholas was not sure he would have seen the man as naked as this. The veneer of steel was gone, and it was deeply, deeply unsettling to him to see Ironwood's desperation rise to a pitch of such barely restrained frenzy.

"Say yes, Nicholas," Ironwood said. "She's not lost to you. This is your inheritance. This is what you deserve."

A sureness took his heart, lightening it enough for him to breathe for the first time in days. With each thud of his pulse, he felt the poison inch through his system. He moved toward the window, looking down into the garden where the candlelight from the ball seeped out, highlighting where Sophia was hiding in the bushes. Her face was turned up like a stargazer's in the darkness, searching for his.

When their eyes met, he gave the slightest shake of his head and pulled the curtains shut on her confusion. *I'm sorry.*

"I accept your offer as given," he said, turning back. "But I would ask for ink and paper, so that I might write a letter to Captain Hall, and assure him I am well."

Cyrus Ironwood looked up, eyes gleaming. He moved to his own secretary desk, retrieving the necessities.

"Of course," he said. "Of course. You'll come to find you have a great deal of paper and ink now, as much as your heart desires. My man will search him out to deliver it. I'll have him bring a physician to repair whatever it is you've done to your arm. Better yet, you'll join me in the twentieth century. Medicine is remarkably improved by then."

"No, it's not necessary," Nicholas said, his voice loud to his own ears. "I am already healing."

"Good," he said, "good. There's a bed for you down the hall. Rest. We'll discuss plans to retrieve the funds necessary to enter the auction in the morning.

"My God," he heard the old man say as he reached the door. "My God, my boy, this is almost at its end."

Indeed.

Nicholas wandered down the hall, past the startled guards. He walked along the carpet, not hidden in the walls like the unwelcome secret he'd been. But when he arrived at the staircase and heard the dancing, the airy melody of crystal and glass gently colliding, he turned toward the entrance to the servants' stairwell and wound his way down it.

He was unsurprised to feel Li Min's hands on his throat the instant the door shut behind him. Good. He could face her in the darkness.

"What is the meaning of this?" she hissed. "You'll serve him now?"

"You heard it all?" She nodded. "Good. I haven't much time to explain. I'll take on the role of his heir only long enough for him to find the astrolabe, and for me to then take it from him and destroy it."

It was an easier thing to tell Li Min, who, in her way, always seemed to see the path they undertook from several steps ahead. Sophia would have turned back and finished the old man herself.

"I did not expect you to choose artifice," she said. "Can you maintain the deception long enough to reach your end?"

He nodded. What else did he have now but this one goal?

"Do you despise me for this? It'll mean an end to your way of life. If you've accumulated wealth in other eras outside of your natural one, now is the time to collect it."

And to prepare for the worst of it.

"If this is my last—my only—opportunity to say so, I am grateful to call you my friend. No, please hear me on this," he said, seeing her begin to speak. "I generally consider those who save my life friends, and hope that doesn't offend your mercenary sensibilities. I'm grateful for all that you've done, and that I've known you, even if that bond is broken by what comes next."

"I believe that nothing breaks the bonds between people, not years or distance," she said. "But you seem to simply take his word for it? What if his claims about its destruction prove false? I have heard—" She caught her next words, taking a moment to reconsider them. "It's been a rumor for years that destroying it would revert the timeline back to the original. But the other points sound like fear tactics."

He was too tired to argue this with her. As it was, he could hardly keep himself upright, and had to lean against the corridor's wall to support his own weight. *Too quickly, all of this is coming too quickly—*

I need more time—please, God, more time—

"The man I saw in that room was afraid," he said finally. "I do not know what to believe now. The world is upside down and this is the only way I can think of to right it."

"All right, my friend," she said. "We will follow you and assist in any way we can. If we need to meet, unknot your sling."

Nicholas, in truth, had not expected this, and he was moved by the fact that she'd made the decision so easily.

"What if you need to speak with me?" he asked.

"We will find a way."

"As you always do," he said, with a ghost of a smile. "Until then."

She raised her hand, touching his shoulder just for a moment before pulling back. His vision had adjusted to the darkness enough to make out the pale moon of her face as she stared hard at the buttonless jacket she'd stolen for him only a few hours before. "What would you have done . . . if she had survived? If you had found her?"

He couldn't bear to say Etta's name; it was a thorn on the tongue, as much as it bloomed in his heart. "I think . . . it does not matter much now. If the chance doesn't present itself, tell Sophia I'm sorry it's come to this. That I hope she'll understand."

"She'll understand; she may yet even appreciate your cunning in destroying the old man," Li Min said, drifting further from him as she found her way back to the same window she'd entered by. "But she'll tear down the gates of hell and drag you back by the throat if you allow yourself to die."

That, at least, was absolute in his mind. But he felt pleased in knowing that Sophia would never allow herself to be constrained by the limits of her natural time in the twentieth century. She would carve a way toward the same independence that had eluded him for so long. He had been so very wrong to assume that their uneasy alliance would rest on nothing more than a mutual hatred.

He had been wrong about so many things.

Rather than continue down the stairs, past the glittering souls dancing into the morning hours, past the cooling kitchen, he began to climb. The steps bore his weight with quiet protest, and he drifted up to the attic that had been his home for the first years of his life.

The support beam came within a hairbreadth of cracking against his temple. Nicholas sucked in a surprised breath and ducked through the entryway, bent at the waist to avoid skinning his back against the rough roof.

The old man must have completed some sort of renovation—the rafters couldn't have been so low as this, suffocating the attic so it was little more than a crawl space. He tried to recall if his mother or any of the other five house slaves who had slept with them in this room had been forced to make themselves smaller to enter, to contract their bodies to fit inside what little space they'd been granted.

Now there was no bedding on the floor, only the bed jammed up against the wall below the window. Straw exploded out of the bare mattress through a hole some industrious rat had likely chewed in it. Dust carpeted the floor, undisturbed for many years.

The room coiled around him, nearly unrecognizable from the vantage point his height gave him; he knelt, trying to reclaim some semblance of memory, to understand why this room had once felt like a kingdom. There had been so many times he'd sat beside the room's low window and watched the wide, pale sky above the townhomes, tantalizingly endless beyond the glass. Nicholas wondered if that was the reason Ironwood had given them this room and not the cellar—to show them that everything in their lives would remain just as far out of reach.

The lacework of spiderwebs spread from corner to corner, catching the fragile moonlight. Time began to slip around him, peeling back the years, mending the cracks in the floor and the scuffing on the wall, filling the room with soft candlelight and whispers of life. The bed linen still smelled as he remembered it, of starch and leather and polish. Even in this small sanctuary, they hadn't been able to fully escape their work. They lived it.

He sat on the bed and, using his left hand, finally went about writing a short missive to Hall. But after the salutation he stopped, uncertain of what to say, beyond, *I am well. I will find you when I am able.* Both were lies, and he couldn't abide the thought. But if Ironwood himself didn't break the seal to read it, one of his men would, and report on its contents. So, instead, he gave Hall all that was left to him now: gratitude.

For all that you have done for me, I thank you. I have been warned of the regret of being too sentimental in the face of an uncertain outcome, but I would be remiss not to take this opportunity to say this to you, if nothing else. I have lived a life of vast fortune owing to the generosity of your heart. I will never cease fighting to be the sort of man who will honor those values which you have so graciously bestowed by example. If there is a way back, I will find the bearing and come posthaste. —N.

Nicholas folded the paper and stowed it inside of his coat.

How strange it was, to be near the end of one's journey, and to find oneself back at the place one began and see it as if for the first time. To remember that small rebellion that had lived inside him at the thought of the untraveled world that lay beyond these walls.

The name Carter had come from his mother's first master, and he had kept it, even as he'd chosen a new given name for himself at Mrs. Hall's suggestion. It had been the sweet lady's idea, a way to make him feel as though he had some mastery over his life. But he had kept the surname as a way to honor all that his mother had endured, and all that she had risked in hiding him. If Ironwood had sold him away down to Georgia with her and the others, he knew he likely would not have survived it.

This was the bed he'd slept on with his mother. Here she had cradled him in her arms, her scarred hands smoothing his hair, soothing his spirit. Here she had sung that song from her faraway home, thousands of miles from the cramped, dreary room. It had filled his ears like a fervent prayer, the only weapon she'd had to drive the darkness away from him. It had breathed life into his unconquerable soul.

He had lived so many lives, and yet the sum of his existence felt like so much more than any one part of his history. Even now—even *now*, in the face of the poison he felt inching through his veins, that same rebellion burned inside of him. That same demand for the distant horizons summoned him to fight.

Nicholas, he named himself on the deck of that ship, in the light of a sea of stars.

Bastard, the Ironwoods declared.

Partner, Etta swore.

Child of time, the stranger beckoned.

Heir, the old man vowed.

But here, in this hidden place, he had only ever been *Samuel,* the son of Africa, the legacy of Ruth.

REYNISFJALL MOUNTAIN
IIOO A.D.

TWENTY-SIX

Your presence is requested at the auction of a rare artifact of our history: one astrolabe, origin unknown. October 22, 1891, at the cusp of midnight. Kurama-dera Temple, north of Kyoto. The entry fee remains a hundred pounds of gold or jewels per bidding party.

Etta read the note again, ignoring the soft patter of freezing rain on her hair and face. They'd gone upstate, to a cabin that sat like an afterthought in the woods, and waited a day, watching its doors for any Ironwoods. Hungry and frustrated, she'd broken away from Julian and gone to where he said the key would be: buried beneath the root of a nearby tree.

By the time she'd gotten the door open, he'd been brave enough to join her in sorting through the endless piles of letters and notices that had been slipped inside of its mail slot. Some were torn, clearly battered by their delivery; others showed the era in which they were written by the quality of the paper and the ink. Most were sealed with the same wax seal, bearing the sigil of the Ironwoods, except for one: blank wax, marked with a *B* that rested inside the curve of a crescent moon. Julian had picked it up between two fingers and shaken it, as if afraid it might suddenly reveal a set of teeth.

He had gone through his travel journal to try to locate the nearest passage, but she'd found a small reference book of passages, left on the empty cabin's table for anyone who dropped in and needed help in navigating away. A passage in Brazil would take them directly to Mount Kurama, but one rather weighty problem remained.

A hundred pounds of gold or jewels—not just difficult to locate, but difficult to carry to the auction site.

"I don't want to alarm you," Julian began. He pulled back from the hulking outcropping they'd hidden behind, observing the black beach below. "But there seems to be a gaggle of Vikings rowing up to shore."

That startled her out of her thoughts. Etta pulled him back by his simple tunic and took his place, scanning the fog spreading its pale hands across the sea. A carved wooden face appeared ahead of the rest of the ship, slicing silently through the heavy cover of gloom.

The figurehead was a serpent, a dark specter, all teeth and long, curving neck. Etta sat back, flinching as it broke through the gloom, gliding forward like a knife through a veil. The rush of the tide and the birds circling overhead covered the sound of the oars splashing through the water.

"I thought you said he picked this place for his gold reserve because it was deserted—your exact words were 'untouched by time and man,'" she said, glancing back over her shoulder.

"All right, I've been known to embellish my tales with a touch of drama, but do you honestly believe I wouldn't pay special attention to where I could find my shiny inheritance?" Julian said, leaning over her shoulder. "This was the safest place to keep the loot because of how little play it got with the timeline. No one is supposed to actually like this place enough to come visit."

Several other caches they'd checked had already been emptied and moved to an unknown location, or the timeline had shifted so severely that they had faded out of existence entirely. "Except Vikings," Etta said.

"All right, except Vikings."

"And the Celts," Etta said. "And other Scandinavian peoples. Why didn't he go way back—beyond ancient times? Prehistoric. Actually, how far back *do* the passages go? Could you see, like, the dinosaurs? Cavemen?"

Julian leaned back against the rock, pressing a hand against his chest, his expression one of pure astonishment. "My God, Linden-Hemlock-Spencer. I believe you've just given me a new purpose in life."

Etta's brows drew together. "Finding new passages?"

"No, hunting for dinosaurs," he said. "Why did I never think of that—oh, right, the eating thing. Big teeth and all. Well, never mind."

"How quickly the dream dies," Etta said wryly, turning back toward the beach.

For an hour now, they'd kept watch on the cave, hidden just out of their line of sight by a curve in the mountain. All they could see of it through the mist and fog was the edge of the entrance: towering stacks of stone, some round like pipes, others as straight and narrow as bone, had seemingly splintered from a rough rock face. From a distance, Etta had thought they'd merely been piled closely together, like ancient offerings for whatever king had ruled the mountain and beach below.

The longship navigated between the narrow, towering black rocks jutting up from the water, before driving up onto the shore itself. The landing was quick work; the oars were tucked inside, the sails drawn up so as not to catch the whistling wind.

A half dozen men poured out of the belly of the ship, their feet striking the black sand, moving swiftly to catch the five empty leather sacks thrown by the others on the deck. The depressions their feet left in the black sand filled with rain, shining like scales from a distance.

Finally, a tall figure jumped down from the deck of the second ship, struggling for balance with one arm cradled against his chest. He was darker than the others, both in skin and dress, wearing none of the fur they did. The men around him gathered slowly, as if with reluctance, their heads bobbing up and down with whatever instructions he was giving them. Then he began his long strides toward the very cave Etta and Julian had come to clean out, his shoulders set back, chin raised, the way—

She was on her feet before she could think to rise. Etta choked out something between a gasp and a laugh. "Nicholas."

Julian reached for the back of her shirt, trying to pull her down, but Etta twisted away, frantic. He was too far away, *too far*—her whole body trembled in protest at being forced to remain where it was.

She edged as close to the line of the cliff as she dared, starving for a better look at him; her heart was thundering so hard, she was half worried it might suddenly give out on her.

How long his hair had grown, how thin and battered he was in the face. The distance between them was more than just air and sand and mountains; it manifested in all of those missing days between them, creating a deep valley of uncertainty. The sling for his arm—what had happened? Who were these men, and why—

One last man was lowered down from the first ship, with the assistance of two other men. He was hunched at the shoulders, adorned with leather armor and gray fur, and she knew him—not because her mind put the impossible pieces together, but because Julian did. He recoiled, going bone-white in the face.

Cyrus Ironwood looked like a different beast without the finery he'd wrapped himself in to give the impression of civility.

Oh God, she thought, pressing a fist against her mouth to keep from making another sound. *He's got Nicholas.*

She'd been so focused on finding the astrolabe, so sure in her belief that Nicholas was in Damascus still, that she had somehow never considered the possibility that Ironwood would have snared him again. But then—the men were going where Nicholas was pointing, hauling the sacks toward the hoard inside the cave at the end of the beach.

When Ironwood came up to him, when Ironwood put a hand on his shoulder, Nicholas did not run. He did not flinch. He nodded, pointing to the cave.

He . . . *smiled.*

"What in the name of *God*?" Julian began. He shook off the surprise first, pulling her back down to a crouch beside him. "He's—that's Nick, isn't it? But then, that's Grandfather, and they're . . . they're together."

Walking side by side to collect the reserve of Ironwood treasure.

For one terrible moment, Etta could not feel anything below her neck. The cold air seemed to ice over the inside of her lungs, making it painful to breathe.

"He must be—the old man must be forcing him," she managed to say. The Nicholas she knew could barely stand to be in the same breathing space as the man, let alone tolerate his touch.

The Nicholas you knew for a month?

No. No. *No.* Etta shoved the thought away. He'd handed her his heart in complete trust, and she knew the shape of it, how heavily it was weighted with hatred and shattering sadness toward this family. This wasn't a betrayal—the only betrayal would be hers, if she believed he was doing anything other than finding a way to survive.

She blew out a harsh breath, gathering up her small bag of supplies. The landscape of Iceland had a cool, reserved kind of beauty, but its terrain was unpredictable, roughly hewn, as if shaped by the travels of giants. They'd come down a worn path that would eventually lead to the beach below, and, if she continued down it just a bit more, she might be able to get close enough to somehow catch Nicholas's attention without any of the Ironwoods noticing.

"He's treating him like . . ." Julian began, still sitting on the ground where she had left him.

"Let's go," she said. "Come on."

He turned, and for once she couldn't read his expression. "He's treating him like the way he used to handle my father."

"Nicholas is?"

He shook his head. "Grandfather. That's not a prisoner on that beach. That's an *heir*."

The words flew at her like an arrow. Etta took off, continuing up the path, to avoid it landing. She wrapped the heavy, drab wool coat around her tightly, and looked up to find that the rain had turned to snow, and was catching on her shoulders and hair.

Etta took the bend in the trail at a run, scrambling on hands and feet to avoid slipping on the ice and moss. The waves broke below her, snapping against the earth, sounding more and more like the blood rushing through her ears. She kept her eyes on Nicholas below, trying to keep up with him and the others before they disappeared into the cave.

Two hands caught her by the shoulders and swung her back around, hard enough that her feet slipped out from beneath her. Etta slammed onto the uneven ground, the air exploding out of her in a cloud of white. She wheezed painfully, trying to fill her lungs, to rise back up, but she was pinned in place by the kiss of a blade against her exposed throat.

It pulled back suddenly, and the weight that had crashed down on her chest lifted with a gasp. By the time the burst of light cleared from Etta's eyes and she could lift a hand to clear the snow from her lashes, a familiar face was gazing down at her in horror, partially disguised by an impressive-looking leather eye patch.

Her mind understood what she was seeing—who she was seeing— but couldn't make sense of it: the short hair, the shirt and trousers, the boots. Etta scrambled back as best she could, trying to put distance between her and Sophia, until her hand closed around a shard of stone. She thrust it between them to ward the girl off.

"Soph . . . ia?" came the weak voice above them.

Julian stood on the path, a short distance from them. When Sophia turned toward him, rising to her feet, his face seemed to crumble. He didn't just look remorseful—he looked as if he wanted nothing more than for a bolt of lightning to blow him off the face of the hill.

"I guess the obvious question is, how the hell are you alive?" Sophia's voice sounded as if it had been rubbed raw.

Julian dared to take another step toward her, holding out a hand, as if he expected her to take it. Sophia stared at it the way a wolf would assess whether or not it was worth chasing a hare.

"Oh, that—well, old girl—Soph, light of my life—" Julian seemed unable to tear his eyes away from the eye patch. There was an unhealthy sheen to his face, almost feverish, when the attention of the group finally shifted to him.

"You," she interjected, "I know about. I'm speaking to *you*, Linden."

"Me?" Etta repeated. "I'll admit I had a couple close calls, but— wait, *what?*"

"You were dead. D-E-A-D. As in, finished, gone to meet your maker, et cetera," Sophia said. "Your father issued a challenge to Ironwood. He demanded satisfaction for your murder at his men's hands."

"My murder?" Etta repeated, hauling herself back up to her feet, only to have Sophia tug her and Julian back down to their knees.

"Oh," Julian said, turning to her. "Didn't you tell me that your father said he had a way of keeping Ironwood off your tail? How better to do that than to confuse Ironwood into thinking you were already dead?"

"That's a leap," Etta said, even as something squirmed in her stomach.

"He kept it secret from you?" Sophia asked, looking unimpressed. "It's true, though. The only reason Ironwood would ever leave you alone is if he thought you were already dead, and he'd missed out on the fun of killing you himself."

Etta's eyes narrowed. "Ironwood, huh? Not *Grandfather*?"

The other girl drew back, her visible eye narrowing. In Etta's experience, Sophia had defended herself by deflection, by attacking. This time, Etta was prepared for it.

"Aaaand I'm just going to stand over here," Julian said, inching away. Etta cast him an irritated look. He cocked a brow in reply. "You court the dragon, you get burned, kiddo."

"What are *you* doing here?" Etta asked. "Why are you in disguise?"

Sophia laughed then. An ugly, exhausted sound. She flicked her leather eye patch up, revealing a scarred, empty socket. Julian either coughed into his fist or tried to muffle his retch. In either case, it wasn't well received.

"Cute," Sophia said in a cold voice. "I would guess you'd want me even less now, except you already went so far as to fake your death to get away from me."

Julian startled. "What? No—Soph, believe me, it had nothing to do with you—"

"I don't want your excuses," she said. "I want to know why you're here now, and what you're doing with *her*."

"I went to the Thorns," he said quickly, "which was a rotten idea all around. They despised me and I slept every night with one eye open— oh God—I heard the words leave my mouth and I couldn't stop them, Soph—"

Something dark bobbed at the edge of her sight, just past Sophia's shoulder. Everything was in harsh relief here, from the icy sky and feathery clouds to the browning moss that covered the black mountains and cliffs like flaking skin.

But there was another person there with them. In her dark cloak, with her dark hair, the land seemed to claim her as its own. Etta might not have noticed her at all if she hadn't moved.

Recognition linked with memory.

"You."

She was dressed differently from the last time Etta had seen her, in San Francisco. Her soft silk suit had been replaced by a linen tunic and baggy trousers, both held in place by a tightly knotted leather belt weighed down with scabbards and pouches.

There were a number of things about her great-aunt Winifred that Etta had willed herself to forget. Her penchant for vile turns of phrase wasn't one of them.

That creature you insist on working with is here to make her report.

Sophia turned, looking between her and Li Min. "What are you doing? Get over here before they spot you from the beach."

The girl did not move.

"You were wrong after all," Sophia said. "This is Etta Linden; not so dead, it seems."

Li Min was watching Etta, her head already bowed in resignation. Guilt was its own beast, Etta had learned. It took up residence beneath your skin and moved you to things you never thought possible, all to try to appease the discomfort it caused. Etta saw how they had all converged on this place. Fury leaped through her like a bow skidding off the strings of a violin.

Etta understood now.

"Funny that you told her I was dead, considering I saw you less than a week ago in San Francisco," Etta said coldly. "Did you finish your job for my father, or have you been working for Sophia this whole time to undermine him?" Another thought, almost more terrible, arose. "Did he tell you to keep us all apart?"

"Working for me? You're not making sense, as usual, Linden," Sophia said. But Li Min remained impossibly still. She couldn't tell if the other girl was breathing.

"Oh, *cripes!*" Julian figured it out a moment later, his brows shooting up to his hairline. "Li Min, you are one naughty little dame. I was wondering how the two of you ever would have met."

"What is going on?" Sophia demanded, an edge to her voice.

"What job is this, exactly?" Etta continued. "Have you been reporting back to her on the Thorns? Or did my father send you to watch her, on the off chance she found the astrolabe first?"

To her credit, the girl didn't retreat into silence to protect herself, as a coward would.

"I was hired by Hemlock," Li Min said, "to take the astrolabe, if either she or Nicholas Carter reached it first. Report back any useful information." She turned, meeting Etta's gaze. "He did not give me explicit orders to keep you apart, only to use my judgment in what would keep you safest. In the end, that was keeping your paths separate."

"What?" The word was so faint as it escaped Sophia, Etta wasn't sure it could be considered a whisper.

"You have to understand," Li Min said to her, a small, pleading note in her voice. "The Hemlocks found me again, after I escaped the Shadows, after I finished my training with Ching Shih. Her father is the head of my own family's line, yes, but, more than that, he believed in me. He arranged for jobs that helped to build my reputation. He provided whatever resources I needed to live my life on my terms, and he has never once asked for anything in return. I could never be one of them, not the way he hoped for—I could not tell him the things I told you. I was . . . afraid. Set in my ways. But I owed him a debt that demanded to be repaid. I offered to do this job for him and would not have committed to it for anything less than that; you must believe me."

"You—" Sophia stood, her feet carrying her toward the girl. She reached for the long knife at her side, yanking it from the hilt strapped to her leg. "*Believe* you? After everything else you've said and done was a lie?"

Etta understood that Li Min had perpetuated her father's lie and inserted herself into Sophia's life under false pretenses, but . . . Sophia wasn't just furious. Etta had seen fury in her before. She was *shaking*.

"Not everything," Li Min swore. "Not everything was a lie."

"The Thorns—the ones who beat me and left me for dead in the middle of the desert?" Sophia continued, stopping just short of the other girl. "You must have had a laugh, telling me all of that mystical nonsense about revenge. All the while, you were going to stop me."

"Not stop you, join you," Li Min said, her serene expression finally breaking. "I only—it—it all got rather complicated, you see—"

"It's not complicated at all," Sophia said, drawing the freezing air to her, turning her words to ice. "You showed me exactly who you were from the moment we met: a thief and a con artist. You were right. You are not my friend. You are *nothing*. Get out of my sight. *Leave!* Otherwise this time I really will kill you."

There was a long moment where no one spoke at all, not even Julian, who looked like he had a few thoughts on the matter. Li Min turned, shifting the bag on her shoulder as she passed the three of them. Whatever she whispered to Sophia seemed to enrage her further. The breath was steaming in and out of her, her pale face blooming a vicious red. Her one visible eye was screwed shut.

"Well, this has been a day of, ah, fascinating revelations," Julian said, daring to approach his former fiancée. He put a gentle hand on her shoulder, which she immediately knocked away.

"She was watching both you and Nicholas separately?" Etta asked. The question seemed so ridiculous that she almost couldn't get it out. "Or were you . . . *are* you working together?"

Sophia crossed her arms over her chest, turning her gaze out over the water. Her face mirrored the rough, jagged lines of the mountain, rendering her unrecognizable to Etta.

"Should we be preparing to catch her?" Julian murmured out of the side of his mouth. "Grab for the shirt, I'll try for an arm—"

Etta thumped him across the chest. Hard.

In Etta's mind, Sophia was always burning, always straining toward something. Now she stood with her face toward the bitter wind and welcomed it. She tilted her chin up, the way only Ironwoods seemed able to, and a smirk slid into place.

"You're hilarious, Linden," she said. "Work with him? I wouldn't let Carter polish my shoes."

"Soph!" Julian said, his voice sharp.

"Do you really want to take issue with that, considering all those things you called him in the past?" Sophia said. "Whoreson, gold-digger, ratfink—"

"Enough." Julian took a step forward, his face pale, his hair ringed by snow. "Enough! I know what I said in the past, and I was wrong for it. It doesn't excuse you to say any of it now."

"Aw," she said, cooing at him in a repulsive way. "Have I upset you? Or are you struggling with the reality that your bastard brother is now enjoying all of your old spoils of being heir?"

This was a trick Etta was familiar with—Sophia's uncanny ability to zero in on a chink in a person's armor and slip a blade through it. If Etta had had anything remotely sharp on her, it would have been wedged in the girl's windpipe in return.

"Liar," Etta said simply.

"Am I? I've been following him for weeks, that's all. I've watched him drift back into the old man's arms happily. Willingly. He's oversee-ing all of Ironwood's business ventures, repairing the changes caused by the timeline shifts, *advising* him. It's absolutely precious how well they work together. The old man actually looks happy. He's leaving Carter in charge of things, while he goes off to the auction."

Julian swallowed hard, glancing over at Etta, as if to gauge how possible this might be. She shook her head.

"He certainly didn't come looking for *you*, did he?" Sophia said.

A thin, hot thread began to weave itself in and out of Etta's chest.

"He thought her dead," Julian cut in. "As you did."

"And yet he's working for the man who was supposedly responsible for her death. It shows you exactly who he is, doesn't it? You had it in your head he was so good, such a hero, but he's no better than the rest of us. Your whole 'relationship,' your *love*—your *infatuation*—was based on deals and transactions. Payment to bring you to Ironwood. Payment to stop you from taking the astrolabe. Shall I go on?"

Etta's stomach turned so sharply that she tasted bile. Not true. *Not true.* Sophia didn't understand. She wasn't there to see his regret. She didn't know Nicholas *at all.*

"Do you want to know why I'm here? The same reason you are: I want that gold they're carrying out, in order to attend a little auction for something stolen from me."

Of course she was. It was all about her, always. And just like that, Etta reached the end of the frayed patience that she had been clinging to. She lunged forward, ripping the knife out of Sophia's hand, and slammed the girl back against the rock behind her. Etta braced one arm over Sophia's chest, and brought the blade up just beneath her chin.

"Good *lord!*" Julian said, half in appreciation, half in horror. "The two of you bring out the worst in each other."

They ignored him.

"Too high," Sophia said, the words curling around Etta like smoke. "Lower. Did you already forget what I taught you?"

Etta's grip didn't ease. "You still don't see it, do you? The astrolabe *has* to be destroyed."

Sophia laughed—actually *laughed.* "Would you still be saying that if you knew what would happen, I wonder?"

"I've accepted that my future can't exist," Etta said. "You're the only one who still thinks she can get everything she wants in life."

"If you destroy that astrolabe, you'll have *nothing* you want in life," Sophia said. "Of course you don't know. You're nothing but a sweet little sheep being led by the nose, bleating on about right and wrong—wake up, Linden! There is no right and wrong, only choices. And you've made a decision without even having all the facts."

"What are you on about?" Julian asked, ineffectually trying to separate the two. "Sophia, come on. We'll go together—between the two of us, we know enough about the Ironwood holdings to scrape together the entry fee. There *is* a wrong choice in this, and that's letting Grandfather get his hands on it. You haven't seen what we've seen of the future, what's at stake. I don't know what Nick is on about, but it can't be helping him. He's too obnoxiously good."

Nicholas can't be helping Ironwood, Etta thought, her hands curling at her side. But then—he had made that agreement with Ironwood behind her back, hadn't he? Nicholas was supposed to follow her, ensure that she returned with the astrolabe. In exchange, he'd receive Ironwood's holdings in the eighteenth century.

She straightened. No. He'd turned his back on that. He'd confessed, he'd told her that he loved her. *Loved* her.

The small, dark wisp of a voice in her mind returned. *Infatuation.*

"I don't need to hear another word from you, you bloody selfish coward," Sophia snapped. "You've lost the right to care about me. In fact, why don't you just walk off that cliff now, finish what you started? At least Grandfather will have a body to bury this time."

"You don't mean that," Julian said, and Etta was almost surprised by how calm he sounded, how he didn't retreat from any of the ugly looks Sophia sent his way, the hissing words. "Tell me what's the matter, what's hurt you so badly. We've been friends our whole lives—do you honestly believe I can't tell when you're just lashing out?"

"It doesn't matter," she said, finally pulling free of Etta's arm. Sophia stalked over to pick up the bags she'd dropped. "None of it matters. Jump now, or destroy the astrolabe—your life is over either way. Since you can't seem to do anything yourselves, allow me to paint the full portrait for you: the Ironwood timeline won't just disappear. We will all be returned to our own godforsaken times, and the passages will slam closed behind us forever."

"God," Etta said, "you're such a liar."

Sophia had begun up the path, ignoring how Julian's hand reached for her. At Etta's words, she turned. "Am I? I guess you'll see, won't you."

"Wait," Julian called, following Sophia along the trail. "Soph, please—"

The two of them disappeared around a bend in the rocky path, and took that last small need for control with them. Etta's breath left her like she'd taken a punch to the lungs, and she brought both fists to her eyes, pressing the freezing skin there to cool the thoughts racing behind them.

Infatuation.

Returned.

Closed.

Forever.

If what Sophia said was true, and Etta had every reason to doubt her, then Henry clearly had never got the full story. He never would have risked separating the Thorn families from one another. God, what if a child was born in a completely different century than his or her parents—what if one of those children running wild in the house in San Francisco found themselves locked inside a violent time, in a place where they had no friends, and couldn't speak the language, much less ask for help?

Etta remembered what it felt like to have Nicholas's hands on her face, the way his fingers had run along her skin as if he could paint his feelings onto it. She remembered the way Nicholas had trembled, just that small bit, when she'd lain down beside him in the darkness. The warmth of his lips on her cheeks, her eyelids, every part of her, and how he'd given her his secrets. She remembered the way her fear had broken and dissolved against him, how carefully he had held her together each time she came close to shattering.

How quickly his mind worked, how earnestly his heart believed, how desperately he'd fought for everything in his life, including the belief that they could be together. In her heart, Nicholas was a song in a major key, bold and beautiful.

But Etta remembered, too, the way it had felt when the Thorns had reached for her, embraced her, claimed her with a thousand smiles and questions, trying to defeat the lost time between them. She remembered hearing her father's music join her own. She remembered her city, how its occupants and streets and trees had been blown into the same shifting, swirling cloud of ash.

She needed to talk to Nicholas; she needed to touch him, and kiss him, and know how he had hurt himself, know how she could help him. But there were a hundred men between them on the beach, and now, even more dauntingly, a hundred questions between them that Etta couldn't begin to answer.

There's so much darkness to this story, there are times I feel suffocated by it, Henry had said. How these things came back around. How everything circled back to the astrolabe, again and again and again.

A pattern.

No— Etta shook the thought away as hard and as far as she could.

Julian jogged back to her, running his hands back over his hair, breathing hard. "She wouldn't listen. There's something else going on that she's not telling us, I'm sure of it."

Etta nodded, keeping her back to the rock as she circled back to watch what was happening on the beach below. She found Nicholas immediately—it would have been impossible to miss him standing beside the old man, a short distance from the cave's entrance. He stooped slightly, to better hear what Ironwood was saying. Nodding, he stepped forward, cupping his good hand around his mouth to relay the message to the others.

What are you doing? she wondered. *What can you possibly be planning?*

There had been so many moments on their search together when Etta had felt like she understood his mind better than her own. But for the life of her, she couldn't understand why he'd taken this role in a game he'd never wanted to play in the first place, unless something had forced his hand.

"What should we do?" Julian said. "If she's right, then we'll get the original timeline, but then . . . that's the end for us, isn't it? Without the astrolabe to create the passages again, we're stuck."

Nicholas looked up toward them suddenly, as if searching through the mist and snow. Etta ducked before she realized she was doing it, her heart slamming in her chest as she leaned into the hard, jagged ground. She squeezed her eyes shut.

The one thing she had never doubted, never once questioned, was the constancy of her feelings for Nicholas; it was the part of her heart that kept a steady beat, that drummed a song only she could hear. By leaving Nicholas behind so she could chase the astrolabe with the Thorns, had she damned him to this choice, to survive the only way he could—through twisted loyalty?

The snow built around them, flake by flake, blanketing the black rocks and their twisted formations, smoothing them over until their wrinkles and crevices disappeared. When the idea came, it wasn't new; it was repurposed.

"How long would it take us to get back to San Francisco from here?"

Julian felt around the pocket of his coat for his journal. "If we hurry, maybe three, four days? Why? You want to try to link back up with the Thorns?"

"From there, how long to get to the auction site?" Etta pressed.

"If we use the direct passage that's in Rio de Janeiro . . . maybe three more days?" He thumbed through the pages again, checking his math.

"Then there won't be enough time," she said, sitting back on her heels, rubbing her muddied hands against the rough wool of her coat. "Especially if we're going to find a hundred pounds of gold. You didn't happen to notice any Thorn stockpiles, did you?"

"They spent everything that came in on food and water," Julian said. "Your father might have a reserve or two somewhere, but I'm not sure how we'd locate them and still make the auction date."

Etta nodded, recalculating. "And there are no other Ironwood reserves?"

"He's already cleared out the others—"

There was a sharp whistle from below, from the longship, as the men climbed aboard with the overstuffed leather bags. Nicholas followed suit, cupping his hand around his mouth to call out some order that was lost to the wind. Ironwood, it seemed, had already climbed aboard.

"Look at that," Etta breathed out, her heart giving an excited kick. "Did that look like more than a hundred pounds of treasure to you?"

"No," Julian said. "A hundred and a bit extra, maybe. But there's definitely more than that in the cave. They're not moving this cache, then, or clearing it out, are they? They only took what they needed."

"Which means we can take whatever he's left for our entry fee," Etta finished.

If Sophia doesn't beat us to it.

"And then what?" Julian asked. "Etta . . . I know you don't want to believe her, but Soph is never more truthful than when she's aiming for the heart."

"I know," she said, unable to take her gaze off Nicholas as he walked beside Ironwood back toward the vessels. One hand was tucked behind his back, and it reminded her of the way he had walked the length of the *Ardent*'s deck, so completely in his element.

Henry and the others had only known that destroying the astrolabe would revert the timeline, and prevent any new passages from being created to replace those lost by age and collapse. They had no idea that it would close *all* the passages, and strand everyone back in their natural times. She had to think he wouldn't want that—that Henry would come up with another, middle way.

Until she was able to figure out what that could be, she would have to try to keep the astrolabe in one piece. Once they confirmed that what Sophia had said was true, then she and the Thorns could turn their attention back to using the astrolabe to reach history's many linchpin moments, and nudge the timeline back to its original state by influencing them. It would send the Ironwoods lurching into panic, destabilize the old man's rule, destroy him with the knowledge that the astrolabe would remain just out of his reach forever.

It would be slow, dangerous work that might take years, but they could do it. *She* could do it, if Henry could not. It was a stark, disorienting reversal of their original plan, but Etta took comfort in the stabilizing thought that this, *this* would help her make amends for everything her family had done to contribute to the world's suffering across history.

They could start again. They could be better.

"I know," Etta repeated. "We'll get the astrolabe and try to regroup with the Thorns again to decide what to do with it. We can't destroy it, though, not until we know for sure what the consequences will be."

They did not have to sacrifice their families for the good of history and the future. Those two things didn't have to be mutually exclusive. There was a way to have both, and she would find it.

"And what of Nick?" he asked. "I hate leaving him with Grandfather—not because of what Sophia said. Being the heir is a curse, not a blessing. It just feels like, as much as he can handle himself, he's standing in the open mouth of a crocodile."

Etta drew back from where she'd been watching over the edge of the cliff. She felt light all of a sudden, as if she'd left something crucial there. "He's safe for now. We'll find the astrolabe, and then we'll come back for him."

If there was a path back to him in all of this, she would find it, or she'd carve a path where none existed—meet him halfway, as she

409

always seemed to. There was a place for them, for all of them, to live with their families, and love and care for one another, but it couldn't exist in the world they lived in now.

They waited only until the longships had disappeared into the swirl of fog and snow before continuing down to the beach. Etta tried to shake the feeling that Nicholas was still there, that she was somehow walking beside an imprint of him. There were too many footprints on the beach to tell which were his, and she didn't want to cover his tracks with her own; not if it cost her proof that he had been here. That he'd been alive, and so close.

The cave was darkness incarnate, the mouth of a thousand-toothed creature. Ice-coated stalagmites shot up from the ground, the freezing wind whistling between them. It was as if the steps had been intentionally carved into the cave, and she followed them down, stepping with intent, ignoring the splatter of freezing water dripping from above.

"All right, then," Julian said, stopping a short distance ahead of her. They were at the very edge of the natural light emanating from the entrance, but there was a crack of sorts in the mountain above them. Etta looked up at it in wonder, watching the snow drift lazily down to her. She imagined each flake was a note falling against her skin, and the music in her began to stir once again, coaxing out a tentative, sweet song of hope. Nicholas hadn't gotten to see this. She would bring him back here one day.

"It looks like we'll have enough, though it might be close," Julian said, tossing Etta one of the sacks he'd brought with him. "Come on, Linden-Hemlock-Spencer. Gawking is my job. Appreciate the beauty of the world later, will you?"

Etta shook herself out of that reverie, crossing the distance between them. It was obvious where the Ironwoods had hidden their barrels beneath false rock covers. They'd been in such a hurry, they had left the empty ones to slowly rot. Julian popped the lid off a barrel stowed beneath a pile of rocks, cooing at the bright gold inside.

"The lost treasure of Lima," he told her, as if this explained everything. "He's greedy as sin, but lord, does the man have taste."

"Let's just hurry," she said, her fingers digging into the cold metal. There were days ahead of them before the auction, and too many chances for her plan to fail. But here, in the darkness, in the midst of their silent work, it felt safe to think of Nicholas on the beach, to wish that she had been there to warm his hands while the cold air nipped at his skin. She could almost remember what his voice sounded like as it whispered secrets into her hair.

Etta could be grateful even as she felt longing rise in her like an unfinished crescendo. One look had been enough; one reassurance that he was alive would sustain her. And whatever would come in the temple on the mountain, in the darkness of midnight, she hoped that he, at least, would be spared.

RIO DE JANEIRO
1830

TWENTY-SEVEN

SEAMEN WERE A SUPERSTITIOUS LOT, AND IT DID NOT surprise him in the least to find that stories were being traded in the confines of the forecastle, trailing him like sharks now that death had its fingers on him.

A ship's bell, as Hall's old sailing master Grimes had once explained, was the soul of the vessel. It was why they were meant to make such an effort to retrieve a bell from a wreck; over the course of its tenure, it served much in the way a church bell might: it marked the time for watches, and its bold sound was, to many of the men, a ward against evil and storms. But when it rang on its own, or when that same sweet tone seemed to rise from the depths of the dark water, it was an omen— it was a signal that a man was bound for his eternal reward.

Nicholas lay awake in his rented room, listening as the storm that had blown in at supper battered the city. The violent winds made playthings of the shutters and signs and roofs; it should not have surprised him that they were strong enough to shake even the nearby church bell, but it did. He felt the sound move through him as if it were striking each of his bones in turn.

The rain lashed at the window as Nicholas tried to sit up. Every joint in his body felt inflamed, locked into place. He attempted to roll himself over and put his feet down on the carpet, only to realize his left hand and wrist could no longer support his full weight without collapsing. It was slow, hard work to edge over on the mattress, and harder still to quell the disorienting feeling of foam sloshing around inside his skull. He regretted lying down for the night. It was always more difficult to begin again when you'd ground yourself to a halt.

"It's worse now, isn't it?"

Nicholas jerked back, forgetting yet again he couldn't lunge for the flintlock he'd placed beneath his pillow.

But it was only Sophia. She sat in the far corner of the room, shadowed. The steady drip he'd been aware of for a few minutes now hadn't been coming from a hole in the roof, but from her drenched overcoat. Beneath her, a puddle of muddy water was gathering around her feet.

"I feel as if I've been keelhauled, but it is manageable." Nicholas coughed, trying to clear the sleep from his voice. "How did you get in?"

"The guards downstairs are drunk, and the ones outside the old man's door are asleep," she said, crossing her arms over her chest. "What's that face for? There's a tree outside your window I can use to climb down, if you're going to be a grump about this."

At least one of them felt in command of the situation. The past few days of gathering and moving obscene amounts of gold and treasure from all of the old man's various hidden hoards to more secure locations had reaffirmed for him that he would never have a solid grip on the extent of the resources Ironwood had at his disposal. It only further served to reinforce his belief that another man or woman would simply seize control of it in the event of Ironwood's death, and the cycle would perpetuate itself.

"Where's Li Min?" he asked, waiting for his eyes to adjust to the darkness. With the storm clouds knitting themselves together so thickly, he couldn't rely on the light of the moon.

Sophia glanced toward the rivers of rain pouring down his window. "Out . . . finding food."

Suspicion stirred, rising in him like the winds outside. Somewhere, at some point on this journey they had undertaken together, he'd begun to develop the ear to pick out the subtle tones of her voice. He recognized this one all too well. It was the one she used when she was lying.

"Did he get the gold he needed?" she asked faintly. "For the entry?"

"That and a bit more to pay off the men for their silence on the cache's location," Nicholas said. "The old man assumes the astrolabe is as good as won, and has had us moving various stores and supplies to different locations. He wants access to them when he changes the timeline again."

Sophia nodded, rubbing a finger over her top lip. "That makes sense . . . so it's on, is it? Have you finally convinced him to let you accompany him to the auction?"

The old man had wanted to go alone with a small group of men and women for his protection. He claimed to need Nicholas to keep an eye on things at home, to fend off any attacks the Thorns might launch. Nicholas thought it more likely that some part of the old man still was struggling to fully trust him after what had happened with Etta, and did not want the astrolabe within Nicholas's reach.

But it had been far easier than anticipated to prey on the old man's rampant fears of theft or assassination. "He's so suspicious of everyone that it wasn't difficult to plant the seeds of the idea that he might need me to watch the guards watching him. With the twelve-hour time difference, Ironwood wants us to leave here no later than ten o'clock in the morning." He added, "I would keep back at least ten minutes, in the event Ironwood tarries near the passage to see who his competition might be. I will find a way to move him along."

"What's the old man's mood like? How has he been treating you?"

In the most disgusting way of all: like a prodigal son. "It's as if the past few years never existed. He wants nothing more than to discuss his shipping fleet. He lies and dreams in the same breath—I hear all about how much wealth and power I'm to inherit and how best to manipulate

417

those around me if I'm to keep it, and yet I know for certain he wishes to save his first wife. I am a placeholder in his mind."

In truth, the man's property was astounding, but his collections of rare books, ships, and artifacts from across the eras were breathtaking. And he could not deny how truly alarming it was to find himself seated at a candlelit, food-laden banquet table with the old man's closest advisors and inner circle, when before, he had only ever been allowed to wash their plates.

Sophia hummed in thought, still fixated on the window, the swaying of the tree branches as they scratched against the glass. With all of the agility and strength of a man three times his age, Nicholas rose from the bed, ignoring the jabbing aches in his back and the hot blood needling through his veins. He felt himself on the hazy cusp of a fever, but the longer he remained awake and upright, the sharper it became. Using the bedpost for support, he came to stand directly in front of her.

"Have you seen any Shadows about?"

"No," she said. "Now that everyone knows where the astrolabe is, I imagine they've finally turned their attention away from us. But if Ironwood could never find any of the witch's hiding places, I doubt they will."

Sophia still did not look at him, but he was seeing *her* now. The dark ring around her visible eye, the sunken quality of her skin. Either she had spent far too long in the cool rain and was shrinking, or there was a knot of something painful inside her, deep enough that her body was curling itself around it.

"Is that all?" he asked. "I'm glad to see you well, but . . . I thought we were in agreement that it was too much of a risk to meet unless there was some crucial bit of information to exchange."

Sophia said nothing, only stood and wrung out the ends of her oversize coat, as if preparing to go. "You're right. It was . . . it was very stupid to come. I think—well, I thought—that is, we should talk about what will happen in Japan. I'll stay as close to the Ironwood bidding party as possible. If you spot someone about my size, do whatever you can to draw them toward the back of the group. I'll try to pull him or her away from the others and take the robes that the Belladonna supposedly makes everyone wear to make the bidding anonymous."

I'll try to. Singular.

"That sounds simple enough," he said slowly, waiting for her to continue.

She looked down at the back of her hands, her bottom lip caught between her teeth. Stepping to the right, as if to begin her usual listless pacing, she was startled back into place by the loud *squeak* of the floorboard.

"Sophia," he began quietly. "Li Min is not out gathering supplies, is she?"

The girl swallowed. After a moment, she shook her head. His breath stilled in his chest. "Is she alive?"

The devastation on her face pierced even the numbest parts of him. She had gone a sickly shade of pale, one he associated with someone about to cast up their accounts or swoon. Nicholas took a stiff step forward as she swayed on her feet, and urged her to sit down in the chair again. Though it made his body speak in ten languages of agony, he knelt down in front of her, joints popping with the effort. Black spots swam in front of his vision at the movement, forcing him to shut his eyes tightly until they cleared.

When he opened them, a single tear had escaped down her cheek, dripping off her chin like rainwater.

"What's happened?" he asked, gutted. "Sophia, please; tell me what's happened."

"She's alive," Sophia managed to squeeze out. "But I wish—I wish I had killed her myself. She's been lying to us the whole bloody time. She was working for the Thorns."

Li Min was a mercenary, and he could not say that he was surprised to hear she'd been on a job when they'd first crossed paths. "What does that have to do with us?"

Sophia gave him one of her humorless smiles, the one that curved with self-loathing. "*We* were her job. She was supposed to—to follow us. Keep us from finding the astrolabe before them."

"What?" Nicholas took her by the shoulder, forcing her to turn toward him fully. "She told you this?"

Her lips pressed into a tight line, her breath harsh as it wove in and out of her. He put his hand over the place where her hands were curling, tearing at the fabric of her coat.

Sophia turned her face up toward the ceiling, but to her credit, she was looking him in the eye when she said, "Yes, while you were on the beach in Iceland. That's also when I found Julian. And Etta."

"What does—" Nicholas heard her, but it was only several moments later that her explanation landed. It exploded through him like a mortar round, and the damage it caused was mortal. He could not move. He could scarcely gather the wherewithal to remember to breathe.

"They were both with the Thorns this whole time," she whispered. "Julian must have been caught by them or gone willingly in the hope they'd hide him, maybe. And they found Etta first—her father put out the false death notice to protect her, I guess. Etta was the one who recognized Li Min. Because they *saw* each other, just a week ago. And she still lied to our faces, she kept up their ruse that Etta was dead, even though she saw how you suffered from it. If we had gone after the astrolabe, she would have taken it out of our hands before we could have ever decided what to do with it."

Etta was the one who recognized her.

Etta was . . . *Etta is alive.*

But how—how was Julian with her?

"Are you listening?" Sophia was saying. "Do you even *care*?"

She was seething, her anger holding her hostage. Her face blurred in his vision, but he was not crying. That would have required feeling something at all. This swift churning of expectations, of reality, left him hurtling toward the barbed edges of horror and fury. But he never landed. With nothing solid to grasp, he could not seem to break out of the free fall. He fell back, sitting on the ground in a bid to get the world to stop tearing around him in a blur of darkness and rain.

Alive. Impossibly, beautifully alive. If there was ever a moment he might have pulled Etta from thin air, it was this one, when he felt so illuminated, so bold with the knowledge of her, that he could have reached through the darkness of the centuries and fetched her to him.

"Why were they in Iceland?" Nicholas asked with urgency. So close, damn it all. They had been so close to him. "Were they all right?"

"They were there for the same reason you were," Sophia said, her voice flat. "Only, the Ironwoods beat them down to the cave."

If only the fog had delayed the longship even one hour . . . *No.*

He shook his head. It was too dangerous, too seductive a thought. Nicholas would have seen them for himself, yes, but Ironwood would have done so as well. They'd have been reunited under the worst of circumstances, and his plan to destroy Ironwood would have unraveled the instant he saw her.

"They wanted the entry fee for the auction?" To attend with the Thorns, he presumed. But the thought did not seem to follow through logically. Sophia would have met with a larger party than just the two of them. And given what Ironwood had said of Henry Hemlock's personal wealth, it did not seem like they'd need to skim from Ironwood's holdings.

Etta's father's wealth.

The man had clearly known what Nicholas had known from the very moment he and Etta had come to terms with needing to destroy the astrolabe: Ironwood would never cease hunting her if she took what he wanted from him. He would never stop until she was dead by his hand, or someone else's.

But did the old man believe she *was* dead, with the bloodied clothes as his only proof? His anxieties about double agents in his family ran deep, and with good reason. Perhaps some of his men were truly in Hemlock's pocket, and had claimed responsibility for the death to perpetuate the lie.

That, or the old man had known she was alive all along and had decided to use the pain of it to turn Nicholas to his side, dropping the hollow promises of wealth and respect as additional lures. He thought he knew his grandson's heart so very well, didn't he?

"That's the third time," he said softly to himself, shaking his head. Seeing her inquisitive look, he clarified, "That I've allowed myself to be deceived. It's remarkable we've made it this far, given what a fool I've been."

"If you're guilty of being a fool, it's only because you expect the rest of us to be as honorable as you are," Sophia said.

"I actually expect the world to be fairly miserable in its handling of me," he said. "Over the past week, I've allowed desperation to speak louder than my better judgment. It's had me on a leash this entire time."

He glanced down at the ring on his finger, avoiding her gaze. Nicholas had paid the price for it, certainly.

"Do Etta and Julian still intend to participate in the auction?" he asked carefully.

"I think I might have scared them off," Sophia said, sinking down onto the floor in front of him. "I did something—you're going to hate me for it."

He found his mind stilling again, fixating on her words. His gaze narrowed slightly. "What did you do?"

She pressed her lips tight together, as if she were drowning, trying to save that last bit of precious air.

"What did you do?" he repeated.

"You won't understand—I was *so* angry, so bloody furious, and I went to this place inside myself I don't like, that I can't help but

422

disappear into, and I could hear myself saying all of these things, all of these lies. I wanted to *kill* them for ruining everything, the two of them; I hated them for shattering Li Min's lie; but I was scared, too."

"Of what?" he asked. "*Sophia*. What did you tell them?"

She pressed her hands to her face. The panic in her voice gripped him and held him there, at her next words' mercy.

"That you were—that you were the heir now, and happily working for Ironwood. I told them that you never bothered looking for Etta, and that you were happily won over by the old man, because whatever was between you and her wasn't real to begin with."

Was that all? Nicholas shook his head with a dismayed laugh. "She didn't believe you."

The girl pulled her hands away from her face with a look of surprise.

"There is an understanding between us," he explained. "She knows the whole of my heart. But why would you say such a thing? Why try to send them away?"

"Because," she said, struggling to keep her voice down, "because of a *hundred* reasons! Because you would have reconsidered following through with the plan to destroy the astrolabe, knowing there was a chance you could be with her now. Because she would have interrupted you, distracted you, and cost you precious time when that loathsome ring could steal you at any moment and leave me to finish this all alone. And because I will be *damned* before I let you lie down and die without at least trying to give us the time to break the ring's hold over you."

Nicholas sat back, silenced by the force of her words.

"You can bloody well hate me for it, too, but I can't be sorry," she said, wiping at her face in disgust. "And now you have me weeping like a child! If I liked you any less, I would beat you senseless for this."

"I'm not surrendering to the poison, Sophia," he said. "I fight it every single day. This has been our plan—"

"This was *your* plan. Yours and Li Min's. You told me I wasn't allowed to die," she said. "Do you remember? In the desert, in the hospital, over and over again. Each time I wanted to slip away you were there, with your annoying 'You owe me a debt, you are not finished with your life, this is not your end' nonsense. It made me want to die just to irritate you, but I didn't. So why should I sit here and watch you make the same slow farewell?"

Nicholas's left arm began to shake under the strain of holding his weight. He shifted, leaning forward with a grimace. "Then why did you agree to follow me to the auction?"

She looked at him as if he'd asked her why chickens lay eggs. "Because I'm going to find the witch and stick a bunch of knives in her until I find the one soft, fleshy spot that makes her take your blasted ring off!"

He did not want to tell her that she was in the deepest sort of denial if she truly believed she could convince the witch of anything. The stories Ironwood had told him about the woman made his skin crawl, and he had very little doubt that killing her or wounding her would only cause the poison to work faster. She was as merciless as they came, and the only way to truly get his revenge on her would be to take the astrolabe and ruin her chances of adding another secret or soul to her collection.

He wasn't surrendering the ship; he was going down with it, and on his own terms.

"You said they . . . that Julian and . . . Etta," Nicholas said, trying to stamp out the ember that began to glow dangerously inside him again, "that they were planning to attend the auction? Or at least apply for entry to it?"

"They *were*, though judging by Linden's expression, I think I put her off the idea," Sophia said, with one last confession. "I told them what's going to happen when the astrolabe's destroyed. Neither of them took it very well."

It was amazing that, for all of their similarities, neither Etta nor

Sophia could decipher each other or understand the other's minds. Nicholas translated Etta's reaction for her: "That only means she'll be there to try to steal it."

"There wasn't enough gold left in the cache for an entry fee, anyway," Sophia said. "I came back and checked about an hour after you'd left. And Ironwood's cleared out the other ones Julian would know about."

That would pose an actual problem, though he had little doubt that Etta could think her way through the situation. "Then you're likely right, and they won't be there. You've kept them safely away from any trouble we might cause."

"Stop trying to make me feel better," Sophia ordered. "It won't work. I'm determined to be angry and guilty about this for at least another two days, and then again when I'm punching your corpse."

He tried his best to smile. "Though I sincerely doubt they believed you, you attempted to keep my pretense to maintain our plan, even in the face of great emotional turmoil. Ma'am, I regret to inform you that you now have honor in spades."

She pulled a hideous face. "Ugh. Is that why I feel so terrible? Take it back, it's awful."

Nicholas shook his head ruefully. "Can you not see it, though? How your situation might align with—"

"I don't want to hear this—"

"How it might align with Li Min's?" he pressed on. "She kept up a pretense on behalf of another that only served to keep Etta safe and alive. This whole situation might have taken a different direction, certainly, but it wouldn't have changed the manner of the deal I made with the Belladonna. Nothing but Ironwood's death or her mercy will take the ring off, and neither will ever come to pass. At least now . . . at least now something good might come of it."

She rubbed at her forehead. "I don't really want logic right now, Carter. I mostly want murder."

"Will you settle for an end to this?" he asked. "It's all I can offer at the moment."

"How can this not change anything for you?" Sophia asked, that same pleading note bleeding back into her words. "Why can't you be selfish like the rest of us?"

Etta's alive.

Julian is safe.

Li Min is gone.

All of these facts should have tilted the earth itself, upended him. But it changed . . . nothing.

It was better if Etta did not know about the ring, about the bargain, about his choice. She would fight him every single step of the way, and he couldn't risk being taken off that path now, not when he was so close to seeing everything through.

But the weight of that, knowing he was intentionally keeping her in the dark yet again, felt as though it might crush his entire chest. He had to fight for his next breath.

"I'm . . ." He tried to give a name to the quiet storm inside of him, but the moment he grasped what it was, it slipped away again, and all that was left was weariness.

Resignation.

He felt now like he was taking on water, moving forward sluggishly, toward an inevitable end. The thought of Etta breathing, fighting, filled the dark sky of his thoughts with stars. If he stretched out on his back, closed his eyes, he could imagine himself back on the deck of that ship. He would be able to see those stars falling once more, arcing down in one last flare of brilliance. It was seared upon his memory as she was.

Whatever would come the next night, Etta was still in possession of her life. He was unspeakably grateful, even as he knew once more the fear of his heart lying vulnerable outside of himself. She would continue on without him, blazing through the darkness in her way. If he could not give her back her own future, he could make a life for her that was safe, free from the retribution and strife between their families. He would end this cycle, wash the blood away.

But, oh, he was a coward, because he found himself seizing on that thin hope that Sophia was right, and Etta had been turned away from this task. It was harder to die than he imagined it would be, and desperately humbling. He did not want her to see him like this, no more than he wanted her in harm's way should things come to blows.

He did not think he could survive a final farewell.

The single power that time travel truly held over them was regret. If he could simply move back through the weeks, sift through the days, to arrive at that moment in the Belladonna's shop, of course he would have steered as far away from it as he could. But hindsight had given him something undeniably precious: insight. Into Sophia, into himself, and into their bitter, beautiful world. All he had ever wanted to do was travel, seek out those horizons; and he had, hadn't he? He had gone farther in these weeks than the limits of his own imagination.

"If we must act quickly, and there is no time tomorrow," he told Sophia, "I would like to say that I am proud to have fought beside you. I would never again presume to tell you how you ought to live your life; I would only say, as your friend, that there's no pain more acute than words left unsaid, and business which can never be concluded—"

She reached forward, pressing her hand against his mouth to silence him. Nicholas started to tug it away, exasperated, but in the next moment he heard it, too. Footsteps. A curt knock on the door.

"Everything okay in there, Carter?"

The Ironwood men didn't defer to him so much as guard him. Watch him. Judge him. He had seen the looks flying around the table, after Ironwood's proclamation declaring him heir during their last—and, please, God, final—family meeting.

"Fine," Nicholas called back. "Reciting . . . my prayers."

"Whatever you say," the man—Owen—grumbled. "Just keep it down, will you? If you wake him up, it'll be the end of all of us."

Too right.

Nicholas waited until the footsteps receded before turning back to Sophia, but she was already at the window, unlatching it. A slap of wind and rain struck him across the temple.

Right. The damned tree.

"You'll break your neck," he said, trying to stand. "Wait for the rain to settle. I'd rather not have to explain the presence of your broken body in the morning."

Sophia's lips curled ever so slightly upward. "Don't be ridiculous."

She sat on the window ledge, swinging one leg over, then the next. Her gaze roved over the tree's shaking limbs, the rivers of rainwater washing the street below clean.

"She might yet return," he told her as he came to stand behind her.

Sophia turned to him one last time, the mist of the storm collecting on her face. "No. She won't."

OUR LADY OF CANDELARIA WAS A STATELY PAPIST— Catholic—church, with all the embellishments the Baroque style of architecture had to offer. Two towers sat proudly on either side of an unfinished dome, dark granite accents contrasting neatly with its white-washed walls. Inside, however, the design was neoclassical, its pillars and statues of angels, saints, and the Virgin Mother carefully carved with an eye for the size and beauty of the place of worship.

It was blessedly far, at least, from the all-too-prosperous slave market on Valongo Street, the fattening houses where weak and thin "merchandise" were cajoled into gaining weight to increase their value, and the dock itself, which had no doubt been built by the hands of slaves to welcome each subsequent shipment of innocents. Of course, that had not stopped Ironwood from walking their party of an even dozen men right through it, with all the care and sensitivity of a monster.

"What's the matter with you?" the old man asked.

Wonders abounded—the man had finally broken away from the narrow lane of focus that was the astrolabe. The last five days had proven that when the old man was not speaking of it, he was thinking of it; and when he was not thinking of it, it was only because he was asleep and dreaming of it. It was the first word out of his mouth in the morning, and the last one he spoke in place of his evening prayers. Conversation with Ironwood was already forced, but it had become so rote and tiresome, Nicholas actually found himself missing the man's vile threats and bitter oaths.

Nicholas shifted his eyes away from the church. "Nothing. Am I not allowed to admire beauty when I see it?"

Ironwood snorted at that. "A terrible liar, now and forever. It's how I know I can trust you. How's the arm? Back in fighting form, I see. Good, good."

Rather than risk being left behind as a liability, someone who wouldn't be able to protect the old man from any enemies who might appear, Nicholas had removed his sling and tucked his useless hand into his coat pocket.

"It is—"

"Wonderful, yes," Ironwood said, in a voice that practically sang with glee. Nicholas was instantly repulsed by the heavy hand that landed on his shoulder. The added weight of it might as well have been a mountain, for how quickly his knees threatened to buckle.

Owen—the short, stocky guard—emerged from the church, signaling it was clear to enter and take the passage to Japan.

"One more step," the man said, as he urged the two of them forward. "One more night. Imagine her face; the future you wish to create is within your reach."

Owen held the door for them, allowing Nicholas to duck inside without moving his paralyzed arm. And, whether he wished it or not, he did see Etta there. He saw her in the flickering of the candles. He saw her in the smooth, pale lines of the arches. He saw her in the singular way the light struck the stained glass behind the altar and colored the world.

A hymn to her. A requiem to a future that was no longer his to claim.

"Yes," he said finally. "The end is in sight."

MOUNT KURAMA
1891

TWENTY-EIGHT

THE CENTURIES AND CONTINENTS MOVED AROUND HER IN dark waves, and the passage's usual bellow was more of a long, continuous whistle. The difference, while pleasant to Etta's ears, was rather disconcerting. But before she had much time to consider this, her feet struck the ground, and the full weight of the gold she carried in her leather backpack brought her down to her knees.

Julian tumbled out behind her, rocketing into her and sending them both down in a heap of limbs and bags. The gold plates and chalices dug into her spine.

"Ow," she said.

"Ouch," came the weak response. "Not one of our better landings."

"Better than the last six," Etta said, rolling out from under him.

Julian lurched up to his feet, struggling to stay vertical under the weight of his pack. "Time?"

Etta squinted at the wind-up watch they'd found tossed in with Ironwood's other treasures, still breathing hard from the run. "Half past ten?"

Julian punched the air in triumph. "Told you we'd make it in time, didn't I?"

While there had been enough gold and precious stones left in the

433

cave, Julian had previously mislabeled one of the entries in his journal, which had subsequently sent them on a hair-raising journey through Jerusalem during the First Crusade, with twentieth-century clothing and more gold than anyone had any right to.

The passage's whistling receded, but the drumming continued to pulse through the darkness. The vigor of the drums and chiming cymbals was breathtaking; as Etta stood, stumbling to maintain her balance on the soft incline, she was surprised to find the ancient music wasn't the heartbeat of the mountain itself.

The passage had deposited them behind a line of flames that snaked up the mountain's cleared path. Etta crawled through the damp, cool mud for a closer look.

"Sai-rei, sai-ryo!" That same phrase was being shouted, over and over, for all the wild, dark world to hear. She turned to Julian for a translation.

"I think . . . 'good festival'? Something like that?" Julian scratched at his mussed hair.

The smell of pine and smoke bled through the line of trees, carrying with it the voices of young and old alike. Stripped to their loincloths, men carried torches over their shoulders. Small ones, yes; carried by boys, really, who looked exceedingly proud to have the task. But as the torches increased in size, so did the men who carried them, until a few bore the staggering weight of torches the size of—motorcycles, and likely as heavy. The men staggered beneath their weight as they wound through the one-street village below, ascending up the dirt path. Cheers of encouragement followed from the villagers walking in their footsteps, their faces lit, glowing warmly in the face of an encroaching midnight.

Etta's brow furrowed. "What is this? Why would this Belladonna person pick a place where we'd be more likely to bump into the people of this time?"

"To your first question, a festival of some sort, clearly," Julian said, turning to the task of trying to pick the dirt out from under his nails. "In deference to whatever spirit or god is enshrined at the temple. To answer your second, it's best not to dwell on the dark, spider-infested maze of the Belladonna's mind, but I assume the festival will be ending soon."

She blinked. "That was . . . surprisingly useful."

"As I like to say, always aim to disappoint in life," Julian said. "That way you'll never fail to be a delightful surprise when you don't."

Etta snorted. "All right, let's go."

They began their climb through the trees, up and over the rocks, until at last they saw that more villagers were flowing down the mountain than up it. Soon that number sputtered to a few, and finally, none.

They moved onto the cleared trail without a word between them, shuffling through the black ash left behind by the fires. Etta caught a glimpse of Julian in a narrow pocket of moonlight—the smear of dirt across his cheek, the stains on his hands and knees, the way the waves of his hair seemed to stand on end. She already knew she looked like she'd been nearly trampled by horses in a street of melted manure and mud . . . because she had been.

"I'm worried you're not going to be enough of a distraction," Etta said quietly, "for me to get behind this Belladonna woman and grab the astrolabe. I might get out, but you won't."

"I am a *very* fast runner," he told her, "when sufficiently motivated."

"I was thinking . . . maybe I should just make a bid. Win it legitimately." She glanced over at him in the darkness.

"She only takes favors and secrets," Julian said, stopping to adjust the weight of his backpack. "Do you think you have something Grandfather doesn't?"

Etta had one thing none of the others did: she had grown up in a distant future, whereas no other traveler still alive had been born after 1945. But that future was gone, and any information from her future was worthless now. Which left one secret—one she wasn't sure the woman didn't already know. "We know the real reason why Ironwood wants the astrolabe. If the woman knows that, then she can use it against him. I think it's valuable, but it still doesn't feel like a concrete plan."

"I told you," he said. "You're not supposed to be able to plan anything at these things—no thefts, no murders, no business deals beyond purchasing the witch's wares. You'll be as much in the dark as Grandfather, if that's any reassurance."

Beyond the good work of irritating Cyrus Ironwood by forcing him to travel, the Belladonna was smart to pick a time and location where there might be witnesses, as a deterrent against bad or outlandish behavior from the travelers.

As they continued up the path, Etta began to take account of the stone markers, the lanterns, the small, open shrine-like structures with their slanting roofs and rich crimson paint. Their journey spent more and more minutes, their most precious currency, but it was a relief to see the lights were fading in the village below, like a hearth reduced to silent coals after burning through the last of its wood. In time, the only sound she could detect was the rustling of the forest's night-dwelling creatures.

She breathed in the smell of the damp greens around her, comforted by the familiarity of the traces of woodsmoke. Her body ached, but it was a good hurt, an earned one. Etta had fought through these last weeks and felt no small amount of pride for surviving.

"We're doing the right thing, aren't we?" Etta whispered. "I've wanted it gone for so long that the thought of keeping the astrolabe intact feels unnatural. Maybe it's cursed—it infects the lives of everyone who comes in contact with that same darkness."

Julian sighed. "I don't know. You're the moral compass, you're supposed to tell me that."

She elbowed him lightly. Inside her pack, the gold coins sounded like heavy rain as they rubbed against each other.

"I guess in my mind, it's like this, Linden-Hemlock-Spencer: the astrolabe itself has never been evil. For better or worse, it only answers to the heart of the person using it, but there isn't a person alive unselfish enough not to take advantage of it in some way. If destroying it destroys us, then we have to . . . I don't know, we have to hide it again once we straighten the timeline out."

What Mom did years ago.

Etta had been so quick to blame this journey on Rose's madness, her trauma, that she felt heartsick now just considering this. Rose might have known all along that destroying it would destroy the travelers' way of life, and that was initially why she had only hidden it.

But it didn't excuse her for keeping the truth from her daughter, it didn't forgive what she had done to Alice, and it didn't explain why she had become so bent on Etta destroying it.

Halfway up the mountain, her legs burning and her back aching from the weight of her pack, Etta saw a glimmer of light. The ring of it grew until she could make out the distinct shapes of lanterns twinkling in the trees above the path, and a young boy with golden hair sitting on a stool beside a large brass scale and several baskets. Behind him, a large white curtain had been hung to cover whatever lay beyond.

Julian slowed beside her.

The boy wore an oversize white robe, but had tugged it up when he'd crossed his legs, and she could see the fine stockings and velvet breeches underneath. At their approach, he merely flipped to the next page of the book in his lap.

Julian cleared his throat, but the boy held up a finger, still eyeing his book.

"Hello?" Etta tried.

Finally, the golden child lifted his gaze, and she almost laughed at the annoyance on his face. She knew what it was like to be interrupted in the middle of a particularly good page.

"It's just the two of us in the bidding party," Julian told him, finally sliding his backpack off his shoulders with a relieved sigh.

This only served to further irritate the boy, who slid from his stool and motioned to the scale. He stepped onto one side, leaving the other for them to pile their sacks on top of, and they began their prayers that they had not misjudged the weight.

"How do we know you weigh a hundred pounds?" Etta asked.

The boy glowered back, bobbing like a ship on a wave as the scale balanced. Etta caught herself holding her breath as their side dipped lower than the boy's, only to straighten in triumph. They'd brought more than enough.

"Oh, thank goodness." Julian rushed forward to remove some of the gold. "Would've been a shame to let all of this—"

"Welcome! Welcome, my young beasties."

A woman pushed through the pale curtain, careful to close it again behind her before Etta could see what was there. Her long legs devoured the distance between them in two quick gulps, stopping uncomfortably close to Etta. She fought every natural instinct to take a step back and reclaim some semblance of comfort.

Instead, Etta looked up and met the woman's dark gaze over the silver veil that covered the lower half of her face. Her full-figured body was dripping with black lace that looked as if its ornate floral patterns had been cut from the shadows themselves. And, as if she thought the occasion might call for it, she had added a silver-and-diamond diadem that sat on her head like a row of wolf's teeth.

She exchanged a look with the golden-haired boy, who nodded some sort of confirmation.

Julian wobbled a bit on his feet with what Etta believed might have been a bow that he thought better of halfway through. "Good evening, madam. We've brought the requested entry fee."

"And not much else," she said, her catlike eyes flitting from his face to Etta's.

"It doesn't matter," Etta said, with what she dearly hoped was something resembling confidence, "when we have the secret we do."

"Indeed." The veil fluttered, as if she'd given a silent laugh. "Only two of you, when others have tried to bring in nearly a dozen."

"I know your rules," Julian said. "Only eight per party."

She ignored him, her gaze still fixed on Etta. "How curious, beastie. Yours is a face I have seen before."

She waved the other woman off. "Yeah. Been getting that a lot recently."

"And such a pleasant temperament to match. Now, if you'll each please take a robe and a mask from the basket and don them—yes, you'll need to put the hood up as well. Safety in anonymity, as I always say."

"A jolly good policy if I've ever heard one," Julian said, placing the mask on his face and quickly knotting it behind his head. It covered the whole of his face, save for his eyes.

The woman cocked her head to the side. "Aren't you—"

"The previously-believed-to-be-dead Julian Ironwood?" he said, with the eagerness of someone who'd been longing to be recognized.

"—going to close your robe?" the Belladonna finished, and without any sort of preamble, took up the task of knotting the series of ties that ran down its side. Etta quickly laced her own, and tried not to laugh when the woman ran her spindly fingers down Julian's front.

"I believe you are our last bidding party. If you would follow me . . . You have set us back several precious moments. I cannot delay the start of the auction any further."

The woman cut in front of Etta and pulled the curtain aside.

If Etta had been asked to guess what was behind it, she would not have gone with two dozen other white-robed, golden-masked travelers and guardians, all of whom remained facing forward, packed together like cattle in a stall. The Belladonna reached up for one of the silver lanterns hanging in the trees and held it in front of her as she pushed her way up through the ranks.

Julian started to follow her, but Etta held out an arm, shaking her head. It was better if no one took particular notice of them, and moving to the front would give everyone ample time to guess who might be under the robe. As it was, no one dared to utter a single word as the pack began to follow the Belladonna and her lantern up the rest of the path, toward the temple several hundred yards away.

Only one figure, bringing up the rear of the first group, risked a look back at them. He or she was the only one who allowed themselves to break from the quick march of the others, moving slowly, with an almost labored gait. Hurt, or old, maybe. Etta narrowed her eyes, wishing it wasn't so dark. Because it looked like, it seemed like . . .

That person is slowing down. Drifting back intentionally. Etta felt for the small dagger she'd plucked off a knight in Jerusalem, dread combing its cold, clammy hands through her hair, down her neck. She was so wholly focused on the figure that she did not see the movement in the forest just to the left of Julian, until something lashed out, hooking a black-cloaked arm around his neck. His shout of alarm was smothered by the gloved hand smashing against his face.

Etta dove into the forest after them, the dagger in her hand. It was just like the attack in Russia. The attacker was shrouded in black, and the blade was pressed against Julian's throat, even as he struggled to disentangle himself from the powerful grip. She was a step behind the attacker, and drew her blade back to stab—

The weight hit Etta's back and brought her down before she could catch Julian's attacker, but it was the mountain itself, its sharp decline, that sent her rolling, spinning over the soft earth and ferns, until finally her back collided with a tree big enough to catch her weight. The blow knocked the dizziness from her mind, enough that she ignored the bruising she'd taken and climbed back onto her knees, searching for Julian in the darkness above her. A short distance away, tangled in the ferns and obscured by the small stone marker, were the twisted, white-robed legs of her own attacker.

440

Etta scrambled up the hill on hands and feet, the blade of her dagger clenched between her teeth until the ground flattened out enough for her to stand. She swung around the edge of the stone marker, her gasping breaths steaming the inside of her mask. At the very last second, rather than stab with her right hand, she threw her left fist forward, smashing into the attacker's mask and knocking them flat on their back just as they made to rise. She dropped to her knees on their chest, ripping their mask off and bringing the blade up to their jugular.

She knew this face.

She loved this face.

"Oh my God," Etta gasped, flying back, pulling her own mask up. "Oh my *God*—"

His eyes widened, equally stunned by the sight of her.

Her hands sank into the dirt, shaking. She pulled up leaves and roots, trying to ground herself in that moment, to make it feel real to her. That valley between them that had devastated her with his absence, the one she hadn't let herself fall into, opened up again.

One single, soft word reached her: "Hi."

Etta's heart broke open, and the relief was as painful as it was necessary. The way he looked at her now, like she was a pearl in the darkness; the way his hand reached for her, waiting for her hand, its twin—she crashed into him just as he sat up, her lips on his, stealing his breath, his surprised laughter. Stealing him back into herself.

"Hi," she managed, her hands cupping his face, kissing him, kissing him—

"Where . . . have you been?" he asked when he could.

"Where have *you* been?" she demanded back, feeling his hands sink into her braid, weaving sweetness into it.

"I've been quite occupied . . . with looking for you," he said. "Had a . . . damned time of it. I might have known you'd find me first."

"Saw you—the beach—" She tasted blood from his split lip, but she didn't care, she didn't care—

"I know, I know—thought you were—"

"I know, I'm sorry—why did you chase me now? Why are you here?" Etta forced herself to stop, to pull back and wrap her arms around him so he'd have the opportunity to answer. His arm came up to lock around her waist, and his forehead rested against her shoulder; he was breathing hard.

"Are we incapable of meeting under remotely typical circumstances?" Etta heard him wonder. The damp ground was soaking through her robe, straight to her skin, but she hardly felt it. Nicholas's pulse was fluttering against her cheek, nothing at all like the steady, driving beat she remembered from even their most desperate moments.

It was the darkness, she was sure of it—it was only the hunger, the exhaustion, and the shadows that made him look so frail. But when her hands skimmed over his back, she felt each knob of his spine. The ridges of his ribs. Etta leaned back so she could brush a half-open kiss against his lips, his labored breathing mingling with hers.

"I can't even hold you," he whispered. "It's too much, it's all too fast—I wasn't afraid before, but I find myself—I find myself just that slightest bit afraid now."

"What are you talking about?" she asked, trying to shift so she could study him, see his face. He only held her tighter, his arm shaking with the effort. Her hands came up to slide through his tufts of hair, and his scalp was warm against her palms. Nicholas strained to kiss her again, his mouth grazing the soft corner of her lips.

"—I was just going for whoever looked to be about my—" Sophia's voice said behind them.

"I am *not* your size!" That was Julian.

"Well, would you prefer I said I went for whoever looked easiest to take down?"

She heard Sophia and Julian approach, felt the moment they were seen. The silence that followed was its own century.

"What are you still doing here?" Sophia aimed the words at

Nicholas, coating them with anger. "He's going to notice you're gone if you don't hurry back."

"Thought she—that Etta was—someone who could—hurt you—"

It was difficult to piece together the soft fragments of his words. Her mind did the best it could: Sophia had unwittingly snared Julian to steal his robes for the auction, and, seeing a disguised Etta pursue them, Nicholas had panicked, worrying that Sophia wouldn't be able to fight two people at once.

"Why are you—?" Etta asked. "Tell me what's happening—*Nicholas!*"

The cold wash of fear as he sagged against her was nothing compared to the hurricane that came with Sophia's sharp oath. She leaped over the fallen tree that stood between them and seized Nicholas's shoulders, giving him a hard, jaw-snapping shake.

"Damn you, Carter," she said, "not *now*, damn you—"

"Nicholas?" Etta couldn't stop saying his name, as if that would be enough to pull him back to consciousness. "Tell me what's happening!"

"We're running out of time, that's what's bloody happening," Sophia said, and with no other warning, slapped him across the face.

TWENTY-NINE

Even as he came to again, the darkness in his vision remained like a halo around her face, as if to dash away the dream of her. But she was still there.

Etta was still there.

She knelt in front of him, smelling of fire smoke, warm, sweet bread, a home. The mud that was smeared across her face had caught a single strand of her hair, sticking it to her cheek. For the life of him, he could not say why he found this unbearably endearing.

"You're not okay, are you?" she whispered.

He knew it was Sophia behind him, propping him up so he could face them—*them*, because Julian was hovering a few short feet away, looking so uncertain he was nearly unrecognizable to Nicholas.

"Julian," he said, letting his relief bleed into the words. He hadn't realized it until now, how grateful he was that these two had found one another. Etta would protect Julian; and Julian would ensure Etta didn't have to be alone.

Hearing his name, his half brother drew closer to their small circle. "This is the part where I tell you I'm a fool and an ingrate, and you punch me."

Meeting his gaze, seeing Julian's face, Nicholas thought of the rage that he'd always imagined would pour through him, boiling with years' worth of resentment and ill-humored thoughts and words. But what he felt now was simply peace. That small part of him was resolved, and thankful, and above all, glad; this was his brother, and not even death had changed his love for him. "Perhaps another time?"

He gave Sophia a meaningful look, then glanced at Etta.

"Fine," Sophia said. And then, to Etta: "I'm sorry about the way I treated you. I'm also sorry your mother is a demon from hell."

"I'm sorry about what happened to you, and the things I said, except for when you deserved them," Etta said, her words wavering, even as she tried to steady them. "But why won't anyone answer my question? What's happening?"

His abominable pride did not let him ask for help to stand, but the others offered it regardless. Etta held both of his forearms, keeping his balance for him. The fear on her face tore at him. Nicholas turned to look at Sophia and Julian. "I need a moment."

"We don't have long," Sophia said. "I can explain it to them. Just *go!*"

He shook his head. *God grant me time enough for this.* "It'll only be a moment. *Please.*"

He was sure she would fight him until the breath left both of their bodies. But instead, Sophia let out a small huff and nodded. She drew Julian away, back up toward the edge of the trail.

Etta turned his face back toward her own.

"Tell me," she said. "*Please*, just tell me what's going on. Why were you with Ironwood? Are you all right? What happened to your arm?"

Of course she had noticed.

"I am not completely myself at the moment," Nicholas admitted. "There isn't time for it all, only what is necessary. If I could pluck this moment out of time and keep us here forever, I would. But we cannot stop time; we can only right it again."

"That's what I'm trying to do," Etta said. Her heart shone in her face, lit softly like a candle, as she brought it close to his, as if trying to give him her light. He burned with the regret of it, not trusting his body to hold her the way he wanted to, without collapsing again.

"But our plan," she continued, her lips close to his ear, "it has to change. We can't destroy it."

And he knew devastation. Pure, unadulterated pain. Etta saw it flash in his face, and knew from the way denial pooled in her eyes . . . on this, they could not be reconciled. He captured her mouth again, trying to soften the blow, to find the words he needed. The cool night bit at his skin, but her lips were hot, insistent, moving over his own as if to launch her own argument.

Nicholas tore himself away, trying to still her long enough to reintroduce her to reason.

"It has to be destroyed, you said as much yourself," he said. "I know the consequences, I know what might come of it, but Etta—do you see? Do you feel how much of this is outside our hands? If this is ever going to end, let it be now. Your mother—she came to me in the desert, just after you were orphaned. She spoke of a war to come."

"I know all about this," Etta interrupted.

"She wasn't wrong. *This* is the war which never ends. The one that exists between the families," he said. "There's a shape to this, a pattern."

Etta flinched at that word, already shaking her head, trying to capture his lips again, keep him from finishing. "No, no, no—don't say that, don't use that word—"

He deserved a bloody medal for having the will to stop her from kissing him.

"I cannot help but think there is no lasting peace between the families because there is something deeply unnatural about us, what we can do," he continued. "It must be time's revenge that we inherently repel one another. It feels to me as if these conflicts are trying to force us back to our natural times, where we're meant to be."

She lifted her pale eyes, hardened now like chips of ice. "There is nothing more *natural* than families. You haven't seen what I have.

These are people who love and need one another. We can still fix the timeline—it'll take longer, yes, but it's possible to do it one piece at a time."

"And then what?" he prompted. "The astrolabe is hidden again? We risk someone else resuming the search, finding it, unraveling everything we've done? This is the only way to hold Ironwood accountable, to make him answer for what he's done to us all. If not for that reason, then think of the millions upon millions of lives he's toyed with, the disregard and apathy he's shown them. He is not the exception, Etta, he is the *rule*. There is too much power in what we can do."

Nicholas knew it was unfair of him that he could make this decision with the callousness it required, knowing it would be one of his last. But only days before, he'd been running toward vengeance like a man on fire, burning up the last parts of his soul. Some part of her, at least, seemed to see the truth in his last argument. Her whole body tensed in frustration.

He was staring down another loss, and, though he had been so logical, though he knew her to be logical, he saw the stricken look of betrayal on her face, and all of those arguments threatened to fly away from him. What was history anyway but the lies of the winning few? Why was it worth protecting, when it forgot the starving child under siege, the slave woman on her deathbed, the man lost at sea? It was an imperfect record written by a biased hand, diluted to garner the most agreement from competing parties. He was tempted to see her point, to imagine that she could realign the past and present and future into something beautiful. God, if anyone was capable of it, it would be her.

But their history, the one forged by travelers, was one of violence, war, and revenge; they had not simply made it. They were made by it.

"And what about us?" she asked, running her small, lovely hands up to his shoulders, his neck, his face. Nicholas leaned into the callused tips of her fingers. "What if I love you, and I need you? What was the point of this? Why did we fight so hard, if you were only ever going to give up?"

"*Carter!*"

The man's voice echoed down to them, still a distance away. *Owen.*

Etta made as if to draw him behind her, and he wanted to kiss her then more than he wanted his next breath. The seconds unraveled around him, blistered his raw heart.

"Stay with me," she begged. "Stay with me. This isn't over yet."

"This is freedom—*this*, the freedom from fear, is what it means to rewrite the rules," he said. "A world in which the astrolabe exists is a world in which either of us could be taken at a moment's notice. If nothing else, I'll know you'll be safe."

"*Alone,*" she corrected sharply.

"Never alone," he promised. "Did you not feel me with you in all of our days apart?"

Can you not feel my heart beating for you?

"It's not the same," she said, her eyes flashing again. "And you know it."

"I only know this: our paths were separated by centuries, but we converged. No matter the outcome, my destiny has always been joined to yours."

"*Carter! Where the hell are you?*"

Etta leaned forward into him, her face against the curve of his neck. "Don't do this—please don't do this."

"Do you believe in that world you spoke of, the one made for us?" She swallowed, nodding. Her soft lips were against his bare skin, and he was a man, damn it all, and he was burning for her. The words that escaped him were choked with emotion. "If we aren't to have it in this life, then in the next. If not now, then we'll have forever."

She pulled back, only to surge up onto her toes and grip him fiercely by his robe. The kiss shot down his spine like lightning striking a mast, blowing him apart.

It wasn't a retreat, and it was far from a surrender. She invaded his every sense at once, the way the sun first breaks in the morning and illuminates the horizon. The taste of her, the smell of her, those small sounds she made in her throat; all of these things were secrets entrusted to him, prizes he had fought so desperately to retake. Etta seized every part of him at once, and he pushed the deadening dread away, let the frantic joy of *her* rush through him, flooding the empty places, turning him inside out.

His skin felt drum-tight wherever her lips touched, and Nicholas wondered, in those spaces between the battering of his heart, how it was possible that she was so soft, when all of the days that had led them here had been so very hard. She did not cry, his brave girl, but he felt the rage beneath her skin, moving her to fit against his body, to disappear into him.

"*Nicholas!*" Sophia called softly. "He's coming!"

The blade hanging over them fell at last.

Nicholas eased back from her, wondering if this was what death would feel like—the painful release. He had envisioned it so many times as wading out into dark, cool water, letting it rise past his hips, his shoulders, his head. This was a breaking, a thunderclap of agony. How short a person's life was, but how very many times they were asked to die inside.

"I love you," he told her softly. "Time can never steal that."

And somehow, before she spoke, Nicholas knew what she was about to say. Her face was steeled, defiant.

"I'm not giving up," Etta said, the loose strands of her hair flying about her face. A shining storm of a girl. "I won't destroy it. This isn't the end."

Nicholas turned her hand over, pressing one last burning kiss into her palm. "Then may the best pirate win."

———

"Hurry it up, will you?" Owen wasn't a large man by any means, but his voice could absolutely thunder when the situation called for it. He had lifted his mask, and was scanning the dark line of the forest for Nicholas. Sophia was right, then. The old man had noticed he was gone, and more quickly than he would have expected.

"I managed to get turned around," Nicholas said, limping up to him.

The other man took in the sorry state of his stained robes. "What kind of fool falls while taking a piss?"

"You do." Sophia had moved so quickly, looping in a large circle back up to the trail behind Owen, that neither man noticed her until she brought the rock crashing down on his head.

The whites of his eyes flashed as he crumpled. Nicholas watched in appreciation as Sophia stripped the robe and mask off him and set about rolling Owen off the trail, into the forest, where the mountain did the rest of the work in carrying him away.

"Did you finish your business?" she asked innocently.

"Did you?" he pushed back. Julian had gone ahead with Etta, and while there was much he wished he could have said to his half brother, there was likely quite a bit more that needed to be spoken between the formerly betrothed pair.

A gong sounded from above, where the graceful temple sat at the top of the trail. Nicholas straightened his mask and accepted Sophia's offered shoulder as support for the last few yards of their climb. They passed through the structure with its airy, open foundations, the upward slant of its roof, to find an enormous white tent pitched in the center of its stone courtyard. So, then; they would not be trampling over a sacred place. Good. Perhaps the Belladonna still had some scraps of decency clinging to her tattered soul.

The scent of wine and spirits floated to him on the next autumn breeze, followed by the sweet notes of fruit. A short distance from the tent, a table was elegantly piled with food, though it had clearly already been ravaged by the others. The Belladonna stood beside it, waiting for them.

"Help yourselves, of course," the Belladonna said, turning to greet a man who, Nicholas thought, must have been a priest or a monk, based on his ceremonial robes, different from the ones the travelers donned. He seemed harried, hovering near the tent but not daring to enter. The woman shooed him away by blowing a kiss.

"Is he a guardian?" Nicholas asked.

"No. Return a few legendary national treasures and you'll be surprised by the favors people will do for you," the Belladonna said. "And the things they're willing to forget."

Sophia snorted, drawing the woman's eyes over to her. The Belladonna hummed thoughtfully but said nothing. "If you are ready, follow me. The rest of your party is already situated."

The tent was far larger than it had appeared on the outside, so much so that he wondered if it might be one of the Belladonna's illusions. The central aisle led up to a raised and gilded table, on which a dark wooden box had been placed. Two masked men stood on either side of it, swords in hand, as if prepared to slice any who dared to reach for it. If he hadn't felt it just then, that chill creeping over his skin, the tremor in the air, Nicholas might not have believed the astrolabe to be inside.

"Do you . . ." Sophia whispered, sounding almost faint. *Feel that?*

The Belladonna jerked her head around. "*Silence.* Here. Here is your place."

Lining the long aisle were stalls, divided by heavy white fabric that looked, to Nicholas's biased eye, like sailcloth. At least one dark shape of a man or woman appeared to be sitting in each, backlit by a lantern or an arrangement of candles. So that was it, then—how she had managed to further the anonymity of the bidders and, likely, the winner who would be taking any of her auctioned goods home.

Where is Etta?

"You," she said, brushing his shoulder with her long, curling nails, "are designated as a bidder. Present your offer when I call for the fourth bidder—should you survive that long." As she leaned in closer, he breathed in that same earthy scent, as if she were a dark forest wearing a woman's skin. "There's still time, of course."

Nicholas ignored the tremor in his heart as he said softly, "Good evening to you, ma'am."

The Belladonna stood to the side, lifting the entrance to their stall. Inside, the Ironwoods were lifting their masks to taste the proffered food and wine, but they instantly slid them back into place. Sophia stepped in beside him, edging around the room to avoid too much notice that she was not, in fact, Owen.

"There he is!" Ironwood said as the curtain shut behind them. Still mercifully in possession of his good mood. "Now it begins."

His footsteps were soft against the rugs and pillows provided; there was little else, beyond a few candles and a small wooden table. Nicholas surrendered himself heavily to the floor. The bruises and cuts he'd acquired were a low throb of pain, but they were nothing compared to the fire searing his veins. Instead of letting himself notice the twitching of his left hand, he focused on the foul smell of the pipe someone was smoking in the stall beside theirs. The Belladonna had placed them directly in the middle of the stalls, but save for that whiff of bad air and the murmur of the Ironwood men around him, he could not hear or see evidence of any of the other bidders. He could not even hear the wind outside.

The gong sounded again. With a kick of his heart, Nicholas turned back toward the curtain draped over their stall's entrance, and beyond that, the muted shapes of the Belladonna and her guards.

"Ladies and gentlemen, I would like to welcome you to tonight's auction. As always, your silence is mandatory. I have taken . . . liberties, shall we say . . . to ensure this. I will be able to hear you, but to protect the privacy of the winner, you will not be able to hear one another."

Ironwood drummed his fingers against his knees, nodding repeatedly in an eager, childlike manner. The man's entire world was winnowed down to this moment, as he stood on the edge of grasping the only thing that had ever been truly denied him.

"The winner of this item will be liable for its transportation and protection outside the barriers of this site. All sales, regardless of satisfaction, are final and binding. Upon the conclusion of the auction, the winner will be allowed to leave first, followed by the rest of you in the order of my choosing. Rather than conduct multiple rounds of bids, please submit your best offer as it stands. I will call each designated bidder forward to hand it to me."

Nicholas's fingers dug into the muscles of his thighs. He dropped his eyes to the floor. *Please, God, keep her safe, let this end—*

"I thank the consigners who entrusted me with this sale. Without further ado, I present lot 427, a purported astrolabe—"

Purported. Nicholas actually laughed.

"—of unknown, ancient origins. First bidder, please."

Nicholas leaned forward, trying to peer through the smallest of gaps where the side of the stall met the curtain. His breathing had taken on that uneven quality that made darkness dance in his vision. Etta—where was Etta?

"Second bidder, please."

Hell and damnation, he thought, wiping the sweat from his forehead, his eyes. He tasted rust in his mouth. *Not yet. Not yet, damn you—*

A dark splatter—deep enough to show through the thick fabric— whipped against the curtain directly across from theirs. Nicholas and Sophia jumped to their feet just as the bidder's lifeless body, still spilling blood, was thrown out of the stall, a darkness deeper than night exploding after him.

THIRTY

As she made her way up to the Belladonna, Etta squared her shoulders, the scrap of paper on which she'd written her offer, *A secret about Ironwood's desires*, soft and damp in her hand. The candles' flames shook in their stands, the dimly flickering light outlining each of the stalls as she passed them. It was the silence that was unleashing her anger, unbraiding the knot of fury she'd wrapped around herself. Her hands clenched by her side again, as if to keep the feel of Nicholas's rough skin trapped there a moment longer.

May the best pirate win.

It wasn't even that they were at odds; she understood his line of reasoning, even as she wanted to strangle him for simply accepting it. It was what he had so clearly withheld: the reason why the fire had left his heart. Why, when she kissed him that last time, had he shuddered, as if on the verge of shattering? *Something's wrong, something is so wrong,* her mind had screamed as her hands skimmed over him, searching for a wound, a bandage that might explain the exhaustion, the weakness.

Pattern. She hated that word now, the lack of control it implied. The way it had hooked into what Henry had told her in Russia, grown through her like a winding, barbed vine. *You will see the pattern, too.*

They were both wrong. Etta didn't have to accept that anything was *meant* to happen. She had been orphaned in Damascus, flung centuries away from Nicholas, but that was nothing compared to being trapped almost three hundred years ahead of him, locked away from her family, from the Thorns, from this hidden life. This wasn't a pattern unless she let it become one.

We cannot possess the things and people not meant for us, we cannot control every outcome; we cannot cheat death. Etta hardened herself, straining to listen to the sound of her feet so she wouldn't have to hear Henry's words rising in her mind again, to see his bloodied face.

Etta stepped up to the table, feeling the icy pressure of the Belladonna's gaze on her. When she was sure she'd released enough of her frustration in order to keep her expression neutral, Etta met her eyes and held out the offer. The woman plucked it out of her hand like a petal off a flower.

Standing near the table, Etta picked up the murmurs of the bidders, the debates they were having with themselves, as if all of their words had been funneled to that exact spot. But even those conversations were lost to the sound of the blood rushing in her ears.

If she reached out, she'd be able to brush the smooth, dark wood of the box that held the astrolabe. The candlelight caught all of the intricate detail, the etchings and marks of the device resting on the box's velvet interior. Etta had held it for only a moment, but she recognized it all the same.

The flames flickered with her next step forward, and the sight gripped her, made her hold the next breath she drew in—because when the flames danced, so did the image of the burly guards.

A projection? An impressive one. *How——?*

Don't do it, don't do it— But she couldn't help herself. She brushed her fingers against the edge of the astrolabe's box.

The lid snapped down. The Belladonna's long fingers, knotted at the joints, held it firmly in place.

"I see your heart," the woman said. "It cannot be you."

The scream set Etta's pulse stuttering long before she saw the splash of dark blood against the curtain. A piercing laugh followed, an attack on her eardrums, and her legs were suddenly weak beneath her.

Them.

The Belladonna merely took a step back, crossed her arms over her chest, and watched as the same bidder's body was tossed through the curtain, landing in a sickening, blood-soaked heap in the central aisle, his mask askew. The force of it blew out the candles at the table and the guards vanished like shadows meeting sunlight.

Etta barely swallowed her gasp of shock as she turned toward the Belladonna. But the woman's face was impassive as she watched a new figure emerge at the entrance to the tent. It must have been a man, for he was broad in the shoulders and seemed almost inhumanly tall. He was draped in a shimmering cloak of gold and silver threads that made him look like a flickering flame. He reached up and slowly lowered the hood, never breaking eye contact with the Belladonna.

His shock of white hair was combed back neatly over his skull, and though Etta recognized his face as human, all of his features seemed to be exaggerated by the desperate way his skin clung to his pointed chin and prominent cheekbones. The arch of his brow was severe, and several veins bulged across his forehead. He looked as if he'd been carved from wax—patches of his skin seemed to gleam as golden as his cloak, while others were gray and flaking.

But even in decay, he seemed . . .

Radiant.

The small boy, the Belladonna's servant, had been sitting to one side of the table, his book open in his lap. Now he stood, calmly shutting the cover, and left through the rear of the tent.

"It's been a lifetime," the Belladonna called to him. "And now we find ourselves here again."

"I might have known it was you. What an intriguing reinvention;

and more intriguing still that you did not consume this one, this time." The man walked with an eerie silence, the only sound was his long golden robe whispering against the stone ground.

"You know, I've been quite content with two lives, the second of which will keep me in comfort for many years yet." The Belladonna's eyes drifted down the length of the man, skimming over the worn edges of his form. "It seems the same cannot be said for you. I wonder, how long would you have without it? I could not have drawn you out if you were anything short of desperate. Unless, of course, you merely wished to see the flock. I admit, they are amusing. From time to time."

"I am as impervious to your words as I am to your blades," he said, the words chiming like a song.

"We shall see." Etta almost jumped clear out of her skin. It sounded as though the Belladonna were standing directly beside her, whispering the words loudly to her for the man to overhear. "Why . . . it looks as though a single spark would set you aflame."

A shadow passed over the man's face. That strike, at least, had landed. "I felt your mark upon that child, that young man, and spared his life only to amuse myself by killing him in front of you. This game is at its end, sister."

The Belladonna gazed back, as serene and still as the moon. "And so it is."

The man's eyes were like sunlight passing through glass, intensifying as they fixated on something. Etta felt the gaze burn through her skin, to her core, as his eyes flicked over to her. They narrowed, as if in recognition, and terror froze her in place.

She sucked in a sharp breath; at that moment, darkness broke loose from the closest stall and flooded the tent with night. Blood slapped the white canvas, the fabric rending, as a body was thrown through. It rolled over to them, limbs flapping, sucking wounds visible, until the stranger—a traveler Etta didn't recognize—gazed up at her, unseeing.

She was pinned by that moment, unable to get her feet under her again. The screams of the other travelers tore through her ears, but she couldn't work up one of her own, could barely breathe.

"Etta!"

Nicholas, Sophia, and Julian tore out of their stalls as she dove for the table, for the box, for the astrolabe. Her fingers closed around it, and she felt the familiar pulse of the astrolabe's power inside. The air pulled around her—her only warning before she was blown off her feet by the impact of someone slamming into her. The ground rushed up to greet her.

No, no, no! The box flew out of her hands as she fell, her vision blanking out with the force of her impact on the stone. She heard the wood splinter; her knife, her sole weapon, clattered as it danced away; but before she could reach for either, a torrent of black fell over her. Hot spittle flew in her eyes; the attacker's weight was oppressive, as if trying to force her deeper into the ground. Etta choked on her next breath as the man leaned low, coming close enough for her to smell the decay emanating from his rotting teeth. His clawlike dagger dug into her upper arm and twisted.

With a cry, Etta managed to unpin one hand long enough to catch his jaw, desperately reaching with the other for the knife she'd lost, muscles straining, fingers grasping—

A sword swung out, its dull edge catching the Shadow on the side of his head. The blow was enough to stun him, but not to knock him off her chest. Etta managed to wriggle that last inch to the left, latch on to her knife, and, without any thought but getting out from under his weight, slam the blade upward, into the only place she could find without armor: his neck. The spill of dark blood made her stomach riot as it bubbled from the man's wound. The Shadow was shoved away from her, and she sucked the smoky air into her already burning lungs.

Etta scrambled to her feet, assisted by a hand that gripped her beneath one shoulder. She whirled—

"Are you hurt?"

Henry stood there, his white robe spattered with blood. A bruise covered his skin from his temple to his jaw, and he couldn't seem to fully straighten to his full, powerful height. But it was him. *Alive.*

Etta felt the burn of tears in her eyes, and choked on her words. His face was so unusually soft as he looked at her that she had to wonder if he'd mistaken her shock for fear. She stumbled forward, surprising both of them as her arms wrapped around his center, and she buried her face in his shoulder.

Alive.

"Are you—are you all right?" he asked, one tentative hand touching the back of her head.

Behind him, around him, men and women burst through the entrance of the tent, in clothing that ranged in style from the twentieth century to the first, weapons in hand. Leading the charge was Li Min, shrouded in black silk. The young woman shot forward, skimming through the carnage, seemingly searching. Nicholas and Sophia were locked in the middle of a blood-soaked circle, the bodies piling around them, choking them off from the rest of the room—from the attackers, the victims, the men and women who clutched their dead, screaming, until they too were silenced. With the smoke filling the space, it was nearly impossible to tell a shadow from a Shadow.

Nicholas stumbled, taking a blow to his back that brought him to his knees. Li Min drew herself back, just like an arrow notched on a bow, and then she was flying again, straight for him. She pulled a small dagger from her boot, launching it at the neck of the Shadow who'd cornered them at the table. The range of emotions that exploded across Sophia's face at the sight of the other girl was indescribable.

"You are not forgiven!" she shouted.

Li Min kicked a silver serving platter up off the wreckage of canvas and wood on the floor. A man—an Ironwood—had taken up a gun and aimed, but she used the heavy platter to deflect the shot away from Nicholas and Sophia, and then to knock the man clear off his feet. In her next move, she seemed to produce a sword out of thin air, driving it through the back of the Shadow who had recovered enough to swing her claw and sword at Sophia's face. Nicholas, his face fixed in determination, ripped the blade out from between her shoulders and proceeded to slash her with the cold dispassion of someone who'd fought, and thrived, in many more battles than his opponent could ever imagine.

Sophia gripped the front of Li Min's cloak, drew her in, and kissed her soundly as the flames from the nearby candles caught the tent and set it ablaze.

"Thorns!" someone shouted above the shrieks, the vibrations of the dark one's speech, the screams of agony and fear as the travelers tried to flee.

Another voice. *"Hemlock!"*

Henry spun Etta away; she heard, rather than saw, the explosion of a gunshot that ripped through the din of clanging metal. He jerked, but didn't fall—Etta reached up, trying to pull back to see where he'd been hit, only to find that a man in a trim suit behind him was already slumping to the ground, shot clean through the skull.

The smoke from the burning stall began to fill the air, but it lifted as her mother stepped forward without a mask, her rifle still raised—pointed now at Henry, who calmly brought up his sword, bringing it to rest at the spot where Rose's long, pale neck met her shoulder. She, too, was wearing the white auction robes, though now she had painted herself red and black with blood and smoke.

Etta pulled back from Henry with a jerk of alarm.

Rose's cool expression slipped at the sight of them, cracking enough for her relief to bleed through.

"Can you get her out of here?" Henry asked.

Rose said nothing, only nodded.

"No—!" Etta ripped herself out of his grip. "You don't understand, the astrolabe—you can't destroy it—"

A familiar cry had Etta spinning back around. Nicholas had taken cover behind the overturned table with Sophia and Li Min. As one, they lifted it and used it as a battering ram, charging into the two Shadows who'd begun taking turns driving their claws through the body of one of the Thorns on the ground, trying to crawl over to another wounded young man.

When she looked toward her mother, Rose was nearly unrecognizable in her bone-pale terror.

Etta turned slowly.

It was the quiet, the way he absorbed the sounds around him like a vacuum, that was so deeply disturbing. The walls seemed to kneel to him, leaning forward, as if with each step he quietly devoured more of the world. The man in gold glided forward through the wreckage. The fighting fell away from him, the shadowed attackers drawing their prey into the stalls like predators wanting to feast on their kills. The hem of his robe was soaked up to the knee with blood.

Henry reached for her, but it was her mother who seized her. Etta found herself tucked between her mother's back and the wall of the tent as the glittering man passed by. This close, his face had the consistency of rice paper. For a terrifying moment, Etta imagined she could see the dark blood throbbing through his rootlike veins.

But she wasn't shaking—her mother was. Rose Linden, who had hunted tigers, betrayed Ironwoods, conquered an unfamiliar future, was *shaking*. As if that same raw fear carried vibrations through the air, the radiant man stopped suddenly, turning toward them, his eyes seeking. Recognition flared as he found Rose, his lips curving into a horrifying imitation of a smile.

"Hello, child."

A whisper.

A curse.

Knowledge flooded Etta, filling the cracks in the picture she had begun to assemble of her mother's life. Henry stepped in front of them both, but the man had no interest in him. As the man passed by, her father recoiled, as if the man had brushed his soul. There was something about the way the air itself seemed to curl and vibrate around the man, bowing to him, that made Etta's stomach clench again.

"My God, my God, Rosie—" Henry said, turning toward her.

"You . . . believe me?" The vulnerability in her mother's words was shattering.

"I'm sorry," Henry said, so softly that Etta wasn't sure her mother could hear him over the swarm of fighting. It felt as if she were standing in the path of two hurricanes finally on the verge of collision, the winds of clashing blades and blood whipping around them.

"Etta!"

Etta pulled herself free from her mother at Sophia's bellow. Sophia was standing back to back with Li Min now, staving off two Thorns who had blades of their own. "Ironwood's got it!"

Etta searched through the blazing fire and darkness until she found the place where the flames had eaten a hole in the side of the tent. There she saw an older man, his mask still on, rushing out into the courtyard, dodging the Shinto priests as they attempted to throw buckets of water onto the flames to stifle the fire before it jumped to the temple.

Between her and that opening, however, was Nicholas, with a Shadow clinging to his back; one clawed hand was on the verge of raking across his throat, no matter how hard Nicholas tried to buck his attacker off. His palm came up to block the next swipe of the claws, and blood instantly pooled where they cut deep into his flesh. Etta rushed toward him, but then Julian seemed to materialize out of thin air, shooting the man with what she thought must have been Sophia's flintlock. The bullet wasn't enough to deter the Shadow for long, but it was long enough for Nicholas to reclaim his sword from the ground.

The Shadow lunged again, but as Nicholas moved, the small leather cord he wore around his neck escaped his robe, and a large bead swung out from beneath his shirt. Etta might have imagined it—smoke was gathering heavily around them, masking them in silver—but when the Shadow stabbed at his heart, the bead caught the tip of the blade. The Shadow seemed almost enraptured by the unexpected sight, and, seizing his chance, Nicholas swung the blade back with as much strength as he had in him, bringing it down on the Shadow.

Astrolabe—Ironwood, she reminded herself.

The last sight Etta had before rushing out into the courtyard was of the Belladonna, standing where she had stood the entire night, watching the blood creep across the stones and absorb the ashes at Julian's and Nicholas's feet. She surveyed the fighting with the long-suffering look of a mother. Then she turned and left through a wall of fire and smoke, disappearing into the star-encrusted belly of the night.

THE MOON WAS HIGH AND BRIGHT ABOVE HER AS SHE RAN, searching for Ironwood's figure down the path, among the trees, in any crevice the snake could have slithered into. The passage at the base of the mountain would have closed up with the first traveler's death, but he had the astrolabe—he could create his own escape, and then seal the entrance and prevent anyone from following behind.

The air was clean and sweet in her lungs, but Etta couldn't stop coughing, hacking up the smoke and spit and bile from deep inside her chest as she ran, her feet struggling in the soft earth.

Damn it, she thought. He couldn't take the astrolabe now, not after everything—

"*Etta!* Etta, where are you?" Nicholas's frantic voice carried down from above, but she didn't stop—she had caught another voice on the wind.

"—face me! Face me once and for all! Let us end this!"

Etta stumbled down the weathered path, stopping just long enough to keep herself upright before picking up her pace again. Ironwood's shouts sent birds launching from the safety of their branches.

The man had torn away his mask and robe, revealing a fine suit beneath. He was pacing up and down the path, his breathing ragged; his hand clenched at what remained of his hair, twisting it. Rivulets of sweat poured off him, along with the stench of blood.

"I know you're out there!" he shouted—to the trees, to the darkness. "It's mine, do you hear me? Come for it again and I'll tear you apart, limb from limb!"

Etta had only had one real interaction with the man, but the frantic quality of his speech, the way he paced and screamed as if the words were being torn from him, made her feel like she was meeting him for the first time. His control over himself, his family, the machinations of the world, had been so tight and refined; she couldn't reconcile that man with the knotted mess of anxiety and desperation in front of her. This was the same person who had bent time to his will? Who had subjected whole families to his cruelty?

"Do you hear me, you devil?" he shouted.

She came up short, a few feet away, but Cyrus Ironwood didn't seem to notice. The empty box lay overturned nearby, and he was waving the astrolabe in the air, holding it up for the moon to witness, as if expecting something to swoop down and snatch it. A torch in his hand nestled him in the center of a shallow pool of light.

"Ironwood," Etta said, walking toward him slowly. She kept the knife in her hand pressed to her side.

He spun toward her, eyes flashing. It was like looking in the face of a child, one who'd been struck once and knew he was about to be hit again. His rage was nearly choking him, polluting the cool mountain air.

She had a knife on her. He had only the torch.

And the astrolabe.

"Give it to me," she said, holding out her hand. "It's over."

Ironwood swung around toward her, his gaze clouding. "Over? The Ancient One is dead?"

Ancient One?

Etta swallowed. Nodded. She reached out her free hand, repeating, "Give me the astrolabe. . . ."

"It's mine," he told her, the rough lines of his face painted with blood and soot. His mouth twisted up in glee. "Years . . . *years* . . . it's mine, finally, and mine alone—"

Her fingers curled more tightly around the knife.

She was close enough to smell his sweat now.

Without giving him a second to prepare, Etta lunged forward, grabbing for the astrolabe. With a speed she didn't expect, his arm flew out, backhanding her sharply across the face. And suddenly, his rage had a target—a focus. Etta stumbled back, swinging her knife between them to try and keep him back. The torch dropped from his hand, but didn't go out as it struck the path.

Ironwood swung the astrolabe toward her temple, heavy and unyielding, and it narrowly missed crushing her skull. But she was off-balance, and Ironwood seized the advantage and dropped his head, charging her with a rough yell, throwing her down onto her back. Etta's breath left her in a rush as she rolled to avoid his next blow, but not quickly enough. Ironwood caught her by the hair and yanked her back down, hard enough to tear a clump of it out at the roots. The knife was out of her hand and in his, the blade flashing in the moonlight.

"You want this?" he cried, holding the astrolabe in front of her face. Etta reached for it, but Ironwood drew it back so sharply, so suddenly, that it went flying from his sweat-slick fingers. With a cry, he dove for it, but Etta yanked his leg back and dragged herself forward, snatching it just long enough to throw it as hard as she could into the dark forest, out of his reach.

Etta couldn't hear the words he screamed at her over her thundering pulse, she only felt him slam her back to the ground, flipping her over again, his spittle flying in her face. She kicked, trying to claw at his face, but the knife was back in his hand and suddenly at her cheek, dragging the blade down against it. He closed his other hand over her throat.

"You did this, all of you, you did this—"

Etta reached up, trying to drive her fingers into his eyes, her broken nails clawing at his face.

"*Rose,*" he howled down at her, his eyes unfocused, "Rose Linden! Are you satisfied? Are you *satisfied*?"

The sound the blade made as it pierced him from behind, the sickeningly wet thump and the spray of blood across her face, would never leave Etta as long as she lived. Then the blade was torn back through his body, and she was forced to watch as he choked on his own hot blood, his hand pressed to the gaping wound in his chest. His head turned as he slumped to the side, his fingers finally becoming lax enough for Etta to scramble out from underneath him.

"No," Rose said, wiping her blade against the side of her tattered white robe. "*Now* I have my satisfaction."

Etta stared up at her from the ground, willing the feeling back into her limbs. Her mother stared down at her, her skin tight over delicate bones.

"*Rose!*"

Henry's voice echoed down from the top of the mountain path. Rose turned—not toward the sound, but behind her, just as the man in the golden robe slashed a clawlike blade over her throat.

THIRTY-ONE

Nicholas heard only Etta's scream.

It flew to him over the sounds of savage fighting and the moans and begging of the wounded.

"Oh God," Sophia said, swinging around, searching for its source. Li Min took her hand and led them both out of the tent at a full run. Nicholas tried to dash after them, but he stumbled, his entire right side limp. He cursed his body, the weakness that threatened to dissolve him at his joints, the Belladonna—

But then there was an arm around his side, and his arm was being thrown over a shoulder, and Julian was there, sweat-soaked and grim. He glanced over at Nicholas, and at his brother's nod of acquiescence, dragged them both forward.

The last of the travelers shoved themselves through the burning mouth of the tent, only to be pursued by the Shadows, who left the massacre inside to claim more lives. Nicholas turned to look back, taking stock—there were dozens of bodies on the floor, both travelers and Shadows alike. Nearly the whole of Ironwood's traveling force, and an equal number of Thorns. More dead than he had ever realized were alive.

How many of our kind survive now?

Near the entrance a woman was crawling, laboring through the gore and flames to an older man, crying, "Father—*Father?*" Beside her, another man rocked the unmoving body of a younger one, weeping.

Julian hurried by, and then they followed the path the silvery smoke was taking, along the mountain path. But no sooner had they taken a few long strides down it than the nightmare claimed them, too.

For there was their grandfather, choking on his last gasps of life, clawing at the ground beneath him.

There was Rose Linden in Henry Hemlock's arms, her hand pressed to the line of blood at her throat.

There was the man in gold, striding toward the dark line of the forest, searching.

There was Etta, illuminating them all with the single torch in her hands. There was Etta, throwing it as hard as she could. The fire spun end over end, striking the back of the ornate robe, right where a powerful sun had been embroidered.

The blaze took hold like a spark on brittle parchment. The sound, the *whoosh* of purifying, ravaging fire as it caught the ends of the man's hair and lit him like a fuse, would never leave Nicholas, however long he lived. Nor would the look of quiet disbelief as the alchemist's son looked back over at his shoulder at a sobbing Etta in the instant before he was fully engulfed.

Li Min and Sophia stood a few feet from them on the path, thunderstruck by the sight. He had to believe it was the stink of scorched flesh that made Julian gag. Voices shrieked from the forest, ragged and almost inhuman. Li Min staggered, clutching at her chest as if feeling something release there. Sophia caught her before she fell, but Li Min could not tear her eyes away from where the body of the man was still burning.

They approached slowly.

"—had to be her." Rose was struggling with each word, her hand clutching Henry's arm, her eyes locked on his stricken face. "My baby—Shadows—"

"Shhh," Henry said, trying to stanch the flow of blood from the cut with fabric torn from his robe. "Don't speak just yet—it will be all right—be still, darling, be still."

Li Min ran to him and the man glanced up, desperate. He shifted to allow her to inspect the wound with careful hands. She reached for the small leather bag draped from her belt, one of her own knives.

"I understand now . . . you led them away from us, didn't you?" he was saying to Rose, distracting her from Li Min's work. "Clever, clever darling. You won't go, now that you've only just arrived, will you? Won't you stay for just one more dance?"

Just beyond them, Etta was on her knees, heaving for air, trying to crawl toward her parents. Julian started toward her, but she waved her hands, trying to control her crying so she could speak. Nicholas thought he had never seen anything so brave in his life.

"The astrolabe—" Etta pointed toward the nearby patch of forest, squeezing the words out between her tears. "I can't, I can't do it, it's—"

Footsteps crashed through the forest; voices cried out, searching for the astrolabe. Shadows, undeterred. Finishing what their master had begun.

He pulled Julian away from her. They were nearly out of time and he loved her, he loved her, he loved her enough to not go through with it, to not leave her side. Which meant he had to go, and it needed to be now.

He and Julian broke apart to search with nothing more than a frantic look between them, Nicholas bracing himself against one tree, then the next, making his way through the darkness. In the distance, he saw two shadowed figures weaving through the trees. Branches and rocks mauled and battered him on all sides, but he kept his eyes on the ground, searching through the pockets of darkness, the shifting dirt, the patchwork of ferns and shrubs. The breath burned in and out of his lungs, and his side began to ache in a way that might have doubled him over if he were not so singularly terrified for the lives of everyone he had left behind on the path, of the way the Shadows around him were beginning to shift and gather.

But he felt it. He felt the vibration, the dread that broke out across his skin; slowly, he turned and retraced his steps to where a glimmer of ancient gold peered out of a small animal's burrow. His left hand was slick with his own blood, from the deep cut which he'd been a fool to get; it had been protesting each time he so much as twitched a finger. He hardly felt it now—hardly felt the cold, or took notice of the way his hot breath steamed out into the air, hardly heard Sophia and Julian calling out to him.

Time seemed to bend around him, encasing his body in amber. Even his movements felt distressingly forced, as if he were struggling to move forward against a great wind without a line to assist him.

But he knelt.

He crawled.

He took the considerable weight of the astrolabe in his hand, staining it with his blood as he removed his dagger from his boot with his other.

Touching it flooded his senses, shot his blood through him with dizzying heat. He felt the astrolabe pulse, as if with its own heartbeat, its pace increasing to match the slamming of his heart. Now that it was in his hand, his reason for taking it slipped out of his mind; he couldn't quite remember it, not with the images that suddenly flooded his field of vision like dreams borne on the wind.

Standing on the bow of his newly commissioned ship, the wind fair and the ocean tame, as he gave the order to change course.

Moving through a great house, chasing a small child across the soft Oriental rugs, beneath the portraits of ancestors and descendants yet to come, sunlight spilling in through the tall windows that overlooked the green lands below.

His mother, taking his arm as he led her away from the fields, from the plantation, from the illness that had killed her.

And Etta . . .

Etta in the silk dress he had seen her wear to dinner on the *Ardent*, the one that had suited her so well, guiding him forward to a passage, her smile dazzling—

All of this. He heard the sweet whisper of words as clearly as if someone were sitting beside him. *I can give you all of this.*

Nicholas did not want to pull back from these dreams. He wanted to live each moment through to its conclusion, to see what other sweet wonders might be offered to him. But the light, the mist hanging over his mind, it all pulled back.

It left him in the darkness again, with a choice.

A man made his own future. He chipped it from whatever hardships insinuated themselves into his life; he carved out the happy, glad moments to capture his gratitude for them. It came from the simple magic of merely living. Of surviving. Seeking.

Not this. *Not this.*

Using his wounded hand, he pinned the astrolabe to the ground and raised his dagger, driving it down hard against the metal surface. If he could just crack it—if he had just enough strength left in him to wedge it apart—

The astrolabe heated beneath his hand, scalding to the touch. Nicholas let out a cry, but held it fast, blinking as it began to glow. He drove the dagger down again, piercing its center; the hotter it became, the more malleable it was, until at last the bulk of the blade broke through its case and black blood burbled up from inside, spilling against his hand, searing it with a pain that whipped him down to the seat of his soul.

He fell back, his jaw working out a scream as the light around him flooded his senses, drowning out the image of Etta racing toward him, her mouth open, calling something to him, trying to tell him something. But the light swept over her, and she vanished, dissolving in front of his eyes.

No, he thought, trying to rise again. *No!*

The sound of thunder and fury bore down on him, drowning out her name. There was a tug at his back, a weight that wrapped around his core, and he felt himself lifted, pulled and tossed, the pressure crushing against his skin. The whole of the world tilted around him as time caught him in its torrential stream.

And, in an instant, Nicholas felt himself vanish.

NEW YORK CITY
Present Day

THIRTY-TWO

SOMEHOW ETTA KNEW EXACTLY WHERE SHE WAS, EVEN before she had the courage to open her eyes and see for herself.

This isn't happening . . . this can't be happening. . . .

The stone stairs were cold against her skin, smelling of nothing more than the museum's old air-conditioning system and the lemon-scented cleaning product the custodians used to wash the stairs down.

Get up, she ordered herself. *You have to get up.*

Did she?

Etta forced her eyes open. Forced the breath to come into her lungs, and then out again. With arms like wet clay she pushed herself up, biting her lip to keep back her grunt of pain as the aches and bruises made themselves known again. The fluorescent light was nearly blinding, after living with sunlight and candles for so long. She shielded her eyes as best she could, lifting her arms, curling her legs toward her as she slid over the last few inches to rest her back against the closest wall.

She was still wearing the white robe. If it hadn't been stained so thoroughly with gore and dirt and soot, Etta might have believed the whole thing to be some sort of desperate dream. That she'd tumbled down the stairs on the night of her performance and knocked herself out. But she wore the evidence of her struggle on every inch of her skin; the bruising and dried blood decorated her like war paint.

Alone, she thought. *Trapped.*

For once in his miserable life, it seemed Cyrus Ironwood had told the truth.

But the last thought lingered as a question. Slowly, she unknotted the hooded robe and used the relatively clean inner side to try to wipe her face and arms. Her clothes were from the last century, but this was New York, where there was always something or someone more interesting to look at.

She tried to swallow the taste of smoke and blood in her mouth, and forced her eyes up to take in the familiar empty stairwell.

This was the passage that had taken everything from her. The same passage that had opened up a link to the past and carried her over land, across oceans, through time. She had arrived at the place she had departed from, back in her native time. *This is home.*

What was left of it.

Etta rose to her feet slowly, struggling for balance. Memories swirled there, all floating colors and sparks; not of the life she had lived, but of the destruction, the devastation of what New York had become in the altered timeline.

Anger climbed in her as her feet took to the steps, blinding her with its intensity. So much so that she had to lean heavily against the rail to keep from falling back.

Nicholas had done it. He had done this to her, to them, to everyone. Her mother was bleeding to death somewhere that wasn't here—that, Etta was sure of. Her father was alone in his own time, wondering what had become of the two of them. Julian would be left to his own devices. Sophia and Li Min, separated. The remaining Thorns, blown apart and scattered to the winds. For a moment, just one, she thought she might actually hate him.

Why had this been worth it? *Why* had he done this to them?

She drew in one breath, then another, trying to control the shaking that wracked her entire body. She smoothed her hair back, wiping the drying tears from her face. As she reached the top, voices drifted to her from beyond the door. The muffled wailing of a child. The endless stream of footsteps squeaking against the floor. But there, inside the stairwell, was nothing. There was devastating quiet.

Etta's breath hitched in her throat as she turned, looking down the stairs again. She hugged the folded robe to her chest. There was no shimmering wall of air to call her back. No thundering drums to announce her arrival. There was no passage at all.

There was only Etta, alone.

AS IT TURNED OUT, THE INSIDE OF THE MET WAS THE SAME, with enough small exceptions that Etta felt as though she were moving through a kind of shadowland version of her city. Exhibits had been moved; the style of clothing she saw around her seemed sharper, shorter, brighter; even the cell phones people carried to snap photos of the artwork were unfamiliar, razor-thin and sliding open like the old mirror compact Alice had carried to check her lipstick. Etta kept her head down and moved steadily past the school groups and couples meandering through the halls, through the blessedly familiar Egyptian wing, down the grand staircase, and out into whatever waited for her beyond the doors.

It was disorienting, the way the skin of the city had changed, even if the bones had not. Etta recognized the older buildings—the old-houses-turned-museums—lining Fifth Avenue, but when she jogged around to the part of the museum that backed up to Central Park, she faced an almost unfamiliar crowded skyline on all sides. Historic landmarks like the Dakota were gone, replaced by ever-reaching skyscrapers that literally blotted out the sunlight and cast impossibly long shadows across the park. The trees had changed color and were burnished with all of their golden autumn glory. Strollers wove through the park's paths.

Men in suits passed men out for a jog in the crisp weather. Women sharing coffee and conversation on nearby benches glanced at others making business calls as they power-walked by. It was a variation on a theme Etta had known and loved, and now she would need to study it to understand the underlying notes that had changed.

She wondered if the city had always been this loud, this clean, this frenetic.

Henry had said the timeline tried to account for inconsistencies and restore as many traveler events as it could. Maybe Etta's life here was what it had been, at least mostly, even if the trappings had changed? She had lost everything and everyone else . . . maybe she could at least have the scraps of her old life?

She felt the pressure of eyes and turned to find a young girl staring up at her, sucking on her thumb as she held her mother's hand, waiting for the light to turn. Etta tried to smile, but she'd noticed others giving her a wide, silent berth, and could only imagine her smell and how out of place she looked, despite having lived the whole of her life on these streets, moving through the veins of the city.

When the little girl and her mother crossed Fifth Avenue, heading home, or to a shop, to some real, concrete destination, the wave of longing and uncertainty and desperation finally broke over her, and Etta began to cry.

You're overwhelmed, but it's all right, she told herself. *You are all right. Give yourself a minute. Give yourself time.*

But there was nowhere for her to go.

There was no one.

Unless . . .

Etta turned, crossing the street just as the signal began to flash. Her jog turning into a full-on sprint through this new, slightly changed version of the Upper East Side. She dodged sleek city cabs in their familiar shade of yellow, delivery bikes, and the parade of evening dog walkers.

The sun was setting at her back as she turned onto Alice's street, and she felt her heart jump at the sight of her brownstone, looking almost exactly as she remembered it, the pots of flowers still alive on her stoop. The front windows were dark, but she tried knocking anyway; she stepped back, and then knocked again, practically bouncing in anticipation.

When there was still no answer, when she was sure her heart would beat its way out of her chest, Etta dug down in the base of the pot of pansies, dumping the dirt out onto the stoop, well aware that Martha, Alice's snoop of a neighbor, was watching her through the window. Her hand had just closed around the spare key hidden at the bottom when Martha's front door opened.

"Etta, is that you?"

She straightened slowly, hoping she'd managed to clean the better part of the blood from her skin. "Yes. It's me."

The old woman, already in her paisley silk robe, pressed a hand to her chest. "My goodness, we were so worried about you and your mother when we didn't see you at the service. It's been months, doll; how have you been? Alice was so excited for you to come back to the city for a visit. And goodness, you look as if you've crawled out of the ground—"

Service.

Months.

Etta had to swallow the bile down, forcing a smile that was more of a grimace. "I've been . . . traveling."

Martha seemed to accept this, at least. "That house has been sitting empty for an age! If you'd like a referral to an agent to sell—"

Etta's hands were trembling so hard, she could barely fit the key into the lock. It was a difficult door no matter the timeline, apparently. She had to shoulder it open.

"Careful, there!"

She stumbled inside, her chest heaving, and slammed the door shut on the woman. Gasping, Etta dropped to her knees, bracing her hands against them until she had the courage to look up. The whole apartment smelled as she remembered it: the cinnamon-apple potpourri Alice favored, and Oskar's pipe smoke, which had lingered long after he'd passed away. Etta leaned forward, pressing her face to the old blue floral rug covering the hardwood, and let it muffle her scream of frustration.

She's dead.

She's still dead.

And her home was as buried as she was—every piece of furniture, every piece of art, every surface was covered with white sheets. Etta breathed in through her nose as she stood, leaving a trail of dirt across the pristine floor in the living room. The floorboards squeaked as she approached the couch and placed a knee on it, pulling the fabric away from the painting hanging there. The city sang its medley of horns and trucks and rattling garbage containers outside, and all the while Etta stared at the impressionist field of red poppies, raising a hand to touch the paint, to brush the dust from its frame.

She moved from room to room, uncovering pieces of Alice's life. Photos of herself smiling naively, unscarred in and out, with her mother; neat stacks of bills; an unfinished novel on the bedside table. Her violin, the one she'd gifted to Etta years ago in the old timeline, rested in its case on the bench at the foot of the bed. Etta sat beside it, flipping open its latches, and for a long while did nothing but stare at it. Brush the glossy surface, breathe in the wood and rosin with her filthy fingers.

"*I'll be seeing you. . . .*" The words emerged broken, battered. *In all the old familiar places.*

But there was one painting she had never seen before, resting just outside the floor of Alice's closet, as if she'd gone to hang it up and forgotten about it. Having grown up in the halls of the Met, Etta recognized the Renaissance style of the piece, from the pose of the young woman to the warm, vibrant tone of its colors.

It was so unlike the other pieces in the apartment that it drew Etta forward for closer inspection. The ivory dress with its square cut was detailed with gold thread, but otherwise simple in style. The subject's golden hair was plaited down her back, crowned by a circlet of lush red roses. In one hand, she held a map; in the other, a key.

The eyes staring back at her were her mother's.

Her fingers touched delicate brushstrokes, and the roses blurred in her vision like an open wound. *This* was Rose Linden's natural time. Alice had indicated it to her the only way she could, by keeping this relic of the past. Sensing, or knowing, that Rose would never get around to telling her daughter herself.

Etta couldn't push the chill out from beneath her skin, any more than she could stop the shaking that overtook her as the vicious reality set in. She did not think she could ever forgive her mother, not fully, for taking Alice's life, no matter the reason. But she pitied Rose deeply; she felt an unwanted empathy trying to imagine making that decision with the trauma of her past, and the promise of more death to come, ringing her neck like a noose. She understood now that Rose was as much the hero as she was the victim of her own story, blooming in blood.

Etta wanted to speak to her, to understand, to finally clear the air between them, even if it was only one last conversation.

And now it would never happen. At least five hundred years and a single deadly cut had stolen their last chance. If her mother had survived . . . somehow survived, there was no way of finding her.

Etta sat on the carpet for hours, considering her mother, considering the life they'd had together. The sun tracked around Alice's bedroom like the arm of a clock. *Alone.*

Finally, thirst won out. Etta rose, carrying the portrait back across the apartment with her to its new place in the living room. In the kitchen, she went straight for the refrigerator. She'd already noticed that the water was running when she'd stopped to wash her hands and face, and the electricity, too; but she was surprised, somehow, to find that the food stocked inside the fridge had already been cleared out, leaving only a few water bottles.

Who had done that for her? Who had cleaned this place and covered everything inside of it?

Her answer came in the form of a letter, resting on the kitchen table beside two heavy letter-size envelopes. One was labeled with her name, the other with Rose's.

Dear Spencer Family:

My name is Frederick Russell and I have been appointed by my firm to handle Mrs. Hanski's estate. I was recently asked by Mrs. Hanski to serve as the executor of her will. As you may already know, the bulk of it has been left to your family in a trust, but I have been unable to reach you by means of phone or Netgram to confirm this.

Netgram? Whatever passed for e-mail in this timeline, most likely.

I'm leaving these envelopes here per Mrs. Hanski's request, and against my better judgment, as I believe they may contain personal material both sensitive and valuable. Funds to maintain the utilities and upkeep of this home, as well as its taxes, will be paid out of the trust until you specify otherwise. Please notify me the moment you arrive, so that I may explain these next steps to you.

"Still taking care of us," Etta murmured, folding up the letter and the man's contact information. She reached for the envelope bearing her name, and dumped the contents out onto the table, finally taking a seat.

Inside, as the lawyer had expected, were personal documents—a

482

birth certificate, a passport, a Social Security card, and vaccination records. Real, copies, or forgeries, Etta wasn't sure. She turned her attention to the letter itself, hoping for some clue. It was dated July 3.

Dearest Etta,

I don't know where to begin. It has been only minutes since I last saw you. Both you, and to a lesser extent, your mother, have been appearing and disappearing almost at random throughout the years. There have been moments where we are sitting together at a meal, and I'll rise to refill my glass of water, only to return and find you both gone. I cannot tell what has become of the timeline, only that it must be very bad. Your great-grandfather tried to explain the idea of "imprinting" to me once—how the timeline adjusts around the travelers' actions, and when it can't, it leaves impressions of them behind to maintain consistency. I wish I had paid better attention. The great gears of time are shifting, and I am powerless to do anything other than watch.

I remember our encounter in London as if it were yesterday. I remember the look on your face when you saw me—when you spoke of what our life would be together. I believe I have lived it in pieces. Not the whole, perhaps, but I am grateful to have been your instructor, and your friend. I am grateful I saw you become that young lady with my own two eyes. But I am afraid for you now. I've seen the world shift around me in tremendous waves—destroyed one moment, healed the next. I know it must be tied to your search, and I know my own end, the one I saw so plainly in your face, must be near. And so I have taken precautions for you, should you return to an unfamiliar city. These documents should suffice in establishing a life here again, should you choose to.

"Should you choose to . . ." These words strike me as odd, because it seems as if there has always been a kind of inevitability to your and Rose's travels. Those of us left behind, perhaps, can see it

483

more clearly, the way it all eventually weaves together and connects.
There are patterns; loops are opened that ultimately must be closed.
The choice is whether or not to open new ones, I suspect.

Duck, you are the pride of my life. I should very much like
to hear you play again, and I hope to see you return to me soon;
if not here, then in the past. I've tickets to a concert at the Met in
September, a night of Bach, but the only question is whether or not
this blasted timeline will straighten out again before then, and weave
you back into my days in time for us to go together.

Oh God. Of course the timeline would restore that moment to the best of its ability—she clearly wasn't a part of the concert, but what were the chances that she and Alice had still gone—that she had heard the sounds of the passage—that she had bumped into Sophia and followed it . . . ? Fairly good, if she had to guess.

But if something should happen before then, or if you are reading this
years and years from now and I've merely kicked it from age and
whatever else life has decided to throw at me, I wish to tell you only
this: I love you and your mother beyond time and space.

Etta read and reread the letter before returning it to its envelope. She arranged it at the center of the circle of documents she'd laid out and began to consider her options.

The passage was closed. Whether there was another one in this year, or any forthcoming year, remained to be seen.

If any still exist at all.

Her mother, as far as she knew, was not here. Nicholas was not here. The only name she had that might be able to help was a lawyer named Frederick Russell, and what news he had about this supposed trust, this apartment, might turn out to be bad. Alice and Oskar had done well for themselves, but neither was astronomically wealthy. This fund would not last forever.

But it might last long enough to get her through school. Until she found a job to support herself.

Don't be afraid, she told herself. *It will be okay.*

She would do what any traveler would in a foreign place and time. She would blend into the life around her, to the best of her ability. She would disappear into it, observing, learning, living.

Etta would wait.

The only question now was . . . for what?

NEW YORK CITY
1776

THIRTY-THREE

NICHOLAS AWOKE WITH A MOUTHFUL OF DIRT AND THE sounds of fife and drums battering out a march nearby. Despite the rawness, the crustiness of sleep, he cracked one eye open to take in the gray, hazy light. The dirt beneath him had soaked through his robe and his shirt, and created a freezing cast over his skin.

Cold, he thought.

Pain, his body relayed back.

It was as if that one word was enough to wake it in him, the agony. His left hand burned as he flexed it, bringing it up to wipe the dirt from his face. Looking directly at the wound, he discovered, only made it bloom hotter and quicker. He turned the palm of his left hand up, staring in horror at the slices that ran from the base of his fingers to the heel of his palm, and the mutilated flesh of the burns that covered the rest of it.

Nicholas drew it closer to his face because—yes, *there.* The swelling had yet to subside, and the tender pink of the raw flesh seemed to burn its way down to his bones, but he saw the pattern in it. He recognized the looping lines and nonsensical symbols, the mysterious secrets they held. He carried a nearly perfect brand of the astrolabe on his flesh, and, if his past history with scars was any indicator, likely would for the entirety of his life.

The white light—

All at once, the memory pierced him and he jerked up out of the mud with a desperate gasp. He ripped the white robe, or what remained of it, off his person and threw it as far as he could manage with an arm that felt like mortar. It fluttered like a great white bird, sailing over the edge of the land, into the familiar gaping mouth of the river.

His right arm swung freely, with a strength it hadn't had in weeks.

"No," he breathed out. "It cannot be. . . ."

The ring was missing from his finger.

Nicholas turned and turned again, his gaze passing over the trees around him to the lively sounds of war emanating from the Royal Artillery Park just beyond. From where he stood, he could make out the lines of drilling soldiers, their red coats made more vibrant by the odd, stormy gray light. He searched out the passage, strained to pick up its usual rumble.

He could not hear a thing.

Holy God.

Gone, as if it had never been there at all.

He paced through the small spread of trees in circles, as if expecting it to pop up like a snake disturbed from its hole.

He'd done it. The pressure at the center of his chest sharpened, unbearable.

It is finished.

And Nicholas wasn't just alone now; he was *alive*. He was whole, as if the closing of the passages had burned the poison from his body, wiped the last weeks away like a stain on his life. He found himself instinctively reaching for his memories, to cradle them close on the off chance they might be taken. Carried off, the way the crimson and gold leaves falling around him were eased along by the wind.

Nicholas stood still, simply breathing, trying to grip the life around him. All of his decisions . . . they had all been based on hypotheticals, speculation. Knowing that death was walking two steps behind him, it had felt somewhat like trying to shape air. The actuality of what would come had never felt substantial until this moment.

He could not simply reach for Etta, or turn to Li Min or Sophia, or make certain Julian had come through it all unharmed. He could do nothing but stand there, his thoughts drifting through the growing void inside of him like clouds.

It had to be done. It had to end.

Perhaps Sophia was right, and he was a coward for giving up on his life, even to serve this end. He certainly was a coward for choosing this finality while he believed he wouldn't live to see it affect him.

"You there!"

Nicholas looked up, meeting the gaze of a regular patrolling the edge of the Artillery Park. The man was young, younger than himself, and while there was suspicion embedded in his expression, there was also genuine concern.

"What business do you have here, sir?"

Nicholas straightened, clearing his throat. "I . . . came to appreciate the view. My apologies."

"I see," the soldier said, but a new tone in his voice left Nicholas wondering what, precisely, he *saw.*

Likely thinks I've escaped to freedom. The state of his clothing, his wounds; they all spoke to that very notion. The thought sent a prickle of alarm from the base of his skull down his spine. He hadn't merely returned to this era, he had been swallowed by it, sent back to drown in all of its hypocrisies, its cruelty. To be . . . *muzzled* by it. What proof did he have to offer this man if he was pressed on the matter?

His freedom papers, which he had carried with him every moment of his life after Hall had procured them on his behalf, were gone. Unless the original timeline was severely altered to something beyond what he'd known, the only copies were with the captain, presumably out at sea or imprisoned, and in his former employer's office in New London, Connecticut.

The all-too-familiar bitterness rose in Nicholas's throat like bile, and he fought to keep his expression neutral. He had faced darkness, shifted the timeline, and traveled to the ends of the world, and yet—his word would never satisfy those who believed he should still be in chains.

But Nicholas did not cower. He did not turn and run, though his instincts begged him to reconsider. He was a freeman—here, now, and everywhere. Any man who dared to question the point would be met with equal malice.

"Move along, then," the soldier said, returning Nicholas's nod with one of his own.

And so he did. What spare gold Ironwood—*Ironwood!*—had insisted he carry on his person as heir bought him a clean shirt, a buttonless coat, a skin for water, and a bottle of whiskey—the latter both for courage and, moments later, to clean the searing wound on his hand. The fact that he remained standing long enough to bind it with a clean cloth and did not soil himself in front of the entirety of the Dove was a miracle in its own right. The Dove's innkeeper was none too pleased to see him reappear, and all too happy to send him on his way again with the small bag of belongings he had abandoned in his hurry to follow Etta through the passage to London.

"Here it is," the man said, tossing it to him. "Kept everything you and your party left behind. Wouldn't dare to cross that man."

Nicholas lifted a brow. It looked full, but he had no doubt what few valuables were inside had been carefully assessed and possibly taken. Still, he thanked the man profusely, shifting the bag to his left hand to dig in his pocket for one last gold coin.

The flash of color and sight and sound at that touch blew him back off his feet. A crack of thunder whipped through his skull. He saw the tanner in Charleston he'd purchased the bag from years ago, as if the old man were standing directly in front of him. The shop began to take form, as if dripping into place around him, smearing down over the tavern's tired walls. There was the pressure, the insistent tugging at his core. . . .

Holy God.

He dropped the bag to the floor, feeling as if his bones were on the verge of turning to sand. The Dove's owner leaped back at the moment Nicholas did, his eyes narrowing in suspicion.

"Thought I heard . . . a rat," he said, his voice sounding far away. "In the bag. Just now."

The man tilted his head toward the door. "Best be off, then."

Nicholas stooped, hesitating a moment before picking the bag up again, this time with his right hand. When he was sure the world wasn't about to shatter to pieces around him, he made quick strides toward the door and stepped out into the cold grip of the late-October air. His skin felt as if he had been sitting too close to flames, and rather than see his original plan through—wait and see if he might be able to convince a passing wagon to let him trade work for a ride in the direction of Connecticut—he wandered farther down the road, away from the Dove, from the Royal Artillery Park, until the only sounds were the birds in the old oak above him and his thrumming heart. He pressed his back against the tree, sliding down until he sat again, his palms turned up against his knees.

That was a passage.

Impossible.

With considerable care, he went about the work of unwrapping his burned hand again, laying it side by side with his right one. He looked at the mark of the astrolabe on his skin, the raw, blistered, and scabbed image of it. *I saw the past.*

More than that, there was no other way to describe it, except to say he had felt himself begin to *go*. The world had shifted around him, and if he had only reached out, held on, the darkness would have reached out and taken him.

"Don't be ridiculous," he said, because Sophia was not there to.

But . . . how to test this? He needed to prove himself wrong. Remus Jacaranda's explanation for the astrolabe rose in his memory, creating a quake of horror in him: *to create a passage, legend holds that you must have the astrolabe, but you must also have something from the time and year you wish to go.*

He sorted through his bag, searching for something he might have procured in Nassau over the past year. The weapons were gone; the buckle from his shoe, sold; everything—

Everything except the thin leather cord around his neck, the one that held Etta's earrings and a small, broken bead. He reached up with his aching hand and closed his fist around it, letting his eyes slip shut.

The first drip of color brought the turquoise of the clear, pristine water; the next, the ivory sands of the beach; the third, the unstoppable, vibrant green of the palms that had shaded him and Sophia on their spot at the beach. The air began to stir, pinching at each of his muscles, until, in the distance, that dark spot appeared, twisting, flying toward him. Nicholas forced himself to stay in place, to meet that darkness as it came alongside him, gripped him by the collar, and dragged him forward.

There was nothing to do save surrender himself to the sensation of being buried alive. The darkness was as oppressive as the nudging pressure that raced toward him from every direction, and the high whistle accompanying it trilled ceaselessly, even after he was launched forward into sunlight and sand, the briny scent of the ocean rising to greet him.

"Bloody *hell*!" he swore, staggering to his feet. The tide rushed in behind, crashing against the beach and sending up a spray of foam that whipped him back to his senses.

"Aye," said a familiar voice behind him. "I think that's about the right of it."

Nicholas spun around, half-desperate with hope. There, standing less than three yards away, surveying the spot where he and Sophia had made camp, was Captain Hall.

His unruly whiskers had grown in, a stark contrast to the neat queue of his hair. The afternoon sun drove nearly all traces of silver from it, creating a crimson halo around his skull. Nicholas found himself choking on his next, surprised laugh. The Red Devil, alive and well and stalking toward him.

"What are you doing here?" he managed to rasp out. His legs had not quite steadied enough to gallop the distance between them as he wished. It was left to Hall to come to him, to take careful, obvious stock of Nicholas as he approached.

"Correct me if I'm wrong, Nick, but we were to expect you in New London 'shortly,' or am I misremembering?" His voice, while not harsh, bore an edge beneath its cheerful note that Nicholas recognized all too well.

"Did you receive any of my letters?" Nicholas asked in a ragged voice. He thought his heart might blow like a grenade in his chest. "Everyone—Chase—are they all alive? Sound?"

Hall took a step back, startled possibly for the first time in his life. "There have been a number of shifts; I've felt them all pass like storms. But, Nick, nothing's happened to us. Not in this timeline, at least."

Nicholas pressed his face into his hands and laughed and laughed until he was so near to tears he practically choked on them.

"Nick, my God, come here, come—is it as bad as all that?" Hall said. "We were worried for *you*. Tell me what's happened!"

When he steadied himself, Nicholas said, "I ran into . . . unexpected circumstances."

"*Unexpected circumstances?*" Hall placed his hands on his heavy belt, the flintlocks and flasks swaying as he began to pace. "All along, I'm hearing stories, terrible stories—the kind that put a guardian ill at ease. The winds of change over the later centuries were foul enough for word to reach me at sea. Imagine my surprise *again*, lad, as I arrived here to question Ironwood's guardians about whether or not they'd taken you into their custody, only to find them all a-fluster over that very same passage disappearing. *And then*, here you are, appearing right out of the air."

Nicholas fell back, shaking his head, staring down at his burned palm.

"God defend us!" Hall said, seizing his wrist, turning his palm up. "Lad—what is this? What's happened to you?"

Nicholas blinked fiercely, trying to reconcile the torrent of disbelief. Hall wrapped an arm over his shoulder. "It is over now. All of it. He's dead. The passages have closed."

His adoptive father took his meaning instantly. Shock coursed through him.

"You'll tell me on the way, then," Hall said. "And tonight you'll dine with Chase and the crew. They'll be beside themselves to see you well. Nicholas, *I* am beside myself to see you whole."

The emotion that wove through his heart at the thought made his chest impossibly tight. He had dreamt of that moment. But he had dreamt of many others as well.

"That is just it," Nicholas said, looking down the beach. "I'm not sure I can rightly say that I am."

THE STORY EMERGED IN FITS AND STARTS OVER THE COURSE of weeks, as the *Challenger* prowled the Atlantic for new prey. Nicholas supposed some part of him felt that, if he did not acknowledge what had happened, the past weeks would eventually be consigned to memory and stop haunting his waking hours.

Of course, he was never so lucky.

The Revolution continued as it had before; the men of the crew sang songs as familiar to him as the sky; his routine of work became the very plaster that kept him together. Everything had a rhythm, he realized; a recognizable ebb and flow. Love, separation. Work, rest. Pain, rum.

Hall granted him a wide berth, with a patience that somehow shamed Nicholas into feeling like a child. But even that had its limits. His questions—about what had happened, about what would happen—became more pointed. Nicholas found himself grateful for the ever-constant presence of the crew. It provided him with cover, a legitimate reason to not speak of it. As a guardian, Hall was the only one who had ever possessed a key to their hidden world. And now, he was the only one who knew the girl who'd emerged in the smoke and chaos on the *Ardent*, the very same one who had charmed her way into the hearts of men who no longer remembered her.

So he smiled with Chase; he allowed the gentle rocking of the sea to cradle him; he relished the feeling of warm sunshine spreading its fingers through his dark coat as he walked the length of the deck on watch. The sea, he knew, was his remedy. And time, no longer an enemy, simply existed in tandem with him, not to vex him. Only occasionally did he feel the tug of something else deep inside of him, the burn of the healed scars in his hand.

But sometimes, when he was tired after a day's work, or deep into his cups, or when he let the strict discipline of his heart lapse, he was clumsy with his words.

"Looks like a packet boat in the harbor port," Chase said, handing him the spyglass. "They might have news of the war for us, then."

The crew was restless for a night on shore in Port Royal, but Chase had grown hungry to track the progress of the war, and the growth—or lack thereof—of the Continental Navy. They'd narrowly escaped pursuit by a seventy-four-gun man-of-war only days prior, and Chase was still stewing in the disappointment of the missed fight. His fingers drummed now against the rail like a war summons. Impatient for something he'd yet to articulate.

"When did you become such a Whig?" Nicholas asked, glancing up at his friend's face. "Surely you're not that eager to hear about Washington's latest defeat."

Nicholas was, in fact, rather curious to see if anything had been altered in the course of the war, due to the timeline shifting to its original state. But he was equally as frightened to search out the answers.

"He wasn't *defeated* on Long Island." Chase's lower jaw, heavy with blond whiskers now, jutted out as his pale blue eyes narrowed on Nicholas. "It was a strategic relocation of his forces."

Nicholas laughed, his first true laugh in quite some time. "Now you sound like Etta, turning over manure and calling it soil."

Nicholas did not understand the rise of Chase's brows, the suggestion tucked into his smirk. *"Etta?"*

The spray of seawater against Nicholas's face did nothing to ease the rush of hot blood there, the clench of his heart. "That is—"

"Ehhhh-tah. *Etta, Etta, Etta.*" Chase toyed with the name, rolling it over his tongue. "Who is this lovely Etta? Oh, do not be cross with me about that—of course she's lovely, if she caught your eye. Where is she? In Charlestown? Is *that* who was keeping you from us?"

Nicholas pressed his hand to his throat, pulling the tie loose to bring more air into his chest. Hall was a guardian, but Chase and the rest of the crew were not. And now there was no recognition at all on Chase's face as he spoke, as he'd turned Etta into a stranger.

"I said to the others, a simple sickness would not have kept Nick from the fight, I did! Tell me, did she issue tender . . . ministrations?"

He closed his eyes, the feel of her smooth cheek against his own still so close to him. The gates were down now, and the flood of feeling and memory devastated him as any hurricane would. His mind had not let him dream of her, unless it was a nightmare—her mother slowly bleeding to death, her wrenching sobs, the future she returned to alone.

He was caught by those thoughts, hooked clean through his center, and he could no more escape being wrecked by them than he could avoid Chase's concerned gaze.

"Nick," Hall called from behind him. "A word, please."

Chase put a hand on his shoulder, but Nicholas dodged it neatly, his eyes fixed on the black ribbon that gathered the captain's faded red hair. He trailed several steps behind him to the cabin, and let the man shut and lock the door behind him. Without needing to be prompted, Nicholas took one of the seats in front of the imposing table that served both as a place to eat supper and a place to spread out the charts and maps.

The captain pressed a glass of amber liquid in his hand, and came around to lean against the desk. Nicholas sniffed at it, but was too wary of the knots lingering in his stomach to drink it just yet.

"You look worse than when I found you," the captain said at last. "I cannot bear to see you this way. If you won't tell me what's the matter, I'll keelhaul you until you're picking barnacles out of your teeth."

"I've healed," Nicholas said, his eyes on the map of the colonies, on the narrow harbor of Manhattan. "Even my hand."

"However, the bruising runs deep," Hall said. "You told me of your travels, the auction, Ironwood's death. But nothing of what you intend to do now with your . . . newly acquired gift."

"And I never shall," Nicholas said.

"My dear boy," Hall began, crossing his arms over his broad chest, "am I wrong to say that perhaps something unexpected has happened? That, if we were to take account of the night of the auction, we might discover that you walked away with . . ."

"*Don't,*" Nicholas begged, his voice cracking. "Don't put it into words. I cannot understand it any more than I can understand the stars. I cannot . . . It cannot be."

He could not hope for it. If his resolve cracked just once, he would scour the earth for the means to open a passage to Etta, to her future.

And that would defeat the very reason he had destroyed the astrolabe in the first place.

I cannot be selfish. No man is meant to have everything.

His life had merged with the very thing his family had hunted and killed for. This ancient thing—the astrolabe—born again. As stubbornly resistant to death, it would appear, as Nicholas.

Was Etta alive? Was she safe in her future? Sophia, Julian, Nicholas, Li Min . . . all of them flung across the centuries, forever out of one another's reach.

But not mine.

Nicholas batted the thought away, gripping the arms of the chair tight enough for the wood to creak.

"But you worry for the others, don't you?" Hall had read him flawlessly. "It weighs on you, not knowing their fates, when it is within your power to."

My power. When he considered the weight of that, his heart seemed to thunder as the passages had.

"It is not as easy as that," he managed to say. "The passages were the source of strife, the heart blood of it. I would need to open them again, to spend years searching out the others, and by then, anything might happen to the other travelers." The skin of his palm was still stiff, thicker than it had been before. He clenched his fist again, trying to hide the markings burned into it. "I understand so little of what's happened. The terms of it are beyond my fathoming. The ancient ones who toyed with us extended their natural years by consuming the other astrolabes. Is that what's to become of me?"

"Did they bear a mark like yours?" Hall asked. "Or did they consume the power of the astrolabes some other way?"

Nicholas could not recall any such markings on the ancient man, though he vaguely recalled markings of some kind on the Belladonna, who—he was sure of it—had drawn them all to that temple for some purpose other than an auction. The true picture eluded him, but he could guess. He wondered if, perhaps, the alchemist's daughter had survived in the same manner the son had.

He did not care. He didn't care a single whit about them. Nicholas had taken stock of himself and found, in the aftermath, he was a selfish sort after all. He wanted Etta beside him. On a ship, in a home, in a city, in the jungle—he didn't care, so long as her small hand had possession of his own, and he could lean down and kiss her whenever he damned well pleased, which would be often, and always.

He'd been quick to scorn the sickly poets and playwrights who wrote of dying from love, but he saw now that this was a form of grief. A loss that stole some small bit of gladness from him every day until what was left of his heart was as cold and hard as flint.

As cold and hard as Ironwood's.

One could survive without a heart, but a life like that was stunted, like an unopened flower, never receiving the necessary sunshine in order to bloom.

And it was not just Etta. There was Julian, there was Sophia, there was even Li Min, who now owed him two farewells. That was a family of sorts, wasn't it? Perhaps not the most graceful example, but it bore all the necessary ingredients of one: care, concern, friendship, guidance, love.

"I used to dream of traveling, of what it might mean to me—that I might master skills enough to find a place for myself in the world beyond what this time was willing to give me." Nicholas stopped, testing Hall's reaction, afraid of the disappointment or hurt he might see there.

Instead, the captain nodded.

"There is good in it, Nick," he said. "There is wonder. You can sit and ponder the nature of morality and corruption, like all the old, moldy philosophers. But it was never the passages themselves that were evil. It was the way they were used."

"But that's my point. The fact that they exist—that they *existed*—and that some of us have this ability . . . it does not mean we have to travel," Nicholas said. "We do not have to risk causing further instability."

"You're thinking aloud," Hall noted, "but you're dancing around the heart of the matter. You recognize that there is an inherent threat in their existence, that just by being used, they open the timeline up to change. And yet . . . ?"

"These are *families*," Nicholas said. Etta's words that night on the mountain had never left him; they'd only crystallized in his mind. "You did not see the massacre. I don't know how many of us survive now, but it seems a crueler thing to keep apart those of us who did. I never felt the Ironwoods were my own, but I have people now I consider near enough to be my own blood. If others are stranded in their natural times, trapped there . . . How do they go about living their lives, knowing they will never again see the ones they love?"

"I suppose Miss Spencer is included in these ponderings," Hall said, innocently enough. "Perhaps you might make one more passage, to her time? It would allow easy access to return when you feel the call of the sea, or wish to see this old man."

But as soon as that warm thought settled, guilt rose to dash it to pieces. "I cannot. It's . . . Isn't it self-serving? And in truth, I'm not sure I'd be able to reach her at all. To create a passage, I would need something from her time. She is not just from the future—she is from the *far* future."

There was nothing in his possession that had originated in that place, not even Etta's earring. The Lindens seemed to be collectors of the first order, if the home in Damascus had been any indication. There might be something there he could use. So there were two passages needed, at least. How quickly this could spiral beyond his control.

Hall's brows rose sharply as he stroked his beard, considering this.

"If there are as few travelers left as you say, then would it not be easy to establish rules and hold others accountable? It was always my understanding that the greater portion of traveling was done innocently, for the experience of it, or to see the guardians who had to remain in their natural times."

"What you're speaking of is a new system of order," Nicholas said. "Simply considering it is overwhelming. The judgment about where and when to open a passage would fall to me, time and time again."

"And I'm grateful for that," Hall said. "For there is no traveler alive who would torture himself and labor over each decision the way you will. There will be sacrifices, no matter what you decide. You may spend your days tunneling through the years to link travelers to their families, and never know the life of a captain. You may risk persecution for what they'll discover you can now accomplish for them. Or you may choose the dream of your youth, and one day, perhaps, learn to live with knowing your choice has affected more than just your life."

Nicholas took a sharp breath in. "I did not ask for this. I never desired it—I only wanted to live my life as any man would."

It was too much power for any one person to hold. Was this not the *exact* reason he had fought so hard to keep Ironwood from seizing control of the bloody thing? To make a decision to act in his own self-interest, to save only Etta—how was that different from the selfish ends Cyrus Ironwood would have used the astrolabe to pursue?

He would not simply be able to stop after searching for the other travelers. He knew his heart too well, and thanks to Hall's searching, he knew where his mother had been sent after she'd been sold from Ironwood's service. He knew where she was buried. He had been gone, traveling with Julian, the very year she wasted away and went to her reward.

I can save her.

No—*no*—not without risking the stability of the timeline. Bloody hell, he needed to get out of there. Hall was chipping away at his logic, and soon he'd have none left to counteract the greed in his soul. He started to rise, but was startled by a knock at the door.

One of the ship's boys slipped inside at Hall's "Enter!" with a bundle of letters clutched between his hands.

"From the packet boat, Captain," he explained, then dashed back out before Hall could utter a thank-you.

"Am I really as frightening as all that?" the man wondered aloud, cutting the string that bound the letters together. He sorted through them quickly.

"Positively ferocious," Nicholas said wryly, noticing for the first time that the man had spilled ink down his shirt again. "Is that the one who struck you with the spoon on the *Ardent*?"

"No, that wicked little imp refused service—" Hall's jaw clenched suddenly, the words falling away.

"What is it?" Nicholas asked, leaning forward.

"There's a missive in here for you," Hall said, holding up a small yellowed envelope, then turning it backward to show the black wax seal. A single *B*, surrounded by creeping vines and flowers. He felt himself shudder.

"Yes, that's the correct response," Hall said. "This is the Witch of Prague's mark."

Nicholas took it from him, hesitating only a moment before breaking the seal. The smell of earth and greens rose off the page; a look at the date told him the letter was over three hundred years old. The brittle, withered quality of the parchment seemed to confirm this. How it had found its way to Port Royal was anyone's guess.

Darling Beastie,

I told you before that everyone has a master. As you may have sensed the night of the auction, so had I. Not a man, nor a woman, but a

certain dark history which threatened to repeat itself once more,
cycling endlessly through generations, until at last none of our kind
would survive. It is a cunning businesswoman who plucks at the greed
in other hearts, and a wise woman who acknowledges it in herself. I
searched many years for the answer, only to find you. A mere boy. I
have enjoyed watching your progress from afar these many years.

Indeed, a boon has been granted to you. Rather than despair,
consider the fact that this was by my design; that you were tested,
your heart measured and found worthy to bring this ancient story
to an end. The copies of the master astrolabe, when consumed,
prolonged life by hundreds of years. However, my brother sought the
master for its raw power, the ability which you now possess. Had he
seized it, everything would be ash and cinders, with only his chosen
few left to survive his dreams of a total rebirth of the world. With
him, naturally, as its god. The ego, beastie; honestly.

"Honestly," Nicholas repeated, his pulse thrumming in his veins.
Hall's eyes never left him as he read, but he could not bring himself to
say the words aloud.

The only soul deserving of such an ability is one that refuses
everything it desires, in the face of death and great loss, to protect the
lives of the many from untold strife. I applaud your decency, which is
rare and formidable, and something to be prized in a world that has
struggled so terribly to make you aggrieved. Whatever you choose
to do with this gift, take comfort in knowing that it will die with
you. You will live long, but you will not be impervious to harm or
unnatural death. A fine limitation indeed, should you choose to open
the centuries. Or, perhaps, simply seek a single girl. To that end, I
have something useful in my collection. You may find me in a willing
mood to negotiate on it.

The short letter concluded with *As always, your business is greatly appreciated. Please visit again soon.*

Wordlessly, he passed the letter to Hall, who devoured its contents like a man knowingly swallowing sour milk. His brows seemed to inch up his face with every successive line.

Nicholas's mind was a whirlpool, one that threatened to draw him into its depths and drown him forever. This had all been a game between a man and a woman—between a family. No one, save the Belladonna and the Ancient One, held all of the cards, but the truth had been scattered across the generations, waiting for someone to fit it together. He saw a thousand points of light connecting one traveler's life to the next as if they were stretched out in the room before him.

He understood, too, the source of Rose's great plan, its mysteries and contradictions stripped away. She knew—she *must* have known—that whoever destroyed the astrolabe would take its ability into him- or herself. That was the reason she had allowed Etta to be taken into the past, why she hadn't destroyed it herself or merely hidden it for her to find. In Rose's heart, the only one worthy of the power was Etta, in all of her goodness.

Hall leaned back in his chair, a whistling breath escaping his teeth. For a long while, they merely stared at one another, ignoring the ship's bell as it rang for the next watch.

"I knew from the moment our lives crossed, Nicholas," Hall began softly, "that yours would eventually lead to a road I could not follow you down. You have been on it for many years, with you none the wiser. Tell me, aside from saving the others, if you knew that it would not alter the timeline beyond repair, if you released yourself from the prison of right and wrong, what would you do? No—don't argue it with yourself. Just tell me."

"I would save my mother, purchase her freedom, set her up with a comfortable life," he said without hesitation. "But it's impossible. I can't risk an alteration."

"Impossible," Hall agreed, reaching out to take his hand, his eyes lit from within. His words spilled out of him with the force of a river dammed for far too long. "But tomorrow you leave this ship. You travel five years into the past, where you found—will find—me in Norfolk, force me to swear to God to keep this infernal secret, and then, my boy, we do *precisely* that."

NEW YORK CITY
One Year Later

THIRTY-FOUR

Etta's debut as a concert soloist came months after she'd released that dream to the wind and let it soar away for someone else to claim.

"You'll do great. Don't be nervous!"

Etta glanced over at Gabriela. They stood in the wings of the stage, listening to the intermediate orchestra sail through its rendition of Mendelssohn's Symphony no. 4—the "Italian Symphony," as it was also known. They were playing only the first two movements, giving Etta about fourteen minutes to mentally take stock of her nerves and decide whether or not she really did need to throw up or if it would pass, as it usually did, once she was actually onstage.

She forced herself to smile at her friend, giving her a weak thumbs-up before she turned back to listen to the symphony. She breathed in and out, as Alice had taught her, but inside she was a little girl all over again, the one who burst into tears from fright the moment she stepped out onto the stage. It had nothing to do with whether or not she would be able to remember nearly thirty minutes of music, and everything to do with the fact that it was the same piece she should have played six months before with the New York Philharmonic, in Avery Fisher

Hall in Lincoln Center, with Alice sitting directly in front of her in the audience.

"I'm more nervous about the interview for the tutoring gig on Tuesday," she whispered back, needing to bolster herself a bit. Whether Gabby actually believed her was up for debate.

The strings caught her attention again, with a vibrancy and joy that breathed life into the tiers of Carnegie Hall's audience. She felt them stir, responding to the triumphant call of the first movement. And in that moment, she let *herself* resonate with that tone; she let the piece lift her out of the quiet, small existence she led.

It was an odd thing, she'd discovered, to haunt your old life. A year before, Etta had waited until the fourth of November, her eighteenth birthday, before self-enrolling late in the fall semester at Eleanor Roosevelt High School using the meticulous, not entirely truthful homeschooling records Alice had kept on her behalf. For the first two weeks, she'd walked past the music room, daring herself to go in, to see if there could be a place for her in the orchestra.

There was. She very much liked the idea of playing as part of a group, of disappearing seamlessly into a whole, but the challenge wasn't there, and Etta had felt herself settling into a complacency that frightened her. The teacher, Mr. Mangrave, recommended her to the director of the New York Youth Symphony, who allowed her to gladly take a seat left open by some poor boy who'd managed to break both of his arms falling off a bike. After graduating high school and spending the summer teaching violin and waitressing, she had auditioned again for a second year with the program to fill the time that wasn't spent applying for college.

Only sometimes did she let herself go to the Met. On days when it rained, or she was caught in a black mood, or it somehow seemed that enough time had passed to check again. She would always pay the full suggested donation to enter, walk through the exhibits she did not recognize, and sit at the top of the stairwell, waiting.

Now Etta was finished waiting.

The intermediate orchestra moved flawlessly into the second movement. Next to her, Gabby began to shift from foot to foot, adjusting the collar on her black dress. Etta had pulled her own plain, floor-length gown from Alice's closet. She wondered what her old instructor would have made of all this. Sighing, Etta reached up to smooth a stray hair back into her low chignon, and glanced over at her friend.

Gabby was the only other member of the senior orchestra from her school. She seemed determined to befriend everyone, even the shell-shocked blond girl who would only be in school for about seven months, and she had dragged Etta through all of the introductions in the group. She'd walked her home the night after their first practice, just talking, filling her in on the intricate hierarchy of who was who in their school. And then she'd managed to draw Etta right into her family's life, where they had welcomed her like another child, and never once mentioned how odd it was that her mother was constantly traveling and never available to take calls.

It was the oddest thing, because the more time Etta spent with Gabby, the better she came to understand her mother. She caught herself managing that same careful distance Rose had cultivated, not only between herself and her daughter, but with everyone in her life save for Alice. Etta tried to fixate on the memories of the life she'd had with Rose before all of this, but inevitably the image of her on the ground, bleeding, *dying*, was close behind.

The finality of the realization that her father, Nicholas, all of the others, were not just lost to her, but dead, had left her unable to leave Alice's apartment for days. It was easier to think of time, of their lives, as the loop Alice had written of—that, although they were not with her now, they were still alive in the past.

As much as she understood why Nicholas had done it, understanding did nothing to beat back the piercing loneliness, or the devastation of its finality.

There were moments Etta felt suffocated by the secrets and scars, times she'd had to dig her nails into her palm to stop herself from telling Gabby the truth: that her frequent nightmares weren't about stage fright or even failing school, but about ancient cities long dead, deserts, and shadows in a dark forest.

There were nights Etta dreamt of drowning, of sinking further and further into the black heart of the sea. No one came to rescue her.

She'd had to rescue herself.

It was only that . . . now and then, she caught a fragment of a memory long enough to examine it, each a lesson in heartbreak. Nicholas's secret smile in the rain. Henry's eyes, watching her play for the tsar. Her mother's pale hand reaching for her, just as the timeline reset.

The sudden roll of applause startled Etta out of her thoughts. She straightened, shifting her violin out from under her arm, feeling something like a warm buzz move against her skin. The orchestra cleared out through the other stage wing, allowing the senior orchestra members to flood out to claim their seats.

Gabby flashed Etta a huge smile as she stepped out with the others to renewed applause, taking over Etta's post as the concertmaster. The rest of the students whispered words of good luck and encouragement to Etta as they passed by.

"All right, here we go," Mr. Davis said, coming up behind her. "I'm so grateful this worked out—I can't thank you enough for stepping up like this."

Sasha Chung, a celebrated violin virtuoso new to this version of the timeline, had been slated to perform Mendelssohn's Violin Concerto in E Minor for the concert; the idea being, Etta supposed, that Sasha would be an additional audience draw and help further raise the profile of the program. On the way to the airport in Paris, however, she'd been in a car accident that had sent her to the hospital, leaving them without a soloist.

514

"Thank you for the opportunity," Etta said sincerely.

She liked Mr. Davis; it was easy to return the smile he gave her, to chuckle as he nudged her and whispered conspiratorially, "I think you play it better anyway."

The orchestra fell silent, leaving only a few stray coughs from the audience to fill the darkness.

"That's our cue," Mr. Davis said, motioning her to step out first. Etta ducked around the curtain, half-blinded by the lights at the stage's edge as she approached her spot near to the conductor's stand. Because she knew it would make her laugh, Etta reached out and gravely shook Gabby's hand, the way she would greet any concertmaster, and her friend turned pink with the effort to hold her giggles in. Mr. Davis situated himself at the front of the orchestra, and glanced her way.

She looked out into the audience one last time, at the way the lights under each tier of seating looked like necklaces strung with stars.

In most concertos, there was some small slice of time before the solo violinist entered the piece. But Mendelssohn broke with convention, and the solo violinist was present from the beginning, playing the tune in E minor that he once told a friend gave him "no peace" until he finally situated it in a concerto. Etta had always loved that story. There was something beautifully human in trying to capture a feeling, a fragment of notes, and translating it all into the universal language of music before it fled.

Mendelssohn's Violin Concerto in E Minor fluidly shifted between three movements: *allegro molto appassionato* in E minor, *andante* in C major, and, finally, *allegretto non troppo—allegro molto vivace* in E major.

All right, Etta thought, lifting the violin to her shoulder, *I hope you're listening, Alice.* Because she was going to play the hell out of this piece. She was going to bleed every last ounce of emotion out of it that she could.

Mr. Davis raised his hands.

Etta took a deep breath into her belly.

Felt the ripple of excitement race along her bare arms.

They began.

It was hard to describe exactly what she felt when she played. The best she had ever come up with was a feeling of being whole, though she hadn't been aware something was lacking to begin with. She became a drop in a larger stream, driving steadily forward without hesitation. It was a voice of beauty when her own faltered.

Etta knew this concerto so well that she barely needed to think through the bravura of ascending notes, which led to the orchestra restating the opening theme back to her. By the time she reached the cadenza, moved through its rhythmic shifts from quavers to quaver triplets and semiquavers, her muscles were warm from the ricochet bowing, her blood thrumming. Etta moved with the music, twisting, dipping, eyes closed. Relief flooded her—that she could still feel Alice nearby when she played, that it was still possible to know the joy of it when Alice wasn't there to experience it with her. And she wondered again what had ever been the point of holding back when it felt so good to fly.

Out of the corner of her eye, she saw Mr. Davis relax and lose himself in the piece. When she hit her first brief rest, Etta risked a glance out to the audience. Something pale caught and drew her gaze to the right end of the front row.

Rose.

The word swung wildly through her mind. But she was impossible in every way, by every definition: impossible to tame, impossible to capture, impossible to stop.

Her mother wore a navy dress, the bandage around her throat half-hidden by a scarf, gazing up at Etta with a faint smile on her face. Etta sucked in her next breath as a quiet gasp, the sight of Rose working through her like a lightning bolt, stunning her so greatly she nearly

516

missed her next entrance back into the piece. But once she'd seen her, Etta found she couldn't stop looking at her, at her mother's expression of pride. When Rose turned to look to the other end of the row, Etta nearly dropped her violin.

Henry sat on the edge of his seat, his elbows braced against his knees, his hands covering his mouth, as if trying to hold something— some word, some feeling—in by force. Etta's heart began to pound, and she felt as if she were rising off the stage as she coaxed the music from her violin. She wanted to shut it off, that swell of emotion in her chest, but the moment she saw the light catch the tears in his eyes, Etta had to look away to keep from crying herself.

How?

The tempo picked up again as they flowed into the second movement, and the question was lost to the flurry of notes—but then the rest came, and she looked again, searching for their faces to ensure that they were still there.

The key changed from the E minor opening to a slower C major movement as they moved into the *andante*. The tone shifted to A minor, becoming darker. Her accompaniment took on a tremulous quality that required the entirety of her attention before they shifted back to the C major theme and glided to a serene conclusion.

They're here.

How are they here?

After the second movement came a fourteen-bar transitional passage back into E minor for her and her fellow strings, and Etta braced herself for the fast passagework of *sonata rondo* form. When she looked up from her strings, her eyes drifted to the back of the auditorium, where a lone, shadowy figure leaned against the wall. Etta squinted, trying to make out the face. The set of his shoulders . . . the way he held his head—

As if sensing her gaze, he leaned closer to the dim light fixture on the wall behind him.

And suddenly, Etta knew joy. It passed through her like a thousand fluttering feathers.

She felt it explode inside of her as the orchestra moved as one through the effervescent finale, and the music became demanding again. Her mind could scarcely keep up with her fingers, and she had to tell herself, *Slow down*—she had to tell herself, *Don't rush—*

Nicholas.

Etta soared through the ascending and descending arpeggios, trying to keep herself rooted to the stage, to the music. By the time she reached the frenetic coda, she was smiling, near to bursting with the rapid way her world had colored itself back in. She was playing now for the world to hear, and it didn't matter that she might never have the opportunity again, it didn't matter that the still life she'd built for herself over the last few months was on the verge of collapse. Etta reached the final note and felt as if the roof had cracked open and finally let the starlight back into her world.

She couldn't hear the applause over her own heart. Some part of her remembered shaking Mr. Davis's hand, him saying something to her that was lost as she turned to thank the orchestra. Gabby had to point to the front of the stage to remind her to take her bow.

Etta was the first one off the stage, setting her violin down in its open case backstage and bolting to the green room, and then to the west gallery, which ran along the auditorium seating. The man working the concession stand looked up, startled by her sudden, frantic appearance as she moved past him, exiting at the back of the house and all but exploding through the doors into the lobby.

Nicholas stood a short distance away, hovering near the closed ticket counters. To anyone else, he might have been the portrait of nonchalance, but Etta read the uncertainty in his stance as he tried to take in the lights, the sounds of this world around him. He kept one hand tucked into the modern, relaxed black slacks he wore; he used the other to smooth down the front of his crisp white button-down.

"Hi," she managed.

"Hi," he said, sounding slightly out of breath himself. "That was . . . astonishing. *You* are astonishing."

She took another step toward him. Another. And another. Slowly, until he could no longer stand it, and met her halfway. Etta felt unbearably raw, as if her chest had been cut open and her swollen heart was there for all to see.

"And you're . . . here."

The smile that crept across his face was mirrored in full effect on her own. "I am."

"And . . . my parents?"

How?

Nicholas laughed softly. "We might have been here to greet you before the start of the concert, but neither could agree on how best to arrive, and by then, there were few seats left to be had."

Etta was almost dizzy with the sight of him after so long. "I don't understand—the passage closed."

He slipped his left hand out from behind his back and turned the palm up to face her. What she saw there was a scar, a whole network of them, that crisscrossed and wove through one another, creating what looked to her like . . .

"The astrolabe," she breathed, reaching out to grip his hand, to take a closer look. He'd been holding it when it was destroyed, keeping it in place.

"It took me some time, pirate," he said quietly, stepping close enough to her that she could see his pulse flutter in his throat. "To find your father in Moscow, and your mother in Verona, and wait for her to be strong enough to travel once more. Li Min did something to keep her breathing before we were all scattered across the years. I'll not pretend to understand, and while it's cost her the ability to speak, she is whole, and well. Then there was the not-insignificant matter of finding something from your time to create the passage here. A separate journey unto itself entirely."

Etta was so close to him now that she had to crane her head back to look up past the strong line of his jaw into his beautiful face. "What did you use?"

He dug a hand into his pocket and pulled out a cheap plastic key chain with the I ♥ NY logo, dangling it in front of her. Etta laughed, taking it from him. "Okay, I need this story."

Nicholas's smile was so unguarded, so freely given, she nearly cried at the sight of it. "The Belladonna had it in her vast collection. She was attempting to fetch a king's ransom for it—or another favor. The resulting destruction to her shop as your parents dueled for who had the right to take the favor caused her to throw it at me and banish us."

"You're joking."

"Sophia called it the most breathtaking display of stupidity she's ever witnessed—and passes along her regards," he said.

"So you tracked down Sophia," Etta said, understanding. "And Li Min?"

"We separated only so she could search for her on her own." His hand hovered above her face for a moment, tracing the shape of it into the air. His throat jumped as he swallowed hard, bringing the tips of his fingers to brush the loose hairs back out of Etta's face.

Etta wanted to always remember the look on his face as she kissed his smiling mouth, kissed his jaw, kissed his cheek, whatever part of him she could reach, until she felt like she could dissolve into scattered, incandescent light.

"It was my turn," she said at last. "To find you."

"I consider us remarkably even on that score," he said with a soft laugh. "But I thought, perhaps, you might like to accompany me to find the others who might be in need of rescue?"

Etta took a small step back, feeling hope shimmer around her like a trembling note.

"You're opening them all," she breathed out.

He nodded. "At least, trying to bridge those gaps between what was, what is, and what should be. I think we'll try again. The families. I think we ought to make a life of it, and if there's a better way, I think I should very much like for you to help me find it, Miss Spencer."

She stroked the scarred skin of his palm again, letting her fingers slide down to interlace with his. A thread of doubt wove through the swirling mass of joy. Nicholas ducked his head to meet her gaze, and she saw the question in his eyes.

"Miss Spencer," she said softly. "Is that who I am?"

Over the last year, she'd tried to piece together her old life, only to find that most of its pieces no longer existed, and the ones that did exist felt like they might choke her if she tried to wear them again.

"You could be a Hemlock, as I could be an Ironwood; or you could sign your name with Linden, as I might sign mine with Hall. Or perhaps you are Miss Spencer, and always will be," he told her, his thumb skating over her cheek. "Or you could choose, one day, to be a Carter. Or we might be nothing beyond *you* and *I*, and be done with this business of names once and for all, for they have never once had a true bearing on who we are or who we intend to be."

And with that, the tension bled from her limbs, and the knot of confusion in her heart finally loosened.

"Then, yes, I think I should like that very much, too," she said, mimicking the formality of his tone. "But first . . . there's someone we need to see."

He nodded, plainly curious. "Name the horizon, and it's ours."

By the time the auditorium doors opened, they were gone.

LONDON
1932

EPILOGUE

THERE WAS A MAN IN THE GARDEN, HIDDEN BEHIND MAMA'S rosebush. She noticed him only because the sun was setting, but the gold of his long robe caught the light and seemed to burn behind the branches and bramble like a sunrise. And because she, too, was hiding in the garden; only, she was the one smart enough to choose to crouch behind the hedge.

There were always travelers arriving without warning, and never dressed properly. Fewer now, and soon none, if Grandpapa had his way.

You're in the twentieth century, she wanted to whisper to him. But when he turned, she did not recognize the stranger's face—not from memory, and not from any of the books of photographs her parents had compiled of the Ironwoods, Jacarandas, and Hemlocks for her to memorize.

The only reason to hide was for fear of being discovered, and the only reason to fear being discovered was if you'd arrived with bad intentions.

Rose drew herself deeper into the hedge, but the man heard the subtle shift of the leaves. He slowly turned his head toward her, revealing himself through the flowers. Her Mama had declared her brave so many times, but Rose found she could not move, not with his eyes locked on her face, glimmering like gold coins.

It was painful to look anywhere else. She saw only pieces of him. A long, thin nose. The skin over the curve of his forehead; tight, the way a snake's might be. Neither handsome nor hideous. Something else entirely.

"Hello, child," he called softly. "Are you frightened? I have only come to help you."

Rose knew the response to this was to run back into the house and call for Grandpapa. But she could not look away from him, the way his skin glimmered with light as he came toward her. His footsteps made no sound as they passed over the stones and grass.

Rose crossed her arms over her chest, shrinking back against the high wall that separated their town house from the neighbor's.

"S-stay back!" she ordered, reaching down to pick up a stone to throw.

The man's gliding path came to a halt in front of her. He towered, taller than any man she had ever seen, but he cast no shadow over her. Standing there, staring into his eyes, Rose felt only . . . warm. The hungry parts of her were suddenly full, calm. For a moment, she could not remember the reason she had come into the garden at all.

"I would never harm you," he told her, his voice drifting between her ears, soothing like an ointment over a cut. "There is such sorrow in your heart. Tell me, have you lost someone?"

She hesitated, but felt herself nod. "Mama. Papa."

"Death is an enemy few defeat," he said, coming closer. "But there is a way to save them, child. They should never have died."

Rose felt her eyes sting with the truth of his words. Her voice wobbled as she asked, "How?"

"There is a special object your family possesses. It is the key to saving not only your dear Mama and Papa, but all those around you."

Rose shook her head, trying to bring her hands up to cover her ears. Her arms would not move, not while the man's words wove around her, coiling and coiling around her until her chest was too tight to breathe.

No matter how hard she squeezed her eyes shut, Rose could not shut out images of the things he spoke of. Each word painted the images inside of her mind. Smoke, not the smell of wet grass, filled her lungs. Something hot and metallic-tasting filled her mouth and nearly choked her.

A cool hand closed around her wrist softly, leading her. It was only when Rose heard the distant honk of a horn that she realized she was standing at the open gate, the edge of the darkened street. She tried to tug her hand free, but there was a fever in her, painful and cloudy. His face was blotted out in her vision, a smear of ivory and gold.

Grandpapa.

"All I need is that special gift your family was given. Only that, and you can save everyone. *You.*"

The images raged through her now, flickering like colored film. Mama, Papa, the blood, a great city shuddering with flames, an explosion, bodies charred to bone and piled as high as mountains, her hands spilling over with tar, a rising dark river of drowning animals, children, blades flashing, tearing through skin and bone—they burned their way through her, searing her mind. The pain slammed into her, plucking and pawing and tugging at her until blackness rose in her vision and she felt hands cupping her back, her legs—

The astrolabe. The golden disc. Grandpapa had drawn it for her to see, but she had never touched it, never seen it pass through the house.

She realized she had been saying all of these words aloud when the man, at the end of a long tunnel, nodded.

"Rose!"

That voice . . .

"*Rose!*"

That was . . . Rose tried to think of whom the voice belonged to, but nothing existed outside of the man's face, the long, elegant fingers that stroked her cheek.

"Rose! Where are you?"

Afraid.

There is a place where you will never feel hurt. Where you will become strong.

The words slithered through her, unstoppable. When she opened her eyes again, the street was gliding past her, streaked with night.

"Rosie! Rosie! Come out, Rosie, this isn't funny!"

Alice. Why did she sound so far away? Why did she sound so frightened? *Who is hurting Alice?*

The man's face came into focus, glowing against the darkening sky. It felt good. So easy. So very safe here. He would protect her. He would make her strong, like Mama.

But who would protect Alice?

Rose struggled, squirming to break from his grip. He did not put her down. If anything, his grip tightened and, all at once, the soft blanket of contentment he'd wrapped around her was stripped off. Rose, suddenly, was fighting. Kicking, clawing, slapping, screaming. The images of death and destruction slammed into her again, tearing through her mind, but she did not stop. Rose screamed until her throat turned raw and she fell to the ground on her hands and knees. The darkness swelled up around her, over her head, crashing down the way she'd seen the tides of fire break over an unfamiliar city.

"Rosie!"

"Rose!"

Alice. Grandpapa. Someone—anyone—please—

Help me.

WHEN ROSE WOKE, IT WAS TO SUNLIGHT AND JASMINE, ON A bed of cushions and silk, centuries and continents away. She remembered Grandpapa easing her up, carrying her through the passage, but her mind had been soft with sleep.

Her heart began to beat madly when she saw that neither Nanny nor Grandpapa were with her. This was a room she'd never seen before.

He took me. The words were like claws in her mind. Rose flew to the corner of the room, crouching down, her arms above her head. *He's come back for me.*

The breath whistled out between her chattering teeth. For a moment, Rose could not move at all, not even to swallow.

But then she remembered.

Grandpapa's worn face as he'd told her again and again, *Hush, darling, nothing happened, you gave yourself a fright.*

"It wasn't real," she told herself, the way Grandpapa had barked at her when she'd tried to describe the man. "Not. Real."

But then, why could she still feel the sharp press of the man's fingers on her wrist? Why, every time she shut her eyes, did she see that same burning world?

"Stop it," she ordered herself, hating the tremor in her voice. She scrubbed her fists over her eyes. She'd only upset Grandpapa; he'd been so angry at her for wandering away from the house. He'd thought she'd run intentionally, because . . . yes, they were leaving London. He had bought them a new home, far from her mama's garden. She wouldn't upset Grandpapa anymore by crying and hiding like a baby.

He was all she had left.

Rose stood, breathing in through her nose, and ventured outside of her room, exploring the house. She called for her grandfather, for her nanny, but the rainbow of tiles in the enclosed courtyard only echoed her voice back to her.

Safe.

But alone.

Rose returned to the room she had awakened in, searching through the trunks at the far end of the room for books. Instead, she found her small easel and a neat stack of canvases and paint. Nanny had remembered to pack them.

She set everything up, but before she could begin to think of what she would paint, she heard voices on the street below. Pulling back the bedroom shutters, she leaned out. Down the dust-filled alley, the other children were playing some sort of game with a ball, women in rainbow veils and tunics hovering over them, clucking like chickens. Rose scoffed at the sight.

She swung her legs out of the window so that they dangled, pale and long, over the world below. The street emptied and silence returned.

When the tears burned her cheeks, Rose knew they were because of the wind and the heavy dust it carried. It had nothing to do with the man, the dreams of fire and blood. That was all. Grandpapa had told her to be brave, and so she would be. Rose Linden was not afraid, not ever.

"Not real," she whispered again, squeezing her eyes shut.

A *crack* from behind her caught her attention, and Rose turned, searching for Grandpapa's face, or Nanny to call her to supper. She would have even accepted silly, stupid Henry, if he'd be nice just once and not pull her braid. But no . . . she was not supposed to play with the Hemlocks anymore. Rose needed to remember this now. Not with the Jacarandas, either. And never, ever with the Ironwoods.

Instead, there was a woman at the door, staring at her.

"Ma—"

The word was swallowed back down her throat. This girl—this young lady—wore a simple cornflower-blue tunic of sorts, with a short jacket over it. She hadn't thought to do her hair, or even wear a hat, which was most improper.

But she was not like the man in gold. She was nothing like him.

Now that the young woman was coming closer, Rose found herself swinging her legs back into the room. She saw the echoes of Mama's face in the girl's eyes and her mouth. Reaching down, she picked up the small letter opener Grandpapa had left on the room's table and held it up. "Who are you?"

The girl stopped where she was and let out a startled laugh. She held up her hands. "I'm . . . like you."

Her accent was American. Rose had not expected that, either.

"There's no one like me," she said.

The girl laughed. "That's very true. I meant that I'm—"

"*Don't* say it!" Rose hissed, shocked at her carelessness. Anyone might hear. "I know what you are. You're doing a terrible job of it. You didn't even buy the right kind of shoes!"

The girl looked down, then back up again, her face flushed. "Well, you've got me there."

Rose slowly lowered the letter opener. "What do you want? Grandpapa isn't home."

The girl took a step closer. Rose allowed this. She took another step closer. Rose allowed this as well.

"I came to talk to you, actually," the young lady said. "I wanted to see how you are—to talk to you about what happened."

Rose shook her head, slapping her hands over her ears. "No, no, no! We aren't supposed to tell, we aren't—"

"I know, I know," the girl said, crouching down in front of Rose. "But . . . I could use someone to talk to, too. And there's no one I trust more to help me, to keep my secrets."

Rose could not tell her what the man had said. It would be like pulling splinters out from under skin that had already healed over them. It hurt so very badly to think of it.

But this stranger—not her Grandpapa, not any of the other travelers—believed her to be someone to speak to, not speak down to. She liked this idea, that she was strong after all. It was a very sad, hard thing, her Papa had told her, to be a traveler, for there were so very few people who knew what they could do, and fewer still that they could talk to.

"I'll listen," Rose allowed, her voice trembling only a little.

The girl's face clouded, her pale brows drawing together as she knelt down on one of the cushions, watching Rose come toward her, almost in awe. "I'm sorry about your parents. That must have been beyond terrible for you, and you were so brave. I've lost someone I love, too. My heart still hurts, even though I understand why it happened."

Rose stood with her back straight, clasping her hands in front of her as she met the girl's blue-eyed gaze with her own. "I'm not afraid."

"I know you aren't," the young lady said, almost in a whisper, "but I heard that you had another visitor recently, and that some of the things he said might have been upsetting. I promise you, though, everything will be . . . okay in the end."

Rose swallowed hard. Whenever she closed her eyes, she saw that man, the one who'd visited her before they left London. He had told her about terrible things, *horrible* things. She dreamt of what he said, the burns, the suffering—the—the *blood*.

"Will it?" she whispered, even though she knew it was wrong to press about the future.

The young lady nodded. "I promise." She turned toward the corner of the room, where Grandpapa had set up a small easel. "Do you like to paint?"

Rose hesitated a moment, then nodded. She had not painted since Mama and Papa had . . .

She closed her eyes, scrubbed at her cheeks. The girl rose up off the ground and touched her hair gently, stroking it down. "Would you paint something for me? Maybe . . . maybe something from your memory?"

"Something . . . happy?" Rose asked, looking up at her.

"Yes," the girl said softly, taking her hand. "Something happy."

ACKNOWLEDGMENTS

SOME BOOKS ARE BORN MAGICAL AND SHINY FROM THE FIRST draft, but this one proved to be a true labor of love. I'm so grateful for the friendships I've made this year, both with my fellow authors and with my amazing readers, for keeping me going on the journey from first draft to the finished book you're holding in your hands.

First and foremost, I'd like to thank my agent, Merrilee Heifetz, who fights so hard for her clients every single day and is always there to pick me up, dust me off, and set me on the right path. I'm so grateful for your unfailingly good advice, kindness, and patience. Thanks also to Allie Levick for being so reliable and wonderful—I don't know how you stay so on top of things! I'd also like to send some major love to Cecilia de la Campa, Angharad Kowal, James Munro, and the many subrights coagents who have ensured that readers around the world can find my stories. Rock stars, all of you!

Emily Meehan, Hannah Allaman, Laura Schreiber . . . thank you for navigating the absolutely insane world of time travel with me. I'm so grateful for your help in shaping this story and helping me find its heart. Thank you to Andrew Sugerman, for being such an incredible champion (Go Tribe!). Mary Ann Naples, Seale Ballenger, Dina

Sherman, LaToya Maitland, Holly Nagel, Elke Villa, Andrew Sansone, Sara Liebling, Guy Cunningham, Dan Kaufman, Meredith Jones, Marci Senders, and the entire team at Hyperion: you are all so, so, so amazing. I could fill an entire book with thanks for you.

I would have been completely lost this past year without Erin Bowman and Susan Dennard. Thank you both so much for your invaluable thoughts, your support, and for not letting me give up on this story. I'd say more, but we're probably already on Gchat talking . . . and, well, I think you know (#cattleprod). Massive love to Victoria Aveyard for staying up until the wee hours of the morning brainstorming alternate history with me. To Anna Jarzab, I love ya, buddy—thanks for putting up with me and my neuroses all these years, and for being the kind of good friend I aspire to be.

I'd also like to thank Sabaa Tahir and Leigh Bardugo for their caring, much-appreciated check-ins, and for whatever psychic ability they possess that allowed them to know exactly when I needed moral support most. To Amie Kaufman: your guidance through rocky waters is always spot-on, and I'm honored to call you my friend.

A special thank-you to my two favorite Kevins: Kevin Shiau for your help with honing Li Min's character and checking my Mandarin, and Kevin Dua for being kind enough to give me your thoughts last year on Nicholas and his journey. Likewise, my eternal gratitude to Valia Lind for helping me nail the right Russian phrases and to Evelyn Skye for helping fact-check.

Thank you SO much to my family. I love you guys which, duh, you know, but I thought I'd put it in print. (And Mom, I promise Rose isn't based on you.)

Finally, to the readers who came on this journey with Nicholas and Etta: thank you, thank you, thank you. You are the reason I'm able to do what I love, and I'll never forget that. Now go out there and make history.

Don't miss

THE
DARKEST
MINDS

also by Alexandra Bracken

Keep reading for a sneak
preview of the first book!

PROLOGUE

When the White Noise went off, we were in the Garden, pulling weeds.

I always reacted badly to it. It didn't matter if I was outside, eating in the Mess Hall, or locked in my cabin. When it came, the shrieking tones blew up like a pipe bomb between my ears. Other girls at Thurmond could pick themselves up after a few minutes, shaking off the nausea and disorientation like the loose grass clinging to their camp uniforms. But me? Hours would pass before I was able to piece myself back together.

This time should have been no different.

But it was.

I didn't see what had happened to provoke the punishment. We were working so close to the camp's electric fence that I could smell the singed air and feel the voltage it shed vibrating in my teeth. Maybe someone got brave and decided to step out of the Garden's bounds. Or maybe, dreaming big, someone fulfilled all our fantasies and threw a rock at the head of the nearest Psi Special Forces soldier. That would have been worth it.

The only thing I knew for certain was that the overhead speakers spurted out two warning blares: one short, one long. The skin on my neck crawled as I leaned forward into the damp dirt, hands pressed tightly against my ears, shoulders tensed to take the hit.

The sound that came over the speakers wasn't really white noise. It wasn't that weird buzz that the air sometimes takes on when you're sitting alone in silence, or the faint hum of a computer monitor. To the United States government and its Department of Psi Youth, it was the lovechild of a car alarm and a dental drill, turned up high enough to make your ears bleed.

Literally.

The sound ripped out of the speakers and shredded every nerve in my body. It forced its way past my hands, roaring over the screams of a hundred teenage freaks, and settled at the center of my brain, where I couldn't reach in and rip it out.

My eyes flooded with tears. I tried to ram my face into the ground—all I could taste in my mouth was blood and dirt. A girl fell forward next to me, her mouth open in a cry I couldn't hear. Everything else faded out of focus.

My body shook in time with the bursts of static, curling in on itself like an old, yellowing piece of paper. Someone's hands were shaking my shoulders; I heard someone say my name—*Ruby*—but I was too far gone to respond. Gone, gone, gone, sinking until there was nothing, like the earth had swallowed me up in a single, deep breath. Then darkness.

And silence.

Also by
ALEXANDRA BRACKEN

THE DARKEST MINDS SERIES
The Darkest Minds
Never Fade
In the Afterlight
Through the Dark

THE PASSENGER SEQUENCE
Passenger
Wayfarer